I0565535

Printed in the United States of America

Published by MARLvision Publishing
Sarasota, FL

ISBN: 978-0-9833763-4-7

Pornocopia

A collection of erotic stories by Carl Hose

Contents

4

Banging in the New Year

Belinda Walters looked at the clock hanging on the wall to the left of her desk. It was an old clock. One of those round ones you always see in school classrooms. The kind with the big hands, which meant there was no chance of not being able to see what time it was. Big hands that never let you miss the hours and minutes ticking away.

The clock was a reminder. It was the clock she'd had since she opened her business, back when she was still struggling to make a go of it.

It was only ten p.m., but Belinda was already tired. There was a good possibility she would be here all night. That was one of the bad things about being in business for yourself. When there was work that had to be done, holiday or not, you had to do it.

It was New Year's Eve. All of Belinda's employees had taken the day off, and none of them would be coming in tomorrow either. There were year-end accounts that had to be cleared, orders to process, and bills to be paid. Belinda couldn't afford to take time off for holidays. Not if she wanted to stay in business.

Belinda was a bitch, no two ways about it. In the cut throat world of business, a girl had to do what it took to stay on top of the game. Still, even she wasn't bitch enough to force her employees to work holidays. Well, she was, but she never did, simply because it would make it hard to keep employees around, and that meant she sometimes worked long hours to pick up the slack.

She enjoyed it, though. She was a workaholic. Driven was how she preferred to think of it, but the truth was, she was a workaholic. She was inspired by comfortable living, and comfortable living was only brought about by ample cash flow, and ample cash flow was achieved through hard work.

Belinda Walters was in the business of sex. Her company specialized in high-tech sex toys, virtual reality sex games, and some of the old stand-bys done with the latest in realistic rendering. She was on the cutting edge of the sex industry, with clients ranging from porno stars and sex club owners to the rich and famous.

Sex was money. Actually, *pleasure* was money. People were willing to pay big bucks to be pleased, and sex was simply one way to get pleasure.

She turned her attention to the stack of work in front of her. Maybe she needed to start thinking about relaxing a little. She really didn't have to work so hard anymore. The company pretty much ran itself, and really, was one night going to make a difference?

Next year, she thought. My New Year resolution. I won't work so hard, I'll at least take the holidays off.

She rubbed her eyes. Damn, she was tired. She went over to the coffee pot and poured herself another full cup. Strong and black. That's what it was going to take to get her through the rest of the night.

She sat back behind her desk and began going over some proposals regarding the production of her company's newest line of dildos. The production costs had come down due to the line's popularity.

She glanced at the prototype sitting on the desk next to her computer. It looked so real and inviting that she had trouble resisting the urge to touch it.

She picked up her coffee cup instead.

Her eyes kept shifting to the dildo. She picked it up and closed her fist around it as best as she could. It warmed to her touch.

This one was nine inches long and nearly half that size around. It was a Caucasian model, second only in sales to its ebony counterpart, made of a new type of material that conducted body heat and distributed it evenly. Beneath the fleshy "skin" were tiny sensors that detected both pressure and moisture, causing the dildo to react to individual users in different ways.

Belinda ran her fingers up the full length of the dildo and down the other side. She closed her eyes, leaned back in her chair, and brought it to her mouth, letting her tongue slide around the smooth, soft tip of it. She closed her eyes and slipped one hand inside her blouse, letting her fingers travel under the silky edge of her bra cup until she found her nipple.

She caressed it. It was so sensitive to her touch. It felt like a thousand tiny little charges of pleasure shooting through her. It had been so long since she'd had any sort of sexual encounter. That was one of the drawbacks of putting all your time into work. It left no time for personal pleasure.

She unbuttoned her blouse and tugged her bra down below her breasts. Her pale pink nipples stood up hard and eager. She stroked and pinched them as she licked the head of the dildo and took it in her mouth.

She unsnapped her jeans and thrust one hand down the front of her pants, into her panties, curling the finger into her damp opening, plunging it all the way inside her. She wasn't getting any work done this way, but what the hell, you only live once.

She withdrew her finger and brought it up to press it against her clit. She lifted one leg and propped her foot on the edge of the desk, opening herself wider. She gasped as she found her pleasure spot and manipulated it with deft strokes, spreading her silky slick juices around.

She came quickly, releasing pent-up sexual desires she'd kept in check for too long. She withdrew her hand from her jeans and licked her wet finger, tasting the sweetness of her climax.

The phone rang, startling her from the afterglow of orgasm. She tossed the dildo back on the desk.

"Hello?" she said into the receiver, brushing thick blonde hair from her face.

Gina Martin was on the other end of the line. She'd almost forgotten about the meeting she'd scheduled with Gina and her husband Rick.

Gina and Rick were exotic dancers whose show drew major attention across the United States. Both were in their mid-twenties, both had the same dark shade of red hair, and both were extremely attractive people. It was easy to see why they were so successful.

Belinda's company had a contract to provide them with some of the high-tech props they used in their shows. Additionally, Gina and Rick wanted to contract Belinda's company to design a special set for the show. Belinda had decided up front that she would handle their account personally.

"We just finished a show," Gina said. "We'll be there in fifteen minutes."

"I'll see you then," Belinda said.

She hung up and went into the bathroom to clean herself up. She brushed her hair and pulled it up into a ponytail, touched up her makeup, and then started a fresh pot of coffee. When Gina and Rick arrived, she let them into the building and ushered them into her office, offering them something to drink.

"I just made coffee," she said. "Or I could get you something a little stronger."

"I'll take something stronger," Rick said.

"Me too," Gina added. Belinda poured Bacardi Gold, a dark, slightly sweet rum that always put her in a sexy mood. Not that she needed any mood alteration. If she felt any more sexy, she wasn't sure what she'd have to do to alleviate the problem.

She concentrated on business. Rick and Gina sat on the Ocean Avenue leather couch she'd purchased for the office. She'd also purchased a plush matching chair, which she now sat in, crossing one leg over the other.

"First, I'd like to thank you for stopping by. I know you had a big show tonight, and this could have waited until tomorrow . . ."

"It's no problem," Gina said. "We're actually interested in getting this project off the ground as soon as possible. We're grateful you were willing to see us on New Year's Eve."

As Belinda listened to Gina and Rick discuss their vision, she couldn't help but steal an occasional glance at Gina's long, shapely legs. Gina wore a Catholic schoolgirl blouse and a very short plaid skirt. When Gina crossed or uncrossed her legs, Belinda caught glimpses of the modest white panties she wore underneath.

Gina caught her looking. She continued talking about business unabated, but the way she looked at Belinda suggested that she was not only aware of Belinda's attraction to her, but that she encouraged it as well.

"Would you like another," Belinda asked, indicating their empty glasses.

"Please," Gina said.

Belinda retrieved the bottle of rum and filled everybody's glass, including hers. "We're also carrying a new line of sexy outfits," she said, sitting back down in her chair. "Some of them would fit in well with your shows."

"I'd like to see some of them," Gina said.

"I don't suppose you'd model?" Rick suggested.

Belinda blushed and waved the suggestion aside. "I don't think I'd be comfortable doing that," she said.

"Why not?" Gina asked.

Belinda was only thirty-five, and she knew deep down that she was sexy, but she didn't feel confident enough to expose herself in skimpy outfits to a pair of professional dancers—two people who made their living turning other people on.

"I'm not very good at modeling," she said, bringing her glass to her lips to sip her rum.

"That's nonsense," Gina said. "A woman as attractive as you could model a burlap sack and make it look good."

Belinda blushed again, this time so much so that she could feel the heat flushing her cheeks. "No, really—"

"Come on, just one or two outfits," Rick said. "Just enough to give us an idea what the line is like."

Belinda finally consented. Not because these two represented so much business, which they most certainly did, but because the thought of being nearly naked in front of them excited the exhibitionist in her.

She disappeared into another room. When she came back, she was wearing a tight, very form-fitting black leather dress, fishnet stockings, and shiny black shoes with stiletto-type heels. Her thick blonde hair, which she'd had back in a ponytail, now fell over her shoulders in a wild tangle. The front of the dress was cut low enough to expose the creamy round edges of her breasts.

"Wow," Gina said.

Rick whistled appreciatively.

Gina moved over to Belinda. "I love that," she said. "What's it made out of?"

"It's leather," Belinda said.

"It's so soft," Gina replied, sliding her hand over the curve of Belinda's waist.

Belinda shivered slightly at the touch of Gina's hand. When she made no move to reject Gina's overt come-on, Gina ran her hand over the front of the dress caressing the swell of Belinda's right breast.

Rick lit a cigarette and settled back on the couch to watch.

Gina kissed Belinda, at first brushing her lips over Belinda's mouth tentatively, then letting the tip of her tongue flick across Belinda's lower lip.

Belinda responded by parting her lips slightly—just enough to allow Gina's tongue to gain access.

Gina pulled Belinda close, sliding her arms around Belinda's waist. The kiss grew more insistent. Belinda melted against Gina, accepting Gina's wet tongue into her mouth.

Belinda slid her hands, lifting Gina's tiny plaid skirt, cupping Gina's panty-clad ass in her hands. She pulled Gina tighter against her, squeezing Gina's bottom. Gina pressed closer to Belinda, rotating her hips, grinding against her.

They finally broke their kiss, both of them gasping and flushed. Gina unbuttoned her blouse and took it off, then her bra, letting her tits fall free.

Belinda turned around, lifting her hair from the nape of her neck. Gina unzipped the dress, and Belinda slipped it from her shoulders and peeled it down to expose her sexy figure, naked now except for panties, fishnets, and heels.

Rick joined the girls in the middle of the room, pressing himself against Belinda from behind, slipping his hands around her waist.

Gina knelt in front of Belinda, kissing the soft swell of her mound through her panties. She tugged the panties down just far enough to uncover the silky blonde tangle of Belinda's pubic hair.

Gina moved lower, sliding Belinda's panties down as she went. She flicked her tongue between the plump lips of Belinda's pussy, which Belinda kept smooth shaven. Gina's tongue found the little pink nub of Belinda's clit. She ran her tongue across the top of Belinda's clit, then ran her tongue in circles around it. She finally caught it between her lips and nibbled.

Rick brought his hands up over Belinda's belly. He cupped her breasts, one in each hand, and squeezed them, taking her nipples between thumb and forefinger.

Gina dragged Belinda's panties to her ankles, and Belinda stepped out of them, hands on Gina's shoulders for support.

Rick took off his clothes and dropped to his knees behind Belinda, pressing his face against her firm, pale ass. He kissed one cheek then the other. He slipped a finger into her pussy and pushed it all the way inside her.

Gina thumbed open Belinda's pussy lips and flicked her tongue between them, teasing the ragged pink folds of her labia. She teased Belinda's clit with light strokes of her tongue, and when Rick withdrew his finger, Gina took it in her mouth and sucked it clean.

Belinda turned around. Rick stood up, stroking his thick cock with one hand. Belinda took it from him, tilting her eyes up to watch his face as she slowly ran a tight fist up and down the length of his erection. She sucked him hard, making wet noises as she took him to the back of her throat.

Gina kissed Belinda's ass and teased her asshole with the tip of her tongue. She took off her panties but left her skirt on, then she lay on the floor beneath Belinda.

Belinda settled back on Gina's face, moaning around a mouthful of cock as Gina's tongue disappeared into her hot, damp opening. She drew Belinda's smooth, plump lips apart with her fingers and licked every inch of her pink pussy, occasionally wandering back to slip her tongue into Belinda's wet hole or tease her asshole with gentle little strokes.

Belinda lowered her mouth down on Rick. Her blonde hair spilled over his cock as she expertly deep throated him, going down to the base of his shaft in one fluid motion, then coming up slowly, making her lips tight around his meat as she did. She'd always been good at sucking cock, ever since she'd started doing it at a young age and learned she loved the way a hard dick felt in her mouth.

Rick closed his eyes and threaded his fingers through the silky blonde strands of her hair, groaning as he reaped the benefit of her skilled mouth. She squeezed his cock at the base and bobbed her head on it, occasionally pulling her mouth from his cock to circle the head of it with long, wet swipes of her tongue.

Gina continued to work her tongue in and out of Belinda's pussy, probing deep, tasting the sweet wet honey that ran into her mouth.

Belinda rocked her hips, sliding her wet pussy against Gina's face. She tightened her mouth around Rick's cock and drew the thick, hot shaft all the way into her mouth, reaching up to massage his heavy balls with one hand.

She was so close now. Her belly fluttered as she felt the pleasurable tingle that began in her clit and emanated throughout her body. She took her mouth away from Rick's cock. She kept one hand on him, giving his dick an occasional squeeze or a few tugs, but her focus was on what Gina was doing to her.

"Oh my god," she gasped.

She climaxed, her hips jerking spasmodically, tits bouncing up and down. Her knees scraped the carpet. She knew she'd regret the rug burn later, but for now it didn't matter. Nothing mattered but the exquisite, mind-numbing orgasm that brought all of her senses into play at once.

When it was over, she managed to stand up, though her legs were weak. She stroked Rick's cock with her slender fingers as she kissed him, leaning against him for support. He slipped his tongue inside her mouth and explored.

Gina knelt beside Rick and began to lick his balls. Belinda pushed Rick's cock into Gina's mouth, and Gina slowly went down on him, allowing the thick shaft to disappear gradually.

Belinda dropped to her knees beside Gina. She took great pleasure in watching Gina suck Rick's cock. The way Gina looked up at him as she sucked, her eyes full of love, hungry and eager to please. It was very arousing.

Belinda reached between her legs and began rubbing her own pussy. She was so hot down there, so wet and sensitive. The touch of her own fingers sent tiny spasms of pleasure racing through her again.

Gina took Rick's cock from her mouth and offered it to Belinda. The two women teased the head of his dick with their tongues, licking all around it.

Belinda took it into her mouth and nibbled the head while Gina worked her way up and down one side of his shaft.

They passed his cock back and forth for a few minutes, then Belinda kneeled on the couch and Rick stood behind her, placing his hands on her hips and drawing her back to him. The head of his cock nudged her, pushing the lips of her pussy apart, slipping into her slick, pink opening.

Gina knelt beside Rick, wrapping her arms around his legs. She stroked his balls as his dick slipped in and out of Belinda's wet cunt. Her fingers brushed his thick shaft as it filled Belinda stroke after stroke.

Gina got up on the couch beside Belinda. Rick reached over to finger his wife's pussy as he continued fucking Belinda.

Belinda and Gina kissed, soft lips brushing together, tongues slipping into each other's mouths.

Rick pulled his cock from Belinda's pussy, slick and glistening with her juices. His dick bobbed in front of him as he took up position behind Gina. He pushed her skirt up over her ass and penetrated the silky auburn curls. The coral pink flaps of her labia opened, clinging to his cock as it slid deep into her pussy.

Belinda reached over to play with one of Gina's tits. Gina covered Belinda's mouth with hers, thrusting her tongue into Belinda's mouth.

Rick ran a hand over Belinda's round, smooth ass. He slipped a finger into her soaking-wet pussy and moved it around inside her, then he dragged the finger up and smeared her juices around the pale pink pucker of her asshole.

Belinda moaned her approval. Rick worked his finger into her ass. She shifted her ass and his finger slipped in a little further. He moved it gently inside her at first, relaxing her anal muscles, and then he slid a second finger in.

Gina pumped her ass back against him, grinding her pussy up and down on his cock. He glanced down and watched her slick lips cling to his thick shaft as she began to rock back and forth on him.

He took his cock from Gina's pussy and got behind Belinda, taking his fingers from her ass as he did. He rubbed his cock along her pink labia, wetting the head of it with her slick honey.

Gina pumped his cock and guided the purple tip between the cheeks of Belinda's ass. Belinda eased backward, pressing her puckered opening down over the head of his cock. There was brief resistance before his dick slipped beyond the tight ring of muscle and slid deep into her ass.

Rick's wasn't the first cock Belinda had ever taken in her ass, but it was by far the largest. The first few strokes hurt like hell, but then she relaxed and got into it, moaning as he pumped her ass with steady strokes, his balls slapping an even rhythm against her pussy.

Gina stayed on her knees beside Rick, leaning down to lick around where his cock and Belinda's asshole met, keeping Belinda's anus well lubricated with lots of slippery saliva.

"Ohhh, yeah. Oh god, come in my ass." Belinda grunted the words as Rick pounded into her, digging his fingers into her hips to keep her close.

"Come on, baby," Gina encouraged him. "Show her what you got."

He came with a grunt, thrusting all the way into Belinda's ass, groaning as his hot come filled her tight bottom. When he finally withdrew, a flood of thick cream dribbled from her well-fucked ass. Gina grabbed hold of Rick's cock and took it in her mouth to suck it clean, then she got behind Belinda and licked the come from around her ass.

Rick retrieved the prototype dildo from Belinda's desk. He knelt behind Gina and ran his tongue along the pink folds of her labia, nibbling on them a few minutes, and then he inserted the dildo into her pussy.

Gina continued licking the come out of Belinda's ass, working her tongue in deep. She shifted her ass, pushing back to take the dildo deeper into her pussy. It wasn't long before she was fucking it, working her hips up and down, the dildo slipping in and out of her wet cunt.

Rick's cock hung limp and wet against one leg. He took it in his fist and stroked it, working up another erection. He was a professional, so multiple erections were no trouble for him. He prided himself on that fact.

He handed the dildo to Gina, who slid it into Belinda's pussy. As she fucked Belinda with it, she teased and licked

Belinda's clit. Belinda squealed as the combined pleasure of tongue and dildo sent her soaring.

Rick pushed his dick into his wife's pussy and fucked her with long, hard strokes, swatting her on the bottom now and then for effect. When he knew she was close to coming, he reached around and fingered her clit, bringing her right over the edge.

Belinda soon followed, crying out in pleasure as Gina drove the dildo in her pussy to the hilt and pulled Belinda's clit into her mouth.

Belinda glanced up at the old clock on the wall. It was past midnight. Another year gone, a new one just beginning. She just happened to have a good bottle of champagne in the refrigerator. Plastic cups were all she had to drink from. Rick popped the cork on the champagne and filled their cups.

"Here's to banging in the new year," she said, holding her cup out so Rick and Gina could join her in the toast.

And looking at her new, still-naked friends, Belinda had a feeling it was going to be a good year for more than just business.

Blast from the Past

My wife Lori has never been one to talk about her sexual fantasies. We've been married for a few years now, and still I know very little about what turns her on. Me, I'm another story altogether. I'm an open book. I talk about my fantasies every chance I get, to just about anyone who will listen.

Last week, though, after a particularly wild bout of fucking, Lori decided she wanted to talk about fantasies. We lay in bed, both of us naked and glistening with a fine sheen of sweat, and she asked me if I wanted to hear about one of her hottest fantasies.

"Are you kidding?" I said. "I've been waiting for this since the day we met."

She proceeded to tell me how she fantasized about being fucked by two men at the same time. Nothing fancy. Just a good old-fashioned threesome. I thought about it for a minute and realized the idea of sharing my wife with another man appealed to me.

I wanted to keep her talking, so I tossed around suggestions as to who we might get to join us if we were to go through with it. She rejected all of my friends, saying it would be too awkward afterward, and picking up a stranger was out of the question because it wasn't safe. That didn't leave many options.

"What about your ex-husband?" I asked in an offhanded manner.

"That might work," she said.

"I was kidding, baby," I told her, grabbing a pack of cigarettes from the nightstand and lighting one up.

"It's actually a good idea," she said. "Mike would do it, I know that much, and after it's over, we can send him on his way."

"You don't even like the guy."

"That makes it even better," she said. "I don't have to like him to fuck him. It would be strictly sex. He was always pretty good in bed."

"I'm not sure I needed to hear that," I said, making it sound as if I were joking, but meaning it just the same.

She plucked the cigarette from between my lips, took a drag, then climbed on top of me. She leaned over and stubbed the cigarette out in the ashtray.

"It's settled, then. We'll ask Mike."

Before I could offer further debate, she reached back and stroked my cock. I was already hard again. She raised her ass slightly, aimed the head of my cock at her wet pussy, and sat down on it.

She started riding me, sliding up and down on my cock as she leaned up to dangle her breasts in my face. She bounced hard, gasping and moaning when she reached her climax, and just before I came inside her, I found myself wondering if she was thinking about her ex-husband now, already anticipating the things they would do together in our bedroom.

* * *

Lori was right about one thing. Mike was willing. I called him the next day, just like I promised, and arranged for him to come to our house the following Friday. It was all I could do to keep him from hanging up and driving the distance to our house right then, and he couldn't have sounded more grateful for the opportunity to fuck Lori again.

The Big Night came quicker than I felt comfortable with, but the plans had been set into motion. Lori didn't get all dolled up in some sexy fuck-me outfit like I expected her to, and quite frankly, I felt better that she hadn't. Still, she looked great. Her blonde hair was pulled up in a ponytail, she wore a casual blouse, jeans, and tennis shoes—she looked like a mild-mannered soccer-mom, which couldn't have been further from the truth.

Not that I'd call my wife a slut, but I saw a side of her that night I'd never seen before.

The evening started with imported beer in the living room. Lori and I sat on the couch and Mike took the loveseat. The conversation was limited at first, even a little strained. We intentionally stayed away from discussing the main event. It would happen when it happened, and talking about it beforehand would only make it more complicated.

Half an hour or so into the evening, Mike went to the bathroom.

"Are you still okay with this?" Lori asked.

"Yeah, I'm okay with it."

"Good," she said.

There was a slight pregnant silence. She had something else to say. I waited, and when she finally spoke, I could tell by her tone that she was nervous.

"There's something I want . . . if it's okay with you," she said.

"Name it,"

"I wanna feel both of your dicks in me at the same time."

The comment caught me by surprise, but before I could respond, Mike came back from the bathroom.

Lori was ready to go. She was beginning to fidget like she always did when she was eager and anxious about something at the same time.

"Why don't you go sit by Mike," I suggested.

She looked at me for a long moment, giving me another chance to change my mind, then she went over and sat beside Mike. She leaned over and kissed him. Her lips brushed his mouth tentatively at first, and then she began to nibble his lower lip, finally working her tongue into his mouth.

She dropped one hand on his lap and fumbled with the button of his jeans, then she shoved her hand down inside his pants and came out with his stiff cock, letting it flop down against his stomach. She continued kissing him as she rubbed her palm up and down the length of his cock.

She unbuttoned Mike's shirt and pushed it open so she could lick his nipples, then she said, "Get naked."

While he clumsily removed his clothes, Lori stood up and started undressing. She took off her blouse first, then her shoes and socks, then her bra. She reached back and unhooked the bra clasp, then leaned forward slightly, shaking the satin cups away from her tits. Her boobs are big and heavy, and they bounced and jiggled as the bra fell away. She took off her jeans last, leaving her purple lace panties on for the time being.

Mike stroked his hard-on as he stared up at Lori. He had a big, stupid grin on his face, looking at her as if he'd never seen her naked before.

Lori knelt on the floor in front of him and moved between his legs, sliding her hands over the tops of his thighs. She looked over at me for encouragement. I gave her a slight smile and a nod. *Sure, honey, go right ahead and blow your ex-husband. That's what we're here for, right?*

She lowered her head between his legs and licked his cock, dragging her tongue along the length of it until she reached its fleshy helmet-shaped tip. She slid her fingers under his cock and lifted it, flicking her tongue against the underside a few times before she took it in her mouth and started sucking.

She jerked him off while she sucked, moving her mouth and fist in unison, occasionally twisting her hand on his dick. Her blue eyes tilted up to watch his facial expressions, which bothered me more than the actual sucking did. For several minutes she made love to his cock orally, and during that time I didn't seem to exist at all.

She finally glanced my way, as if suddenly remembering I was there, and pulled her head back, letting his cock slip from her mouth with a wet slurp

She stood up. "Take off your clothes, honey," she said to me.

She climbed onto the loveseat and lay down, planting one foot on the floor and draping the other over the back of the loveseat. She tugged her panties aside and asked Mike to eat her out.

He dove in, pressing his face into the soft blonde curls of her bush, wiggling his tongue between her plump lips. His hands disappeared under her ass and he lifted her to his face, lapping her pussy like a dog laps water in the heat of the day.

I discarded the last of my clothes and went over to stand next to the loveseat, placing one knee on the arm and leaning up so my cock bobbed next to Lori's head. She opened her mouth and grabbed my cock to guide it into her mouth.

Mike was enthusiastic about eating Lori's pussy. He made sloppy wet noises as he sucked and licked her. His cheeks were shiny with her juices. Lori made muffled moans around my cock, which told me she was pleased with what Mike was doing to her.

He pulled her panties off so he could have unobstructed access to her pussy, then he pushed two fingers inside her and nibbled her clit with renewed vigor.

I fucked her mouth, angling my cock so it went to the back of her throat without difficulty. I got a little overexcited a couple of times and went too far, causing her to gag, and finally I quit moving and let Lori suck instead.

It wasn't long before she was thrashing her hips up, grinding her pussy against Mike's mouth. She turned away from me, letting my cock slide from her mouth, gasping and panting as she watched Mike.

"You miss that pussy, don't you?" she said breathlessly, her tits rising and falling with the uneven rhythm of a fast-approaching orgasm.

Mike nodded and grunted something unintelligible.

"I'm gonna come . . . stick that tongue inside me . . ."

Her ass bounced against the cushions of the loveseat. Her boobs shook like Jell-O. She reached out and grabbed hold of my cock, squeezing and jerking her hand up and down erratically, then she put it in her mouth again, swirling her tongue around the head of as she took it down her throat and started sucking.

She lifted her ass all the way off the loveseat, her legs trembling as she came, her pussy bumping against his face, and then she collapsed back down on the loveseat. Her hand drifted away from my cock and she sat up, leaning over to kiss Mike, tasting herself on his lips.

"Let's take this to the bedroom," she said decisively.

She hopped up and hurried off. Mike and I followed. She was already on the bed waiting for us. She patted the bed with two hands, indicating we should come up and kneel one on either side of her.

"Let me suck your cocks," she said.

We climbed onto the bed, Mike on her left, me on her right. She took our cocks, one in each hand, and leaned over to lick and nibble the head of my cock first, then she moved over and did the same to Mike. She alternated between us, always jerking one cock while she sucked the other.

"Let me see if I can suck you both at once," she said.

She pulled us to her by our dicks, pressing them together so she could run her tongue over both cocks at the same time. She rubbed the head of each dick against her cheeks, then she began forcing both into her mouth.

She tried sucking both cocks at once without much success, so after teasing us with her tongue a little longer, she let us take turns fucking her mouth, Mike first, then me, then Mike, then my cock again when he withdrew, each cock sliding and withdrawing at once, only to be replaced immediately by the other.

She put both cocks in her mouth again, determined to swallow more of them this time than she had the first. She grabbed our asses and pulled us to her, forcing our cocks further into her mouth than seemed possible. Her cheeks bulged like a squirrel hiding nuts and saliva ran down her chin, but despite her best effort, she had to give up, gasping for air as our cocks slipped out of her mouth.

She wasn't finished with us yet, though. She moved back and forth between us, licking our cocks, popping them into her mouth one at a time to suck on them, and licking our balls.

"Somebody eat my pussy," she gasped. "The other one can fuck my mouth."

Mike straddled her chest. She stuck her tongue out. He smacked it a few times with his cock, then slid his dick deep into her mouth. He raised up slightly, giving himself a better angle, then leaned up to hold on to the headboard for leverage.

I wasted no time getting between Lori's legs. She pulled her knees back and dropped them flat on the bed, opening her pussy wide for me. Her little pink opening winked invitingly. I teased around the opening with light strokes of my tongue, then I slowly worked my tongue inside her.

She was soaking wet. My face was drenched by her juices as I immersed it in the slippery heat. As I fucked her pussy with my tongue, darting it in and out, I found myself wondering, maybe a little paranoid, if this was what it would take from now on to keep her happy. Would she always need two men?

Crazy thoughts, I know, but one of the dangers of sharing someone you love with another person, sexually or otherwise. Human beings are possessive by nature. We like to hang on to things. If we feel threatened, we start to think those crazy thoughts, and then jealousy sets in. It's the reason most threesomes don't work out well. Somebody usually gets fucked in the end, and not in the way it was originally intended.

I reminded myself it was sex, nothing more or less. It was one of my wife's fantasies. I was helping her make it happen. It was something we were doing *together,* as a couple.

I looked over the blonde mound of Lori's pussy as I nibbled her hard little clit. I couldn't see her face because Mike's ass was blocking my view. Her hands were on his ass, her fingers squeezing tight as she brought him into her mouth. I could hear his balls slapping against her chin. The bed shook with the rhythm of his cock slipping in and out of her mouth.

Lori's hips bucked against me and she started rotating them, rubbing her pussy against my face. I slid two fingers deep inside her pussy and fucked her with them as I flicked my tongue back and forth over her clit.

She arched her back as she came again, her legs trembling as she held herself suspended above the bed. After it was over, she dropped her ass back down on the bed, pushing Mike away from her as she did.

"Give me a minute," she gasped.

A minute was all she ever needed. She could come multiple times, and with a minute in between, she was always ready to go again.

"You guys want another beer?" she asked, rolling off the bed and heading for the kitchen before we had a chance to respond.

When she came back with the beers, the three of us stretched out on the bed, with Lori between Mike and me.

"Are we having fun yet?" she said, following the question with a sip of beer.

"Hell yes," Mike said.

"I bet you are," Lori said, laughing. "You finally got me to suck your dick."

"You never sucked his cock when you were married?" I asked, surprised by the revelation.

"Not once," she said.

"How come?"

She shrugged. "Don't know, really. I just never did."

"It wasn't for lack of trying on my part," Mike put in. "I begged her to suck my cock, and not just once in a while . . ."

Lori grabbed hold of his cock, which was still fully erect. "Poor baby," she said, massaging his erection. "But I made up for it today, huh?"

"Don't forget me," I said.

I took her beer away from her and set it on the nightstand, then I took her newly freed hand and placed it on my cock.

"Jealous?" she asked, smiling at me as she stroked my dick.

"Maybe a little," I answered.

I tried to *sound* like I was joking, but there was, in fact, some truth to it.

The entire exchange went right over Mike's head. He was busy fingering Lori's pussy. He moved a finger deep inside her, pulled it out, and dragged it along the folds of her pink slit, bringing it to rest on her clit, which he began to rub in a slow circular motion.

"Yeah, that feels good . . ." Lori said in a whispering half moan.

She gave my cock a good, hard squeeze. I stuck a finger in her pussy while Mike continued to massage her clit. It wasn't long before she was worked up again, undulating her hips, pushing her pussy up and down on my finger . . .

"Remember what we talked about earlier?" she panted.

Mike was confused.

"Yeah . . . I remember," I said.

"I wanna do it now," she said, her words tumbling out in an excited rush.

"What am I missing?" Mike asked.

"She wants both our cocks at the same time," I told him.

"Both of us . . . the same time?"

"I want both of you to fuck my pussy," she said. She got up on her knees and patted the bed. "Lay down," she said to Mike.

He stretched out on the bed, resting his head against the headboard. Lori climbed on top of him, straddling him in a reverse cowgirl position, then reached down and lifted his erection, pressing the tip of it against her wet opening. She sank all the way down on it, sighing with pleasure when she was fully impaled.

She fell back and put her arms behind her, pressing her hands flat on the bed for support, then brought her pussy to the tip of Mike's cock, rotating her hips to work her pussy around on him before dropping down again. The lips of her pussy stretched wide to accommodate his girth. Her slick pink folds clung to his glistening shaft, folding in and out as she rode up and down.

"Oh yeah . . . that feels so good," she said, half grunting the words.

She suddenly threw herself forward, putting her hands on the mattress in front of her, pumping her ass up and down.

Her tits swung down and scraped Mike's thighs, swinging back and forth as she put every ounce of effort into riding him. For a long moment the only sounds in the room were the sounds of her ass and pussy banging away at Mike and her tits slapping back against her ribcage.

I was kneeling on the end of the bed, pumping my cock in my fist, watching my wife ride her ex-husband's cock. It worked for a while, but then I started to get that old familiar feeling—the left-out feeling—and then Lori raised her head and met my eyes. She knew right away what I needed.

She sat up and leaned back, offering her pussy to me. "Now," she said. "Put your cock inside me."

She was breathing heavy from her workout. Her skin glistened with a thin sheen of sweat. Some of her hair was plastered to the side of her face.

I moved between Mike's legs and leaned over Lori, grasping my cock in my right hand and guiding it up to her pussy.

"You sure?" I asked her, more for my benefit than hers.

"I'm sure," she said.

Mike hooked his hands behind her knees and drew her legs back, opening her pussy as wide as he could. I angled my cock and slowly pushed into her, inching forward until I was all the way inside.

It was a snug fit, with not much room to move around, but we did the best we could. Mike and I took turns moving thrusting into Lori. She squirmed around between us and worked the muscles of her pussy on our cocks.

"How's it feel, baby?" I asked.

"Good . . . " was all she managed to say.

Mike and I alternated strokes. The friction caused by our cocks rubbing together in the confines of Lori's cunt added to the overall pleasure. We established a sort of rhythm, grinding our cocks around inside her, and pretty soon she was moaning and groaning and breathing heavy.

"I can't do this much longer," she gasped. "You need to hurry up and come."

"I'm almost there," Mike said.

I wasn't far behind. The tight grip of Lori's pussy coupled with the friction of Mike's cock slipping and sliding against mine was quite the incentive.

"Shit . . ." Mike grunted.

I felt his cock jerk as he unloaded inside my wife. A couple of thrusts later I added my come to the mix. The extra lubrication paved the way for both our cocks to push deep inside Lori.

I collapsed on top of her, my weight pressing her down on Mike. I withdrew my cock, dribbling come onto her pussy, and rolled over to one side of the bed.

She lifted her pussy off Mike's cock. There was a wet sucking sound as his cock slipped out of her cunt and fell back against his stomach. A flood of milky come washed out of Lori, soaking her thighs and spilling onto the sheets.

"Yuck . . . I need a shower," she said.

She hopped off the bed and ran out of the room. A moment later the shower was running in the bathroom.

Mike and I sat naked together, our erections quickly fading away. The heat of the moment was gone, leaving us in an awkward position.

"Think we'll do this again?" Mike asked.

I needed a cigarette. I found a pack in the drawer of the nightstand. I offered one to Mike, lit mine, then tossed him the lighter.

"I don't think so," I said in answer to his question. "That was what you'd call a once-in-a-lifetime deal."

He nodded as if he understood completely.

Booze, Toys, and No Boys

Heather had started selling Dr. Love products to just a few select girlfriends a couple of months ago, but she hadn't been making the sort of money she'd hoped for. A few of her girlfriends, as horny as they were, weren't enough customers to pay her rent. She needed to do what the Dr. Love brochures suggested. She needed to host parties and invite all her friends, and she needed her friends to invite their friends, and so on down the line. She needed clientele.

She scheduled her first party on a Saturday night. She planned it a month in advance, sent out invitations, and promised free gifts to all who attended. It was going to be an all-girl event—booze, toys, and no boys.

Casey and Liz, both married to men who wouldn't know romance if it bit them on the balls, confirmed their attendance right away. Angie, who had plenty of boyfriends to experiment with, called to say she'd be there. Michelle was coming too, promising to bring a few of her girlfriends with her. Rachel, who'd recently been dumped by a cheating boyfriend, tentatively accepted the invitation.

Heather wanted the party to be a success. She had a wide selection of naughty samples for the girls to look at, a case of pink champagne, and three huge party trays. She'd even rented a couple of porno movies for entertainment.

The party started at seven, but quite a few girls showed up early.

"Wow," Angie said, immediately heading over to a table covered with an assortment of lotions and lingerie. "This is some pretty cool stuff."

"Try anything you want," Heather said. "Those are samples."

Angie began opening bottles and smelling the contents. "This stuff smells good enough to eat," she said. "Put it in the right places and it could be fun."

The women poured champagne and began to look at some of the product samples Heather had laid out.

Angie picked up a long, thick double-ended dildo. "Holy shit," she said, a big smile plastered across her face. "This thing could be dangerous." She waved the big dildo around, and some of the other women started laughing.

"There's something about you that's not right," Margo said.

Margo was a plump blonde who looked as if she'd be more at home at a PTA meeting than here at a Dr. Love party. She blushed and turned away from Angie's antics, occupying herself instead with some of the lingerie items on display.

"Anybody want chocolate?" Heather asked, producing a foot-long cock made of milk chocolate and wrapped in a giant pink condom.

"I *love* chocolate," Michelle said.

Heather handed her the chocolate cock. "It's all yours," she said.

"Who uses something like this?" Angie asked, still swinging the double dong around. "I mean, shit, I like 'em big, but this is crazy."

"I think they're for lezzies," Casey said.

Casey was pretty and petite, blonde with blue eyes, and a little flighty.

"See, I really don't get that," Angie said. "If you're a carpet muncher, why the hell would you want to fuck each other with a fake *dick?* Does that make sense?"

"Sure it does," Margo said, pouring herself more champagne. "The dick isn't the problem. It's the men attached to them that lezzies avoid."

A loud burst of laughter filled the room.

Rachel checked out the DVDs and put one in the player.

"Wow, I haven't seen one of those since college," Liz said.

On the TV, a busty blonde was doing a striptease for a naked man who was lying on a bed and stroking his cock as he watched.

Michelle sat down in front of the TV to watch the movie. She unwrapped the chocolate cock and took a bite.

"I sure hope you treat your men better than that," Angie said. "You could've at least *licked* it first."

Rachel sifted through a selection of lingerie. She found a pair of black panties with red lips imprinted all over them. "Now these are cute," she said, holding the panties up for inspection.

"I think there's a bra that matches them," Heather said.

Rachel found the bra, which was lacy and had holes cut out for the nipples. "I wanna buy this," Rachel said. "It's just too cute."

"Try it on," Heather said.

Rachel wasn't the least bit shy. She stood up right there in front of everybody, took off her clothes, and put on the bra and panties. Her nipples were small and pale pink. They stuck out of the little openings in the front of the bra. A few wispy curls of red pubic hair peeked out around the edges of the panties.

"Whattaya think?" she asked, doing a pirouette to show off the outfit.

"Sexy," Liz said.

Casey tried several bottles of champagne and found them all empty. "Any more of this?" she asked, tipping an empty bottle upside down.

"In the kitchen," Heather said. "I'll get some."

The action on the TV was heating up. Michelle was still engrossed. Angie joined her. The blonde from the beginning of the movie was now servicing two well-hung porn studs.

"Now *there's* a lucky girl," Angie said.

"You're such a slut," Casey said, then as an afterthought, "Have you ever done that, though? Fucked two guys at once?"

"I have, and it was awesome," Angie said.

Liz came up behind Angie and leaned over her shoulder to look at the TV.

"How do you get into a situation like that to begin with?" she asked.

"Lots of booze," Angie said. "I was dating this guy, and one night he brought a friend of his to my house. We all started drinking, one thing led to another, and voilà, they were both fucking me."

"I wish I had half the sense of adventure you do," Casey said.

Heather returned with more champagne and some pretzels.

"Let's play dress up," she suggested, rifling through some lingerie.

Casey joined her and selected a simple white bra and panty set made of sheer fabric, complete with ruffled garter belt and stockings.

Angie decided on a black leather bustier and crotchless panties that matched.

Liz, who chose a sheer blue baby doll, glanced over at Angie and saw that Angie's pussy was completely shaved.

"Do you keep it that way all the time?" she asked.

"Yep," Angie said. "It drives the guys wild. Don't ask me why, but it does."

"It makes 'em think they've got a sweet young thing," Michelle said, taking a red fishnet bodysuit from the lingerie display. "I used to shave, but it got to be a pain in the ass."

"It *is* a pain in the ass, but I like the reaction I get from the guys."

The blonde in the movie was doing a sixty-nine with another girl. Casey glanced at the TV and said, "Damn, *every*body gets to fuck her."

Several silent moments passed as the women watched the two girls in the movie eat each other out. Rachel finally broke the silence.

"That looks kinda fun," she said. She poured more champagne. "Anybody here ever had sex with another woman?"

"Not me," Angie answered right away. "I like dick too much."

"You saying you'd never even think about trying it?" Margo asked.

"I never say never," Angie said. "I've just never had the opportunity."

"I did, back in college," Liz said. "I had a roommate. We fooled around, you know, fingered each other, made out . . . nothing serious."

Rachel seemed impressed. "I've thought about it, but I've never tried it or anything. It's just one of those fantasies I figured I'd never do."

"I'll tell you what," Casey said. "All this sexy talk is making my pussy wet. I haven't gotten any in three months."

"Tell me about it," Liz said. "I'm pretty good with my fingers, but playing with yourself only goes so far."

Heather opened a box of chocolate candies, took one, and passed the box to Michelle, who took a piece and then handed the box to Angie.

Angie took a chocolate and said, "So let's have an orgy," then popped the candy into her mouth.

The women all looked at her as if she'd come from another planet. There was an awkward silence. She looked from one to another. "Oh, come on," she said. "Don't tell me it hasn't crossed your minds. It'll be our little secret—a sort of girls'-night-out thing."

Looks were exchanged. There seemed to be no objections, but no one was eager to make the first move either. Angie finally shrugged, scooted over beside Rachel, who just happened to be closest to her, and kissed her on the mouth.

Rachel didn't hesitate to respond. She opened her mouth to allow Angie's tongue to explore. Angie ran a hand over Rachel's flat tummy and moved it up until she found one of Rachel's small breasts. She cupped the breast and slid her thumb over Rachel's exposed nipple.

Casey and Michelle, both sitting on the floor, paired up and began to undress and fondle each other.

Heather, Liz, and Margo were on the couch. They looked at one another. Heather said, "Guess we've got a threesome, huh?"

Liz and Margo sandwiched Heather between them and took turns kissing her. Liz pulled her nightie over her head and offered her tits to Heather, who began to suck eagerly on the nipples.

Margo got down on the floor and pushed Heather's legs apart. She began kissing the insides of Heather's thighs, working her way slowly to the damp crotch of Heather's panties.

Liz lay back on the couch, draping one leg over the back of the couch and letting the other dangle over the side. Heather stroked Liz's thighs and then worked a finger under Liz's panties. She teased the outer lips of Liz's pussy and then slid her finger into Liz's moist, hot opening.

"Ummm," Liz moaned. "That feels good."

Liz arched her back, giving herself to Heather's probing finger. Heather pushed her finger as far in as possible, then she added another, opening Liz wide.

Margo tugged Heather's panties aside and started licking her pussy.

Rachel reached behind her back and unhooked her bra. She cupped her tits, each no more than a handful, and pushed them together, offering them to Angie, who went to work on them with her tongue.

Angie reached over and grabbed the two-headed dildo. "This is ours," she said to Rachel. "Let's have some fun. Come on, lay down."

Rachel fell back on the floor, raising her butt so she could take off her panties. She opened her legs wide, slipping a finger into her pussy.

Angie straddled Rachel in a sixty-nine and lowered her head between Rachel's legs. Rachel pulled Angie to her, sliding her tongue through the opening of Angie's panties and between the smooth-shaven lips of her pussy.

The room was filled with the combined sounds of seven women giving one another pleasure. Soft moans and sighs, the occasional squeal, and lots of gasping and panting. If there had been any second thoughts among them, those thoughts had given way to wild abandon.

"Oh shit," Michelle said, tangling her fingers in Casey's hair as Casey brought her to the brink of orgasm and then took her over the edge.

Casey lifted her head from between Michelle's legs. Her cheeks glistened with Michelle's pussy juices. She watched Michelle's face as she slid a couple of fingers into her pussy and began to fuck her with them.

"For somebody who's never eaten pussy, you sure know what the hell you're doing," Michelle said. "Now let me return the favor."

By now Margo, Liz, and Heather had joined the others on the floor. All seven of the girls gathered together in a big grope fest, tongues and fingers working on the nearest pussy, mouths sucking the closest nipple.

Angie licked both ends of the two-headed dildo, then lay sideways, scissoring Rachel with her legs. They rubbed against each other for a little bit, then Angie inserted one end of the dildo into Rachel and the other into her own pussy.

"Oh, fuck," Angie groaned.

The soft red curls of Rachel's pussy separated as the dildo pressed into her. The lips of her coral-pink vulva blossomed and the dildo slid effortlessly inside her. Angie rocked her hips gently as she worked her pussy further down on the dildo, inching her way closer to Rachel. She reached over and began rubbing Rachel's clit with her thumb.

"Oh yeah," Rachel gasped. "Oh, *shit* . . ."

Michelle leaned down and started kissing Rachel. Casey was on her knees beside Michelle, pushing a chrome vibrator in and out of her pussy. Margo crawled over and occupied herself by spreading Casey's ass and licking her asshole.

"Check this out," Heather said, snatching up a bottle of champagne.

She tipped the bottle and poured some of the bubbly liquid over Liz's pussy. Liz couldn't resist a quick giggle. "It's cold," she said.

"Gimme," Casey said.

Heather handed Casey the bottle, then she went down on Liz, licking and probing her pussy with her fingers and tongue, lapping up the sweet mixture of champagne and pussy juice.

Casey poured champagne between Michelle's ass cheeks. It dribbled down her crack and over her pussy. Casey pushed the vibrator in and out of Michelle a couple more times, then she removed it and used her tongue, teasing around the outer perimeter of Michelle's taut, wrinkled asshole and then working her way down to push it into Michelle's pussy.

Heather continued using her tongue on Liz. Alternately pushing it inside her, then dragging it along the length of Liz's pink folds until she reached her clitoris.

"You're making me come," Liz said, placing one hand on the back of Heather's head just in case Heather decided to pull away prematurely.

More moaning and groaning filled the room. Angie and Rachel each had taken about half of the double-dong into their pussies, and they were now mashing their clits together around it, thrashing their hips as they began to climax.

Margo appeared beside Angie and Rachel, watching as their pussies bumped together. She reached out to massage one of Angie's tits while she fingered her own pussy. When Rachel and Angie finally stopped thrashing against one another, Margo removed the dildo and leaned down to lick Rachel's pussy first, and then she moved over to Angie's pussy.

"Easy," Angie said, jerking her hips slightly as Margo's tongue teased her clit. "I get sensitive right after . . ."

Heather and Liz were finished for the moment. They sat side by side, both flushed and out of breath.

Michelle started moaning and then cried out sharply as Casey, who was once again using the vibrator on Michelle's slick pussy, made Michelle come.

"Anymore to drink?" Margo asked.

She found two champagne bottles, both empty.

"Here's a full one," Liz said, taking a bottle from the table.

Heather tossed her the corkscrew and she opened it. Thick foam bubbled from the bottle and ran down the sides, dribbling over Liz's fingers.

"Now that's symbolism," Angie said, scooting closer to Liz.

"Where's my glass?" Liz asked.

"I don't think we need to worry about glasses," Angie said. "If any of us have germs, we've already thoroughly shared them. Give me a drink."

Liz tipped the bottle and took a swig of the bubbly before handing it to Angie.

"Hey, an orgy," Margo said. She was watching the porn movie's big finale.

The same blonde who'd been in all the scenes was in this one too, now joined by an Asian girl with grapefruit-size tits, a light-skinned black girl, and a tall, slender brunette. Two lucky men were doing their best to service the girls.

"That girl has to be worn out," Heather said.

"You're telling me," Casey said, heading over to look through some of the assorted toys Heather had laid out.

"I'm not sure I could enjoy fucking if I had to do it like that, you know, as a job," Michelle said.

"I could," Angie said.

Casey picked up a long red jelly dildo. "Who wants to play?" she said.

"Over here," Angie said.

Casey carried the dildo over and kneeled beside Angie. She put the tip of it in her mouth to get it wet.

"Wait . . . try some of this," Heather said. She grabbed a tube of lubricant. "It's fruity flavored."

"Great, just what I've always wanted," Casey said. "Fruity-flavored pussy."

Heather laughed. "Just try it. It's really good."

38

Casey opened the tube, gave it a quick sniff, then squeezed some over the head of the dildo. Angie lay back on the floor with her knees bent and wide apart. Casey rubbed the bulbous tip of the dildo up and down between the lips of her pussy and very slowly began working it into her.

The rest of the girls gathered around to watch.

Casey worked half of the dildo into Angie's pussy and bent down to lick Angie's clit as she started pushing and twisting the dildo inside Angie, going a little deeper with it each time she pushed in.

Margo moved up beside Angie and took one of her nipples in her mouth, sucking hard on it. Michelle went to work on her other nipple, circling it with her tongue a few times before drawing it into her mouth.

Heather and Rachel kissed. Liz moved up behind Rachel and reached between her legs to stroke her pussy. Heather kissed Rachel's tits, licked around her nipples, and then moved down to kiss the mound of her pussy.

"Wait . . ." Rachel said.

She stretched out on the floor. Heather and Liz took up positions, one on either side of Rachel, and started sucking and licking her nipples, occasionally stopping to kiss each other before going back to Rachel's tiny, hard nipples.

Heather started down first, and Liz followed her lead. They took turns licking her navel before finally converging on her pussy, attacking her clit simultaneously with quick pink tongues. Their combined efforts had Rachel moaning in no time.

Angie's legs were high in the air, feet wide apart. She propped herself on her elbows to watch as Casey sucked her pussy and pushed the jelly dong in and out.

"You're good at that," she said.

Margo lifted her mouth from Angie's tit and leaned up to kiss her, then she moved down to take Casey's place. As Margo bent down to lick Angie's pussy and work the dildo into her, Casey got behind Margo and pressed her hands against Margo's ass, squeezing the soft cheeks as she pulled them apart.

Margo shifted her bottom slightly and moaned into Angie's pussy.

Casey dragged her tongue between Margo's plump pussy lips, pressing aside the slick red folds of her vulva and pushing the tip of her tongue into Margo's wet entrance. Margo pressed back against Casey and shifted her ass again, settling herself on Casey's tongue.

"Let me eat you," Angie said to Michelle.

Casey stopped eating Margo long enough to get a strap-on cock. It was a latex model with a leather harness. She fixed it to her waist and took Margo by the hips, guiding the latex cock into her pussy, and then she began to fuck Margo.

Michelle lay back on the floor, scooting her bottom as close to Angie as she could get. Angie had to twist her upper body to comfortably reach Michelle. She slid two fingers into her pussy and pressed her thumb down on her clit, applying circular pressure with her thumb as she pushed her fingers in and out of Michelle's slick pussy.

For a long time the room was filled with soft moans and gasping, the wet sounds of licking and sucking, and intermittent squeals of delight as one after the other of the women found pleasure.

Another round of orgasms and more champagne.

"I'm not so sure I wanna go home to my husband after all this," Liz said.

"You're telling me," Casey agreed. "I might just turn lesbian all the way."

"I should've stuck with it in college."

A couple of the girls giggled.

"You should've majored in pussy eating, huh?" Margo said.

"You're terrible," Heather said.

More laughing. They were having the time of their lives. Heather went into the kitchen and came back with two more bottles of champagne.

"Last two," she said.

She handed a bottle to one of the other girls and popped the cork on the other bottle, licking up some of the foam that spilled down its side.

"This reminds me of sleepovers when I was a little girl," Rachel said. "Except for the sex, I mean."

"We really should do this more often," Liz said. "Hell yes," Angie added.

"Well, it's not over yet," Heather said. "Let's play Twister naked."

Everybody thought it was a good idea, and after passing around the last of the champagne, they climbed into a naked pile on the Twister mat and began to tie themselves into a sweet, sexy knot. . . .

Bumping Monkeys

Traci and Caitlyn ended up at the Pink Palace, a lesbian bar known for great dancing. They picked the bar because they wanted to be able to dance and drink without having to fend off a bunch of drunk guys while they were trying to have a good time. They made a pact before they went into the club to pretend to be lovers, that way they wouldn't have to worry about being hit on by a bunch of lesbians either.

It seemed like a good plan.

They attracted lots of attention as soon as they walked through the door. Both were blonde, each was cute in a girl-next-door sort of way. Traci was skinny, with small boobs and dark blonde hair. Caitlyn, by contrast, had longer hair, a little more blonde than Traci's, a fuller figure, and huge boobs.

They made their way to the bar, ordered drinks, and went in search of a table. The place was packed with a wide range of women, some obviously dykes, others more feminine and very pretty.

They found a corner table and sat down to enjoy their drinks. It wasn't long before a dyke approached them. She wore torn jeans and a T-shirt that read *I clean carpets.*

"Wanna dance?" she asked Caitlyn.

"We're together," Caitlyn said, nodding at Traci.

"Oh, cool, sorry," the dyke said, turning away with a shrug, making her way back across the dance floor.

"See how well that works," Caitlyn said.

Traci lit a cigarette. "Want one?"

She held the pack across the table. Caitlyn took one. She'd quit smoking a long time ago, but she still did it when she drank. It was the only time cigarettes tasted good to her.

They finished their drinks and went to dance. The first couple of songs were fast. They faced one another on the dance floor, bumping and grinding to the music, shaking their asses, and having a good time.

A slow song came on. Some of the women on the dance floor coupled up, their bodies pressed together, grinding and kissing as they danced to the music.

Traci and Caitlyn went for another round of drinks. The dyke from earlier joined them. She offered to buy both of them drinks. They declined, not wanting to give her the impression they were open to anything kinky.

"I don't believe you two are together," the dyke said, taking a drink of her beer.

"Sure we are," Caitlyn insisted.

"You haven't touched each other since you came in."

"We're just not affectionate in public," Traci said defensively.

"Bullshit," the dyke responded. "I can spot a couple of straight chicks a mile away."

"Whatever," Caitlyn said, turning her back to the dyke.

"So prove it," the dyke said. "Kiss her."

Caitlyn turned around again, ready to knock her on her ass. "You know what, bi—"

Traci grabbed Caitlyn by her shoulders and spun her around, kissing her before Caitlyn knew what was happening. Caitlyn surprised herself by opening her mouth to let Traci's tongue slip inside.

The kiss was hot enough to convince the dyke she was wrong about them.

"My bad," she said, once again going off to another part of the bar, presumably to harass somebody else.

"What the hell was that?" Caitlyn asked when the dyke was out of earshot.

"You were about to start a fight in a lesbian bar," Traci said. "How else was I supposed to stop you?"

"You didn't need to stop me. I could've kicked her ass," Caitlyn said.

"And then we'd have a bar full of dykes on us. No thanks."

Caitlyn picked up her drink, looking at Traci over the rim of the glass as she sipped it.

"What?" Traci asked innocently.

"That kiss," Caitlyn said.

"What about it?"

"Pretty hot shit."

"Oh."

Traci blushed.

They finished their second round of drinks and went back to the dance floor. The first song was fast. The next was slow. Traci started to leave the dance floor.

"Wait," Caitlyn said.

Traci turned and looked at her.

"Let's slow dance."

"Really?" Traci asked.

"Sure, why not?" Caitlyn said. "We've already made out."

She held her arms out, palms up. Traci took hold of her hands. Caitlyn pulled her close. They slipped their arms around each other and began to sway to the sensuous music, their bodies pressed together, the two of them looking into each other's eyes.

Then they kissed for the second time that night. A hot, passionate kiss, tongues dancing together and darting into each other's mouth. It was a kiss that seemed as if it would never end—a kiss that left them both flush with excitement.

They had one more drink before they left.

"Where to?" Caitlyn asked, starting the car.

"Um . . . I don't know," Traci replied with uncertainty in her voice. "Not home."

She smiled.

Caitlyn smiled back.

"No, not home," Caitlyn agreed.

They stopped at a grocery store, bought two bottles of wine, and got a motel room. They were only half way through the first bottle of wine when they started making out, peeling off their clothes a little at a time, until both of them wore nothing but panties.

They finished the first bottle of wine, which, in conjunction with the drinks they'd had earlier at the Pink Palace, had them feeling pretty good.

They fell back on the bed, facing one another. Traci draped one leg over Caitlyn and they kissed.

Caitlyn reached down and rubbed Traci's pussy through her damp panties.

"Ummm," Traci moaned into Caitlyn's mouth.

Caitlyn slipped a finger under the elastic of Traci's panties and stuck it into her warm, wet cunt. Traci moaned as Caitlyn's finger slid deep inside her, probing, wiggling around . .
.

"Ohhhh, yeahhh . . . I like that," she said.

"You like that?"

"Yeah, nice."

Caitlyn withdrew her finger and got up on her knees, removing her panties, tossing them over the side of the bed. She hooked her fingers in the waistband of Traci's panties and tugged them down.

Traci pulled her knees back and opened them wide, exposing the slick pink folds of her vulva. She ran her hand over her mound and cupped her pussy, inserting a slender finger inside herself.

"I'm so wet," she said.

Caitlyn put her head between Traci's legs and slid her hands under her bottom. She pressed her mouth to Traci's pussy, licking the opening, running her tongue between her outer lips and over her slick, pink vulva.

She caught Traci's clit between her lips and nibbled, working her tongue against the smooth surface, back and forth and in tiny circles. She drew it into her mouth, sucking gently, teasing it until Traci was moving beneath her, slowly pumping her hips, rubbing her pussy hard against Caitlyn's mouth.

"Oh, God . . . shit, that feels good."

Caitlyn watched Traci's face over the mound of her pussy, gauging her reaction to various techniques. Caitlyn had no idea what she was doing, but she knew what she liked done to her, and those were the things she did to Traci.

Traci arched her back, thrusting her pussy at Caitlyn, moaning as she felt the first waves of her orgasm. She grabbed the back of Caitlyn's head with two hands, tangling her fingers in her hair, screaming with pleasure as her climax reached its peak.

She fell away from Caitlyn when it was over, her chest rising and falling unsteadily as she fought to recover from the intensity of her orgasm.

"God, you're good at that," she said.

"Thank you," Caitlyn said.

"My turn," Traci told her.

They switched places.

Traci went down on Caitlyn, holding her plump outer lips apart as she slid her tongue into Caitlyn's pussy. She pushed her tongue deep inside Caitlyn and wiggled it around, then she pulled it out and flicked it over her clit.

"How's that?" she asked, her lips hovering against Caitlyn's clit, her breath warm against it as she spoke.

"Perfect," Caitlyn answered, rocking her hips slowly at Traci. "Just don't stop."

She reached down and slid her fingers through Traci's hair, gently urging her to get back to work.

Traci nibbled Caitlyn's clit, then she slid her tongue back into Caitlyn's pussy and fucked her with it.

"You're making me come," Caitlyn panted. "Don't stop."

She pushed her pussy against Traci's face, rolling side to side as her orgasm swept through her. Her muscles tightened as she reached the apex. She clamped her thighs around Traci's head, holding her in place as she shuddered with release.

They lay together afterward, working on the second bottle of wine. Caitlyn rolled onto her side, facing Traci, her head propped in her hand. She took a drink of wine and handed the bottle to Traci, who was leaning against the headboard of the bed.

46

"I've got an idea," Caitlyn said, getting up on her knees as she took the wine bottle from Traci and set it on the dresser beside the bed. "Let's bump monkeys."

Traci laughed hard. "What the hell is bumping monkeys?"

"You've never heard of that? It's a lesbian thing. It's when two girls grind their pussies together."

"Oh my God, that's hilarious," Traci said, still laughing.

Her laughter was contagious. Caitlyn laughed with her, and soon they were both laughing so hard they had tears in their eyes.

"Okay," Traci said, trying to pull on a serious face. "let's bump monkeys."

The laughter came again, just as hard as before. It was several minutes before they were able to keep straight faces and talk again.

"Don't say it," Traci said. "Let's just do it."

A long moment passed where they fought the urge to laugh anyway. They struggled to keep it together.

"Okay," Traci said, putting on a serious face, "How do we do it?"

"We lay down and, you know, just sort of scissor each other," Caitlyn explained.

"Oh, you're an expert?" Traci said, teasing her.

"No, I just know that's how lesbians do it."

They lay facing each other, legs scissored, coming together until they were pussy to pussy. They shifted and squirmed until their clits bumped and rubbed together, causing them to moan with satisfaction.

They began grinding, thrusting their hips, rubbing their pussies together. The room became silent except for the long, low moans, the soft panting, and the rhythmic squeak of mattress springs.

They worked their pelvises in slow, grinding circles . . .

"God, that feels good," Caitlyn moaned.

Their taut bellies undulated with the effort . . .

"I'm about to come," Traci panted.

They slammed their pussies together, filling the room with the soft, rhythmic slap of their bodies in their frenzied pursuit of sapphic pleasure.

"I'm coming," Traci said, her breath coming in short, panting gasps.

"Ohhhh, yeahhh," Caitlyn said, moaning as she pressed her pussy against Traci's and grinded back and forth.

They locked their legs tight around each other, humping and rubbing their slick cunts together as they came. Hot moans and heavy panting filled the room as they reached the peak of their orgasms together.

They clung to each other for a while, basking in the afterglow of the best sex either could remember having had in a long time. Their bodies, slick with perspiration, slipped together. Their breasts flattened between them, hard nipples against hard nipples.

They shared a deep kiss, their tongues exploring one another's mouth, and then they rolled apart, each of them flushed and fully satiated.

"I didn't expect this to be so fun," Caitlyn said.

"Yeah, you're telling me."

"Now comes the tricky part," Caitlyn said. "I have to tell my husband."

* * *

They were sitting on the couch together, snuggled up, watching TV. Caitlyn wore a short negligee and panties. Mike was in his boxers.

She slid a hand down the front of his boxers and fondled his cock until he got hard, which didn't take long.

"Honey, I have a question," she said.

"Hmm?"

His eyes were closed and he was enjoying the attention she gave his cock.

"Would it be cheating if I had sex with another woman?" she asked.

"Huh?"

"Would I be cheating on you if I did it with another woman?"

"Well, yeah, technically it would," he said. "Cheating's cheating."

She jerked his cock faster.

"Would it be grounds for divorce?" she asked.

"I guess in a court of law, but I wouldn't divorce you over it," he said.

She continued to masturbate him as she told him what had happened between her and Traci. By the time she finished her confession, Mike had a real mess in his boxers. She took her hand out and licked her fingers clean, then she leaned up and gave him a long, deep kiss.

"You wanna watch us?" she asked.

"Hell yes . . ."

She called Traci and invited her over, explaining the situation to her on the phone and asking her to stop on the way and pick up a special toy.

Traci arrived half an hour later, the special toy tucked away inside a bag.

Caitlyn fixed drinks for the three of them, then she and Traci sat together on the couch and started making out.

Mike sat in a recliner, sipping his drink with one hand, stroking his dick through his boxers with the other.

"Am I going to get to join in?" he asked.

"Un-ungh," Caitlyn said.

She raised up on her knees, pulled her negligee off, and pushed her soft tits at Traci, who lifted them to her mouth one at a time to suck the swollen nipples.

Mike reached down into his boxers and stroked his cock.

Caitlyn pulled her tits away from Traci. She lay back on the couch, lifted her ass off the cushions, and slid her panties down. With one foot on the floor and her other legs resting on the back of the couch, she was wide open.

"Eat me," she said, sliding one hand between her legs and spreading the lips of her pussy with two fingers.

Traci turned on the couch, directing her ass in Mike's direction as she lowered her head between Caitlyn's legs and started licking her pussy.

"Yeahhhh," Caitlyn moaned, pumping her hips in wild abandon.

Traci whipped her tongue up and down the length of Caitlyn's pink slit a few times before settling on her clit. She teased the smooth little button with quick strokes of her tongue, then she hooked her lips around it and sucked hard, pulling it deep into her mouth.

Traci raised up and undid the buttons on her blouse. She slipped it from her shoulders and took it off, tossing it aside, then she reached behind her back and unhooked her bra, sliding the straps from her shoulders.

Caitlyn slid her hands up and cupped Traci's small tits, giving them a gentle squeeze, then she rolled the taut nipples between her thumbs and forefingers. She sucked one of Traci's nipples, then moved to the next, flicking it with her tongue before taking it into her mouth.

"Take off your pants," Caitlyn said.

Traci lay back on the couch, kicking her shoes off as she unbuttoned her jeans. She pushed her jeans down to her knees, then Caitlyn took over, pulling them the rest of the way off. She took Traci's panties off next, tossing them across the room to Mike.

"You can play with those," she said.

She settled between Traci's legs and started eating her pussy. Her tongue darted in and out of Traci, around her clit, over the slippery pink folds of her inner lips. She stuck a finger into Traci's cunt and fucked her with it as she sucked her clit. It wasn't long before Traci was moaning and pushing herself against Caitlyn's face, right on the verge of coming.

Caitlyn suddenly stopped and sat up, leaving Traci with her hips pumping at the empty space recently occupied by Caitlyn.

"Let's try the toy," Caitlyn said.

The bag sat on the floor, right next to the couch. Traci reached down and stuck her hand into the bag, bringing out a long, thick rubber dildo attached to a harness. She turned and looked into the bag, reaching in again, bringing out a small bottle of lubricant.

Caitlyn took the dildo and strapped it on. Traci opened the bottle of lubricant, squirted some in the palm of her hand, and smeared it up and down the full length of the dildo, working her fist on it as if she were massaging a real cock.

"You wanna see me fuck her?" Caitlyn asked Mike, who now had his boxers down far enough to expose his hard-on.

He was stroking himself with one hand. With his other hand, he held Traci's panties to his face so he could sniff them.

Traci turned around and got on all fours, facing the end of the couch, resting her weight on the arm of the couch. In this position, she could watch Mike jack off while Caitlyn fucked her.

Caitlyn got on her knees behind Traci, stroking the dildo as she eased it into Traci's slippery pink pussy.

"Ohhhh, yeahhhhh, fuck me," Traci groaned. "Give it to me hard."

Caitlyn held Traci by her hips, squeezing her tight, and began to pump the thick rubber cock in and out. Traci's pussy lips split wide, her pink hole stretched around the dildo, clinging to every thrust.

Mike wrapped his cock in Traci's panties and jerked off with them. He looked directly into her eyes, holding her gaze, watching her face as Caitlyn gave it to her from behind.

"Oh yeah, fuck me," she panted, rocking her ass on the dildo as it plunged in and out of her. "Make me come . . ."

Caitlyn reached around and under Traci to rub her clit.

Traci threw her head back, mouth open, gasping as her orgasm took over, shaking her body with its intensity. She cried out in pleasure, panting and gasping, grinding back against Caitlyn, pushing her pussy all the way down on the dildo.

She finally collapsed, falling across the arm of the couch. The dildo slipped out of her pussy, bobbing in the air, slick with her juices.

"Bravo," Mike said, clapping and whistling.

Traci turned over, looking up at Caitlyn. She ran her hand down between her legs, over her pussy, and jumped. She was still a little sensitive down there.

Caitlyn unhooked the harness and handed the strap-on over to Traci.

"My turn," she said, lying back on the couch.

Traci strapped on the harness and climbed on top of Caitlyn, situating herself between Caitlyn's legs, guiding the dildo inside her.

Mike was still jerking off with Traci's panties.

Caitlyn wrapped her legs around Traci's waist, pulling Traci toward her, taking the full length of the dildo into her pussy.

Traci pumped her hips, fucking Caitlyn with long, deep strokes. It wasn't long before Caitlyn was breathing hard and gasping, hanging on to Traci's ass and thrashing her hips as she reached her own climax.

Traci collapsed on top of Caitlyn, kissing her hard on the mouth. Both of them were out of breath and temporarily spent.

Mike, still stroking his cock with Traci's panties, went over to stand beside the couch. The girls looked up at him, smiling.

"Any chance I can buy a ticket on the next ride?" he asked.

"Nope," Caitlyn said. "This ride's for girls only."

"Yeah, girls only," Traci said.

He stood looking down at them, his cock waving in the wind, throbbing and in need of a little release. Caitlyn and Traci exchanged a quick look between them, then Caitlyn said, "Okay, maybe just a blow job."

He grinned. That was enough for him.

Traci reached up and took hold of his cock, pulling on it as she sat up and leaned forward to take it in her mouth.

Caitlyn joined her, running her tongue along his shaft as she tugged his boxers down to his feet. He stepped out of them and the two girls took turns sucking his cock, passing it back and forth, one sucking and licking his balls while the other took his dick down her throat.

"Girls . . ." he said, moaning as both of them ran their tongues around the head of his cock while Caitlyn stroked his shaft and Traci squeezed his balls.

"You like that?" Caitlyn asked in a soft, seductive voice.

"Hell yes . . ."

They attacked his cock from both sides, running their tongues along the length of his dick from top to bottom, meeting again at the tip.

"Shit, I'm going to come," he said.

Traci pushed his cock at Caitlyn, who took it in her mouth and sucked hard, making loud gulping noises as she swallowed. Her fist slid up and down his shaft as she jerked all but the last few drops of his come into her mouth, which she shared with Traci in a long, deep kiss.

"Okay," Caitlyn said, slapping her husband playfully on his leg. "Now that you've had your fun, you need to give us girls a little time alone."

"Right," Traci added, looking at Caitlyn with a mischievous gleam in her eyes. "It's monkey-bumping time."

Caitlyn and Traci broke into a fit of laughter.

Mike understood the joke. "If your monkeys get hungry for another banana," he said, "I'll be in the living room."

He shut the door on his way out and stood listening as the rambunctious laughter in the room gave way to soft moans.

. . .

Cold as Ice

The snow storm caught everyone by surprise. It's not that we're not used to snow in the Midwest, but this snow came fast and hard, knocking out power across the state and leaving everyone paralyzed.

Jenny and I had been fighting for several weeks and were on the verge of a breakup. In fact, I was in the middle of packing my shit when the snow started. I figured I'd take what I needed for the time being, rent a motel until I could find a new place to live, and then get the rest of my things.

Jenny's a beautiful woman. Extremely beautiful, as a matter of fact. Long, curly brown hair, green eyes, pouty mouth, nice legs, a tight ass, and perfect C-cup boobs. It's her personality that ruins everything.

She didn't used to be so bad. She used to be a warm, caring woman. She used to have a heart. She lost all of those wonderful traits somewhere along the way. She became cold and emotionless. She started looking at life negatively. Nothing was ever good enough for her anymore.

Needless to say, our sex life suffered greatly. When we did make it to bed, all we did was fuck. Don't get me wrong. There's nothing wrong with fucking, so long as there are real emotions attached to it. I know a lot of guys don't care one way or the other, but me, I'm the kind of guy that likes a little emotional attachment with my sex, and emotional attachment was something that didn't exist between Jenny and me anymore.

The snow storm was about to change everything. Neither of us knew it at the time, but our relationship was about to get much worse, then like the blizzard, the rough weather would pass and things between us would begin to clear up.

The power went pretty quickly. It was dark. We lit as many candles as we could find in the house and threw some logs in the fireplace.

It could have been worse. We had food, coffee, and a fire to keep us warm. It wasn't the best of situations, but like I said, it could have been worse.

That wasn't good enough for Jenny. She started bitching, and when Jenny bitches, there is nothing to compare to it. She gets a hold of something and she will not let it go. Being stranded in the house with no power in the middle of the biggest snow and ice storm the Midwest has seen in more than a decade is a walk in the park compared to being around Jenny when she's bitching.

"I'm bored," she said.

"Read a book."

"I don't want to read. I want to watch TV."

So I went up into the attic and searched until I found a little battery-operated TV. There were no batteries, of course, so I searched the house until I came up with the batteries it would take to operate the TV for what would probably be a maximum life of about an hour, at which time I would have to go through the whole I'm-bored routine again.

In the meantime, though, Jenny was entertained. I smoked and read a book. I was actually enjoying myself. A good Stephen King book in the middle of a blizzard in front of the fireplace was actually quite comforting.

Then her TV died, like I knew it would, and Jenny was bitching again.

"Why can't you just make the best of the situation," I said.

"There's nothing I can do to make this situation good," she replied.

"You can appreciate the fact that we have a fire, that we're not starving, and that you're not alone here. . . ."

"I might as well be alone," she said. "It would be better than being stuck here with you."

"You think so?"

"Yes . . ."

I thought I saw hesitation on her face—a slight softening of her pretty features that betrayed her real feelings.

"It doesn't have to be like this," I said.

She didn't respond, but yes, she was definitely warming up to me. I decided to turn up the heat. It wasn't often I saw her this vulnerable, and quite frankly, I found it rather appealing.

I wrapped my arms around her. She felt stiff at first, a little hesitant, but as I rubbed her shoulders, I could feel her loosening up. I kissed her on the lips. She kept them tight, still trying her best not to give in.

"Come on, let's keep each other warm," I said.

I kissed her harder, teasing her mouth with the tip of my tongue. I slid my hands up over her breasts, squeezing them through her sweater. Her lips parted slightly, enough to allow me to get the tip of my tongue between them.

She slid her arms around my waist. Her mouth opened wider. I felt her tongue sneaking out, exploring my mouth. I sucked it gently. It tasted sweet and felt so damn warm . . .

The fireplace was roaring. The crackle of the fire seemed magnified and the flames danced invitingly.

We moved in front of it, holding on to one another, still kissing. Her tongue moved into my mouth, my tongue into hers.

I pulled her sweater over her head and she turned her back to me. I unfastened her bra and slipped the straps from her soft shoulders, then I lifted her hair and kissed the back of her neck.

I moved my hands over her hips and up, cupping her breasts, lifting them in my hands. I moved my thumbs over her nipples and rolled them between my thumbs and forefingers.

She faced me and we kissed again. This time she was more aggressive, kissing me hungrily, forcing her tongue deep into my mouth.

We undressed one another fully. I knelt in front of her and kissed her belly, teasing around her belly button. I flicked my tongue in the little indent, then I moved downward, kissing the soft curls on her pubic mound.

The scent of her was sweet and exciting. She smelled a particular way when she was turned on, and the more aroused she became, the stronger the scent was.

I opened the outer lips of her pussy with my thumbs and ran my tongue over the swollen bud of her clit. She moaned. I could feel her shudder with pleasure.

I turned her around and kissed each of her smooth, pale ass cheeks, letting my tongue delve between them to explore the tight opening of her anus.

We stretched out on the floor, our legs entwined, my erection hard against her belly. I could feel her cunt opening against my leg, smearing its slick heat on my thigh. I reached down and slipped a finger inside her.

She slowly moved her hips, rolling her pussy around on my finger, sliding up and down on it until her breathing began to quicken.

"Another . . ." she gasped.

I added a second finger and pressed my thumb down on her clit.

The memories began to come back. When things were good in the sack between Jenny and me, they were really good. She was coming alive again, responding to me in a way she hadn't for so long now.

She wrapped her hand around my cock and started jerking me off. Her fingers closed just tight enough around my dick to provide friction, but not so tight that she couldn't move effortlessly.

She stroked me until I was on the verge of coming all over her hand, then she stopped and let my impending orgasm recede before she continued. She was in tune with me that way. She could feel every twitch of my cock. She knew by the way I breathed when I was going to come. She could keep me on the edge for hours if she wanted to. I loved that about her.

"Can I suck your cock?" she asked.

Her voice was sweet as honey. It was as if she were asking me if I wanted a second serving of dessert.

"Yes," I said.

She moved down and licked the head of my cock, swirling her tongue around it like she was licking candy. She flicked her tongue against the opening, then she brushed it several times against the sensitive underside.

Every nerve in my body was alive, on fire with the heat of my desire. Jenny took me in her mouth and sucked gently, slowly pulling me deeper, using her tongue and mouth in conjunction, driving me out of my mind with her expertise.

God, I wanted to come so badly. I wanted to fill her mouth with my come and hear her swallowing it. I wanted to kiss her afterward and taste myself on her lips and on her tongue.

She sensed the urgency of my need. Her hand quickened. Her grip became a little firmer. Her thumb found the right spot beneath the head of my cock.

I warned her, but she didn't stop. She wanted me to come as much as I wanted to. I closed my eyes and placed one hand on top of her head. I didn't apply pressure because that was something she didn't like. She didn't like feeling forced. I was careful about that, but my hand was on her head just the same, touching her silky hair as my cock jerked in her mouth.

She tightened her mouth around my cock and swallowed hard as I exploded. I could hear the deep gulps she took to get it all.

We lay together afterward, me stroking her hair and kissing her. I didn't go fully soft, but I wasn't quite hard enough to be inside her yet. She played with my cock, stroking the length of it, cupping my balls in her fingers to squeeze them with just the right amount of pressure.

I lit two cigarettes. Jenny only smokes after making love. She hates the smell and taste of cigarettes any other time.

"You know . . . I don't like being a bitch," she said out of the blue.

"I don't like it when you're a bitch," I joked.

She gave me a playful jab with her elbow.

"I know you don't," I said.

It wasn't the complete truth. There were times I was absolutely certain she liked being a bitch—relished it, in fact—but I wasn't about to spoil the moment.

We finished our cigarettes and then Jenny straddled me. She leaned down and let her hair fall in my face. I could feel the warm, damp lips of her pussy against my cock as she rocked her hips gently.

She stopped suddenly and lifted her bottom, reaching down as she did to get a firm grip on my cock. She put the head of it right against her opening and very slowly lowered herself. I could feel her opening around me, stretching to accommodate me, then tightening around me until I slipped inside her.

I have to believe that was as close to heaven as a man could get on earth. Her pussy was made for my cock. I believed that too. There was no other cock in the world that would fit so perfectly inside her, and not another cock in the world her pussy would do such things to.

Oh yes, I believed that.

I slipped my hands under her firm bottom and brought her up once she reached the base of my cock. I held her there, with the head of my cock all that remained inside her, and then I lowered her again, taking my time, drawing the pleasure out for as long as I could. I did this several times, until I was sure one of us would go out of our minds, if not the two of us together.

She took over after a while, riding the length of my cock, bringing herself up and then dropping down again. She kept a nice, steady pace at first, closing her eyes as she enjoyed the way my cock filled her, but then she began to go faster, riding me harder . . .

Her breasts shook above my head like Jell-O. I tried to capture one of her hard, coffee-with-cream colored nipples in my mouth. When she realized what I wanted, she lowered herself to make it easier. I sucked the nipple firmly into my mouth and bathed it with my tongue, lapping and swirling until the nipple came away all slick and shiny with my saliva.

I did the same to the other, and then I took a firm grip on her hips and took over, arching my back as I drove up inside her and came down again. . . .

I rolled her over after a while, keeping my dick embedded in her pussy. She locked her ankles together behind my back and opened herself to me, moaning with every thrust of my cock.

We made love like that for a while, with me stopping every so often, trying not to come again too soon.

We switched positions again. She got on her hands and knees. I licked her pussy from behind, easing my tongue inside her, then I licked her asshole. She tasted sweet there, unlike what those who never venture to that area might think, and I took my time, working her up with the tip of my tongue until I could get it to slip just inside her ass.

I eased my cock into her from behind, then ran my hands over her waist, bringing them up and around. I took one firm, beautiful breast in each of my hands, squeezing them gently. Her nipples were hard against my palms.

"Ohhhh, yes . . ." she moaned.

I took her by the hips and steadied her, pressing my fingers into her soft flesh as I withdrew my cock almost all the way and sank into her again. The wet, slippery opening of her pussy worked on my cock like a mouth. The silky wet folds of her inner lips clung to my shaft, spreading like wings as I withdrew, then folding in as I entered her deeply.

She always liked it that way, from behind. She said she could feel me inside her better that way. She said I went deeper. I don't really know, but I do know how it felt to me. Her pussy was tighter. It caressed my cock differently when I fucked her from behind.

We switched positions again.

"Let's take our time," I said.

She was on her back again, looking up at me with a love in her eyes I had not seen in quite some time. My ice princess was completely thawed.

I bent down and kissed her nose, then her chin . . . I tilted her head back and kissed the soft indent above her collarbone.

We fell asleep under a thick blanket. I don't know how long we were out, but I woke up because I felt the chill of Winter seeping in on us. Most of the candles had gone out. A few of the bigger ones were still flickering. The fire was beginning to die out.

"Honey . . ."

I shook Jenny. She opened her eyes and raised her head, looking around as if confused about where she was. She pulled the blanket around her.

"It's so cold," she said. "Aren't you cold?"

I was still naked, and yes, I was pretty damn cold. I tossed the last of the logs into the fireplace and got the fire roaring again. Jenny moved closer and soaked up the heat. I poured us coffee and joined her. We sat looking at one another through the steam that rose from our mugs. She looked so sweet.

"I still love you," I said.

"And I still love you."

"Then what are we doing?"

She seemed unsure about how to answer. Maybe she didn't know the answer. Maybe she was as confused as I was.

"You deserve better . . ."

"You're all I want," I said.

I looked out the window and saw that it was snowing again. The windows were iced over. The crackle of the fire was comforting.

"I'll try to do better," she said.

"And I'll try to be more understanding."

We sipped our coffee and set the mugs on the ledge in front of the fireplace. She opened the blanket and leaned up, wrapping it around the two of us. I enjoyed the way her breasts spread flat against my chest and her nipples, made even more stiff by the temperature, drilled into me.

We shared body heat.

She nibbled my lower lip. Soft, gentle nipping at first, and then she bit down. It wasn't hard enough to do serious damage, but hard enough to make me open my eyes wide.

"What was that for?" I asked.

"I love you, that's all."

Her tongue snaked into my mouth.

We lay before the fireplace. warming up once again, and I entered her, moving slowly . . . taking my time this time.

She draped her arms over my shoulders and wrapped her legs around me, bringing me back inside her each time I pulled back. Her hips moved in little circles beneath me. Her pussy caressed the length of my cock. I paced myself so I wouldn't come before her. I wanted us to be one, to come together in an orgasm that would end all orgasms. It was best when we did it that way, as we always had in the beginning of our relationship. Somewhere over time that had changed. Jenny and I had lost track of one another. We'd grown apart until we were strangers, but she was no stranger to me now.

Her hips rocked against me. The rhythm of her breathing became more erratic. I felt her fingernails digging into my back, leaving marks I knew would be raw and stinging in the morning.

I didn't care. I'd deal with the scratches later. All I cared about at that moment was making love with Jenny like we used to. All I cared about was the way my cock felt slipping in and out of her, the noises she made that let me know she was enjoying it as much as I was.

All I cared about . . .

"I love you," she said, panting the words.

"I love you too," he gasped.

I wanted to come with her. I felt it building inside me, bubbling to the surface. She begged me not to stop. She was getting close . . .

I knew I wouldn't last much longer . . .

I *couldn't* last much longer.

Somewhere in the distance I could hear the wind picking up. I saw through the window and the snow was coming down so hard and thick now that it appeared as if a giant white sheet had been draped over the house.

I didn't care about that either, just like I didn't care about the scratches on my back. All I cared about was Jenny beneath me, warm and shuddering as she reached her climax.

She screamed out and arched her back. I plunged deep inside her and let myself go, spurting my hot come into her pussy . . .

. . . thinking about how good it was to have her back again . . .

. . . how sometimes life was surprisingly funny . . .

. . . and about how a snow storm had heated things up for Jenny and me.

Confessions of a Heel

We were born in the 1940s, black leather with velvet etchings, custom made for the wife of a mob boss. She bought us (we were still a pair then) for three hundred dollars—a lot of smackola in those days, believe me, but this dame only bought the best.

Molly McGreer.

Great gams, delicate feet, and cheeky enough to make it.

The boss was always away on mob business, usually banging some other dame, but that was okay by Molly. She preferred women. In particular, a busty blonde named Candy. The two of them logged lots of hours together, using my six-inch tapered heel in some very creative ways. Insertion was the key word.

Then Molly was caught in the act. She left the marriage with one bag. My better half and I ended up in there, along with some lingerie and a few pieces of jewelry she was able to smuggle out.

Molly did okay after that. Married a nice guy, had a daughter, and stored us away in a dark closet.

Her daughter Shelly wore us to her high school prom. This was the 1950s, when rock 'n' roll was young and those awful saddle shoes were the rage. A girl wears a pair of stilettos to her prom, you can bet she turns a few heads.

She lost her virginity in the back of a '55 Chevy that night, windows fogged up, her legs in the air, her prom dress around her waist, and yours truly on one foot, my partner on the other.

Shelly kept us through the 60s. Flower power and peace. We were at Woodstock. Great music, lots of free love. Oh, the free love. Orgies, women with women, guys with guys, everybody fucking everybody.

Shelly tuned out like most kids in the 60s. By the time she tuned in again, she had a daughter of her own, sold us at a yard sale, and settled into suburban life.

Our new owner, Chet, took us through the 70s, using us in a campy burlesque act. We drew huge crowds. We had the fever, baby. We were stayin' alive. Forget Travolta, we were the superstars.

Chet's act gave out in the early 80s. Bummer, dude. He passed us on to a bubbly blonde, Bambi (can you believe that shit?), who made it big in video porn. She wore us one time, left us on the set, and we ended up props in the biggest porn adventures of the decade. Blondes with big hair doing unnatural things with unnaturally hung studs, brunettes with big tits and puffy nipples, whips and handcuffs, and, of course, stiletto heels. . . .

My better half and I got split up in the 90s. I've been sitting here in this attic ever since, thinking about the glory days. Now and then some pervert comes up and sticks his cock in me for a cheap thrill, but I don't mind. It beats being alone all the time. . . .

Cupid's Confession
(The Little Prick with the Big Bow)

I'm pissed. Can ya blame me? I mean, come on, think about it, pal. I spend all my time gettin' people together, and what do I get for my trouble? I get to run around naked with my little dick swingin' in the wind, I got wings like a fairy, and I get to watch all the couples *I* hooked up bangin' their brains out.

That's right, I said *watch*.

Do I ever get invited to join in? Not even once. Not one damn time has anybody ever said, "Hey, Cupe, wanna get yourself a piece of the action?" Where's the fuckin' gratitude? No, this business ain't all glamour. In fact, I ain't seen glamour since I wiped my ass with the cover of the magazine back in '96.

There's benefits that go along with the job, sure. I can't be seen by anybody, so I can pretty much go where I want to, and since I dig watchin', I always got the best seat in the house. I can sit right up on stage in the best strip joints in the world, so close to the pussy I can smell it, and tug on my little dick all night long while I watch naked babes strut their stuff.

I can't touch, though. That's one of the rules of the job. No touching the mortals. Get as close as you want, but keep your hands (and your dick) away from them, period. It's in the contract, which, by the way, is in serious need of renegotiation if you ask me.

Nobody ever does.

Wait, let me get a beer here. I need a fuckin' beer. I really do.

Where was I?

Oh, yeah, so it's a hands-off policy. You're probably wonderin' why I bitch about not bein' invited to join in, right? I couldn't participate anyway, so what's the big deal if nobody asks?

Principle, that's the big deal. So what if I'd have to decline. The point is, nobody ever asks. There's no appreciation for the work I do, and that bothers me. It really does. I work my little raisins off, and for what? So everybody else gets laid while I stand around with my dick in one hand and a beer in the other.

You see my work everywhere. I'm a fuckin' artist. Take, for instance, that ugly porn star still makin' movies with all the hot young talent. You think he does that on his own? Give me a break. His cock's big, sure, but that stopped bein' an attraction a long time ago. Big cocks are a dime a dozen in the porn business, and on better lookin' men.

That guy gets all his work 'cause yours truly steps in and works his magic. If I didn't shoot my arrows, trust me, he wouldn't get to shoot his. All those young starlets would see his fat ass and run the other way. He'd be sellin' Hoovers door to door. I *made* that man. I gave him his career, I don't even see an agent's cut.

I know what you're thinkin'. I get the joy of makin' people happy, right? Gimme a fuckin' break, okay? Pass the Kleenex while I write a fuckin' Hallmark card. I couldn't care less about makin' people happy.

What have you done for *me* lately?

You mortals don't even believe in me. Oh, sure, my name gets brought up now and then, but only metaphorically, just to bolster your belief in fate, destiny, and all that other goofy shit.

Take a look at that chick over there. Pretty face, but she is F-A-T, know what I mean? And dig the GQ-lookin' stud with her. He's gettin' into it, ain't he? Got his head between those jiggling thighs, his face pressed into that big hairy bush, lickin' away at the wide pink flaps of her pussy . . . You think fate has anything to do with that? You think the guy just likes his women big?

I take credit for that one. Again, folks, that's my work. I engineered that little fuck scene. One well-aimed arrow and he was climbin' the mountain of love. Hell, I'd settle for a piece of her pie. More cushion for the pushin'. It's cliché, but it's gotta be true.

And what about that skinny little dweeb with the glasses and the oily hair? Look at the blonde babe he's doin' doggy-style. You think she picked him out of a lineup? Not before she tasted the tip of my arrow, that's for sure.

Here's another winner, thanks to yours truly. See that guy with the receding hairline and the beer gut. He can't even see his dick past his belly, but look at the two gorgeous babes swappin' his cock back and forth, damn near fightin' over it. You think they do that 'cause he's got class? Not a fuckin' chance. I took 'em both with one shot. Got 'em while they were standin' together. The slob just happened to be walkin' by. He thought he'd won the fuckin' lottery when they approached him with a proposition he couldn't refuse.

Way back in the day—we're talkin' 13th century BC—I was still able to partake in some of the pleasures of the flesh. It wasn't until much later the Gods made my job official and wrote the contract I now work under.

Back then I was still doin' this shit as a hobby, so it really didn't take up much of my time. I could enjoy life a little bit. I banged a lot of nymphs and muses— especially one cute Dryad nymph named Daphne.

I met Daphne one day while I frolicked in the woods. That's what I did, I frolicked. I mean, if you read the literature, I'm a frolickin' kinda guy, and that's exactly what I was doin' on that day—the day I met the nymph chick.

Daphne was a hot young nymph who liked to do some frolickin' of her own. She wore a skimpy piece of cloth around her waist, which was as far as her modesty went. She had big, soft tits, wide hips, and legs that went on forever.

"Hey, Eros," she called out as I cavorted (hell, I like that better than frolicked) in the woods.

All right, I know what you're thinkin'. Who the fuck is Eros, right? Well, check it out, Eros, Cupid, it makes no difference. I'm both dudes. It depends on whether you go with the Greeks or the Romans. Cupid works better on you mortal types, but to me, I don't know, Eros is just more manly.

Anyway, I had to look hard to find where that sweet voice had come from. I found Daphne wedged between two thick trunks of an oak tree, hidden from direct view of anybody who might happen by. She slid out of her hidin' place and gave me a coy little smile. I was a sucker for that kinda shit back then.

"You wanna play with me?" she asked.

She slid her hands over her tits, pushed them together, and lifted one at a time so she could lick and suck her nipples. She dropped her cloth and sat on the ground, pullin' her knees back and opening them wide. She leaned against the huge oak she called home, sliding one hand down between her legs. She opened the lips of her pussy with two fingers, showin' me the slick pink folds hidden under her thick brown pubes, and then she slid one finger inside her pussy and started movin' it in and out.

The tree came to life. Its big limbs embraced Daphne, slithering around her and pinning her arms against its trunk. Another branch wrapped around Daphne's waist and two more threaded around her legs, draggin' her knees even wider.

I watched as a limb bearing an uncanny resemblance to a certain part of the male anatomy slithered up between Daphne's legs and started fuckin' her. I was a little steamed, let me tell ya. A fuckin' tree horning in on *my* action.

Sloppy seconds to a tree. Can you believe that shit?

But I *did* get to nail Daphne, so what the hell, right? And there were plenty more after her. There were sea nymphs and mountain nymphs, river nymphs and forest nymphs. I sampled 'em all, you better believe that. There was a time when bein' Cupid meant somethin'.

But those days are long gone. Now I get about as much respect as a garbage man. When was the last time you thanked your garbage man?

Like I said before, I'm pissed. I ain't exactly blessed with the kind of equipment a guy in my business oughta have. I carry a big bow, though (hey, a guy's gotta compensate), and I do my best to make this gig work.

Bars are the best. What I mean is, I get some of my best raw material when I cruise the bars and nightclubs. Gimme a fuckin' break. You ever checked out the bar scene? Man, what a circus. It ain't the booze that sends unlikely couples home together for a one-night stand from Hell. That's yours truly at work, sendin' out those love potion-tipped arrows.

Check it out. See the plain-lookin' chick sittin' by herself at the bar? Look at that guy over there. Executive type, thinks he's too good for anything but a cover girl model, except there's the cover girl model with the rich foreign guy. She's goin' home with him tonight. I already sent the arrows out. It's a done deal.

So, 'round about closin' time I'll send out another arrow (a low-potency version, designed for temporary lust), straight into Mister Executive's ass, and guess who he's goin' home with? That's right, my friend. The plain chick at the end of the bar. He'll take her home, they'll do the horizontal bop, and in the mornin' they'll both be confused. She'll wonder if he'll call again, he'll be askin' himself just what the fuck it was he *drank* at that bar last night.

I've seen this chick in action before, and believe me, she may be plain, but she's got style. Mister Executive ain't gonna be able to resist her after the night they have. Oh, he'll want to, sure. He'll think he's too damn good for her, but then he'll remember those bedroom acrobatics she performs—the way she puts her feet behind her head and locks her ankles together—and he'll call her again.

Tell ya the truth, I've jerked off over her a couple times myself. Her blonde hair and blue eyes, slim build (not alotta tit), plain features, and the whole feet-behind-the-head schtick do somethin' to me.

Hell, a girl like her would be a nice diversion for a hard-workin' stud like me. You wouldn't believe the hours I've been puttin' in lately, and not on new projects either. It's all been maintenance. Married couples that lose the initial spark, that sort of thing. Sometimes the effect of my arrows don't hold. It depends on the brand I use. Some of it's cheap stuff, which means I have to do an occasional reapplication, and if I slack on routine maintenance, the divorce rate goes through the roof, then I got the big guys upstairs comin' down on me, and I don't like 'em lookin' over my shoulder, know what I mean?

Low key, that's the way I do it. Let Apollo and Mars and Mercury take all the heat. Those guys are always in trouble.

Now, where was I?

Yeah, maintenance. Keep the hearts beatin', the love juice flowin', and everything runs smooth, then I get to kick back and take it easy.

That's what I was doin' just before Valentine's Day, kickin' back at one of my favorite strip clubs, a joint called TITS 'N' CLITS. Now *that's* entertainment. Those girls don't waste my time. They come out onstage wearin' nothin' but thongs, and those don't last long. Pretty soon it's wide-spread legs and masturbation. Those babes make use of an arsenal of toys, let me tell ya.

Sometimes . . . and listen, I ain't really supposed to do this . . . sometimes I like to shoot a few arrows indiscriminately, you know, just to see what I can drag outta the woodwork for fun.

The other night I was in a particularly effervescent mood. John Fogerty's song *Centerfield* was playin' and a hot blonde was onstage wearin' nothin' but a baseball cap, white cotton panties, white socks, and a worn baseball glove. She danced around a minute or two, then she started doin' some of the most entertaining things I've ever seen done with a baseball bat.

Let me tell ya, I was downright giddy. I always get a hard-on when I hear *Centerfield*.

What the hell?, I thought, and I fired an arrow at the blonde dancer just as she bent over to give the crowd a nice shot of tight white panties stretchin' across her firm bottom. My arrow found its mark, *bang,* right between her cheeks.

The arrow was a potent one. The blonde turned around and grabbed the first man she laid eyes on—some old dude wearin' the outfit John Travolta wore in *Saturday Night Fever*—and dragged him up onstage.

I turned away from the stage, took aim, and let another arrow fly. A slender little brunette waitress at the bar caught that one. She climbed onto the bar and started doin' her own dance number, grabbin' the bartender by his hair and pullin' his head up under her skirt.

A group of little Japanese guys sat at a table to the right of the stage. I let a couple arrows fly in their direction. My aim is always good. I caught one of them in the ass, the other right through the heart. They looked at each other and smiled.

Another waitress came by, blonde and pleasantly chubby. I hit her with an arrow. She dropped the drink tray and fell to her knees in front of a man at the nearest table, unzippin' his pants so she could get his dick out.

The woman sittin' with the man wasn't too happy to see the chubby blonde stuffin' her mouth full of cock, but before she could create a scene, I hit her with one of my high-potency arrows. She immediately fell back in her chair, spread her legs wide, hiked her skirt above her waist, then slipped her panties off and started playin' with her pussy while she watched the chubby blonde suck.

I went wild, sendin' arrows out at random. The big bouncer at the door took one in the ass and nailed the next chick that came into the club; two businessmen at a table near the stage decided they didn't need female strippers anymore; a computer geek sittin' by himself at the bar suddenly had two stacked babes rubbin' their titties in his face.

Ah, the power of love. I was havin' a blast. An all-out fuckfest, thanks to my artistic renderings, and I was just about to revel in the glory of it when I heard a voice I recognized quite well.

"Where the hell have you been?" she asked, reprimanding me with her eyes.

She, in this instance, is my wife Psyche. Did I forget to mention her?

She wore the clothes of a modern mortal woman, although she'd ceased being one of *them* a long time ago. The top she had on left her flat tummy and pale shoulders bare, her jeans looked painted on to her wide hips. Her green eyes flashed with anger, but damn if I didn't get hard anyway. She always did look sexier when she was pissed.

How'd I meet Psyche?

Long story, but here goes the edited version.

My mom (Venus), in a fit of jealousy, sent me to make Psyche fall in love with the ugliest son of a bitch I could find. See, Venus was pissed off 'cause Psyche was so beautiful she was gettin' all the attention, and that shit didn't fly with my mom. She figured she could use *me* to get back at Psyche.

Here's the catch, though. I was so taken by Psyche's beauty (especially her tits . . . man, she's got great tits) that I stuck myself with my own fuckin' arrow and fell in love with her. I stuck her too, but that goes without sayin'. I mean, how else would a dame like that fall for a wise-ass like me?

The whole deal really pissed mom off, but eventually the higher ups convinced her she had to go along with me and Psyche gettin' hitched, so long as Psyche drank from the cup of immortality, of course. Can't have the son of a goddess married to some mortal chick. It wouldn't look good in the records.

The wedding was the talk of the tabloids for a long time. Cupid and Psyche, the couple everybody wanted to be. We were all the rage, baby, and the marriage was real good at first.

Ain't it always like that? I mean, damn, she was hot to trot, a real nymphomaniac in the bedroom, then BAM, all the arrows in the world wouldn't get me laid by my wife.

I did what I had to do. I started steppin' out. I looked up a couple of old nymph girls, banged 'em on the side, that sort of thing.

Then Psyche found out. She went crazy on my ass, let me tell ya. Threatened divorce, and how the hell would *that* look in the tabloids? I can see the fuckin' headline now—CUPID'S MARRIAGE MISSES THE MARK.

My career can't take the bad press, so I promised Psyche I'd lay off the extramarital pussy, and I did.

Do you have any idea what it's like to be responsible for so many mortals gettin' laid and not to be gettin' any yourself? To be able to watch gorgeous naked babes spread their legs and masturbate without bein' able to touch 'em? To be condemned to a life of watchin' people fuck and suck when all you can do is jerk off?

Now you can see why I'm pissed.

I looked around at the sexual chaos I'd caused at the TITS 'N' CLITS. I'd gone overboard, yeah, and I was pretty sure there'd be hell to pay when the higher ups got wind of my shenanigans.

Tell ya the truth, I was more worried about what would happen to me when Psyche got me home to our little love den. She didn't look all that happy, and quite frankly, I couldn't blame her. Here it was, the night before Valentine's Day, and I'm out on the town throwin' a temper tantrum in a strip joint.

"What's gotten into you?" Psyche demanded.

"I don't know," I said sheepishly.

"Look at how you behaved tonight," she said. "Is that any way for a god to act? How's that going to look in the mythological literature, huh?"

That was the last straw. Fuck the literature, fuck the tabloids, fuck the higher ups, Cupid needed to get laid.

"You listen to me, little Miss Missy," I said. "When you drank that sweet immortality nectar, you did it because you wanted to spend eternity with me. And in the beginning, right after we were hitched, baby, you were the best."

I could see her softenin' up a bit. Her eyes were damp.

74

"I couldn't have loved anybody more than I loved you, and I know you felt the same about me," I said.

I laid it on thick, but it *was* from the heart, and I think she could tell because she started bawlin'.

"I want us to get back to where we were," I finished with a flourish. "Cupid and Psyche, the couple everybody wants to be."

Hercules got the strength, Mercury got the speed. Apollo, he got a fuckin' theatre, but me, I'm the little stud muffin who got the gift of love.

Psyche threw her arms around me. I felt her hard nipples against my chest. She poked herself with one of my arrows and then plunged it into my ass.

Thunder rumbled in the heavens. Jupiter, and Venus acknowledged our rekindled love. I was off the hook with the higher ups, forgiven of my temper tantrum and allowed to continue on. There would be no tawdry headlines, no scandal, no more nymphs on the side, and no more wild-arrow parties.

Life was good again.

I decided to take Valentine's Day off and let nature take its course without me. If the mortals couldn't handle their own affairs, well, tough shit. All work and no play makes Cupid a twitch dude.

I booked the *Hunka-Hunka Burnin' Love* suite at the *Heartbreak Hotel* in Memphis, and me and Psyche played ain't nothin' but a houndog all night long.

Eating Peaches

Mike couldn't get the vision of his girlfriend fucking another man out of his mind. Sara, beautiful and blonde, freckles on her big boobs and a smile that melted his heart—that vision was gone.

Long gone.

All he remembered now were the sounds he'd heard coming from their bedroom—soft moans and grunts, squeaking bedsprings, and the steady rhythm of the headboard against the wall.

Something had told him to forget about it. He should have listened to his gut. He should have turned and walked out the door without looking back. Instead, he'd gone ahead and looked into the bedroom, and there it was, the vision he would never forget.

Sara had been on top of the guy, her head thrown back, sliding up and down on his thick cock. His hands had been on her hips, lifting her up, setting her down again, and it had been clear by the increasing intensity of her moans that she was very near orgasm.

Even then, Mike had found himself unable to vacate the premises. Not until he'd seen the ugly situation through to the end.

He'd watched her shudder with release, then fall over the guy, still grinding her hips as the last of her climax faded.

She'd seen him then, after catching her breath, and she'd done her best to explain the situation to him.

He hadn't given her a chance. He split the scene immediately, gotten into his car, and hit the highway. It was only two hours later that he realized he was heading for Georgia.

Georgia was where he'd met Sara. He'd been there on business. She and a friend of hers had been in the club where he'd gone to cut loose for the night. He'd ended up with Sara instead of her friend Julie, and now he was going back to Georgia to find Julie.

What a stupid fucking idea. He didn't have a clue what he was doing. He knew her last name, but what were the chances she was still there, and even if she was, that she would be interested in him?

Something in his car rattled. He looked at the dash and saw red lights. He was no mechanic, but he knew red lights couldn't be good.

Then he saw the check engine light and knew he was screwed.

"Son of a bitch," he muttered.

He rolled the window down and lit a cigarette.

He was fucked, no two ways about it. He'd come all the way to Georgia in search of some girl he'd never find, he was lost on a dusty back road, and now his car was about to die on him.

He passed a hand-painted sign that featured a huge peach with the words *eat peaches* painted in bright orange beneath it in sloppy cursive.

Yeah, just what I need, a fuckin' peach, he thought.

He drove on, pressing the car until it began to rattle.

Do I sound bitter?

He passed another sign similar to the first. The peach painted on this one was cut open, a glistening drop of juice dripped from the cut. The words under the peach read *fresh, juicy peaches,* and for some reason, Mike got a hard-on.

Holy shit, now I'm getting horny for a peach.

The next few signs were all similar, with directions to the Orchard Inn and "all the peaches you can eat."

He passed more signs, each with crude painted arrows and a mile countdown to the Orchard Inn. Mike followed the signs, figuring the inn was the best bet in his current situation.

By the time he turned onto the gravel drive leading to a white two-story farmhouse he presumed to be the much-touted

Orchard Inn, Mike's car was sputtering, coughing black smoke, and unable to go another inch.

He abandoned the car and started down the gravel road on foot. There were peach orchards on both sides of the road. Mike was dying of thirst. The thought of a sweet, juicy peach made his mouth water, and while the farmhouse was in sight, it was still a damn far walk in this southern heat.

Mike sneaked into the orchard and grabbed a peach. What harm could there be? He planned on spending at least one night at the inn, so surely the owners wouldn't mind if he helped himself to one of the peaches.

He bit into the peach as he continued down the gravel road toward the farmhouse. Sweet, sticky juice dribbled down his chin. He had to admit, it was one of the tastiest peaches he'd ever eaten.

He had it gone within thirty seconds, licking his lips to get the last of the juice.

Just one more, he thought.

He glanced in the direction of the farmhouse, then he slipped into the orchard again, grabbing another peach, which he attacked with fervor.

A sign in front of the farmhouse confirmed what Mike already knew. This place was indeed the Orchard Inn.

Mike went inside.

The foyer was tastefully decorated with what looked like furniture from at least the Civil War era. The floors were hardwood with hand-woven area rugs. There was a dark polished mahogany desk on the other side of the entryway. A guestbook sat open on the desk. Beside it was a bell with a small sign that read *ring for service.*

Mike tapped the bell. Its sound carried through the big house.

"Well, hello," came a voice from somewhere to Mike's left.

A gentle-looking woman in her sixties was coming from another room, smiling as she approached Mike.

"I'd like to get a room for the night," Mike told her.

She was a talkative old woman, friendly in that southern way. She took Mike's money, told him where his room was, and made sure he knew what time dinner would be served.

"I make everything myself," she assured him. "You haven't tried anything until you've tried my peach cobbler."

Mike went up to his room. He needed to find a mechanic who'd come fix his car, but right now all he wanted to do was rest.

He glanced out the window and saw he was at the back of the house, looking out over vast peach orchards. There was a barn in the distance, and just before he turned away from the window, he saw a girl come out of the barn and disappear into the orchards.

Her blonde hair was in a ponytail. She was barefoot, wearing a halter top and blue jean cut-offs. That was about all Mike could really tell in the brief glimpse he managed to steal before she was out of sight.

He hurried from his room, down the stairs, and out onto the front porch. He lit a cigarette and went around to the back of the house, heading toward the barn and the orchards. He still couldn't see the girl, but he was determined to find her. The quick look he'd gotten of her had been enough to set his heart racing.

And that wasn't all. He realized, as he made his way across the back yard, that his cock was pressing hard against the front of his jeans, nearly bursting his zipper with anticipation.

He forgot all the bad shit going on in his life—his cheating slut-of-a girlfriend, his piece-of-shit car, his search for some chick who probably didn't even remember him—all of it gone.

He wanted only one thing—to find the girl in the peach orchard.

He was out of breath when he reached the edge of the orchards. She couldn't have gotten far. He entered the orchards and began searching, moving up and down between the rows of peach trees.

She was here somewhere.

He cut through a stand of peach trees and crossed the open space on the other side, looking left and right, now beginning to wonder if she'd been a mere figment of his imagination.

He was about to quit his search when he found her.

She was standing on a ladder under one of the trees, picking peaches. He stood behind one of the trees, admiring the sweet curves of her bottom so clearly displayed in the tiny cut-offs.

She stepped carefully back down the ladder, cradling her freshly-picked peaches. She set the peaches on the ground, reached behind her back to untie her halter, then slipped the halter off, exposing her small breasts.

She ran her hands up over her tits and squeezed them, then she caught a tiny pale pink nipple between the thumb and forefinger of each hand and tugged them until they stood out nice and hard.

Mike knew he should probably slip quietly away. He was intruding on this girl's privacy. He had no right to watch her without her knowledge.

Still, he couldn't bring himself to move.

She unbuttoned her jeans and stepped out of them. She wasn't wearing any panties. Somehow that didn't surprise Mike one bit. A pretty young southern girl like her (she couldn't have been more than nineteen or twenty) probably didn't even own a bra or a pair of panties.

She sat on the ground beneath the tree and picked up one of the peaches she'd picked. She bit into it, savoring the fruit for several moments. Mike saw the sticky peach juice dribbling down her chin. He imagined her lips and tongue working the soft, sweet fruit.

What she did next made his cock twitch with desire. She held the peach over her breasts and squeezed it, smashing it to a pulp between her fingers and letting the juice splash all over her tits.

Mike unzipped his pants and took out his cock. He slowly jerked his cock as he watched the pretty blonde rub the pulpy peach all over her tits.

She leaned back against one of the trees with her knees bent and wide apart, giving Mike a clear view of her thick, curly blonde bush. She picked up another of the peaches and placed it against her pussy and began to rub it up and down.

Her eyes were closed. Her small breasts rose and fell as her breathing quickened. She cupped one of her tits and squeezed it as she worked the peach against her pussy. It was clear she was on the verge of a climax.

Mike pulled on his cock faster. The sight the blonde girl's tits all slick and shiny with sticky peach juice while she masturbated with a peach was the sexiest thing he'd ever seen in his life. He felt his cock throbbing and his balls getting tight as he approached an orgasm he knew would make his knees buckle.

"Hey, ya'll wanna come over here?"

The sound of that sweet southern accent dripping with sexuality stopped Mike right before his cock erupted.

She was looking right at him, the peach still between her legs, though she was no longer rubbing herself with it.

He stepped away from the tree he'd been using as cover, his erection sticking out of his pants with pride, showing no signs of softening.

"My name's Peaches," she said. "What's yours?"

"Mike," he answered. "I, uh, just checked into the inn."

"That's my granny's inn," she said.

There was a moment of silence between them, then she said, "You like Peaches, Mike?"

"Sure do," he said.

"Why don't you come over here and eat Peaches," she suggested.

She took the peach from between her legs and held it out to him. He went to her, knelt on the ground, and took a bite of the fruit.

"Now this peach," she said, pushing him between her widespread legs.

He worked his tongue through the thick blonde curls of her pubic hair, sweetened as they were from the juicy peach she'd used on herself.

"Ummm, lick me," she said, sighing with pleasure as his tongue danced between the slippery folds of her vulva.

She grabbed the back of his head, sliding her fingers through his hair as she pulled his mouth against her.

"Right there," she told him, breathing quicker now that he'd found her aroused clit. "Oh, Mike . . . you sure know how to please a girl."

Every sexy southern syllable she uttered drove him crazy with lust. Something about a southern accent was just too sexy to ignore.

He sucked her clit into his mouth and nibbled. He flicked it with his tongue, teased her to within a heartbeat of climax, then let her slip away from the precipice of her orgasm before starting in on her again.

He finally allowed her the release she so desperately needed, leaving her gasping for breath and flushed with desire.

He wasn't near finished with the masterpiece of southern charm, though. He kissed her flat tummy and then worked his way up, moving to lick one sticky pink nipple and then the other. He took them into his mouth one at a time, sucking and gently nibbling, and then he pushed her tits together and worked both nipples at the same time, doing his best to give them equal billing.

"Let me suck your cock," she said eagerly.

He stood up and pushed his jeans and briefs down around his ankles.

She got up on her knees, wrapping one hand around his shaft as her tongue snaked its way around the head of his cock a few times before she finally took his dick into her mouth.

Her mouth was sheer heaven, all warm and wet around his cock. She used her tongue, creating an extra sensation that had him on the edge of climax within a couple of minutes.

He stopped her suddenly, gently urging her mouth away from his cock. He wasn't ready to come yet. Not so soon. A sweet thing like her, he was pretty sure he'd have no trouble getting it up again, but he wasn't taking any chances.

He laid her back on the grass and climbed on top of her, settling himself between her legs. He reached down and took hold of his cock, guiding the swollen tip of it up to rest against her slick entrance.

He was inside her all the way with a single thrust. She was tight and hot and slick with pussy and peach juice.

He fucked her with long, slow strokes, bringing his cock almost all the way out of her, then sliding in to the hilt again and again.

She wrapped her legs around him and her hips rose to meet each of his strokes. Their pace began to quicken as each of them built toward their much-needed release.

She screamed as she reached her climax. Her ass came off the ground as she wrapped herself around him and shook with the force of her orgasm.

He allowed himself to come with her. His body tensed as his cock jerked inside her, giving an entirely different meaning to the phrase peaches and cream.

They collapsed together afterward, but their rendezvous was far from over.

Peaches instructed him to lie down. He did as she asked. She grabbed another of the peaches she'd picked from the tree and held it over his cock, which was still erect. She squeezed the peach until it smashed between her fingers. Warm, sticky peach juice dribbled over Mike's cock and balls.

She knelt between his legs and pushed the peach down over the top of his cock, then she put her tongue on his balls and began licking them, using wide, soft strokes to lick up the sticky juice.

"Oh, shit . . ." Mike groaned.

Peaches worked the soft, mushy peach up around on the head of his cock, twisting and turning, moving it up and down, always varying the rhythm. Her tongue flicked gently at his balls the whole time, driving him out of his mind with sensations he could only take in a little at a time without sensory overload.

She took his balls in her mouth and rolled them around on her tongue, then she sucked on them, first one at a time, then both at once.

The peach moving up and down on his cock was soft and warm. He closed his eyes and took in the pleasure it gave him.

Peaches discarded the fruit after a moment, climbing on top of him as she did. She slid up and straddled his midsection, pressing her hot, slick pussy down on his erection. She rocked back and forth, rubbing her slippery pink slit up and down the length of his cock, occasionally grinding her hips in slow, wide circles.

He grabbed her by the hips and pulled her all the way up to his chest. She raised up, moved forward slightly, then came down on his face, smothering him with the sweet peach taste of her pussy.

He pushed his tongue through her damp blonde curls and into her pussy. She rode up and down, back and forth, using his tongue like a tiny cock. He worked it around inside her, bringing it out now and then to tease her hard little clit with it.

Peaches squealed with delight as she reached another orgasm. Mike felt her body shudder. She fell forward, her hands flat on the ground on either side of Mike's head for support, bucking her hips wildly as she rode out the waves of pleasure his probing tongue brought.

Without missing a beat, Peaches slid away from his mouth, reaching back to guide his cock into her pussy. She brought herself up on it, then all the way down, then up again, establishing a slow, easy rhythm.

Mike lay there, letting her do all the work. She didn't seem to mind. This was one little southern belle that had an insatiable desire—a thirst that seemed never to be quenched—and Mike was happy to be of service.

He watched as she threw her head back, moaning as she pushed all the way down on his cock and ground her pussy at the base. She cupped her tits, each barely more than a handful, and massaged them, squeezing and pushing them together, running her thumbs over her stiff nipples.

She fell over him suddenly, pressing her tits against his face, feeding her nipples into his mouth one at a time. Her hips pumped a steady rhythm as she moved her sticky-wet pussy along the length of his shaft.

He grabbed her hips and held her tight, raising her and setting her down on his cock as his tongue worked circles around her taut nipples.

She came up off his cock without warning, turning away from him, putting her pale, soft ass toward him. She lowered her head and took his cock into her mouth, wrapping one hand around it, and backed up until her pussy was once again on his face.

She worked her hips, rubbing her pussy on his mouth. He grabbed a soft ass cheek in each hand and spread her cheeks wide, making easy access to her puckered anus and damp, fragrant pussy. He probed both openings with his tongue, occasionally adding his fingers to the mix for variety, and soon she was moaning around a mouthful of his cock.

Her hand worked up and down on his cock, moving faster and faster. Her tongue teased the underside of his cock, whipping against the sensitive spots. He could feel her mouth open as she plunged down on it, taking him to the hilt, and her lips loosen as she came up. Now and then she let his dick fall from her mouth to work her tongue up one side and down the other, always keeping her fist in motion, bringing him closer with every stroke.

He pushed his tongue into her pussy and tasted the combined sweetness of their juices and of the peach juice. He slid his tongue deep inside her, wiggled it around, then brought it out and sought the puckered ring of her asshole, flicking his tongue around it a couple of times before pushing it in.

She did the bump and grind on his face, working herself back against him with increased frenzy. The sloppy wet sounds she made as she worked on his cock were punctuated by the moans and gasps of pleasure his mouth brought her.

Lying here in the hot Georgia sun with a cute southern blonde squirming on his face and his cock deep in her mouth was just about as close to Heaven as any man could get.

She plunged her mouth down around his cock again, sucking hard as she went, and this time there was no holding back. This time he closed his eyes and went with it, groaning as he pushed his hips at her and his cock exploded into her mouth.

Mike plunged his tongue into the soft ripeness of her pussy and let the sweet nectar spill over it. . . .

. . . and he knew he wanted nothing more than to spend the rest of his life eating Peaches. . . .

Exposure

A ngie and I live in a small town. There's not much to do. We occupy our time with lots of good, sweaty fucking. Water sports, role playing, mutual masturbation—just about anything two people can do together, Angie and I have tried at least once.

Everything that didn't involve outside participants, that is.

Angie is knockout gorgeous. Her long blonde hair frames a face that is the perfect blend of sweet innocence and porn-star promise. Her cheekbones are high and her baby-blue eyes, lightly flecked with green and gray, are as seductive as a waterfall in paradise. Her body, highlighted by an awesome set of 38DDs and a round ass, draws attention from male and female alike.

One lazy Saturday afternoon we decided to explore the exhibitionist in us. We'd talked about it a few times in the past, but we'd never seriously considered getting involved in anything of that nature.

We were on our way into town. The nearest mall was twenty minutes from where we lived. I took Highway 30 because it was a straight shot and I could drive seventy or eighty miles an hour the whole way. This time, though, I got stuck behind some guy who was in no particular hurry to be anywhere.

The guy was driving a pickup truck. He kept glancing back in his rearview mirror like he was trying to test my patience. If he was trying to piss me off, he was dangerously close to succeeding.

"Wait," Angie said, placing her hand on my leg.

An impish grin played across her face that told me she was up to no good.

She slid over beside me. The next time numb nuts looked in the rearview, she ducked down so he couldn't see her. He almost drove off the road trying to see what she was doing.

Never one to waste an opportunity, Angie unzipped my pants and popped my cock into her mouth, and it was my turn to nearly drive off the road.

Angie trapped the head of my cock in her mouth and jerked me off. I groaned and came. She gulped hard, swallowing every drop, then licked her lips as she sat up again. "Watch this," she said.

She slowly undid the buttons on her blouse, exposing the lace edges of her bra. She looked to see if I was going to object, and when I didn't, she undid the rest of the buttons and opened the blouse. Her smooth, creamy tits spilled over the lace cups of the bra, showing off plenty of cleavage.

The guy in the truck was weaving every which way as he tried not to miss anything. I alternated between watching what Angie was doing and keeping an eye on the truck to make sure the guy didn't slam on his brakes.

"Dare me to take it off?" Angie asked.

The thought of Angie exposing her tits to the guy in the truck turned me on. I dared her, knowing full well she couldn't resist a challenge.

I punched the gas and whipped across the yellow line. Angie turned sideways as I sped past the truck. The driver was gawking at us. Angie lifted her bra and her heavy tits bounced free of their restraints. Her nipples were hard. She leaned against the passenger-side window, pressing her tits flat against it, giving the farmer in the truck a tit shot to remember.

I cut in front of the truck and sped up more. Glancing in the rearview, I saw the farmer giving it all he had to keep up with us, but his clunker sputtered and fell by the wayside.

Angie was stuffing her tits back into her bra. Her face was flushed. I could see that her adrenaline was running high.

* * *

We fucked later that night. The whole flashing incident had incited a riot in my balls. I could tell Angie had really gotten into it too.

"You liked flashing your tits, didn't you?" I asked.

I was still inside her, not really moving, just sort of enjoying the warm grip of her wet pussy around my cock.

"Yeah, it was kinda cool," she said.

"The guy probably had to pull over and jerk off. Think about that, some stranger pulling his dick while he thinks about fucking you."

"Ummm, yeah . . ." she moaned.

She began to move beneath me, thrusting her hips up, taking my cock deeper inside her. I slipped my hands under her and grabbed the cheeks of her ass, pulling her tight against me. She locked her legs around my waist and shuddered as she reached her climax. I came with her.

"Go down on me," she panted.

She liked it when I licked my come from her pussy. I probed inside her with my tongue, teased her clit, and pushed fingers inside her.

It wasn't long before she was ready to fuck again.

* * *

We were on our way home from a late-night drive-in movie. We'd smoked a joint during the movie and we wanted Taco Bell. It was right at closing time when we pulled into the parking lot.

Two young guys were working, one tall and skinny, the other short and stocky. They had already locked the doors. I banged on the door to get their attention. One look at Angie was all it took to get them to let us in. She was wearing a white sleeveless top that showed her pink bra underneath and a dangerously short skirt with no panties.

"Really, dude," one of the guys said, "we're supposed to be closed."

"We won't be long," I promised.

We took our food to the back corner of the restaurant.

"Did you see the way they were checking you out?" I said.

"I know," she replied. "It was sort of cute, and it got us dinner."

I knew how excited she'd gotten flashing her tits at the farmer in the truck. I wondered if she was willing to take the whole flashing thing to the next level.

"You give them a real show," I suggested.

Her eyes flashed with excited anticipation. "What do you mean?"

"You know, really give them something to think about," I said.

She gave me one of those wicked little smiles of hers. "Are you sure?"

"Yeah, go for it," I said.

She headed up to the counter and ordered two tacos, resting her elbows on the counter, standing on her toes as she did. Her heavy boobs fell against the front of her shirt, giving the guys a clear shot of her bra and her cleavage.

The guys stood rooted to their spots, neither making a move to get the tacos. Angie's skirt rode up, giving me a good view of the lower cheeks of her ass. I had a sudden urge to go right up and fuck her while she leaned across the counter and chatted with the two Taco Bell employees.

Angie grabbed a handful of napkins and started back to our table. She smiled at me and dropped the napkins. She bent over to pick them up, pausing long enough to let the guys get a good look at her blonde pussy.

"You're such a slut," I told her when she got back to the table.

"You ain't seen nothin' yet," she said.

I saw the guys in back, working on the tacos. They whispered back and forth, now and then glancing our way. I could imagine the conversation between them.

Angie went back for the tacos. I was floored by what she did next. She climbed onto the counter, faced the two guys, and spread her legs wide, exposing her wet, pink pussy. How's that for health-code violation?

I went up to the counter to stand beside her. I wasn't comfortable with her being so close to the guys without me. She was treading on dangerous ground. The guys gave me a nervous glance. I nodded toward Angie, indicating they should enjoy the show.

Angie was more than ready to perform. She had one foot on the counter and the other dangling over the edge. She parted the plump lips of her pussy and started rubbing her clit with her free hand.

"I'd like to bang that pussy," the shorter guy said.

Angie shook her head. "Un-uh," she said, "No touching. Just watch."

She fixed the guys with a sultry stare as she played with herself. Her eyes darted to their crotches now and then, and it was obvious she was curious about what was between their legs.

"Maybe you guys should give her something to look at while she fingers her pussy," I suggested. "It would be the polite thing to do."

The taller guy didn't hesitate. He whipped his cock out. Angie's eyes widened when she got a good look at its size. She worked two fingers into her pussy. "Jerk off for me and you can come on my pussy," she said, pressing her thumb against her clit as she fucked herself with her fingers.

The thought of some strange guy squirting his come all over Angie's pussy made me feel a little uneasy. Flashing was one thing, but Angie was getting into some wild shit now.

The tall, skinny dude pumped his fist on his thick cock. He kept his eyes on Angie's fingers as she worked them deeper into her pussy. Her vulva glistened with excitement. The pink folds clung to her fingers, folding in and out as she fucked her pussy.

The shorter guy took his cock out then, his eyes riveted to where the action was. I sat quietly off to the side, leaning against the counter, and watched the two guys tug their cocks while Angie concentrated on making herself come.

Angie withdrew her wet fingers and licked them clean. "Come on, guys, get over here and come on my pussy," she said.

She was breathing heavy, all hot and bothered and into the game. She stuck her fingers in her pussy again, slamming the palm of her hand against her clit each time her fingers went in.

She watched the guys jerk off, chewing her lower lip as she waited for them to come. I'd never seen her like this before. She was always horny, but the thought of those two guys shooting come all over her pussy had her going crazy.

"Hurry," she said, panting, "Come for me." Her cheeks were flushed. I could see that she was on the verge of her own climax.

The tall guy was first. He positioned himself between Angie's legs, still tugging on his cock. The guy squeezed his eyes closed and grunted as he jerked his dick. The head of his cock was swollen and purple and nearly touching Angie's pussy when he squirted half a dozen thick streams of come over her fingers and pussy.

Angie continued to finger-fuck herself with her come-soaked fingers, "oooing" and "ahh-ing" as she worked the sticky sperm into her horny pussy.

The second guy exploded before he reached Angie, and most of his come ended up on the floor. He managed to squeeze some of it on her thigh, gasping as he did. Angie took hold of his quickly shrinking cock and rubbed it against her leg, then she climbed off the counter.

"Have a good night, guys," she said.

We got the hell out of there in a hurry, leaving the two horny guys with their pants around their ankles and their dicks in their hands.

"I'm soaked," Angie said once we were in the car.

"I can't believe you did that," I said. "That was intense."

"I know," she said, still out of breath.

92

I started the car and pulled out of the parking lot. "You're turning into quite a little slut," I said.

"You love it," she said. "Admit it. It turns you on to watch me act that way."

I couldn't deny it.

"Wanna come in my mouth?" she asked suddenly.

Without waiting for my answer, she unzipped my pants and bent down to slide her wet mouth around my cock. She worked her way down, flicking her tongue against the sides of my shaft and around the base of my dick, then she tightened her lips and came up slow, letting the head of my dick slip from her mouth with a wet sucking sound. She circled the tip of my cock a few times for good measure, then went down on me again, stroking my shaft with one hand while she sucked and nibbled the head of my cock.

We were on Highway 55, heading south. Traffic was light—just the occasional eighteen-wheeler trying to pick up some time.

We were cruising along at moderate speed. I saw an eighteen wheeler ahead of us, in the slow lane, and I figured the guy was probably bored out of his mind. I suggested to Angie that we give him some entertainment.

I sped up until I was running neck and neck with the big truck. Just as I had suspected, the trucker behind the wheel was nearly asleep. I flipped on the overhead light. Angie continued to suck my dick as she repositioned herself on the seat, hiking her skirt above her waist, and pressed her bare ass to the window.

The trucker glanced over at us and his eyes went wide as saucers. He grinned and gave us a thumbs up, blasting his air horn for encouragement. I paced him for a few exits before deciding it was best to call it a night.

Angie was still working on my cock when we got home. She finished me off before we left the car, jerking my dick until I came. She opened her mouth and stuck out her tongue, catching the first creamy shots, then she took me in her mouth and swallowed the rest in huge, deep gulps.

* * *

What had begun as a playful game soon snowballed into obsession. We didn't just go out on weekends anymore. I would go to work during the day, come home and get a shower, and off we'd go to find our latest challenge. It was like riding the biggest, fastest rollercoaster we could find.

One night Angie asked me to take her dancing. She wore a tight black dress (no bra or panties), black stockings with lace patterns, and a pair of black suede boots. The dress clung to every luscious curve of her body. It took all my willpower not to fuck her before we left the house.

The club was packed. We ordered our drinks at the bar and found a table. After we finished our first round, we hit the dance floor. Angie loves to dance. She shakes her ass, pumps her hips, and lets her tits jiggle. We danced through two fast songs, and then a slow song came on and we embraced.

Angie grabbed my ass and pulled me against her, rubbing her crotch against me. My cock was erect and poking at her belly.

"How would you like to fuck me right on the dance floor?" she whispered in my ear.

I thought I was going to come where I stood. She sensed my excitement and kept it up.

"Come on, stick your cock in me," she whispered, and then she licked and nibbled my ear.

I slid my hands down over her ass, ran them up the back of her legs and up under her dress. I squeezed the cheeks of her ass, letting my fingers slide along the crevice of her bottom. I pulled her ass cheeks apart and teased her puckered little asshole, then I slipped a finger into her pussy.

"Think about how good it would feel to put your cock in me right now," she whispered, again nibbling my earlobe.

She slipped a hand between us and fumbled with my zipper. I couldn't believe she was going to do it. She managed to get my cock out and, with a little creative maneuvering, work the tip of it into her pussy. I'm taller than she is, so she had to raise up on her toes to get it inside her.

She continued to grind against me and nibble my ear. The thrill of doing it in public like that, with so many people all around us, was intense. My hands moved like they had minds of their own. My fingers stroked the lips of her pussy. Her dress rode up in back, displaying her bare ass to anyone who cared to look.

The song ended. I put my cock in my pants. We went back to our table for a breather. Angie was still in a horny, playful mood. She slipped one of her shoes off under the table, put her foot between my legs, and pressed her toes down on my cock. She had that playful twinkle in her eyes as she teased me.

"Imagine how many guys in here have hard-ons because of you," I said. "Some of them will probably go home tonight and jerk off thinking about you. Some married guy will probably think about you while he fucks his wife. Does that turn you on?"

"Yes," she admitted. "My pussy gets all hot and wet."

"Not just men either," I said. "I saw a couple of women checking you out."

She moaned when I mentioned women. She'd confessed to me a long time ago that she had sexual fantasies about having sex with another woman.

"Jack off for me," she said. "Right now, under the table."

"Right now?"

"Yep, right now. I wanna feel your come on my toes."

She pushed her foot down on my cock for emphasis. I took out my cock. Angie brushed her toes against the head of it. The lace of her stocking was rough, but it felt good. She slipped her toes under my balls and played with them. I took my cock in my right hand and began to stroke it. She kept her eyes on me the whole time, pretending as if nothing out of the ordinary was happening. To anyone who looked our way, we appeared to be engaged in normal conversation.

Angie signaled for a waitress, who came over to take our order. Angie was purposely indecisive about what she wanted to drink. It was obvious she was having fun using her foot on my dick with the girl standing there.

Angie reached for her cigarettes, knocking them off the table. "Oops," she said, smiling at the waitress. "I don't suppose you'd get those for me?"

"Sure, no problem," the waitress said.

She stooped to retrieve the cigarettes. When she stood up again, she was smiling and her cheeks were red. "Here you are," she said, handing the cigarettes to Angie.

"Thanks," Angie said. "What's your name?"

"Ashley," she answered.

She was a cute little thing, blonde and built about the same as Angie, except her tits were smaller. I could tell by the way Angie was sizing her up that she was thinking dirty thoughts.

Angie finally ordered her drink. She watched Ashley go, and then she took off her other shoe and trapped my cock between the soles of her feet. "I want you to come on my toes now," she said, jerking my cock between her feet.

It didn't take long. I felt my balls tighten and my cock jerk as my come spurted across her feet. She kept tightened her toes around my dick and kept pumping until she'd drained me.

Ashley came back with our drinks. "On the house," she said.

"Let's dance some more," Angie said.

She dragged me through the crowd and onto the dance floor.

"She likes you," Angie said, referring to Ashley.

"I think it's you she likes," I said. "And I think the attraction is mutual."

"You think so?"

"Yeah, I think so."

"Can we take her home?"

"We can ask her," I said.

"Oh yeah . . ."

She pressed close to me, putting her mouth against my ear, and said, "This is what I wanna do to her pussy." Her warm, moist breath was a turn-on. She licked my ear to demonstrate how she would lick Ashley's pussy.

I slid my hands to her ass and raised her dress again, just enough to expose the lower cheeks of her naked ass. Public nudity was one thing. Causing a riot was something else altogether.

I saw quite a few people, both men and women, take notice and jockey for better viewing positions.

"Everybody's looking at you," I said.

"I can feel it. It's making me so hot."

I pushed a finger between her pussy lips and toyed with her clit before sliding my finger up inside her pussy.

"Please make me come . . ."

I inserted another finger in her pussy and slowly worked both fingers deep inside her. She closed her eyes and laid her head on my shoulder, rotating her hips as she fucked my fingers, completely oblivious of the people crowding around to watch our performance. She moaned in my ear. Her juices dripped all over my fingers. I could feel the walls of her pussy milking my fingers.

"Come for me, baby," I said.

She sucked on my neck. Her pussy clenched around my fingers and her thighs quivered as she reached her climax right there on the dance floor.

We got all sorts of propositions as we made our way back to our table. One guy even offered a hundred bucks if he could go down on Angie.

Ashley brought us fresh drinks.

"How would you feel about coming home with us?" Angie asked outright.

She chewed her lower lip thoughtfully, shrugged her shoulders, and said, "Sure, why not?"

Ashley met us in the parking lot after work. She'd changed out of her uniform and into a pair of jeans and a blouse. She left her car and rode with us. We were hardly out of the parking lot and Ashley reached under Angie's skirt to finger her.

"Ummm, you're so wet," Ashley murmured.

She leaned over and kissed Angie on the mouth. Angie responded eagerly by sucking Ashley's tongue into her mouth. It was hard to concentrate on driving with the girls making out and Ashley fingering Angie.

When we got to the house, Angie took Ashley upstairs to our bedroom. I grabbed a bottle of wine from the kitchen before I joined them. Angie was already naked. Ashley was nearly naked.

I lit a cigarette and sat down to watch.

They were on the bed, both topless. Ashley leaned over Angie and started sucking her nipples. She gathered Angie's big, soft tits in her hands and went from one nipple to the next, sucking and biting them, and then she worked her way down, stopping to kiss Angie's belly.

Angie spread her legs and gently urged Ashley lower. She opened her pussy lips with two fingers, offering her coral-pink inner lips to Ashley, who wasted no time running her tongue over the slick, soft folds.

Ashley's ass was facing me, raised into the air. Her pink panties stretched tight over her ass cheeks and outlined the lips of her pussy. The temptation to tug those panties down and eat my fill was almost too much, but I resisted the urge.

Ashley slipped two fingers into Angie's pussy. Angie raised her ass off the bed to give Ashley easier access. Ashley continued to eat Angie while she fingered her, watching Angie's reaction over the mound of her pussy.

Angie pumped her pussy against Ashley's mouth. She pushed her tits together and sucked her own nipples.

Ashley took off her panties and lay back on the bed, spreading her legs wide. When Angie went down on Ashley, I got behind Angie and took her by her hips, pulling her to me so I could lick her asshole and pussy. I could hear Angie's muffled moans as she ate her first pussy.

I took off my clothes. My cock was so hard it hurt. I guided it into Angie's pussy. She was dripping with juice. My cock slid right in. I pulled the cheeks of her ass apart and rubbed my thumb around her asshole as I watched my cock slip in and out of her clinging pussy lips. I pressed my thumb against her tight asshole and felt a slight resistance. Angie shifted her ass and moaned. The tip of my thumb pressed into her bottom.

"You like that, baby?" I asked, easing my thumb a little further up her ass.

I fucked her pussy with long, full strokes. Each thrust of my cock pushed her into Ashley's wet cunt. Ashley groaned and started breathing harder. She twisted her fingers in Angie's hair and pulled Angie to her as she came.

To my surprise, Angie suggested the two of them give me a blow job. I wasn't about to complain. The two of them ran their wet tongues up and down my shaft, swapping it back and forth. When one of them sucked and licked my balls, the other was taking my cock in her mouth.

"Oh, shit, I'm going to come," I warned them.

Angie pushed my cock into Ashley's mouth and jerked me off as I exploded. Ashley gulped hard, swallowing the first creamy spurts. Angie pulled my dick from Ashley's mouth and quickly covered it with hers, taking a splash on her cheek before she swallowed the last few spurts.

They embraced each other and kissed, their sticky tongues dancing together, swapping come back and forth. Angie pulled my cock to her mouth and licked it clean. Ashley kissed her again, then they kissed around the head of my cock.

We played until the sun came up, then we went for breakfast before dropping Ashley back at her car. The three of us made plans to get together again.

After Ashley, Angie and I talked about another threesome, this time with a man. Angie liked the idea of taking on two guys at once.

I had no doubt she could pull it off, and with her penchant for advertising, I figured we wouldn't have any trouble finding a willing participant. . . .

Feeling Sexy

Jillian was soaking in a warm tub of bubbly water, thinking about Barry from work. She had been thinking about him a lot lately. He was single and extremely good looking. She'd been wanting to ask him out for some time now, but she always seemed to back out just as she gathered the courage to do it.

It wasn't that she had no self confidence. She was 5'5" tall and weighed right at 185 most of the time. Her hair was long and blonde, her eyes were a pale shade of blue, and her breasts were a healthy 38DD. She had wide hips and short yet shapely legs. She could attract her share of men when she wanted to, but there was something about Barry that made her shy away.

The front doorbell rang. Jillian got out of the tub and wrapped a towel around her. She hurried to the front door and looked out the window. There was no one there, but the postman had left a package on the door step. Jillian opened the door and quickly grabbed the package, giving it a curious look as she shut the door.

She couldn't remember having ordered anything, but the package was clearly marked with her name and address. She carried it into the living room and sat on the sofa to open the box.

She was more than a little surprised to find a very sexy halter-style baby doll with lots of fringe and stretchy lace.

There had to be some sort of mistake. Jillian would not have ordered such a thing for herself. She wasn't currently in a relationship, nor had she been in one for some time. Even if she were seeing someone, she would never have the confidence necessary to wear something as sexy as this.

She looked at the invoice inside the box. The company was Hips & Curves. The invoice showed the lingerie had been paid for in full. She would call the company to clear up the mistake later, but right now she couldn't resist the urge to see what she would look like in the baby doll.

She carried the package to her bedroom, took the baby doll out, and placed it on the bed. She dropped her towel to the floor, picked up the black string-bikini panties and slipped them on first, then she put on the fringe baby doll halter.

She looked at herself in the a full-length mirror.

"Not bad," she said aloud.

She definitely liked what she saw.

She ran her hands over her hips and up under the long black fringe of the baby doll, cupping her breasts through the lace that covered them. Her nipples responded immediately, growing stiff beneath her palms as she squeezed her ample breasts.

She liked her nipples. They were hypersensitive and responded well during lovemaking. She especially liked to have them sucked and licked as she was being made love to. The sensations were electric and traveled through every inch of her body, intensifying her orgasm when it finally came.

How long had it been since she'd made love? She couldn't remember exactly, but now, wearing the Hips & Curves lingerie, she felt especially sexy and in need of the sexual intimacy she'd been lacking in her life.

She climbed on her bed and opened the drawer of the nightstand beside it. She reached into the drawer and extracted the soft, thick vibrator she'd pleasured herself with on many occasions. It had even been a while since she'd put it to good use, and right now she needed to make herself feel good.

She closed her eyes and thought of Barry. What would he think of her new lingerie? She already knew she wouldn't return it. She felt too good wearing it. The lace against her nipples, just rough enough to tease them to hardness, the fringe slipping across her thighs—it felt so wonderful and made her feel like she could seduce the world.

She pulled the lacy panties to one side and inserted her toy, imagining Barry there with her instead. She would make him wait while she went into the bathroom and changed into her new lingerie, then she would come out into the bedroom and do a slow, sexy striptease. She would straddle him and ride him until he was at his peak, then she would go over the edge with him.

She caressed her nipples one at a time, sending little shockwaves of pleasure to her belly, between her legs, and all the way to her toes.

She could almost hear Barry's voice, deep and melodious, and she could imagine his breath on her neck as he kissed her there.

She was so close now. Her breasts rose and fell as her breathing quickened. She could feel herself getting wetter as she reached the edge and teetered there for just a moment before she went all the way over . . .

Her cell phone rang.

She tried to ignore it, but whoever was on the other end of the line wasn't going to go away.

She let herself finish before she collapsed back on the bed and leaned over to answer the phone.

"Hello," she said, trying her best not to sound like a heavy breather.

"Did you enjoy your gift?"

It was Barry. The sound of his voice re-ignited the flames of desire within her.

"I'm trying it on now," she said. "Would you like to come over and see?

"I'd like nothing more," he said.

"I'll be waiting," she said, and hung up the phone.

Fire Inside

"Would you sign my book?"

Janet Donahue was having a latté and staring at her laptop screen, thinking about what she was going to write next. She'd been at it for several hours now, sitting at the same table in the same Starbucks located in the same Barnes and Noble where she'd completed most of the work on her first book, *Fire Inside*.

The woman standing beside her was slender and not too tall, with a slight build, shoulder-length hair that exhibited the varied colors of an autumn leaf, and green eyes with tiny flecks of gold.

Janet noticed all of this before she even responded to the woman's question.

"Yes, I'll sign it," Janet said.

She took the copy of *Fire Inside* and opened it on the table beside her laptop. The woman produced a pen, and not just any pen either. This one was Janet's favorite—a Mont Blanc Meisterstück.

Janet smiled and took the well-crafted writing instrument in her hand, enjoying the feel of it for a long moment before she finally rested its tip against the page of the book.

"To whom shall I make this out?" Janet asked.

"Rebecca."

"Anything special you'd like me to write, Rebecca?"

"How about 'to Rebecca, the inspiration behind the fire'?"

Janet started to write and stopped suddenly. There was something in the tone of voice that brought her back to another time. She looked up at the woman standing in front of her, studied her a moment, and then smiled.

"Rebecca Sanders," she said. "I can't believe it's you. You look so . . ."

"Thin?" Rebecca said.

Janet shook her head in disbelief. "Yes, that . . . and you've changed the color of your hair."

"I've made a lot of changes over the past several years," Rebecca said.

Janet had so many questions, but the line behind Rebecca was getting long and she didn't want to hold up the fans.

"Listen, I'm staying at the Claymont, in room two twenty-one," she said, signing Rebecca's copy of Fire Inside. "Why don't you come by later, say around six o' clock?"

She closed the book and slid it across the table. Rebecca picked it up, smiled, and said, "I'll see you then."

* * *

Janet smiled at the memories. It was true what Rebecca had said. Janet had based much of *Fire Inside* on those days in college, back when the two of them had been so much alike and so in love. It baffled Janet when she thought about how two people so much in love could go their separate ways. She wondered how often Rebecca had thought about her over the years. She wondered if she'd left the same impression on Rebecca as Rebecca had left on her—a mark so indelible she had to write it in a book, changing the names, of course, to protect the not-so-innocent.

Soon she would be with Rebecca again, and she had not even the slightest clue how she would handle that. For all she knew, Rebecca was with someone else and only dropping by to catch up on life. She didn't think so, but she couldn't be sure. She thought she'd seen something in her ex lover's eyes at the signing. She'd certainly felt her own heated stirrings, and if given the opportunity, she would gladly rekindle the fire that had once been.

She wasn't even sure what she should do. A bottle of champagne from room service? Should she dress casual, for a night here at the hotel, or dress for a night of dancing? Maybe they would have dinner together. She knew Rebecca all those years ago. Choices like these would not have been difficult. Now, though, she couldn't be at all sure what to expect.

Six o' clock came and went. By six-thirty she was starting to get anxious. Rebecca showed up five minutes later. Janet did her best not to let it show how anxious she'd been.

"I'm sorry I'm late," Rebecca said. "I had some things to take care of."

"That's all right," Janet said.

"What things?"

"I made arrangements for dinner, if you don't mind," Rebecca said.

"I don't mind," Janet said. "Should I dress?"

"You look wonderful the way you are," Rebecca said.

The restaurant, it turned out, belonged to Rebecca. It was casual elegance with great food and atmosphere. They sat at a table in a dark corner of the restaurant. A single candle sat in the center of the table. They started with crisp salads, followed by mussels in garlic butter, then on to a cream-sauce pasta dish with shrimp. A bottle of red wine accompanied the meal, which they finished with slices of layered chocolate cake.

Dinner conversation centered primarily on what the two of them had been up to since their days in college. The drive back to Janet's hotel leaned more toward the old days, which had the two of them feeling quite nostalgic by the time they were back in Janet's room.

"I've missed you," Janet said.

They had barely gotten through the door.

"I've missed you too," Rebecca said. "I've followed your career, all of it. The short stories, the poetry . . . and when *Fire Inside* came out. . . ."

Janet couldn't be sure who made the first move. She only knew that Rebecca's soft, moist lips on hers felt good. She slid her arms around Rebecca's waist and pulled her close, kissing her harder.

They continued kissing as they headed into the bedroom, losing their clothes along the way. The two of them were down to their undergarments by the time they reached the bed.

Rebecca fell back and pulled Janet on top of her. Janet bent down and kissed her again, reaching back with one hand to stroke Rebecca's inner thigh. The skin there was as soft as brushed velvet.

Rebecca responded by bending her knees slightly and letting her legs fall open, giving Janet unrestricted access to her most private parts.

Janet took her time, stroking Rebecca's thigh in circles that gradually widened until her fingertips brushed over the outer lips of Rebecca's pussy.

Janet caressed the slick folds between Rebecca's outer lips and teased her clit from beneath its hood. Rebecca moaned and her bottom came off the bed as she offered herself to Janet.

Janet explored Rebecca's pussy as if it were her first time, stroking the outer lips, tracing over the smooth, soft folds of her labia with her fingertips, and finally slipping first one, then two fingers inside Rebecca.

"You're so wet," she whispered.

"You make me that way," Rebecca said.

Janet moved her fingers around inside Rebecca, churning the sweet honey until Rebecca's pussy could no longer contain its copious flow.

"Oh, Janet . . ."

Janet kissed Rebecca's breasts, circling each areola with a gentle touch of her tongue, enjoying the feel of the little pleasure bumps that formed all over. She took each nipple into her mouth and gave it the loving attention it deserved, alternating the pressure of her tongue strokes and the intensity of suction. Rebecca's nipples had always been hypersensitive, and Janet knew by the increasing moans from Rebecca that nothing had changed there.

Slowly Janet left Rebecca's breasts behind, kissing her way downward, taking her time when she reached Rebecca's belly. She kissed the soft skin there and dipped her tongue into Rebecca's belly button.

"Do you remember New Year's Eve?" Rebecca gasped. "Do you remember pouring champagne there and licking it up?"

"Oh, I remember," Janet said, and immediately she reached for the phone on the table beside the bed.

"A bottle of champagne to room two twenty-one please," she said., smiling at Rebecca. "And a bowl of fresh strawberries . . . with a bowl of whipped cream."

She hung up the receiver and moved up to settle between Rebecca's legs. They kissed and fondled one another until room service arrived. Janet wrapped the sheet around her and went to retrieve the cart. When she returned, Rebecca was on her knees, anticipating the coming event like a little girl on Christmas morning. Janet rolled the cart up beside the bed, dropped the sheet, and popped the cork on the champagne.

She filled the two empty glasses with champagne, picked up a strawberry, and then climbed back into bed.

Rebecca lay back on the bed. Janet straddled her, offering her the strawberry. Rebecca took a bite and chewed slowly, licking the sticky-sweet juice from her lips as she swallowed the fresh fruit.

Janet slid backward and kneeled beside Rebecca, tilting the champagne over Rebecca's stomach. She trickled some of the bubbly into Rebecca's belly button and scooped it out with her tongue, then she did it again, this time allowing the champagne to overflow and run down the sides of Rebecca's body.

Janet handed the bottle to Rebecca and situated herself between Rebecca's legs, sliding her hands beneath her as she did.

Rebecca drank from the bottle of champagne and then set it back on the cart. She reached down and ran her fingers through Janet's hair as Janet began licking and kissing her pussy.

"Oh my god, that feels so good," Rebecca said, her words coming out in a harsh whisper. "Yes, right there . . ."

Janet knew the spot. After all these years, that spot had not changed. Not directly on Rebecca's clit, but a little to the right. She focused there, moving her tongue back and forth in short, firm strokes.

Rebecca's breathing quickened. She tangled her fingers in Janet's hair and pulled her close, a little rougher than was necessary.

"Sorry," she gasped.

Janet didn't care. She could feel Rebecca quivering beneath her. She could smell the scent of Rebecca's arousal, feel the pliant flesh of her ass as she dug her fingers in, and all she wanted was to hear Rebecca scream her name.

Rebecca arched her back and shuddered as a wave of pleasure swept over her. Janet felt the spasms of her best friend's pussy as she came.

Rebecca collapsed on the bed, breathing so hard she couldn't find the words she wanted. She held out her arms instead, beckoning Janet to lie beside her.

They held one another without words for some time. Nearly two decades had passed since the two of them had been together . . .

Two decades that could not extinguish the raging flames that ignited whenever they touched . . .

A Good Fucking Promotion

My wife Catrina works for a large company. Her boss is one of the top executives in the firm, outranked only by the Vice President and the President. When an opening came up for a position working under the Vice President, my wife wanted the job. Her record more than qualified her, but she wasn't sure her boss would be willing to let her go, and without a recommendation from him, the Vice President would never consider her for the position.

"There is one way I could probably get Gary to recommend me for the job," Catrina said to me one night while we were having dinner.

"How's that?" I asked.

"Well . . . he's made several passes at me, which I've always put off, but if I were to give in to him, I'm sure he would do anything I asked."

"You mean fuck him?"

I was both appalled and excited by the thought.

"The new job would be a lot more money," she said.

"I thought your boss was gay," I said.

"He's bisexual, not gay," she said.

Nothing more was said during dinner, but we talked about it later that night. I finally agreed to go along with her plan, but only on the condition that I be allowed to watch. I was so turned on by the thought of seeing another man's cock in my wife's wet pussy that I spent most of the night making love to her.

Catrina had never mentioned it before, but I suspected she'd harbored fantasies about her boss for some time. The promotion was a perfect excuse for her to act on those fantasies. It also gave me an opportunity to think about one of my sexual fantasies—sharing my wife with another man and possibly even engaging in sex with a man myself.

Catrina left for work the next morning in high spirits. I noticed she'd dressed a bit sexier than usual, although she always looked gorgeous, and it was obvious she intended to follow through with what we'd discussed.

I spent the day imagining what might happen between she and her boss at the office. Would she kneel down under the desk and take his cock in her mouth? Would she bend over the desk with her skirt around her waist and her panties stretched between her ankles while he fucked her from behind? The images were so clear and powerful to me that I jerked off twice.

When Catrina got home that night, I asked immediately what had happened at work that day. She hadn't fucked Gary, but she had discussed our proposition with him. He was due to have dinner with us the following night.

That night, while Catrina ran her tongue lazily along the length of my hard cock, I decided to let her in on my secret fantasy. I wasn't sure how she'd react, so I approached the subject carefully.

"What's that like?" I asked.

"Sucking your cock?"

"Yeah, sucking my cock. What does it feel like to have it in your mouth? What's it like to feel my come spurting across your tongue?"

"It's nice," she said, kissing the head of my cock. "I love the way it throbs when I suck it. I love the way your come hits the back of my throat and I have to swallow hard to get all of it down."

I brushed hair from her face and said, "Let me see you go all the way down. I want you to deep-throat my cock."

She raised up on her elbows and balanced herself as she hovered over me, taking my cock in one hand and bringing it to her mouth. She opened wide, plunging halfway down the length of my dick. Her lips tightened around my shaft as she slowly came up again, letting my cock slip from her mouth so she could run her tongue around the head of it. She went down again, only this time she went all the way, burying her nose in my pubic hair as her wet lips enclosed the base of my throbbing cock.

As she began to glide up and down on my cock, I imagined myself doing the same thing to Gary. I studied the way Catrina simultaneously sucked me and used her tongue on my shaft. I watched the way she used her fingers to stroke my shaft while she concentrated on sucking the head of my dick. When I came in her mouth, I watched her jerk my cock as she swallowed every creamy drop.

"So . . . why the sudden interest in what it's like to give a blow job?" she asked, squeezing the last of my come onto her tongue.

She knew something was up. I couldn't hide it any longer. I confessed my fantasy, watching her face to see how she would react. She took my dick back into her mouth and went all the way down, then she came up again, releasing my cock with a wet pop. She gave the tip of it a kiss and said, "Guess you'll need a few pointers, huh?"

She stuck out her tongue and smacked my cock against it a few times, then she stuffed my meat back into her mouth and proceeded to demonstrate the proper way to give head. I tried to concentrate on the lesson, but she soon had me groaning and thrusting my cock into her mouth as I reached another climax.

By the time Catrina brought Gary home the next night, I was eager to get things started. I pulled Catrina aside the first opportunity I got, asking if she'd mentioned anything to Gary about what I'd suggested.

"Not yet," she said, "but leave everything to me."

Catrina and I sat together on the couch. Gary sat across from us, drinking a bottle of imported beer. He made some small talk about the office. I nudged Catrina with my elbow, urging her to start the ball rolling.

"Why don't you come over here and let Bill sit over there," she suggested to Gary. "You don't mind, do you?" she asked me.

Gary took my place on the couch and I sat in the chair.

Catrina was wearing a black form-fitting dress, black stockings, and pumps. She turned her back to Gary and asked if he would mind unzipping her. He swept her blonde hair up with one hand and slowly drew her zipper down to the small of her back.

Catrina wiggled out of the dress. She wasn't wearing a bra. Her panties were made of black silk, cut high on the sides and trimmed with embroidered rose petals.

She squatted in front of Gary, pushing his knees apart. Her long, sexy fingers tugged at his zipper. She reached into his pants and took out his cock, stroking it a few times before she took it into her mouth and began sucking.

I rubbed my dick through my pants as I watched my wife suck another man's cock. It was a sexy sight to see, the way she lovingly deep-throated his long, thick tool, making it shine with her saliva, teasing the fat pink tip with long, slow strokes of her tongue.

I got undressed and went back to stroking my cock. Catrina reached back with one hand and pulled her panties aside, exposing her pussy to me. She slid one slender finger inside her wet hole and began fucking herself with it.

Gary lifted his ass so he could slide his pants down, which sent his huge cock deeper into Catrina's mouth. She gagged a little, but quickly got her bearings and continued sucking him.

Gary took off his shirt and kicked off his shoes, then he pushed Catrina away from his cock long enough to finish taking off his pants and underwear.

Catrina motioned for me to come kneel beside her. Gary looked surprised, but he made no objections as I knelt beside Catrina. She gave me a kiss, then told me to suck Gary's cock. I nervously took hold of his shaft and pulled his pink dick into my mouth. After a few tentative licks around the tip, I opened my mouth and put his cock inside.

Catrina went down and started licking his heavy balls. She worked her way up, running her tongue along his thick shaft. She took his cock from my mouth and put it into hers, swallowing it to the hilt. She moved up and down a few times, then she pushed it back into my mouth.

We continued like that for about twenty minutes, taking turns sucking on Gary's cock. Catrina gave me tips and showed me a few tricks, and by the time we were ready to try something else, I was able to give a blow job at least as good as my wife could.

Catrina bent over the couch and Gary got behind her, sliding his dick into her pussy. I knelt on the couch beside her and rubbed my swollen cock on her face, then I slid it past her wet lips and into her mouth.

Gary began moving back and forth inside her, each thrust forcing her hot mouth further down on my cock.

We switched places after a little bit. Gary's cock, being quite a bit longer and thicker than mine, had left Catrina's pussy well fucked. My cock slid right into her. I took her by the hips and began rocking her back and forth on my dick. She still had her panties on and the added friction of the silk was enough to bring me right to the edge in no time. When I couldn't hold back any longer, I drove my cock all the way into her and exploded, pumping my hot come deep inside her.

Gary pulled his cock out of her mouth and asked her to lie down on the couch. He knelt over her in the opposite direction, sticking his big cock back into her mouth as he put his head between her legs and started licking my come out of her.

Lying beneath him like she was, Catrina had to keep her hand around his dick to control how deep it went. She squeezed the thick shaft with one hand and massaged his balls with the other, all the while sucking his knob. After several minutes, she mumbled something about his cock and made a wild motion to me with her hand.

I hurried over and knelt beside the couch. She pushed Gary up until his cock slipped out of her mouth. He got the hint and turned around, getting onto his knees so that Catrina and I could both get down in front of him.

"Put it in your mouth," Catrina said.

She was stroking his cock as she pushed my face toward it. I opened wide, feeling the hot, thick length slide past my lips and straight down the back of my throat. I had barely enough time to get it into my mouth before he came, filling my mouth with the hot, salty taste of come. I gulped and swallowed, trying not to lose any of it. Catrina jerked his cock out of my mouth and covered the spurting knob with her own, swallowing the rest of his load.

The three of us took a long, playful shower. Catrina put us back in the spirit of the night by squatting beneath the warm spray of the water and taking our cocks in her mouth. After the shower, we went to the bedroom for a more relaxed session. Gary and I took turns eating Catrina for a long time, then she watched as he and I sixty-nined, sucking each other off while she used her fingers on herself.

"I want both of you to fuck me," she said, getting onto her hands and knees.

We moved behind her, one of us on each side, and Gary began running his tongue around her asshole while I licked her pussy. Since my cock was smaller than Gary's, I was going to be the one to fuck her in the ass. She straddled Gary and lowered her pussy down on his cock, then she leaned forward, smothering his face with her tits. Gary grabbed one of her asscheeks in each hand and separated them, giving me clear access to her puckered back opening.

Catrina keeps hand lotion in the drawer of her nightstand. I leaned over and grabbed the bottle, squirting a liberal amount on my hand and smearing it over the length of my hard prick. I worked a couple of slick fingers into her ass and fingered it until I felt the muscle relax, then I got behind her and slowly worked the head of my cock into her.

It was awkward at first, but Gary and I soon established a rhythm of alternate strokes that kept one of our cocks buried inside her at all times. Catrina squirmed and moaned between us as we alternately pumped our hard pricks into her tight ass and hot pussy. I was the first to come, jerking my cock out of her ass and spraying her lovely cheeks and gaping hole with my creamy load as Gary pounding into her, driving my dripping come deep into her pussy with each stroke.

When Catrina cried out that she was going to come, I pushed her all the way down on Gary's cock with one hand, holding her there as I slid two fingers into her asshole. The added pressure of my fingers in her ass as she climaxed made her scream with pleasure. Gary came with her, groaning as he lifted his ass off the bed and exploded deep inside her pussy.

Afterwards, while we rested up for round three, Gary said, "I hate to bring up business, but there's a promotion in the company you might be interested in. I could give you a good recommendation."

"Really?" Catrina said, reaching out to stroke his cock. "I hadn't even considered it . . ."

Goodbye Goody Two-Shoes

This was a big day for Andrea Rogers. Today was the day she would be promoted to vice president of the advertising department. As far as she knew, she was the only one in line for the position. She'd been with Martin and Henderson for fifteen years. She'd written some of the company's most successful ad campaigns, and she'd been personally responsible for bringing in some of the biggest accounts.

She was ready to accept the challenge of vice president. In the meantime, she opened her briefcase and sipped her Café breve. She was just about to go over her notes for the day when Garrett Martin, the company president, stuck his head out and called her to his office.

This was her big moment. She'd worked hard for it, and while she generally didn't like to toot her own horn, in this case she deserved it.

But something was wrong. She knew it as soon as she entered the office. The look on Garrett's face wasn't a look she expected. There was no beaming smile, he didn't offer her his hand, he didn't even ask her to sit.

Then she saw the tall blonde sitting off to the side, relaxing on the leather couch. She was glowing with an air of superiority that told Andrea all she needed to know. She had been passed over for the promotion, and worse still, the job had gone to this bitch with the fake tits and fake tan.

Andrea knew her well. She'd been with the company for a little more than one year. She wore her skirts short and her blouses half unbuttoned. Her name was Shawna Philips. She was twenty-five years old, inexperienced in the business, and apparently not above fucking and sucking her way to the top.

"Andrea, I'm afraid I have some bad news for you," Garrett said, and then he actually did ask her to have a seat.

"After careful consideration, I've decided that Shawna is best suited for the promotion." He paused for a moment, waiting for her reaction, and when Andrea said nothing, he continued. "I'm also taking you off the Benton Industries account. I'll be handing them over to Shawna."

"Are you kidding me," Andrea said. "I've worked that account for Six months. She doesn't know the first thing about—"

"You'll hand over your files and anything pertaining to the account," Garrett said. "Shawna will oversee the account now."

Andrea fought back her tears. It wasn't fair. She worked hard to make her way in this business, but just because she wasn't as sexy as Shawna, and just because she wasn't willing to sell out, she was taking a backseat to the bimbo.

"I hope you understand how—" Garrett began.

"No, I really don't think I do," she said, surprising herself with her words. "I mean, my tits are obviously not big enough, and I know I haven't sucked your dick—"

"Wait just a minute . . . I think you've said enough for now. If you want to continue on with the company—"

"I don't think I want to," Andrea said.

She got up and excused herself gracefully. At least as gracefully as she could under the circumstances. Truth was, she was not only angry, she was embarrassed. She felt inferior and foolish . . . and she'd felt rejected.

And now she was out of a job.

* * *

Ricky would be able to get her through this. He always knew what to say to make her feel better. He'd been her rock for three years now.

She slid the key into the lock and let herself into their apartment. He would still be at work. She'd surprise him with a nice dinner, maybe a little romance—

She froze and listened, the door to the apartment still open. Noises coming from the bedroom. Sounds she fully recognized and understood. There was the gentle, rhythmic creak of bedsprings, the light tapping of the headboard against the wall. How many times had she wanted to pull the bed away from the wall?

"Ohhhh, Ricky, oh yeah, oh yeah, give it to me, baby, fuck me!"

Andrea closed the door softly, moved across the living room and down the hallway, careful not to make any noise. Not that she'd be heard above the grunts and groans and all the panting anyway.

The bedroom door was standing open. Andrea could see into the room. Ricky was on his back. A woman with red hair was straddling him, riding him hard. Her tits were heavy and pale. She dangled them in Ricky's face. He squeezed her tits together and went to work on her nipples, sucking one and then the other.

Andrea bit her lower lip to keep herself from screaming out. She was hurt and she was angry. The two emotions raged against one another for control. Andrea wanted no part of either at the moment. She wanted to escape, run away and hide.

She backed down the hall, having a hard time tearing her eyes away from the scene in the bedroom. Halfway down the hall, she turned and hurried out of the apartment, back onto the streets. She got in her car and drove. She had no destination in mind. She was lost. The one person she thought she could depend on had betrayed her. She was on her own now.

Andrea drove to the West End, a trendy part of town where a diverse mix of people moved about twenty-four hours a day. It was still early, so a good portion of the crowd consisted of business men and women out for an early lunch. As evening approached, the business crowd would give way to freaks, hookers and pimps, gay and lesbian lovers, and to the art crowd.

Andrea stopped at a small café and ordered a cup of espresso with heavy cream. She drank the coffee slowly, contemplating her life. She couldn't go home and look at Ricky without confronting him, and she didn't feel like having it out with him right now. In fact, she never wanted to have it out with him. She simply wanted to move on with her life.

Andrea walked. She took in a movie, which she didn't pay attention to, and then she ate a late lunch. It was after lunch, as she was heading back to her car, that she saw them in the window, a pair of stiletto shoes, black with seven-inch heels and thin criss-crossing straps decorated with tiny diamonds.

She stared at the shoes until she was looking beyond them, staring at her reflection in the glass. What she saw was a thirty-eight year-old woman with dull brown hair pulled up in a tight bun and her body hidden beneath a power suit—a woman who'd spent her life working to be a success . . .

. . . and had failed miserably at it.

The shoes came into focus again. The tiny diamonds on the straps caught the light of the sun and put on a dazzling light show.

She needed those shoes.

She went into the shop. A short, heavyset woman approached her immediately. "Can I help you find something?" she asked.

"Those shoes," Andrea said, pointing at the display window. "How much are those stiletto heels?"

"Beautiful, aren't they?" the saleswoman said. She went to the window and brought the shoes out, offering them to Andrea. "They're one thousand twenty-five dollars," she said. "They belonged to the wife of a mobster in the thirties."

Andrea took the shoes and held them up for inspection. They were beautiful.

"The shoes are leather, the diamonds are real," the saleswoman said.

Andrea felt a rush of excitement. It was a lot of money, but she had to have the shoes. "I'll take them," she said, and she handed over her American Express.

* * *

Andrea showed up one day with a moving van and two husky moving men. When she told Ricky she was moving out and why, Ricky's first instinct was to lie to her. When he realized lying wasn't an option, Ricky tried blaming his actions on Andrea, and when that failed, he cried and begged for her forgiveness.

The first night in her new apartment was rough. Andrea wasn't used to the silence. She sat on her bed that first night, contemplating the changes her life had taken in just a week's time. She had no immediate job prospects, and while she had a few thousand in her savings account, the money wouldn't last long.

She took her new stiletto shoes from under the bed. She felt different the instant she had them in her hands. Something about the shoes made her feel powerful and sexy. She had not tried them on yet. All the money she'd paid for the shoes and she still had no idea if they'd fit.

She pulled her nightgown off, slipped the shoes on, and checked herself in a full-length mirror. The shoes made her legs look longer and leaner than they truly were. She ran her hands through her hair, messing it up a little, making it look wilder. She took off her white cotton panties and slipped on a pair of black silk panties with a tiny red rose embroidered at the right hip. She'd bought the panties at Ricky's request, and she'd worn them for him that same night, and now she thought about what a waste it had been.

Her nipples were stiff. She wet a finger and traced it around her areola, causing little tiny goose bumps to rise on her flesh. She teased the nipple with a gentle circular motion, then she let her fingers wander over to her other nipple.

She fell back on the bed, drawing her feet up to rest them on the edge of the bed. One hand found its way down her panties, the other moved over her breasts. She rolled her nipples under her palms and slid her index finger between the lips of her pussy. She was surprised to find herself so wet and hot.

Andrea raised her ass and pushed her panties down. She grabbed an ankle and dragged her foot up, bringing the tip of the seven inch heel to rest against the slick entrance of her pussy. She grabbed hold of her ankle and slowly drew the tapered heel into her pussy.

Andrea was not often horny. She'd never denied Ricky sex when he wanted it, but rarely had she been the one to initiate, and she certainly had never felt the need to masturbate. In fact, she had never in her life, until this very moment, understood the need for masturbation.

She took off her right shoe and pressed the heel against her clitoris. Her back arched and her hips moved in a gentle rhythm as she pressed herself harder against the tip of the heel. It felt so good, she wondered what it would feel like to fuck herself with the other heel. She took off her other shoe and slid the heel into her pussy. The combination of the heel on her clit and the other one sliding in and out of her cunt made her come rather quickly.

This self-induced orgasm signified a change. Andrea was tired of being Miss Goody Two-Shoes. She liked how she felt when she strapped on her new stilettos. She felt sexy and free, and yeah, even whorish, and she wanted to use her newfound freedom and power to come out on top for a change.

* * *

It was easy enough to get into the building. The security guard in the lobby knew her, and one look at the way she looked now, he was practically begging to sniff her ass. She might have let him too, had she not been focused on other business at this moment.

She'd gotten her hair cut, layered, and lightened. She'd bought a new wardrobe. Tonight she wore a short leather skirt, a half-top, fishnet stockings, and her diamond-studded stilettos. She'd neglected to wear panties.

Garrett was working late. The guard had confirmed it. He always worked late on Thursdays. Andrea felt under her skirt as she took the elevator to the tenth floor. She was dripping with juices, so horny she wanted to get herself off right there in the elevator. It would take everything she had not to let Garrett fuck her, but that was the way she had to do it tonight.

Tonight was about baiting him.

The elevator doors slid open. The tenth floor was deserted. She could see Garrett's office at the end of the hallway, a dim light spilling from the open door. Garrett was sitting behind his desk, his head down over an open file folder. He was going through paperwork and making notations.

Andrea knocked on the door.

"Yes?" Garrett said, his tone of voice tired and disinterested.

"Hi, Garrett," Andrea said, turning on the sex appeal.

He looked up, did a double take, and immediately stood up. "Andrea?" he said, and it was apparent by the look on his face that he was shocked.

"I hope I'm not interrupting anything important," she said.

Nothing was more important to Garrett than fucking.

"Not a thing," he said. "My God, look at you. I can't . . . what the hell happened. You're so different, you're—"

"Fuckable?" she cut in.

He was stunned at her frankness. "As a matter of fact, yes," he said. "You look extremely fuckable."

"Good. We're on the same page."

"I don't understand," he said. "You came here to fuck me?"

"Not just yet," Andrea said. "It depends on whether or not you can give me what I want."

"What exactly do you want?" he asked, eager to please.

Andrea went to him. She grabbed his crotch and squeezed. She felt his cock through his trousers, hard and eager. She tugged down his zipper and pulled his dick out, closing it in a tight fist. She fixed him with bedroom eyes as she slowly masturbated him.

"I want an adventure," she said. "I want something new and exciting, something I've never done before."

Garrett was only half listening to her. His focus was on her fingers as they moved so lovingly along the length of his erection. Why hadn't he seen this side of Andrea before? Why hadn't he seen the whore beneath the all-business exterior? Maybe he was losing his touch.

"What about it?" Andrea asked. "Would you be willing to give me something I've never had before?"

He nodded eagerly. He would have given her anything at that moment.

She went to her knees, held his cock in the cradle between her thumb and forefinger, and teased the head of it with a gentle flicking motion of her tongue. He slid his fingers through her hair and pulled her face to his crotch, easing his cock into her mouth. She opened wide, taking it to the back of her throat.

"Oh, that's good," he groaned. "Yes, suck it . . ."

He tightened his fingers in her hair and started pushing and pulling, bobbing her head on his cock. She jerked his shaft too, working her tongue against the sides of his shaft as his dick moved deep into her mouth and back out again.

"Ummm, yeah, suck it . . . suck that cock, make me come," he said.

His breathing was quicker now, he was pumping his hips, thrusting his cock in and out . . . and she suddenly stopped.

"What?" he asked, confused by her sudden abandonment.

"I want what I want first," she said.

"Name it."

"I want a threesome," she said.

She took his hand and stuck it under her skirt.

"I want you and Shawna in my bed, both of you fucking me. I want to lick her pussy while you slide your dick in me from behind."

"Oh, Jeez . . ."

"Can you arrange that for me?" she asked, her voice a sexy whisper. She pushed one of his fingers into her pussy. "Can you give me what I want?"

He promised he would.

* * *

123

Garrett and Shawna showed up as expected. Garrett wore the grin of a man who was too full of himself, who was accustomed to getting everything he wanted. He wore an air of smug confidence. He truly believed he was in control.

Andrea wore a loose camisole made of shimmering black silk, a pair of tight white jeans, and her new stiletto shoes. She wore no bra beneath the camisole and her boobs, all natural, bobbed and jiggled with invitation every time she moved.

Shawna did not look happy. She looked sexy in her short summer dress and sandals, but she was obviously here only because Garrett had insisted upon it. Shawna shot Andrea a look that spelled b-i-t-c-h. Andrea simply smiled back at her. This was going to be fun. Her motives, of course, were not pure, but that didn't mean she couldn't take advantage of the situation too.

"Can I get you a drink?" she asked, directing the question at both Garrett and Shawna. "I made sangria."

"Sounds good," Garrett said.

"Thanks," Shawna said.

Andrea couldn't resist. "Is that thanks as in, no, I don't want any, thank you, or thanks as in yes, please, thank you?"

"I'll have a glass," Shawna replied, barely able to contain her distaste of this entire evening.

Garrett and Shawna sat on the couch. Andrea went into the kitchen, fixed the drinks, and brought them out. She set the tray on the coffee table and sat down between Garrett and Shawna.

"So, have you ever gone down on a woman? Andrea asked Shawna.

"Can't say that I have," Shawna answered. "I like men."

"Well, we have something in common then. I've never gone down on a woman either. Looks like tonight will be the first for both of us."

"And I get the pleasure of watching," Garrett said.

"Aren't you the lucky one," Shawna said, her smile tight and forced.

"Let's take this party to the bedroom," Andrea suggested.

Garrett was more than willing. Shawna went along for the ride, though it was obvious by her demeanor that she was less than happy about it.

Andrea couldn't have been happier. The Sony digital Hi-8 was set up in the closet. She went into the bedroom first, on the pretext of setting the mood. She turned the camera on, checked the angle, and set the zoom best suited for the job. She drew the bedspread down, folded the satin sheets down, and called for Garrett and Shawna to join her.

It started slow and tense. Andrea knelt in front of Garrett to suck his cock. He kissed Shawna and squeezed her tits through her dress. Andrea licked the head of his cock a few times, then she took it to the back of her throat and sucked hard.

Garrett took off as much of his clothing as he could while Andrea gave him head, then he brought her to her feet and pushed her toward Shawna. There was no doubt in either girl's mind what he wanted to see.

Andrea took charge. She pulled Shawna to her and kissed her hard on the mouth, and although Shawna was unyielding at first, it wasn't long before she was letting Andrea slip her tongue into her mouth.

Andrea ran her hands up Shawna's legs, pushing them under Shawna's dress. She slipped her fingers under the edges of Shawna's panties and was pleased to find Shawna's pussy heating up.

Andrea had never in her life dreamed of being with another woman, but the thought of going down on Shawna turned her on. The fact that she hated this slut with her whole being somehow made the entire situation that much better.

She pulled Shawna's dress off and pushed Shawna onto the bed, then she began taking off her own clothes, stripping down to her silky panties. She made a slow, teasing production of removing her panties, but she left her shoes on.

Shawna raised her ass and pushed her panties down, slipping them over her ankles. She opened her legs, bent her knees, and reached down to part the lips of her cunt. She slid one finger inside herself and thrust it in and out. She was so wet now, so much more into this.

"Lick me," she said, her voice catching in the back of her throat.

Andrea went down on her, teased her clit, fingered her and licked her asshole. Garrett watched the episode as he pumped his fist on his cock.

"Wear these," Andrea said.

She tossed Shawna's panties to Garrett. He held them up, baffled by her command. "You want me to put on her panties?"

"If you want to fuck either of us, yes."

Garrett put the panties on and rubbed his cock through the silky material. He felt foolish, but whatever it took to turn these girls on and keep them interested was fine by him.

Andrea climbed over Shawna and they ate each other in the sixty-nine position. They licked each other until hot spasms of orgasmic pleasure took over.

"Come here, big boy," Andrea said, climbing off Shawna.

She tugged the panties down. His erection flopped out, smacking her in the face. She took hold of it and started sucking the tip. Shawna joined in, running her tongue along the shaft. She slid a hand under his balls and gave them a good squeeze.

"You wanna fuck us?" Andrea teased.

"Oh, yeah," he said. "And I'm going to start with you."

"Tell you what," Andrea said, "let me fuck you."

She jerked the panties halfway down his legs. He finished taking them off, then climbed onto the bed. Andrea climbed onto him, aimed his cock at her pussy, and sat down on it.

Shawna knelt between his legs and licked his balls while Andrea rode him, occasionally even managing to lick his shaft when Andrea was on the upstroke.

"Come around here and sit on my face," Garrett said.

"You love it, don't you," Andrea said. "The power, the way you control women by holding their careers over their heads, by rewarding the women who fuck and punishing the women who don't . . ."

"Yeah, power," he groaned.

His words were muffled as Shawna sat on his face, smothering him in the damp heat of her pussy. He stuck his tongue inside her and she ground her pussy down on his tongue, gasping and panting as he got her off.

Andrea climbed off his cock and used her hand on him. "Come here," she said to Shawna, who climbed off Garrett's face and knelt on his other side, her mouth open as she waited for him to explode.

"Now," Garrett said, grunting.

Andrea pushed his cock at Shawna just as the first creamy blast erupted. It splashed her cheek. Andrea grabbed the back of Shawna's head and pulled her down on Garrett's cock. She made loud gulping sounds as she swallowed his semen, then the two women went at him with their tongues, cleaning the last traces of come from his cock before exchanging wet, sticky kisses.

Andrea eventually brought Garrett up for another round. This time he climbed between Shawna's legs and slid his cock inside her. Andrea watched as he established a nice rhythm, pumping his dick in and out of Shawna, his heavy balls slapping steadily against the cheeks of her ass.

Andrea leaned back on the bed, supporting her weight on her elbows, and placed her feet against Garrett's ass. He continued to drive his dick into Shawna. Andrea moved one foot so that the heel of her shoe was positioned between the taut, hairy cheeks of Garrett's ass, and before he had the chance to realize what was coming next, she pushed the stiletto heel into his asshole.

"Shit," he screamed out, and just as the heel fully penetrated him, he came again, this time in Shawna's pussy.

He was too far into it now to stop. He kept fucking Shawna, his ass cheeks flexing with the effort. Andrea worked the tapered heel deep inside his ass, twisting it this way and that. She drew the heel almost all the way out before forcing it in again.

Garrett threw his head back and let loose with a groan that sounded like a cross between pleasure and pain. It came from deep inside him. His balls tightened and his cock jerked.

Andrea finally removed the heel of her shoe. Garrett withdrew his cock from Shawna and collapsed on top of her, breathing heavy, his skin slick and glistening with sweat. Shawna lay pinned beneath him, still in need.

"Fuck this," she said, pushing Garrett off her. "Will you take care of me?" she said to Andrea.

Andrea used both feet on Shawna, fucking her ass and pussy at the same time. Shawna rubbed her clit with two fingers. The combination of both holes being fucked by the slender seven-inch heels and her own fingers caressing her pink pearl was enough to send Shawna over the edge.

"Girls, this is the beginning of a great friendship," Garrett said.

"I couldn't agree more," Andrea replied.

By morning it was a done deal. Andrea made a phone call. The security guard who'd let her into the building yesterday answered the phone.

"I could lose my job for this, you know that?" he said.

"But you won't," Andrea assured him. "You're good. I owe you."

"You don't owe me anything. It was wrong the way they did you."

"Thanks," Andrea said, and hung up the phone.

Tomorrow was the presentation to Benton Industries, a multi-million dollar account. Shawna would give the presentation. Garrett would be there too, along with the heads of Benton Industries. When the taped presentation rolled, everyone in the room would get a private screening of last night's event.

Andrea dropped a duplicate copy in the mail, addressed to Garrett's wife. She deserved a peek as well.

Now there was just one thing left to do. She had a date with Ricky, and by the end of the night, she'd introduce him to a couple of man-hating dykes. . . .

Group Effort

"You finish the manuscript?" Max asked.

It was always about the next book with Max, who'd been my agent for more than a decade. He'd gotten me quite a few deals over the years, but not without driving me half crazy in the process.

"Ready to go," I said.

"Good. That's real good, 'cause if you don't write, we don't eat, you know what I mean?"

"I know what you mean, Max," I said.

"Hey, and when the book comes out, we celebrate, right?"

"Right, Max," I said.

"A great big orgy."

"Sure thing," I replied, humoring him.

"Maybe we can swap wives, huh?"

"Yeah, maybe," I answered, again only to humor him.

That was something else Max was always going on about. If it wasn't my next book he was after, he was chasing my wife. He had a thing for her. It didn't bother me. He's a good guy at heart. A little high strung, but basically a good guy.

I hung up just as Jill came into the kitchen. I watched as she poured two cups of coffee and carried them to the kitchen table.

"All taken care of?" she asked.

"All done," I said.

We sipped our coffee, looking at each other across the kitchen table. Her dark brown hair was in slight disarray, she wore no make-up, and she was still the most beautiful woman I'd ever seen.

She caught me staring.

"What?" she asked, blushing.

"Oh, nothing. Just admiring your beauty. I can see why Max is so hot to get his hands on you."

"Is he going on about that again?" she asked.

"He doesn't stop. He thinks we should have a big orgy to celebrate the new book, which would give him the opportunity to fuck you, of course."

"God, that guy's such a pervert," she said.

"Tell me you don't like the idea at least a little."

She blushed again as she sipped her coffee. I could see her mind turning the idea around. "Oh, I don't know . . . maybe a little," she agreed. "Not because I think Max is all that great, but because I think *you* like the idea."

"You think so?"

"I do," she said confidently.

I shrugged. "I don't need anything that fancy. I like us the way we are, just plain and old fashioned."

She came around the table to stand in front of me. She had on a baby-doll nightie, pink and see-though. Her nipples were hard, poking against the sheer fabric, a slightly darker shade of pink than the nightie. Her tight panties outlined the dark triangle between her legs.

"We're not *that* old fashioned," she said. She hopped up on the kitchen table and opened her legs. Her panties stretched tight against her mound. "Come get your breakfast," she said, pulling my head between her legs.

* * *

It started as a normal cocktail party—a party to celebrate my new novel. Max had insisted on it. There were a few couples present, some of whom were close friends of mine and Jill's, and a select list of guests Max had insisted be there. None of us, except maybe Max, anticipated the events that transpired as the night progressed and expensive alcohol flowed freely.

The lights went down. It was the beginning of our foray into the world of free love. Couples began to stake territorial claims. A bunch of adults acting like teenagers with our parents out of town.

Jill and I have always been a little reserved when it comes to sex. That's not to say we're prudes, but in spite of the wife-swapping jokes with Max, the idea of performing sexually in a group situation was something completely new to us.

Jill and I had consumed our fair share of alcohol, and while we weren't drunk, we were feeling less inhibited than usual. Judging by the soft moans, deep-throated groans, and the gentle shifting of bodies as clothes were removed, we weren't the only two people who'd loosened up some.

Jill moved between my legs, supporting her weight with her hands as she took my cock in her mouth. She tightened her lips and sucked, her moans muffled as my cock slid to the back of her throat.

She cupped my balls in one hand and massaged them, venturing back with the tip of one finger to tease my asshole.

I noticed a rhythmic slapping noise that blended with the wet sound of my wife sucking my cock. Her body began to rock back and forth in time with the slapping sound, and I realized someone was fucking her. I looked beyond her bobbing head and upturned ass, focusing my eyes in the darkness. I could see Max behind her, his hands spread across her butt, his fingers digging in.

Now that he had my attention, he fucked Jill harder, every thrust of his cock pushing her mouth down on my cock. She kept choking every time my dick hit the back of her throat, so she took her mouth away and licked the head of it while she jerked me off instead.

I wondered where Max's Candi had gotten off to. As if reading my mind, she materialized beside me, kneeling next to my wife. They licked it together, their tongues meeting around the fleshy tip, then they took turns sucking me.

Candi turned her ass to me. The lips of her pussy widened as she backed up to me. The damp blonde curls separated, exposing the moist pink interior.

Jill moved away with Max. Candi licked my cock a few more times and then pushed me onto my back, holding my dick in a tight-fisted grip as she straddled me and impaled herself on it.

She leaned up, dangling her heavy tits in my face. I caught a nipple in my mouth and sucked it, then I moved to the other one, all the while squeezing her sweet bottom as I bounced her on my cock.

She rode me for a while, then she climbed off me and got on her hands and knees. I caught sight of Jill and Max as I slid into Candi from behind. Jill was riding Max. I could see his cock every time she came up on it, and I immediately felt intimidated by the length and thickness of it.

Candi suddenly disengaged from me and crawled over to a couple not far away from us. I recognized the man and woman as my sister-in-law Jackie and her latest boyfriend, a big construction-worker type with more brawn than brain.

Jackie was sucking his cock. Candi started eating Jackie from behind, licking her ass and her pussy. She motioned me over, but I joined Max and Jill instead.

Sometimes looking at what you have from an outsider's perspective can make you appreciate it even more, and that's what happened as I watched my wife slide up and down Max's big cock. I saw how much he enjoyed her, the way she pleased him, and I appreciated her that much more for it.

Candi, Jackie, and Jackie's construction-worker boyfriend came over to join us. Jackie's boyfriend stood next to Jill and slid his cock into her mouth.

Jackie and Candi sucked my cock until I came. Candi pulled my dick into her mouth first, gulping hard as she swallowed some of my come, then she quickly pushed my cock at Jackie, who took it in her mouth and finished me off.

Max said he was going to come. Jill climbed off his cock and wrapped her tits around it, letting him unload in her soft, warm cleavage. Jackie's boyfriend jerked himself off until Max was finished, then he added his come to Max's come, leaving Jill's tits sticky and soaked.

Jackie and her boyfriend went off to find new playmates. Candi wandered off to get a drink and ended up with the chubby wife of a poet friend of mine.

Jill got on her knees in front of Max and me, taking a cock in each hand. She took my cock and sucked me as she stroked Max's cock, then she switched off. She worked us like that for a few minutes, then she straddled me and sat on my dick. After she'd ridden me for a minute, she looked back over her shoulder at Max and invited him to stick his cock in her ass.

I dug my fingers into the cheeks of Jill's ass and pulled them apart, exposing the puckered little opening for him. He got behind her and rubbed his cock between her ass cheeks, then he slowly pushed his cock into her ass.

Jill groaned and shifted slightly.

"You okay?" Max said, stopping with his cock halfway inside her bottom.

She nodded, obviously uncomfortable, but wanting to go on nevertheless. Max continued to work his cock into her. I felt him inside her, filling her from behind as I filled her from the front. It was a tight fit, but after a few short thrusts, he started fucking her with long, smooth strokes.

It was hard to move with Max's cock invading Jill's ass, so I lay still beneath her, letting her grind her clit against my pubic bone as Max fucked her bottom. He finally grunted and came, letting most of his come fill her ass. He jerked the last few sticky strings of come over the cheeks of her ass and moved out of the way while I bounced my wife on my cock until we came together.

When Jill and I got home that night, we took a shower together and fucked again. She couldn't seem to get enough. I pressed her back against the wet tiles and pounded into her until I felt like my legs were giving out.

Jill wrapped her legs around my waist and pumped her pussy on my cock until she went into a series of orgasms that left her breathless. I continued to fuck her until she released her hold on me and slumped back against the shower wall, satiated at least for the time being.

I woke up with my cock in Jill's mouth. She deep-throated me, pulling on my dick with her soft lips, her tongue wrapped around my shaft as she massaged my balls with two fingers. I slid my fingers through her thick, soft hair and pulled her down. Just when I was going to come, she pulled her mouth from my cock and moved up to lay beside me.

"Wow, what's gotten into you?" I asked.

"I don't know," she answered in a lazy sort of way. "I'm just thinking about last night, how good it felt to be wild and crazy for a change."

"Yeah, I could tell you had fun."

"Didn't you?"

"I had a good time."

"Can we do it again?" she asked.

She sounded like a little girl begging to ride the merry-go-round.

"You really want to?"

"I really do," she said.

She wrapped her hand around my cock, giving it a good hard squeeze, then she mounted me and pulled her panties aside, rubbing the head of my dick between her slick pussy lips before inserting it.

She kissed me, pushing her tongue into my mouth as she rode my cock, rotating and grinding, riding all the way to the tip before coming down hard. Every once in awhile she came all the way off my cock and rubbed the head of it against her clit, driving me out of my mind.

"Let's do it again," she said. "Just the four of us." she said, rotating her hips as she came down on me again..

She hung her tits in my face and I pushed them together so I could alternate between her nipples, sucking and licking and nibbling them, lathering them with saliva as I pulled each one deep into my mouth.

"Say yes," she panted. "Say we'll do it again."

"Yes," I said.

She rode me hard then, sliding her hips back and forth, keeping my cock trapped in the hot confines of her pussy as she worked her muscles. Her tits bounced as she came up and back down again, slamming her clit hard against my pubic bone. I grabbed her ass and held on. She fell on top of me, pressing her tits down on my chest and burying her face in my neck, gasping and panting as she came. Her pussy tightened around my cock, squeezing like a tight fist, milking the length of it until I let go inside her.

We lay there for a long time afterward, both of us breathing hard, trying to recover from the intensity of our lovemaking. Before long, Jill was ready to go again, and I started to wonder if I'd be able to keep up.

* * *

I called Max a few days later. He didn't hesitate when I told him Jill and I wanted another round. I could feel him beaming on the other side of the line.

"I knew you'd like it once you tried it," he said.

"So when do you want to get together?" I asked.

"Hell, what about tonight?"

"Tonight, huh?"

"Why put off 'til tomorrow what you can do today, right? How's six o'clock?"

"Sounds good. We'll see you then." I said.

* * *

We parked in Max and Candi's driveway. Max met us on the porch, clasping a big hand on my shoulder as I came up the steps. "You start a new book yet?"

"The new one hasn't even had time to breathe, Max" I said.

"It's never too early," he shot back. "Gotta keep the iron in the fire, right?"

I agreed with him, only because I hadn't come to spend my night talking about my next book. Truth was, I hadn't even thought about a new book, and tonight the only thing I was interested in was giving my wife what she wanted.

Candi was sitting on the couch in the living room with her feet tucked under her butt. She wore a red silk robe, open just enough to expose a good portion of her pale, heavy breasts.

"Hi, guys," she said, all bubbles and smiles.

She came straight over and kissed me on the cheek, then she kissed Jill on the mouth, placing her hands on Jill's waist as she did. The move surprised me, and by the look on my Jill's face, she was caught off guard as well.

"Drinks," Max said. "Never have a social gathering without drinks. It's the only way I can enjoy my booze without feeling like an alcoholic."

He went over to the bar, broke out a bottle of expensive white wine, and filled four glasses. "To good friends," he said, raising his glass in a toast.

We retired to the living room and made ourselves comfortable on the couch. It was a huge couch with a *u* shape, giving the four of us plenty of room to play. Candi and I sat together on one end, Max and Jill sat on the other.

It didn't take long for the action to begin. Candi reached over and stroked my cock through my jeans. I was already half hard. She slid off the couch and knelt between my legs, dragging my zipper down as she went, one hand circling my cock, pulling the smooth pink knob into her mouth.

Jill followed Candi's lead and went to work on Max's cock. I watched as she pumped her fist on his thick shaft while she sucked and nibbled the head of his cock. It was surreal in a way, watching Jill give head to Max while his wife blew me.

I watched Jill and Max for another minute or so, then I laid my head against the back of the couch and enjoyed the way Candi ran her tongue along both sides of my cock. She sucked my balls next, then she deep-throated me and sucked so hard I was sure she'd take my cock right off. She came up for air every so often, then she'd nibble the head of my cock before deep-throating me some more.

I checked on Jill and Max again. His jeans had been pushed down past his ass. Jill was running her hand up and down the full length of his cock while she licked and sucked his balls. His eyes were closed, and judging by the big grin on his face, he was enjoying himself as much as I was.

Candi stopped sucking my cock and crawled over next to Jill. As she crawled across the floor, her short silk robe climbed over her ass, showing off her matching thong panties, barely more than a strip of red silk between her plump pussy lips.

The four of us got naked. Jill and Candi went to work on Max's erection, kissing each other around it. Candi shifted her ass invitingly. I stuck a finger under her thong and found her wet opening. She moaned around Max's dick as I slid my finger inside her and began fucking her with it.

She reached back and tugged her thong to one side, uncovering her sweet little box of delight waiting for me there. I withdrew my finger, grabbed her hips, and slid into the velvety heat of her hot box. My stomach collided with her ass, forcing her further down on Max's cock.

Jill straddled Max. Candi grabbed hold of his cock and held it as Jill lowered herself down. His thick cock pressed into her, slowly stretching the lips of her pussy as he filled her.

Candi gave me her full attention, rocking back on my cock. I held her by the waist and drove into her. Her ass jiggled as it collided with my stomach, her tits swung back and forth, and my balls slapped a steady rhythm against her clit.

She threw her head back, gasping and panting. Her body shook violently as she came. The walls of her pussy locked around my cock like a vise, trapping me until the last shudders of orgasm faded away.

I jerked my cock from her pussy and painted her ass with my come, watching as it ran down the insides of her thighs.

Jill climbed off Max's cock and let him come between her tits. His come splashed over her neck and ran down between her boobs. Candi licked some of it from Jill's neck, then she kissed her on the lips, pushing her tongue into Jill's mouth. She ran her hands up and covered Jill's breasts, massaging Max's come into Jill's nipples. I was surprised to see Jill so accepting of the intimacy. She'd always been turned off by the idea of women together sexually, but she seemed more than a little comfortable with Candi's advances.

Candi worked her way down, kissing one of Jill's nipples and then the other. She laid Jill back and kissed her way slowly down until she came to Jill's belly. She looked up to see if Jill might offer any resistance, and when she didn't, Candi gently pushed my wife's legs apart and went down on her.

It wasn't long before Jill responded to Candi's expert manipulations, moaning and gasping as she literally fucked Candi's face. I'd never seen her lose control like that, and by the time she reached a trembling climax that left her breathless, I was so aroused I could hardly see straight.

Jill and Candi exchanged lazy kisses, then Jill dropped one hand between Candi's legs and fingered her. I asked Jill to go down on Candi. She kissed Candi's stomach first, then she kissed her thighs. I thought she was actually going to do it, but then she slid up beside Candi and sucked on her nipples while she fingered Candi to orgasm.

It was sunrise when we got home. We went to bed without a shower. I dreamed about Jill and Max fucking. I woke up the next afternoon with an uneasy feeling I couldn't shake.

* * *

Four months passed. We saw Max and Candi at least twice a week for sex parties, and occasionally there were larger gatherings. We decided we were getting too involved in the lifestyle. I was actually the one who suggested we back off. Jill was disappointed, but she agreed to do whatever I thought best.

Max wanted another book. The man was in his fifties and fit as a fucking teenager. He believed in working hard and playing hard. More power to him, but all the playing had worn me thin, leaving little time to write.

Jill and I had both neglected our careers. We decided mutually to take a week apart to work. She's a painter. The entire attic of our house is her studio. I thought it would be a good idea if I went to our cabin to start the new book, leaving

Jill behind to paint. Being apart would allow us to focus on work and not each other.

I arrived at the cabin geared up to write. It's nothing fancy, but it's a hell of a retreat for someone wanting to focus on work. Armed with enough junk food and coffee to last a week, my Dell laptop, and a cell phone, I spent between twelve and fifteen hours a day writing. I didn't talk to Jill once the first three days there.

I called her late the fourth day. She answered the phone out of breath. She said she'd been painting. She was working on a special project—something she hadn't done before.

There were an awkward silence. I heard a faint, rhythmic thumping in the background, the shift of bedsprings, and there was a slight catch in Jill's voice when she spoke. Someone was in bed with her.

"Is somebody there?"

The question came out before I could think about it. I hadn't meant to sound accusatory. I didn't want to put her on guard.

There was silence on the other end of the line.

"Max and Candi came by," she said.

"Oh," I said.

I really didn't know how else to respond.

"Max asked about the book," she said.

"You can tell him it's going fine," I said.

We said bye and hung up. I tried to write again, but I couldn't shake the image of Jill, Max, and Candi in bed together.

It was after 3:00 a.m. when I pulled into my driveway and parked behind Max's car. I let myself into the house as quietly as I could and found the three of them asleep in the bedroom. Jill lay on her side facing Max, one leg draped over him. Candi was curled up behind her.

A wave of remorse washed over me. I felt like an outsider.

I went back through the living room, heading for the door. I saw a painting hanging on the wall. It hadn't been there before. It was an artistic rendition of Jill eating Candi's pussy. Candi's legs were draped over Jill's shoulders, Jill's hands were under her bottom. Had the painting been inspired by real life or was it simply a product of Jill's imagination?

Max was a salesman. He knew how to talk. He could swing just about any deal. That was the reason I'd hired him as my agent, and if the painting was any indication, Max was capable of selling more than the next bestseller.

I couldn't blame Max completely. He'd been the impetus behind it all, but each of us had played a role. It was a group effort. I'd known the risks all along. Each of us had taken the same risks. I could walk out the door and end my marriage over a situation I'd helped create, or I could lighten up and live a little.

I love my wife.

I headed back to the bedroom, stripping my clothes along the way.

There was still room for one more in our bed.

Hard Proposition To Swallow

Mike and Vicki hadn't been to a club in over a year. The two of them had careers that took up so much of their time that all they did was work and sleep. This little excursion tonight was the first step in a plan to bring back some of the spark that had been missing from their life together—particularly in the sex department.

Thick dry-ice induced fog hung heavy in the air. Strobe lights flashed constantly, accentuated with an array of colored lights. The dance floor was packed tight with writhing, shaking, grinding bodies.

Mike and Vicki exited the dance floor, squeezing their way through the crowd, moving toward one of the many bar areas available.

Vicki had dolled herself up for the occasion. She was a pretty girl—not overtly sexy, but definitely desirable. Tonight she wore a tight black dress, rather short, cut low in front to expose the slopes of her creamy breasts. Her normally straight chestnut-colored hair had been curled for the occasion. She wore lace-patterned stocking and heels.

Mike hung back, letting his wife lead the way to the bar just so he could check her out from behind. Damn, he was one lucky son of a bitch. How he'd gotten so wrapped up in work that he'd neglected a sweet thing like Vicki was beyond him.

Mike ordered a Jack the Ripper and Vicki ordered a Palm Beach cocktail. They found an empty table in a dark corner and sat. Conversation was minimal between them because the noise level was too much.

Mike wasn't really into the club thing. It had been Vicki's idea. She liked to dance. Tonight he wanted to make her happy, so he'd made up his mind to follow her lead, even if it meant sitting in an overcrowded club with her.

They looked around, watching men and women jockey for the best spots. Single men moved in on every new woman that came through the door without a man at her side. Women struck I'm-available poses, waiting to lure in a horny man willing to lay out the cash for the clubs overpriced drinks.

"Nice, huh?" Vicki said, leaning across the small round table and raising her voice to be heard in the noise.

"Yeah, nice," Mike agreed.

"I have to go to the bathroom," Vicki said. "Be right back."

She stood, gave him a quick peck on the lips, and vanished into the crowd, heading in the general direction of the bathrooms.

Mike hoped she would be ready to leave soon. He wanted to take her somewhere for a bite to eat and then home, where he planned to get her naked and spend the rest of the night fucking her. Seeing the looks she drew from some of the guys, and even a few women, gave him a new perspective on her. Sometimes the day-to-day rigors of life had a way of making people take what they had for granted, and Mike knew he'd been taking Vicki for granted for a long time now.

It went two ways, of course. She'd been wrapped up in her own career lately, so she hadn't exactly missed the intimate contact with him. She was doing her best to rectify that situation tonight.

They both were.

Vicki returned a few minutes later with a busty, blonde knockout in tow.

"This is my husband Mike," Vicki told the blonde, then to Mike, "This is my new friend Cindi. She and I had an interesting conversation waiting in line to use the bathroom."

Mike couldn't help giving Cindi the once over. She wore a short leather skirt with a low-cut top. Her long legs disappeared into black suede boots. Very sexy.

Cindi joined Mike and Vicki at their table. "I want to take her home with us," Vicki said over the music.

"Huh?" Mike asked.

He wasn't sure he'd heard her right.

"I want her to go home with us," Vicki repeated.

"Why?" Mike asked.

He glanced over at Cindi, then at his wife again. "I want her to go to bed with us," she confessed.

That threw Mike through a loop. Early in their marriage, back when they were still both very experimental, Vicki had confessed that she had lesbian fantasies, but even then they had never considered a threesome with another woman. Now she wanted to bring a stranger into their bed.

"Are you sure?" Mike asked.

Vicki nodded. "I want to live a little," she said.

Mike glanced at Cindi again. The thought of seeing his wife making love to such a beautiful blonde excited him. How could he refuse? He shrugged.

"Whatever pleases you," he said.

The three of them danced some more, particularly the two women. Mike watched as their dancing gradually became more sexual in nature.

Mike backed off the booze toward the end of the evening so he could drive home sober. He figured Vicki and Cindi could use the alcohol intake to loosen their inhibitions, though by the time they all left the club, Vicki and Cindi acted as if they'd been friends for years.

The first thing Mike did when they arrived at their destination was to pour drinks all the way around. The girls were sitting on the couch in the living room, side by side, already cuddling.

No time wasted.

Mike handed them their drinks, then he sat in a recliner with his own drink, taking a sip as he watched the sexy blonde nuzzle his wife's neck.

"Is this your first time with another woman?" he asked Cindi, his tone as casual as if he'd only asked her where she was from.

"No, not at all," she said. "I love women. I'm *definitely* bisexual, though."

Mike was happy to hear that, though he hadn't considered what Vicki might think about *him* fucking another woman. It was one thing for her to pursue her lesbian fantasies, but quite another for her to watch Mike fuck another woman. She was not the possessive type by a long shot, but that didn't necessarily mean she'd have no trouble sharing him with Cindi.

He lit a cigarette. He'd let the rest of the night take its own course. Whatever happened, happened. At the very least, he'd be watching his sexy wife make love to this beautiful blonde, and hell, that was something, wasn't it? How many men would give a left nut for a chance like that?

He got up and dimmed the lights. Brought them down real low, hoping to set a mood that would encourage Vicki to let herself go. Although this whole thing was Vicki's idea, Mike could see that she was a little bit uneasy.

He lit a couple of candles for effect.

As Mike sat back down in the recliner, Cindi draped a leg over Vicki and began kissing her. Vicki responded eagerly, opening her mouth to allow Cindi's wet pink tongue to slip inside.

Cindi ran her hand over one of Vicki's thighs, sliding it under Vicki's short dress. Her fingers found the damp crotch of Vicki's panties. She caressed Vicki's pussy lips through the thin, silky material, causing Vicki to give a sharp gasp of pleasure. She pushed a finger under the elastic of Vicki's panties and worked it between her plump, soft lips.

Mike shifted in the recliner. He adjusted the quickly rising lump in his jeans. He watched as the hem of Vicki's dress climbed up her legs, eventually giving him a good view of what Cindi was doing with her fingers.

Cindi broke her kiss with Vicki and stood up, pulling Vicki to her feet. She slid the straps of Vicki's dress down one at a time, her fingers brushing Vicki's soft shoulders.

Vicki closed her eyes and sighed as Cindi kissed her shoulders and then her neck. Cindi passed her mouth over Vicki's mouth again, nibbling on Vicki's lower lip as she reached behind Vicki and unzipped the back of her dress.

The dress came off smoothly, sliding over Vicki's hips and falling into a pool around her feet. She stepped out of it, kicked it aside, and then fell back on the couch, drawing her knees back and opening them wide.

Cindi dropped to her haunches between Vicki's widespread legs and grasped the elastic band of her panties. Vicki's ass came up off the couch. Cindi took off her panties, dropping them on the floor beside her, and then leaned down to run her tongue between the thick lips of Vicki's pussy.

"Oh, God . . ." Vicki gasped, pumping her hot cunt against Cindi's face.

Cindi held Vicki's ass in her hands, her fingers digging into Vicki's soft cheeks. She teased the inner lips of Vicki's pussy, rolling the glistening red folds beneath her tongue.

"That feels good," Vicki said.

She rubbed herself against Cindi's face faster. Cindi held onto Vicki as she ate her pussy. She worked her tongue into Vicki and fucked her with it, then she moved up and teased Vicki's clit from its hiding place, taking it into her mouth when it was fully exposed.

Vicki was moaning and nearly shedding tears of joy as Cindi exercised her knowledge of the female pleasure points and how to manipulate them.

"I'm coming," Vicki screamed.

Mike was both amazed and impressed. He'd never been able to get Vicki off in such a short period of time.

Cindi stood up, her cheeks wet with Vicki's pussy juice. She removed her top, letting her rather large breasts tumble free. Her nipples were dark pink and erect, surrounded by puffy areolas the size of a half dollar. She pushed her tits together, lifting one to her mouth so she could tease her nipple with her tongue.

Vicki wrapped her legs around Cindi and pulled her down onto the couch. Cindi fell on top of Vicki, pressing her tits in Vicki's face. Vicki worked on one nipple and then the other, biting and sucking them.

Mike was shocked by how quickly Vicki seemed to be adapting to this whole girl-on-girl thing. It was enough to make a man ask a few questions.

Not that he was complaining. The only complaint he could manage at the moment was that he wasn't naked and doing the horizontal bop with one (or both) of the two gorgeous women. His cock was hard enough right now to cut diamonds, and he was eager to put it to good use.

He unzipped his pants and hauled out his erection. It wasn't what he had in mind, but it would damn well do the trick for right now.

Cindi and Vicki kissed a few more minutes, then Cindi stood up and removed her leather skirt, wiggling her ass for Mike's benefit as she did. She wore tight zebra-striped panties that clung to the delicious curve of her bottom.

Mike couldn't restrain an appreciative whistle.

Vicki scooted to the edge of the couch and, looking up at Cindi's face as she did, she slowly drew Cindi's panties down. As Vicki lowered Cindi's panties past her knees, her eyes fell on Cindi's midsection and registered wide-eyed surprise.

Mike couldn't imagine what had caught his wife so off guard. He leaned up in the recliner to get a better look. From where he sat, he could only see Cindi's backside. He leaned a little to the left, jockeying for a better view. Having no luck, he went to stand beside Cindi, one hand still gripping his hard-on.

"Holy shit," was all he could manage to say.

Cindi looked at him with a did-I-forget-to-mention expression on her face.

"What's that?" Mike asked, immediately feeling stupid and wishing he could retract the question.

"It's a cock," Vicki said casually.

And then she laughed.

"I don't think this is funny," Mike said. "What the hell . . . what are you?"

"I'm a woman," Cindi said. "I've just got a little something extra."

"Not so little," Vicki said, stroking Cindi's cock as it grew thicker and harder.

"Vicki, don't do that," Mike said. "That's not right."

"What's not right?" Vicki asked, her eyes glued to Cindi's dick. "I think it's pretty cool."

"Pretty cool?" Mike couldn't have sounded more put off. "She's . . . he . . . fuck, whatever . . . it's not right."

Vicki leaned up and took Cindi's cock in her mouth. She tilted her soft green eyes up at Cindi's face as she sucked.

Mike watched, horrified to see his wife encouraging this mixed-up monstrosity. "Stop that," he demanded.

Vicki ignored him, taking Cindi's cock further into her mouth.

Mike realized he still had his own cock in his hand. He let it go suddenly, as if it might bite him. He stormed over to the bar and poured himself a double shot of whiskey, throwing back most of it in one gulp.

Vicki pulled back and stood up, still stroking Cindi's cock with one hand. They gazed into one another's eyes. Cindi seemed to be waiting for something.

"Ask me anything," Cindi finally said. "It's okay."

"I don't have anything to ask," Vicki said. "I just want to experience you."

Mike was standing nearby, watching unobtrusively. On one hand he wanted no part of this, on the other he felt oddly fascinated by Cindi. There she was, an absolutely beautiful woman, perfect in every way (if you overlooked her cock and balls, that is), and he couldn't decide what he should do about her.

And then there was Vicki, his sexy wife, naked except for black stockings and heels, fondling that she-male's cock, taking it into her mouth, and Mike was caught between being turned on and sickened at the same time.

Jesus, this world was one fucked-up treasure trove.

"Come here," Vicki said to him, patting the couch. "Come and watch."

He hesitated, finished his drink, and sat next to Vicki, who was kneeling in front of Cindi, slowly running her hand up and down the length of the beautiful, busty blonde's erection.

Mike watched in silence, torn between distaste and excitement. Seeing Vicki's hand moving along the length of another cock made him uneasy, and if Cindi hadn't been a completely gorgeous woman in every other respect, he might have taken serious issue with it.

Vicki couldn't have been more unconcerned with him at the moment. She didn't take her eyes off Cindi's cock as she continued to manipulate it, using two hands at times.

The head of Cindi's cock was pink and smooth, still glistening with saliva left behind when Vicki had taken it into her mouth. Vicki leaned forward and licked it again. She gently swirled her tongue around the rim of it, then she teased the opening, and finally slipped her mouth over it.

Cindi tangled her fingers in Vicki's hair and pushed it back, giving Mike a clear view of his wife's mouth being filled by hard, thick cock.

Mike realized he had an erection of his own. Watching Vicki give Cindi head was turning him on more than he imagined it would. He took his cock out again, slowly stroking it as he watched.

Cindi saw him and smiled. She could see that he was coming around. So many of them did. Not at first, of course. Most reacted like Mike did in the beginning, and some even worse, but usually they came around. They were intrigued.

Vicki pulled her head back, letting Cindi's cock slip from her mouth, all slick and wet with her saliva. She looked over at her husband as she pumped Cindi's cock with one hand.

"Wanna help me out?" she asked.

Mike hesitated a moment, then considered the painfully obvious throbbing between his legs. He moved onto the floor, kneeling beside his wife. She continued to stroke Cindi's cock with one hand as she took Mike's cock in her other hand and began jacking him off.

Vicki took Cindi's cock in her mouth again, moving her hand up and down the lower half as she sucked and licked the top half. She brought her mouth away from Cindi's cock and pushed it at Mike, whose first reaction was to pull back. He locked eyes with his wife, saw that she was serious, and then leaned up to run his tongue over the head of Cindi's cock.

"Suck on it," Vicki encouraged him.

He took Cindi's dick in his mouth and sucked on it. He had no idea what he was supposed to do. He'd been the proud receiver of many blowjobs in his life, but giving and getting were two different things, and for the life of him, he couldn't figure out what it was a women did with their mouths that made him feel so damn good.

He did the best he could. Cindi moaned. He figured he must be doing something right. He took a little more of her cock into his mouth, sucking on it as he did, using his tongue like Vicki often did when she sucked him.

Vicki left him to his own devices as she shifted her position so she could bend down to suck his cock. He felt her warm, wet mouth slide over the head of his cock. Her velvety smooth tongue caressed his knob, teased at the underside of it, and then danced against his heavily veined shaft as she descended.

The pleasure of her mouth on his cock was all the inspiration he needed. He found himself mimicking her moves, trying the same moves on Cindi. It was the best lesson he could get.

Cindi began to pump her hips slowly, pushing her cock in and out of Mike's mouth. He looked up and saw her full tits bouncing, saw the satisfied smile on her pretty face, the sexual hunger in her sea-blue eyes.

It was all so surreal and disorienting, his cock in Vicki's mouth, Cindi's cock in his mouth . . .

They stopped long enough for him to shed his clothes. He was in it for the distance now. He got naked, stroking his cock as Vicki sat back on the couch, spreading her legs wide.

He knelt between her legs and guided his dick into her moist, hot pussy, sinking it into her with one thrust.

Cindi climbed onto the couch and stood beside Vicki, feeding her cock into Vicki's mouth a little at a time. Vicki put her head on the back of the couch and tilted her face up, opening her mouth wide for Cindi's cock.

Mike held Vicki's legs wide apart as he pumped her pussy. He couldn't take his eyes off Cindi's cock disappearing down his wife's throat. Vicki opened wider, taking more of the thick meat than Mike believed possible. All of it vanished until Cindi's balls rested against Vicki's chin.

Mike groaned as he exploded inside Vicki. He gave a few more thrusts, working his come deep inside her pussy, and then he withdrew and fell over her, his sticky cock against her belly.

Cindi took her cock from Vicki's mouth and moved down on the floor, positioning herself between Vicki's legs. She went down on Vicki, licking Mike's come out of her first, then treating Vicki's clitoris to an all-out tongue lashing until Vicki climaxed.

The three of them had a little more to drink, then Vicki lay back on the couch and Cindi straddled her face, pushing her hard dick into Vicki's mouth again. Cindi looked over at Mike, smiled, and indicated he should get behind her.

"Fuck me," she said.

He'd already considered this possibility, and he'd made up his mind that he was going to do it if the opportunity presented itself.

And there it was, presenting itself in the form of a wide, pale, shapely ass.

Mike left the room briefly. He returned with a bottle of K-Y Jelly lubrication—the kind that warmed to the touch. He squirted some into the palm of one hand and smeared his cock with it, then he squeezed a good-sized squirt around Cindi's pink asshole and worked it in with a finger.

He entered Cindi's ass slowly, pushing his cock in an inch at a time, pausing, and then a little more. He'd never even fucked Vicki in the ass. He wasn't sure exactly how much an ass could take.

Cindi moaned. At first he thought he might be hurting her, but when he stopped to make sure she was all right, she reached back and grabbed him, pulling him deeper into her ass.

Cindi began pumping her cock into Vicki's mouth. He began pumping his cock into Cindi's tight ass. Pretty soon he had a decent rhythm established, and Cindi seemed to be enjoying it. He fucked her with deep, even strokes at first, then with gradually harder ones, and soon his balls were swinging back and forth, smacking against hers. Each thrust of his cock pushed Cindi's dick further down Vicki's throat.

Mike gripped Cindi's hips and held on for life, groaning as her tight bottom clung to his shaft, squeezing down on it, working him ever-quicker toward his second orgasm of the night.

Cindi threw her head back and moaned. Her cock jerked in Vicki's mouth. Mike heard the deep, hungry gulping noise his wife made as she swallowed Cindi's come. He felt a sharp stab of envy. Vicki had never swallowed for him.

It didn't matter now, though. He could take that up with her later, and he would, but for now he concentrated on his own pleasure.

"Shit," he said with a grunt, thrusting his cock deep into Cindi's tight bottom.

His body went tense and he trembled. His cock jerked. Cindi' ass seemed to swallow. He dug his fingers into the soft flesh of her hips, threw back his head, and howled like a banshee as he emptied his cream into her ass.

He sat the next round out, watching as Cindi fucked Vicki. She fucked her on the couch first, in the missionary position, then she flipped Vicki over onto her stomach and fucked her. She finally pulled Vicki to her hands and knees and fucked her doggy-style.

Mike watched it all, his cock now limp, his mind lost in a haze. Afterward, when Cindi was gone and Mike had to face his wife in the aftermath of what had happened, he felt ashamed of himself. He didn't confront her about swallowing. Instead, he preferred not to talk about the episode (that's what he immediately began calling it) at all. In his mind, it had never happened.

Vicki wanted to see Cindi again. She wanted Mike to be with her. She told Mike she wanted to feel them both fucking her at the same time. He humored her and said maybe, but he knew it would *never* happen again.

Cindi was beautiful, no doubt about it. Mike even managed to convince himself that her cock was incidental, that she was all woman except for that one detail, so his actions that night were completely justified.

He never did see Cindi again, though Vicki saw her on a regular basis. He would never deny Vicki her relationship with Cindi. To each his own. He buried himself in his work again. Vicki did the same. It worked out better that way.

Her Room

Her room . . .

 . . . is private and distinctly feminine.

The bed is unmade. I sit on the edge and study the crumpled satin sheets. The pillows are side by side, one slightly on top of the other.

I run my hands over the soft, cool sheets, imagining her naked body stretched across them. Knowing her naked skin has touched the sheets arouses me.

I smell her scent all over the sheets and pillows—a mixture of Charlie, shampoo, soap, and something more natural.

Her room is in slight disarray. The closet door is ajar. There are shoes scattered on the floor inside the closet. Lots of different types of shoes: black pumps, a pair of black suede boots, Nike tennis shoes, and even a pair of stiletto heels. Her dresses and blouses are hung neatly.

Her dresser has five drawers. The third is open, its dainty contents spilling over and onto the floor. A nylon hangs over the edge of the drawer, a pair of purple panties form a silky puddle in front of the dresser, and next to the panties is a single white sock. There are more clothes scattered around her room: an odd sock here, a pair of panties there, a skirt left lying where she had stepped out of it after a long day at work. . . .

I open the top drawer and find her flannel nightgowns and flimsy negligees. Her jeans are in the second drawer, each pair neatly folded. The fourth drawer contains bras, panties, socks, and stockings, including a pair of black fishnet stockings I imagine her wearing for one of her lovers.

The fifth drawer is full of stuff: empty perfume bottles, notes, jewelry, an assortment of candles . . .

I touch some of it, careful not to disturb anything. Hidden away at the bottom of the drawer is a chrome vibrator.

I pick it up and visualize the cold metal sliding into her pink pussy. I wonder how she uses it. Is it strictly for her personal pleasure, or has she performed with it for a lover?

I find a pair of worn panties at the foot of the bed.

Dirty panties.

White with rose prints.

I sniff them. Her scent is still there, as if the panties have only recently been removed.

I take out my cock and wrap her panties around it. I imagine fucking her as I jerk myself off that way. The silk feels cool at first but gradually warms as I quicken my pace.

Then I hear her key jiggle in the front door. I continue stroking my cock, knowing I should stop, somehow unable to do so, even at the risk of getting caught in her room.

Getting caught would not be a good thing. She trusts me. To find me in violation of that trust, invading her private space, would end our friendship.

I hear her moving around in the kitchen, putting away groceries. I work faster, eager to finish before she does.

This is her room.

I have no business here. . . .

Higher Education

"How bad do you want it?" Lydia asked. Lydia Miles was Dean of Belmont University. She was in the process of making cuts required by the new budget. Paul Connors shifted in his chair. "My job is important to me," he said. "I'd do just about anything to keep it."

Lydia smiled. It was the answer she was looking for. "Good," she said. "You're just the type of teacher we'd like to keep around. You know what's important, and you know how important it is to go the extra mile. I'd like to give you the opportunity to keep your position here at Belmont."

"I appreciate that," Paul said, waiting for the other shoe to fall.

Lydia came around to the front of her desk and sat on the edge of it. "I plan to give you an opportunity to prove yourself. You'll be tested thoroughly."

"Tested?"

"You're not married, am I right?"

He nodded, still uncertain about where she was heading.

"And rather attractive," she added.

"Thank you," he said, now on guard.

"My job can be quite time consuming, sometimes extremely stressful. I myself don't have a relationship. A mainstream romantic relationship would be impossible for me to maintain. I simply can't afford to give as much as I take. Do you follow what I'm telling you?"

"Not exactly," he said.

"I'm extremely demanding," she said. "It takes a special man to meet my needs, and if you think you can do it, I can assure your future here at the college."

"What would you like from me?" he asked.

Lydia was ten or twelve years his senior, attractive in a stern sort of way, with dark hair, green eyes, and a face creased with minimal signs of age. If fucking her was the answer to keeping his job, Paul would have no problem accommodating her wish.

"Let's start with a show of devotion," she said. "Just something to demonstrate your willingness to obey." She paused a moment, then she instructed him to take out his cock and jerk off for her.

He reached for his zipper, hesitated a split second, then unzipped his pants and reached inside to extract his dick, which was already half hard.

Lydia's eyes fell to his lap. "Well, go on," she said. "Play with it."

He felt his cheeks getting warm. He'd never masturbated in front of anyone. He wrapped his hand around his dick and started stroking it, moving his hand slowly up and down its full length.

Lydia watched without saying a word, measuring his performance. Finally she dropped to her haunches in front of him, taking hold of his erection, lifting it so she could examine the length of it.

"Nice cock," she said.

She ran her hand up and down it a few times, gave it a good squeeze, and then climbed back onto the desk. "Play with it some more," she told him.

She unbuttoned her blouse, pulled one lacy bra cup over her left breast, and started playing with her nipple. It was a small breast topped with a dark brown nipple about half an inch long. Paul wasn't much of a tit man, as many men are, and he preferred them small enough to cover with his hands.

Lydia opened her blouse further, slipping her other breast free. "Do you like these?" she asked, cupping her tits and twirling her nipples between the thumb and forefinger of each hand.

He felt like a schoolboy getting his first look at a woman's naked tits. "I like them," he answered, his voice taking on a raspy edge.

"I want you to come now," she said, and the tone of her voice carried a harsh sense of urgency.

Paul felt the beginnings of an orgasm stir in his belly. He pumped his cock, moaning as his pleasure mounted. His eyes never left her breasts. Come spurted hard and thick, covering the short distance separating him from the woman in charge of his future. It splashed over one of her stocking-clad legs.

She retrieved a towel from her desk, wiped her leg, and handed the towel to Paul. While he cleaned up his mess, she wrote her address on a piece of paper for him. "I'll see you tonight, seven o'clock sharp," she said.

* * *

Paul's career was important to him, and Lydia was an attractive woman, so he convinced himself what he was doing with her was justified. He'd felt a little humiliated in her office earlier in the day, but he'd also felt a degree of sexual excitement unlike any he'd felt before.

It was almost seven. He'd understood her quite well when she'd insisted he be on time. He turned into the circular drive leading to a Tudor-style estate, lavish in its intricate stonework design. He wasn't sure what the salary of a college dean might be, but by the look of Lydia's living environment, she had plenty of money at her disposal. She wouldn't be going hungry any time soon, at least that much was certain.

He parked his Toyota and got out, standing in awe of the beautiful home for half a minute before he rang the doorbell, initiating chimes that played a tune he recognized but couldn't quite place.

Lydia opened the door looking a little less stern than usual. She wore a white blouse, buttoned down far enough to expose the smooth edges of her breasts, a tight pair of jeans, and a pair of strap high heels.

Paul followed her to the living room. An ice bucket with a bottle of Dom Pérignon Rosé sat on a circular glass-topped coffee table. Lydia poured two flutes and handed one to Paul.

"Let me get straight to the point," she said, capturing his eyes with hers. "You're here to please *me*. If there is *any* hesitation on your part, I'll call the whole thing off. Is that clear?"

He nodded. "Perfectly," he said.

"Good."

They clinked flutes and sipped the expensive champagne.

"Undress," she said, all business now.

He set his half-empty flute next to the bucket and began undoing the buttons on his shirt. He undid his belt buckle, kicked off his shoes, then stepped out of his pants. His socks came next, followed by his shirt.

He was naked and had an erection in front of the dean of the university.

"That pleases me," Lydia said, nodding at his cock.

She ran her fingers from the base of his penis to the tip, moving around the rim of his smooth helmet. She tightened her hand around his shaft, stroked it for a minute, then gave it a sudden, hard squeeze, bringing Paul up on his toes.

"Sit down," she said.

She pushed him back on the couch before he could follow her instruction, then she unbuttoned her blouse. "Are you ready to please me?"

"Yes."

She slipped her blouse from her shoulders and drew the satin cups of her bra away from her breasts. She cupped her tits and lifted them in the palms of her hands, caressing her nipples with her thumbs.

"Touch your cock," she said. "I like when a man plays with his cock."

His cock felt harder to him than usual, throbbing hard against his palm. He moved his hand up and down, fixing his eyes on Lydia's face.

She leaned over him and pushed a nipple into his mouth. He sucked hard, pulling it deep into his mouth and lavishing it with sloppy-wet tongue strokes.

She wiggled out of her jeans and made him get on his knees in front of her.

"Lick my panties," she said.

Her panties were white. The dark triangle of her pubic hair was visible through the thin material. Paul pressed his mouth to her mound. She grabbed the back of his head with both hands, pulling him against her, making it hard for him to breathe. He brushed his tongue over the rough fabric, feeling the wiry curls of her pussy against his tongue. She pushed him away suddenly. He sucked in a gulp of air, and with it came the heady scent of her aroused pussy.

Lydia stepped out of her panties and sat on the couch, spreading her legs wide. Paul was still on his knees, gazing between her legs. The sight of her thick, dark bush fascinated him. He went to her on hands and knees. A hint of her inner lips were just visible behind the curly thatch of pubic hair. Lydia separated her hairy outer lips with two fingers, exposing the ragged dark red inner flaps, her center so copiously wet that he couldn't resist sinking his tongue into her.

It was fairly obvious Lydia had seen her fair share of cocks, many of them large. Her pussy was hot, open, and accommodating. Paul slid his tongue in effortlessly, wiggling it around inside her. Lydia tangled her fingers in his hair, pulling it as she forced him down on her cunt. She pumped her hips, bumping her wet cunt against his face, trying to keep his tongue inside her.

"Ummm, good," she said, moaning. "Now my clit . . . lick it."

His lips sought her clit. He hooked it between them and sucked, using his tongue at the same time. Lydia gasped and groaned, and then she pushed him away from her again.

"Fuck me," she gasped.

Paul gripped his cock firmly in one hand and situated himself between her legs. He pushed into her, forcing the lips of her pussy open. Her thick pussy hairs tickled his cock. He held one of her legs in each hand as he sank his cock deep into her pussy. She was soaking wet.

"Fuck me hard," she said. "Come on, *fuck* me."

He held her tight and pumped her pussy with long, steady strokes. Beads of sweat broke out on his forehead and ran down his face. His breathing became more labored. His stomach collided with her pussy each time his cock disappeared inside her.

He wiped sweat away with the back of one hand, not missing a stroke. Her pussy was warm and wet. He felt his balls tightening, felt an orgasm building deep in his groin and working its way up.

"I'm coming," he said, grunting as he continued fucking her.

"Not in me," Lydia said, pushing him away from her.

Paul groped his cock and stroked it, looking like a lost puppy. Lydia slid to the edge of the couch, one hand between her legs, fingers working her pussy as she watched him.

"Come on my stomach," she said.

He scooted closer to her, still pumping his dick. A thick, sticky stream of come spurted onto her stomach. He continued to milk his dick, showering her breasts and belly, squeezing the last few dribbles of spunk over his fingers.

Lydia ran two fingers through the sticky mess on her belly and held them out to Paul. "Lick it off," she said, and before he could refuse, she pushed her fingers into his mouth.

The shock of having his come shoved down his throat caught him by surprise. His initial reaction was to turn away.

"Lick it," Lydia said in a firm tone that left no doubt in Paul's mind that she wasn't simply offering, she was telling him what he needed to do.

He ran his tongue over each of her fingers, licking them clean.

"That's a good boy," she said. "Now, let's have a little more champagne."

* * *

Paul was late for class the next morning. He had planned to lecture, but his mind was occupied with Lydia. He instructed his students to work out of their books, and while he pretended to grade papers, he wondered what it was about Lydia that he enjoyed. He'd been married once and divorced his wife because of her control issues, but for some undetermined reason, he enjoyed the power Lydia wielded over him.

Lydia called Paul to her office at noon. She instructed him to pick her up at seven o'clock that evening. "I have a special night planned," she promised.

"You assume I have no plans of my own?" he asked.

"If you have other plans, cancel them," she said, leaving no doubt in his mind that she expected to be his top priority.

"I'll be there," he said.

* * *

Lydia knew all the underground hot spots. After a relaxing dinner, she took him to a sex club called Dazzler. He couldn't believe the atmosphere inside the place. Naked and half-naked men and women walking around, some of them fucking right there on the dance floor.

A lot of the people there knew Lydia. It was apparent she was a regular. Paul followed her around, nodding and shaking hands when she introduced him to someone new.

"This place is my favorite," she said.

She had to scream to be heard over the sound system. When Lydia took him into the private back rooms of the bar, Paul was relieved to find it much quieter. The music could still be heard, but it was muffled and less obnoxious now.

"This is what membership pays for," Lydia said, indicating glass-walled rooms along both sides of the corridor.

Paul saw that many of the rooms were occupied. His interest fell immediately to the room closest to him. There was a naked blonde on her knees in the room, her hands bound behind her back, a blindfold over her eyes. Four naked men stood around her, jerking themselves off. The blonde had her head tilted back and her mouth open. Now and then her pink tongue danced out.

One by one the men unleashed their loads, splashing the blonde's face and jerking off into her mouth. She let the come fill her mouth before swallowing. After each of the men had finished coming, they took turns letting the blonde lick their cocks clean.

Paul turned his attention to another room, where a naked man was straddling what appeared to be an exercise bench. His hands were tied to a bar that ran straight across in front of him. His ass was propped high. Another man straddled him from behind and was fucking him in the ass.

Lydia appreciated this scene.

"There are two types of people in the world," Lydia explained. "Those who dominate and those who are dominated. I know my place in the world. Do you know yours?"

Paul looked at Lydia for a moment. He tried to read her mind. What was she thinking? What made her tick?

"There are private rooms in the back," she said.

She started in that direction. Paul followed her, glancing one more time at the room with the blonde and the four guys in it. The blonde was sandwiched between two of the men now, taking one cock in her pussy and one in her ass. The other two guys flanked her and took turns sticking their cocks in her mouth.

Lydia led Paul down the hallway. They passed more glass-walled rooms featuring a variety of deviate sexual activity. They passed a room where a woman in black leather was spanking another woman while using the heel of a stiletto in her ass. Another room had a man lying naked on a table while a big-breasted blonde and a gothic-looking redhead dripped hot wax on his cock and balls.

Lydia finally stopped outside of a closed door. "I reserved this room for us," she said. She opened the door and stood aside, motioning Paul to enter the room.

There were two women already in the room. One of them had white-blonde hair. She lay naked on a large table, her arms above her head and her wrists shackled. Her feet were apart and her ankles were also shackled. Her pussy was shaved completely. A brunette in black panties and a leather bustier stood beside the blonde, next to a smaller table adorned with a variety of sex toys.

A large, plush couch sat along one wall. Lydia and Paul made themselves comfortable there. The brunette seemed not to notice them. Her attention was focused on the blonde. She began to run her hands over the blonde's naked body, careful not to touch her breasts or her pussy.

The blonde had her eyes closed. She arched her back as the brunette's hands traveled down her belly and along her thighs.

"This is going to be quite a show," Lydia whispered to Paul.

He nodded but didn't take his eyes off the two women.

The brunette moved one hand over the blonde's smooth-shaven pussy and spread the lips apart with two fingers. She leaned down and kissed the blonde girl on the mouth, then she moved to take one of the blonde's hard pink nipples between her lips, sucking hard on it. She thrust her middle finger into the blonde's pussy at the same time.

The blonde moaned as the brunette's slender finger slid fully inside her.

The dark-haired girl pressed her thumb down on the blonde girl's swollen clit and massaged it as she pumped her finger in and out of the blonde's pink hole.

"I love to watch women make love," Lydia said.

She reached over and stroked the bulge in Paul's slacks. "Apparently you do too," she added. "Feel free to jerk off while you watch."

He realized she was serious and dutifully extracted his dick.

Lydia went to the table and selected a hot pink vibrator. She ran her fingers suggestively up and down the length of it, then she slipped it in her mouth and made it nice and wet.

The brunette pulled the blonde girl's pussy lips apart. Lydia pushed the vibrator into the girl's shaved pussy. She twisted it slowly as she inched it deeper inside her. The brunette continued to manipulate the blonde girl's clit.

"Here," Lydia said, handing the vibrator over to the brunette. "Finish her."

Lydia undressed and straddled the blonde girl's face.

Paul watched it all as he slowly pulled on his cock. It aroused him to no end to see the three women together like that. He liked the idea of women touching and kissing one another. He fantasized about it now and then. To actually see it, though, made his cock harder than he remembered it ever being before.

As Lydia reached the fever pitch of her climax, arching her back and moaning with the pleasure of her release, Paul ejaculated onto the floor.

* * *

She greeted him at the front door wearing a black leather corset laced up the front, skimpy panties, thigh-high stockings, and stiletto heels. The sight of her like that never failed to give Paul an instant hard-on.

He'd been seeing her for five months now. He was completely in her grasp. There was nothing she could ask of him that he would refuse.

He followed her into the living room. They drank wine, as was almost always the opening custom. She took a Sobranie Black Russian from a box on the coffee table and held it to her lips. Paul lit it for her with a hand-carved ivory lighter shaped like a penis.

He watched her lips tighten around the gold filter of the cigarette, imagining those lips around his cock. She hadn't sucked his cock yet. He couldn't help but wonder what it would be like to feel her mouth on him.

They went upstairs, into the bedroom. Handcuffs, a chrome vibrator, a latex strap-on dildo, and a bottle of K-Y warming lubricant lay scattered over the bed.

"I want you to get naked and climb onto the bed, Paul," she said. "Tonight is the night you are initiated. This is the big test. If you pass, your job at the college is secure. If you fail, you'll find yourself teaching elementary school in some hick town somewhere in Arkansas."

Paul took off his clothes and climbed onto the bed. He started to turn around to face her, but she stopped him. "On your hands and knees," she said.

He undressed, trying not to show how apprehensive he felt. He turned back around, presenting his backside to her. This was his make-or-break moment.

This was his future.

Lydia climbed up beside him and reached under him to take hold of his erection. She gave it a good squeeze and picked up the chrome vibrator. She switched it on. The buzz of the thing made Paul's asshole clench.

Lydia touched the tip of the vibrator to Paul's anus, then she pulled it away just as quickly, sticking it between her legs instead, pushing the vibrator against her panties until the panties disappeared inside her.

"Oh, yes . . . oh, that feels good," she moaned, twisting the vibrator deeper inside her.

She jerked Paul's cock as she fucked herself with the vibrator, stopping now and then to allow him to settle down. She didn't want him to come yet. Not until she was ready for him.

Paul's cock stuck straight out in front of him, hard and swollen. His balls felt like boulders. He could remember feeling this horny and unfulfilled only one other time in his life, back when he'd been a kid in high school. He'd made out with one of the cheerleaders in the backseat of his dad's car. She'd given him a hand job almost to the point of climax before she suddenly came down with a bad case of religion. He went home and jerked off later that night, but even that hadn't relieved the pressure.

"I bet you'd like me to suck your cock," Lydia said.

Those words made Paul's ears stand up.

"Is that what you want?" she asked.

She pushed the tip of the vibrator between the cheeks of his ass. It found his puckered anus like a heat-seeking missile.

Paul shifted nervously. This was more than he'd bargained for. He loved his job, but did he want it so bad he was willing to let her shove that thing in his ass?

"Relax," she said, stroking his ass with one hand.

She pushed the tip of the vibrator against his asshole. He tensed up instinctively. She took the vibrator away, lubed it with a generous amount of K-Y, and this time slid it right into his ass. She turned the vibration up a notch and really began to tug on his cock.

"You like that?" she asked. "Does that feel good?"

The pressure created by the vibrator combined with the deft motion of her hand was enough to bring him to the brink of orgasm almost immediately. As if she sensed his oncoming climax, she suddenly stopped everything, leaving the vibrator in his ass and taking her hand from his cock.

She removed her panties, grabbed the strap-on cock, and sat on it, driving her pussy down to the hilt. "Lick me," she said in a breathy tone.

Paul turned around on his hands and knees, the vibrator still lodged in his ass, and put his face between Lydia's legs. He tongued her clit and licked the lips of her pussy where they molded to the shape of the dildo. Lydia came up on the dildo, leaving just the tip of it inside her, then drove herself down on it again. Paul kept pace, never taking his tongue from her pussy as she fucked the latex cock.

Lydia grabbed his hair and held him against her. "Don't stop," she gasped. "I'm coming."

She pumped her pussy against his face and bounced on the dildo. Paul found it hard to breathe, but he worked his tongue up and down on her swollen clit, occasionally sucking it between his lips to nibble.

Lydia impaled herself on the dildo and thrashed her hips when her climax overtook her. Paul licked until his tongue felt like it might fall off. He was grateful when Lydia finally fell away from him, lying back across the bed with the dildo still embedded in her cunt.

Paul became aware of the vibrator buzzing away in his ass. He'd forgotten about it in the heat of the moment. He removed it and turned it off. The absence of the high-pitched buzz brought Lydia out of her post-orgasm euphoria.

"Would you like to come?" she said.

She took the dildo from her pussy and strapped it around her waist, getting onto her knees as she did.

"Turn around," she said.

The latex dildo glistened with her pussy juice, but she smeared K-Y Jelly over the tip of it anyway.

She fucked his ass with long, slow strokes, pumping his cock at the same time. It wasn't long before the deep thrusts of the dildo and her pumping fist made him come, and Lydia continued jerking him off until she'd milked every last drop of his come over her fingers.

She pulled the dildo from Paul's ass. He turned around now, his cock hanging limp against his thigh. Lydia pulled her panties back on.

"It looks as if you'll be teaching at Belmont for some time to come," she told him. "So long as we have an understanding."

Paul understood just fine. There were two types of people in the world. The key to success was finding your place in that world.

Paul had crammed for the exam and passed.

He knew his place.

Ho, Ho, Ho, It's Time to Blow

Amanda slipped into a cute red bodysuit, white stockings, and black heels. She topped it off with a little green elf cap and checked herself in the mirror. Her creamy breasts spilled over the top of the bodysuit. Her long, shapely legs looked great encased in the silky stockings.

Jerry was coming home for Christmas. He'd been away too long, deployed in Iraq with nothing but sand and a nude picture of her to keep him company. She wanted this Christmas to be something really special. She wanted to do something for him she had never done before, not only to Jerry but to any man. She wanted to give him a blow job and let him come in her mouth. She'd never done either. The thought had never appealed to her like it did to so many women, but while Jerry was away at war, she'd regretted never having given him the blow job he'd always wanted.

She was prepared for it now. She'd practiced with her vibrator. She read all the techniques and she'd worked to find the most comfortable position for her. She even practiced deep throat, gradually working her way up to being able to take almost the full length of the vibrator into her mouth. It was slightly shorter than Jerry's cock, but with a little more practice, she was confident she'd be able to take all of him.

Today was Christmas Eve. Jerry was due to arrive at the airport at noon. She would pick him up, they would come home so he could settle in, and then they would light a fire and exchange gifts in front of the fireplace.

She would spring his special gift on him then.

The time spent waiting to pick him up drove her crazy. She couldn't wait to see him again. She'd spent many nights alone with her vibrator. Too many nights alone. The vibrator came in handy, that much was certain, but there was no way it could ever take the place of Jerry's smooth, thick cock.

She arrived at the airport with half an hour to spare. Waiting for Jerry to arrive seemed like it took an eternity, and when she saw him for the first time in over a year, her pussy got wet immediately. It took every bit of willpower she had not to take his cock out and suck it before they even left the airport.

Jerry took a shower when they got home. She couldn't resist peeking in on him, and when she did, he pulled her fully clothed into the shower with him. His tongue found her mouth and she sucked his tongue. He tore her blouse open and dragged her bra down over her breasts, running his palms over her stiff nipples.

"Oh, Jerry," she said, moaning.

She wrapped her hand around his semi-hard cock and stroked. Again she had to fight the temptation to drop to her knees and blow him. She wanted to feel his cock harden fully in her mouth. She wanted to suck him until she felt his hot come hit the back of her throat. She wanted to *taste* him.

She unsnapped her jeans and pushed them down. Jerry helped her remove them as she used his shoulders for balance. Her panties were drenched and clinging to her ass, now so transparent it was as if they weren't there. The lips of her pussy were clearly visible.

She grabbed Jerry's cock and rubbed the head of it against her panties, enjoying the way it pushed between the lips of her pussy.

Jerry reached down and pulled her panties to one side, guiding his cock into the slick, wet heat of her. She wrapped herself around him as he began to pump his hips slowly, pressing her against the wall of the shower.

"Oh, baby, fuck me," she said.

His cock filled her all the way with every stroke. She reached down to play with his balls as he pumped in and out of her. It wasn't long before the two of them were breathing heavy and moaning.

"Come with me," she said, panting.

The cheeks of his ass tightened as she dug her fingers into the firm flesh. His cock jerked inside her. She shuddered against him as she reached her climax.

They got out of the shower and dressed. It was all they could do to keep their hands off one another long enough to put clothes on.

"I've missed you so much," she told him.

They kissed passionately, embracing as they did.

"And I've missed you," he said.

* * *

Lying in front of the fireplace with Jerry was everything Amanda had imagined. The snow drifted outside and the windows were frosted. Two steaming mugs of hot chocolate sat on the fireplace mantle. The fire snapped and crackled as the flames danced to their own rhythm.

Amanda thought about their afternoon shopping excursion. They'd made love again, in the parking lot, fogging up the windows like a couple of high-school sweethearts.

Jerry wore a pair of flannel sleep pants they'd picked up earlier in the day. Amanda was still fully clothed. She excused herself, telling Jerry she had a surprise for him. She went upstairs and put on her sexy Christmas outfit. She looked at herself one more time in the mirror before going back downstairs.

The way his eyes moved over her body, taking in the sight of her with a hunger that made her shiver, told her all she needed to know. He desired her.

"Come here," he said, raising up on his knees.

She stood in front of him. He slid his hands over her hips and drew her close, pressing his mouth against her pubic mound. His hands moved around and settled on the cheeks of her ass, sinking into her as he pulled her tighter against him.

"God, I've missed your mouth on me," she said.

She couldn't have meant it more. Her vibrator, while it could never replace Jerry's cock, at least came close to replicating the sensation, but no way could it produce the same effects as his tongue. Jerry could do things to her with his tongue that made her knees weak and her pussy scream.

He pulled the crotch of her bodysuit to one side and flicked his tongue gently against the outer lips of her pussy. She was sensitive and the warmth of his tongue sent electric shocks through her. There was no way she would be able to stay on her feet for this.

She lay back on the floor and drew her knees up, letting them fall open as Jerry moved between them. He slid his hands along the insides of her thighs and ran his tongue around the opening of her pussy, then he worked his way up, nibbling the lips until he reached her clit.

He removed her shoes one at a time and caressed her feet through her stockings. He removed each stocking and massaged her legs, then he helped her out of the bodysuit and began kissing her from the tips of her toes to her forehead, giving her goose bumps.

He kissed her on the mouth as he pressed himself against her. The hardness of his cock nudged her thigh. She slipped a hand down the front of his flannel pants and wrapped her hand around his shaft, squeezing hard as she found the sensitive spot just beneath the head. She stroked him, moving her hand along the full length of his erection, feeling the blood rush to thicken him even more.

He undressed her and then removed his flannel pants. They kissed some more and he slipped his finger inside her. He moved it around inside her, then he withdrew it and started to climb on top of her.

"Wait," she said.

She pushed him onto his back and got on her hands and knees, moving over him until her head was above his groin.

"I have something very special for you this year," she said.

"You do?"

"Umm-hmm . . . something you've always wanted."

She lowered her head to his cock and tentatively ran her tongue over his balls and then up the length of his shaft. The sudden, direct action took him by surprise. She slid one hand between his cock and stomach and brought the smooth head of his cock up to rest against her warm, moist lips. She kissed the tip and teased the opening with flicks of her tongue, tasting the salty-sweet taste of his pre-come.

She slipped her mouth over his smooth helmet and pressed her tongue against the smooth spot just beneath it, gently brushing him there with soft licks. She circled her thumb and forefinger around the base of his shaft and squeezed, making his dick swell in her mouth as she took more of him in.

"Oh, Mandy," he groaned.

She took him deeper and deeper into her mouth, letting her throat open for his cock. It was much easier than she expected. Soon she had the whole length of his cock in her mouth and she tightened her lips around the base of it, creating a wet suction as she came up, leaving his cock wet and slippery.

Jerry stroked her blonde hair and watched her. She adjusted her position to afford him a better view. She knew he was a visual person and that seeing her with his cock in her mouth had to be arousing for him. She made every effort to make a production out of it for him.

"Baby, that's so good," he said, slowly working his hips up at her.

His cock slipped in and out of her mouth, each thrust going deep, and she did her best not to gag. She'd spent many hours working on controlling her gag reflex and it had paid off. Jerry was able to fuck her mouth. He could go as deep as he wanted and she could handle it easily.

He took advantage of her newfound talents, raising his ass high off the floor with each thrust, pushing his cock faster and faster into her mouth.

Amanda kept her hand around his shaft, stroking him as she let his cock slip in and out of her mouth. She was in tune with him, even after all the time they'd been apart, and she could tell the level of his excitement by the way he breathed.

She applied pressure with her lips and worked her tongue around the head of his cock as it moved in and out of her wet mouth. She started sucking, gently at first, and then harder as his breathing quickened.

She pulled back and let his dick slip from her mouth, but she continued to stroke his cock, watching his face as she did. She could see the look of pleasure in his eyes and knew that he wasn't far from coming. She pumped his cock faster, keeping a firm grip around his shaft. His skin was tight and the veins stood out thick and blue, coursing with blood.

"I'm going to come," he moaned.

His cock jerked in her hand. She felt the first warm splash across her tongue and was surprised that she liked the taste of it. She swallowed the last of it and raised her head, smiling at him as she wiped the last drops from her lips with the tip of her tongue. "Merry Christmas," she said, smiling seductively.

"Merry Christmas back at you," Jerry said, and then he started laughing.

"What?" she asked.

"Look in the mirror," he told her.

She stood and looked in the mirror above the fireplace. Her elf cap was still on but lopsided, nearly falling off her head.

"I look ridiculous," she said.

"You look beautiful," he replied.

She fell into his arms, they kissed, and then she reached for his cock again, stroking until his erection was back in full force.

This was going to be a memorable Christmas for more reasons than one . . .

Hot Chocolate, Whipped Cream

Robin listened as her boyfriend broke up with her on the other end of the line. He told her she was special, but that he wasn't ready to settle down. He still had so much he wanted to explore, he needed to find himself, and he didn't think it was fair to either of them to be tied into anything serious. Oh, and by the way, we can still be friends.

Yeah, right.

She tossed her cell phone down on her nightstand and threw herself on her bed. She stared out the window. It had been snowing most of the day. It was still coming down pretty good.

She'd intended to spend the long Thanksgiving break with Javon. She'd even made up some story to her parents about why she wouldn't be able to make it home for the holiday, and now she'd be spending it alone.

That dumb-ass boy had no idea what he was giving up by dissing her like this. She stood up and looked at herself in the ornate full-length mirror she'd brought with her from home. She wasn't stuck on herself, but she wasn't blind either. She could see how good she looked. All her curves were in the right places, her skin was smooth and milk-chocolate brown, her eyes were wide and innocent, and she had thick, beautiful black curls that hung down over her shoulders.

She could have her pick of guys.

She went to the window and looked out at the white coating over everything. The trees were heavy with snow and the roofs of the buildings were all covered with at least a half foot of the powdery stuff. It was all very serene. Too bad her emotions were a raging volcano waiting to erupt.

* * *

Trish curled up in bed and tried to read. She'd been trying to get through Stephen King's *The Stand* for months now. That guy just didn't know how to write small. She needed to keep a notebook handy just to remember the characters she encountered along the way.

She finally had plenty of time to settle in and get the book read. She'd intended to go home for the Thanksgiving holiday, but her parents were at it again, fighting like cats and dogs, and she didn't feel like going through it. Their constant bickering was the main reason she'd decided to go away to college. The further from home she was, the better her excuse for not being able to come home as often as they would have liked.

She felt a little creeped out. The campus was deserted as near as she could tell. At least, she hadn't yet seen anyone else, though she'd mostly confined herself to her dorm because of the heavy snowfall.

She had everything she needed to get her through the Thanksgiving break. Access to the kitchen, a car if she needed to get to town for any reason (although she was sure she wouldn't be driving in this weather), and good ol' Stephen King.

What more could a girl ask for?

She opened the book and leaned against the headboard of her bed, feet crossed at the ankles. She propped the book up and began to read. It wasn't long before her eyes became tired. She set the book aside, slipped on her shoes, and wandered into the hallway.

Creepy.

She was used to the halls being filled with a bunch of giggling girls dodging in and out of each other's rooms, swapping stories about some of the hot guys on campus, or rushing to get homework assignments finished at the last minute.

She went down to the cafeteria and bought a sandwich, chips, and a soda. She was on her way back upstairs when she ran into Robin in the stairwell.

"Oh my God," Trish said, nearly falling backward down the stairs. "You scared the hell out of me."

"You scared me too," Robin said. "I thought I was alone in the building."

"I was just getting something to eat," Trish said, showing Robin her food as if she were verifying where she'd been.

"That's what I was heading downstairs to do," Robin said. She hesitated a moment, almost as if she were embarrassed to ask. "You wouldn't mind walking downstairs with me, would you?"

"No problem," Trish said.

The two girls walked down to the cafeteria. Robin bought a fruit pie, chips, and bottled water from the vending machines.

"Wanna hang out?" Trish asked Robin as they started back upstairs. "It'll be nice to have the company."

"Sure," Robin said. "This place was starting to spook me."

"You here for the whole holiday?" Trish asked.

"Yep. Looks like it," Robin said.

The two girls went to Trish's dorm room. Trish sat on her bed and Robin sat at the desk. They ate. Trish asked Robin why she hadn't gone home for Thanksgiving. Robin told her about Javon.

"Guys can be real assholes," Trish said. "That's why I'm not in a relationship now. I'd rather not have the hassle."

Trish was a bookish blonde, thin and small breasted. Not cover girl material by any set of standards, but cute in a girl-next-door sort of way. She had pale blue eyes that seemed to suggest a bit of a wild side. Robin picked up on it right away.

Robin glanced at the thick book lying next to Trish's pillow. "What's that you're reading?" she asked.

"*The Stand*," Trish said.

"Damn, girl, why don't you just watch the movie?" Robin said. "It takes less time, and you don't have to work your brain nearly as hard."

"The movie is never as good as the book," Trish said.

177

"Oh, you're one of them," Robin said in a manner that sounded accusatory.

"What's that mean, one of them?"

"You know, all brainy and shit," Robin said.

"I'm not brainy at all. I like to read. I can't help it."

"I read too," Robin said. "I just prefer the sexy stuff. You know, erotica. Dirty stories. The kind of stories that get me all wet and horny.

Trish blushed. She wasn't naïve or anything. She'd had a couple of sexual experiences with guys, and she masturbated a lot. She had an active imagination, probably *because* she spent so much time reading.

Robin said she had some wine stashed in her room. She went to get it. When she returned a few minutes later, she had two bottles of wine and a box of books. The books were mostly thin, well-worn paperbacks. There were a couple of glossy magazines as well.

"Okay, this is the stuff I'm talking about," Robin said, handing one of the paperbacks to Trish.

Trish thumbed through the book while Robin opened the wine and searched the room for something to drink from. When she found nothing, she took a drink of wine straight from the bottle and handed it to Trish.

"We could get into so much trouble for this," Trish said, taking a big drink from the bottle.

"There isn't anyone around to catch us," Robin said.

They passed the first bottle of wine back and forth as they went through Robin's books. They took turns reading juicy passages and then discussing the situations presented.

"What's your wildest fantasy?" Robin asked.

"Oh, I don't know . . . maybe getting spanked. For some reason, I really like the idea of being spanked."

"Girl, are you crazy? Why would you want somebody paddling your ass?"

"I don't know. I was an only child, really spoiled, so maybe that has something to do with it."

"I'd spank your bottom for you, but I sure as hell wouldn't let you do it to me. No way I want my ass smacked."

They drank more wine.

"What's your fantasy?" Trish asked.

"Oh, hell, that's easy," Robin responded without thinking about it. "I've always wanted to do it with another girl."

"Really?"

Trish sounded intrigued.

"Un-huh. Always have. Not that I don't like guys. Believe me, I love spreading my legs for a nice, thick cock. Javon, the asshole I told you about, was good in that department. What they say about black guys is true, at least in my experience. Javon was a prime example."

Trish's cheeks turned pink.

"I mean it," Robin said. "You should try black dick at least one time. Once you go black . . ."

"You'll never go back," Trish finished in unison with her.

They fell into a drunken fit of giggles that soon became wild laughter. They were lying across the bed, both of them propping their chin in their hand, with Robin's box of goodies in between them. They suddenly stopped laughing and stared at each other a moment, feeling the charge of sexual energy between them.

"So, if I spank you, will you play with me?" Robin asked.

"Play with you?"

"Yeah, you know . . . a little girl-girl stuff?"

"Um, I guess so . . ."

Trish didn't want to admit it, but the thought of fooling around with another girl turned her on too. She'd thought about it before. Not in any sort of detail, but enough to know she might enjoy it.

Robin leaned over the box and brushed her lips against Trish's. It was a tentative kiss at first, but then Robin began to nibble Trish's lower lip. Trish responded by parting her lips ever so slightly. Robin flicked her tongue against Trish's lower lip and then worked it into Trish's mouth.

The kiss lasted a full thirty seconds. Trish liked it a lot. It felt good. Very soft and sensual. Nothing about it resembled the sloppy kissing she was used to with the guys she'd been with.

Robin sat up and moved the box to the floor. Trish sat up and faced her. Robin pulled her sweater over her head and tossed it over the edge of the bed, then she began undoing the button's of Trish's blouse.

Trish wore a white bra with pink flower patterns and lace edges. Robin reached around behind her and fiddled with the bra clasp. She slipped the straps of the bra from Trish's shoulders one at a time, then pulled the bra away from Trish's breasts and deposited it onto the floor.

Next she removed her own bra, freeing her slightly larger breasts. Her dark brown nipples were erect, the areolas puffy and covered with goose bumps. She ran her hands up and cupped a breast in each, giving them a slight squeeze.

She reached out and took one of Trish's hands and brought it to her chest. Trish didn't need any more encouragement than that. She traced her finger around one nipple, then she did the same with the other. She bent down and took one of Robin's nipples in her mouth, all the while fondling Robin's other tit.

"That feels good," Robin whispered, placing a hand on the back of Trish's head to guide her. "Don't forget the other one."

Trish switched back and forth between Robin's breasts, taking the chocolate-colored nipples between her lips and drawing them into her mouth. She bathed them with her tongue, making each one nice and wet, sometimes sucking, sometimes even biting gently.

They embraced one another and kissed again, pressing their breasts together, creamy white flesh meshing with smooth, dark chocolate. Their tongues slipped into each others' mouths, dancing and teasing.

Robin guided Trish onto her back. She kissed her way down, pausing long enough to gently suck on Trish's neck before she finally moved on to Trish's breasts. She took one pale pink nipple in her mouth and nibbled it. She moved her head to Trish's other breast and flicked her tongue across the hard little pebble of a nipple, back and forth a few times, then in teasing circles. She slid one hand up and wrapped it around Trish's small tit, squeezing the soft white skin, making the tiny pink nipple stand up as she licked and nibbled it.

Trish moaned. She arched her back, pressing her tit to Robin's mouth. Robin released her hold on Trish's tit and kissed her way down. She licked Trish's flat, pale belly. She dipped her tongue into Trish's navel.

"Are you ready for your spanking?" Robin asked, looking up at Trish, who was now breathless with her excitement.

Trish nodded eagerly.

"You are *such* a naughty girl," Robin said.

"Yes," Trish agreed, playing along with the game. "I'm so naughty. I really do need to be spanked."

Robin unsnapped Trish's jeans, then she stood up and held her arms out. Trish reached up and took Robin's hands, allowing Robin to pull her to her feet.

Robin kneeled in front of Trish and tugged her jeans over her hips, down to her ankles. Trish placed her hands on Robin's shoulders for support as she stepped out of her jeans.

Now wearing just white cotton panties and socks, Trish turned her back to Robin and kneeled beside the bed. She spread her arms in front of her on the bed, offering her panty-clad bottom to Robin.

Robin slid Trish's panties down until they were stretched taut between her thighs, exposing the little blonde's naked ass. She ran one hand over Trish's ass, moving it slowly, touching it ever so slightly.

"You've got such a beautiful bottom," Robin said, still caressing the soft white cheeks. "It's a shame I have to spank it."

She drew her hand back and brought it down against Trish's butt cheeks. There was the sharp smack of flesh against flesh. Trish jumped, surprised by the sudden sharpness of the blow. She wiggled her bottom slightly and settled back for more.

"Naughty girl's need to be spanked," Robin said. "You understand, right?"

Trish nodded. Her heart pounded in her chest. She felt the rush of adrenaline as she tried to prepare herself for what she knew was coming.

Robin smacked her ass again, turning one of her ass cheeks bright pink. Trish shifted her ass in response to the sting of Robin's hand. Robin gave her no time to recover before she brought the palm of her hand down yet again, leaving a deep red imprint on Trish's ass.

Trish made a tiny whimper. She was sobbing, but when Robin asked if she wanted her to stop, Trish wiped her eyes and said, "No, I think I need a couple more swats just to make sure I behave."

That was all the encouragement Robin needed. She delivered two more sharp slaps to Trish's ass, one on each of her cheeks. Trish's skin was bright red now and actually throwing off a bit of warmth.

Robin slid her hands over Trish's ass, spreading her cheeks as she leaned down to lick Trish's taut brown anus. She circled it with her tongue, then she wiggled the tip of her tongue as far into Trish's tight asshole as she could manage. Trish was so tight there (obviously she'd wasn't in the habit of using that hole for anything other than nature's intention), and there was no way Robin was going to get any further without some sort of lubrication.

"Naughty girl's need love too," Robin told Trish, and she went lower, working her tongue between the lips of Trish's pussy, teasing the delicate pink folds of Trish's vulva.

"Let's get these off," Robin said, tugging Trish's panties down.

Trish lifted her knees one at a time so Robin could take off her panties. Robin took off her own jeans and panties, leaving herself naked except for light blue ankle socks. She pulled Trish to her feet and turned her around so they were once again standing face to face.

Robin ran her hands over Trish's hips and brought them up and around, covering Trish's perky tits. She massaged Trish's tits and fingered her nipples while she gave her a deep tongue kiss, then she led Trish onto the bed and had her lie back against the stack of fluffy pillows.

Trish watched Robin with eager anticipation. Robin straddled her. She pulled the lips of her pussy apart with two hands, separating the dark, kinky curls of her pubic thatch to expose the glistening pink inner lips of her pussy.

Trish stared with wide eyes, unconsciously biting her lower lip.

Robin slipped a slender finger into her wet cunt and began to move it in and out, occasionally dragging it up to circle her clitoris.

"Wanna taste?" she asked, holding her hand out to Trish.

"Um-hmm," Trish said, opening her mouth and sticking out her tongue.

Robin placed her finger on Trish's tongue and very slowly dragged it back, letting Trish get a taste of her juices. She slid her finger back into Trish's mouth, and Trish closed her lips tight around it, creating suction as Robin once again withdrew it.

"Do you like the taste of my pussy?" Robin asked.

"Yes," Trish said.

Robin moved up on her knees, straddling Trish's face. Trish slid her hands up and squeezed Robin's ass. She pulled Robin down on her face, working her tongue between the damp lips of her pussy, plunging it deep inside the wet, opening. The pungent scent of Robin's cunt turned her on, driving her to delve as far inside it as she possibly could.

"Yeahhh," Robin moan, settling herself down on Trish's face. "Shit, girl, eat that pussy . . . yeah, just like that."

Robin grabbed the headboard of the bed, tightening her fingers around it for support. She pumped her hips, rubbing her cunt on Trish's face, enjoying the way Trish's tongue probed her pussy, whipping around inside her, coming out now and then to move along the slick folds of her glistening pink vulva.

"You sure you've never done this?" Robin asked, gasping the words.

She really couldn't believe Trish could be so good at it without having had at least one experience.

"Um-hmm," Trish answered, her words muffled and lost in the heat of Robin's dripping chocolate pie.

"You must be a natural," Robin said.

She began moving sinuously, grinding her hips, sliding her wet cunt up and down on Trish's face. She threw her head back and moaned, sliding her hands up to squeeze her own tits. She thumbed her taut brown nipples, then she took them between her fingers and tugged hard on them, twisting them as she stretched them away from her small tits.

Trish found Robin's magic spot and took full advantage of it.

"Oh, yeah, that feels so fucking good," Robin whispered harshly.

Her breathing quickened and she began to pant.

Trish teased her clitoris with little flicks of her tongue at first, then she picked up the pace, whipping her tongue back and forth on Robin's hard pink pearl. She occasionally nibbled it between her lips or sucked on it, making Robin squirm with absolute delight.

"Ohmygod," Robin screamed, "You're making me come!"

Robin shuddered violently as she reached her climax. She grasped the headboard of the bed and threw her head back, moaning at first, then screaming as a wave of pleasure washed through her entire body. It was all she could do to keep from tumbling off Trish as her orgasm made her tremble fiercely.

Robin finally collapsed on top of Trish, gasping to catch her breath. She wanted to return the favor. She slid down between Trish's legs, briefly making eye contact with her over the mound of Trish's pussy, and buried her face in Trish's blonde bush, pulling her lips wide as she pushed her tongue deep inside Trish's cunt.

Trish moaned. It felt so good. She lifted her ass off the bed, pressing her wet pussy against Robin's face. Robin stuck a finger into Trish's sweet cunt right along beside her tongue. She used both on Trish, bringing her to the edge several times before she finally allowed Trish to climax.

There was only a brief interlude before they were at it again, lying side by side, both of them with their knees wide apart. Trish's right leg was draped over Robin's left, their arms crossed over one another as they fingered each other, both girls heaving and bucking, plunging two or more fingers into each others' pussies until they came again, only seconds apart, explosive and exhausting.

They lay together for some time afterward, their breasts rising and falling with the uneven rhythm of their breathing. Robin eventually raised up and then leaned down to kiss Trish. She reached between Trish's legs and slid two fingers into the slick heat of her pussy. She withdrew them and Trish licked the wetness away.

This was a Thanksgiving break the two of them would never forget. No turkey, no stuffing, and no cranberries, but plenty of feasting all the same. It was only the first day of the holiday break. The campus was deserted, and with only each other for company, Robin and Trish planned to give thanks again and again.

Icicles

Cold things made her pussy hot. It had always been that way for her. The colder the better. She grew up in upstate New York. Buffalo, in fact, where six or eight feet of snow on the ground was not uncommon.

Most people hated the cold, but she loved it. She sometimes thought she had ice water running through her veins. Mickey said that about her the day she caught him in bed with her best friend. He told her she was as cold as ice. That's how he justified balling her best friend.

She never liked Mickey anyway.

She liked icicles, though. There was nothing like sliding an icicle into your pussy and feeling the cold, hard ice melt away as your pussy devoured it. She liked to start at the skinny end and work it in slowly, watching her cunt widen as the fatter end of the icicle finally made it inside.

Icicles were disposable dildos. She fucked herself with them until they melted away, just like Mickey had melted away.

She never liked Mickey anyway.

She bought a strap-on dildo and built a snowman. She strapped the dildo on the snowman and fucked him in the middle of a blizzard, wrapping her legs around him and hanging on for life. She named the snowman Mickey. He lasted for a little while and then he melted away, just like the real Mickey, who hadn't been real at all.

She never liked Mickey anyway.

There was nothing like the feeling she got when she slid an icicle into her pussy, though. Long and hard and cold, sinking into her hot pussy and melting down the cheeks of her ass.

She liked being naked in the snow too. She liked fucking in the snow. Most of the time she did it to herself, with the biggest icicle she could find. It was hard finding a lover who liked to fuck in the snow.

Mickey never liked fucking her in the snow. He said she was out of her mind.

She never liked Mickey anyway.

Maybe she was cold inside.

Maybe she was cold . . .

Maybe Mickey was right.

Maybe Mickey . . . was an asshole.

She never liked Mickey anyway.

In the Pocket

Kari bet her ass. It was all she had to offer, but she wasn't worried. She had been playing pool with the big boys ever since high school, and she'd grown quite adept at making her money with the game.

She knew all about Joey Travis, of course, and how good he was, and how all the girls thought he was such a stud. He was a cocky one, that much was certain, but he was also an easy mark for her.

She bent over to line up her shot. Joey stood behind her, far enough away not to disturb her. He couldn't take his eyes off her lovely back side. She wore a short black dress that exposed a lot of leg. It rode up even further as she leaned across the pool table, exposing the skimpy black panties she wore underneath.

Kari could shoot pool. She banked the two ball off the side and dropped it in the right corner pocket. Joey whistled his appreciation, both for the shot and for the sweet ass on display.

"How do you like me now?" Kari said, chalking her stick.

"I like you just fine," Joey said. "And I'll like you even better if you promise to bend over again."

Kari giggled as she walked around the table for her next shot. She was facing Joey this time, giving him a nice view of her tits as they fell against the front of her dress when she leaned down to shoot. The smooth, creamy tops of her titties threatened to spill onto the pool table. Joey licked his lips at the sight of them.

"Are they talking to you?" Kari asked.

"They just about are, sugar," he responded, not the least embarrassed at being caught in the act of ogling her boobs.

Kari dropped another ball.

"You're on a roll tonight," Joey said.

"I'm just good, that's all there is to it," she said.

"I ain't about to argue that one," Joey replied.

Kari came around the table for another shot. When she bent over, Joey ran the tip of his pool cue along the inside of her leg, bringing it to rest against her pussy, teasing her through her panties.

"Now, Joey, that's not fair," she said playfully, shifting her bottom just enough to rub herself against the hard tip of the pool cue.

"Well, now, everything's fair in love and war, ain't it?" Joey said. "And little lady, what you got between them legs is as close to love as I need to get."

"Ummm, you keep that up, you're going to have to fuck me," she said.

"You're readin' my mind, sugar," he shot back.

He slipped the pool stick under the elastic of her panties and rubbed it between the lips of her pussy. She spread her feet apart, allowing him better access to her pussy.

"You like that, babe?" he asked.

"I know what I'd like even better," she said.

Joey worked the tip of the pool stick a little deeper into her pussy, twisting it this way and that. When he finally took the stick from her pussy, it was slick and glistening with her juices.

"I'm going to beat you, Joey," she said.

He glanced at the table. She was right about that. He'd bet a thousand dollars, all of which he was damned willing to give up if he lost. It was not getting to claim what she'd put on the table that bothered him.

"Tell ya what," he said. "Why don't we call the game in your favor, I'll give you your winnings, and we can barter for the rest."

"Why would I wanna do that?"

"'Cause it ain't the money you're really after," he said.

He pulled her against him and kissed her, thrusting his tongue into her mouth. His hands slid beneath the hem of her dress. He tugged her panties over her smooth ass. She grabbed his cock and guided it between her legs.

"Feel how wet I am," she said.

He slipped a finger into her pussy and moved it in and out.

She tugged at his zipper as she fell to her knees, hauling out his thick, beautiful cock. She jerked it a couple of times, then she took it in her mouth, sucking hard on it at first, coming up long enough to lick the purple head a few times before putting it back in her mouth.

"Shit," Joey groaned, tangling his fingers in her hair.

"You like that, tiger?" she asked, pumping her slender fingers up and down his spit-slickened shaft.

She cupped his balls, each of them as big as a pool ball, and fondled them as she went back to sucking his cock.

The bar wasn't as crowded as usual, but those who'd come out for a night of drinking and dancing had begun to gather to watch Kari and Joey's performance.

Kari paid no attention to them. She focused her full attention on blowing Joey, and Joey certainly didn't care who watched. He was into Kari—the girl who could beat his ass at pool and suck his cock like no other woman he knew.

He brushed silky blonde hair from her face so he could watch her take his cock all the way into her mouth. She tightened her lips and came up slowly, sucking so hard that there was a wet pop when his cock left her mouth.

She stood up suddenly, leaving his thick, heavy dick bobbing in the wind for a moment before she grabbed hold of it and began jerking him off.

"You ready to fuck me?" she asked in a honey-sweet voice.

"You gotta be jokin' me," he said. "I've been ready."

She turned around and leaned over the pool table. It was all the encouragement Joey needed, but before he got around to sliding his dick into her, he dropped down behind her for a little taste test.

He pushed her dress up around her waist, pulled the cheeks of her ass wide apart, and went at her with his tongue, darting it around her taut asshole and into her slippery pussy.

Tiny, a big fat man with a ZZ Top beard and a shaved head, was right up at the edge of the pool table, sucking cold beer from a bottle and cheering. Pushing up next to him was Janice, a pretty little brunette waitress with big tits and a small waist. She held a tray of drinks in one hand, balancing it as she leaned around Tiny for a better view of the action.

There were others too. A couple who'd been dancing only a few minutes earlier, the bartender Skaggs, who'd abandoned his post for a front-row seat, and a cute, chubby blonde dressed like a cowgirl.

Kari spread her legs wider, moaning as Joey worked her over. She shifted her ass against his face as he probed her with his fingers and tongue, making sure her ass and pussy were treated equally.

"Ummm, Joey, that feels soooo good," she murmured.

He held her plump outer lips open with his thumbs as he teased her juicy pink entrance, poking his tongue in every so often and working it around inside her.

"Come on, Joey, fuck me," she said. "I want you to fuck me *now*."

"Yeah, fuck her," Tiny called out, finishing off the last of his beer and helping himself to another from the tray Janice had.

Joey glanced at Tiny and grinned, enjoying the spotlight. He grabbed Kari by her hips and pulled her toward him. The head of his cock nudged up against her pussy, pushing her plump lips apart. He sank his fingers into her soft skin and held tight as his cock disappeared all the way inside her.

"Save a horse, ride a cowgirl," Joey whooped.

Kari reached up with one hand and slid the straps of her dress from her shoulders, letting her heavy tits fall flat against the top of the pool table. Joey pounded his cock into her, his balls slapping a steady rhythm against her clit. Each thrust of his cock sent her forward, dragging her nipples across the felt-covered table top.

"Ohhhh, yeahhhh, I'm coming . . ." Kari screamed, grinding her ass against Joey as she reached a shuddering climax.

Joey wasn't far behind. He slid all the way inside her, keeping his cock buried as he came. Thick, hot spurts of come washed up inside her and out again, running down her thighs.

She collapsed across the table. Joey fell over her, supporting his weight on his elbows to keep from crushing her. They were slick with perspiration and breathing hard, trying to regain composure.

"I'd say you sank the eight ball," Kari finally managed to say.

"Right in the pocket," Joey agreed.

She reached back and stroked his still-hard cock, certain there was enough time for at least one more game.

Irish Cream

My name is Sean Gilmour. I'm Irish through and through. My family came to America generations ago, and while America has always been my homeland, I never gave up the dream of one day visiting the lush green hills of Ireland.

But, alas, time has a way of slipping past. I started my own business and worked hard to succeed. I married and divorced two times over. Weeks became months, months became years, and the years became decades.

I was forty-five when I finally reached a place in my life where I had the opportunity to make my long-awaited journey. I arranged to meet with a travel agent, but after looking over several pre-packaged trips, I decided to skip the commercial tour routes and play it by ear.

I arrived at Dublin Airport on Friday afternoon. I planned to spend most of my time in the country, but I wanted to spend a couple of days and nights in Dublin just to take in the sights and sounds of Ireland's capital city.

Dublin is a juxtaposition of beautiful and urban, old and new, and I found myself so caught up in its history that I spent a full week there before I set off to explore the Irish countryside.

The people of Ireland are, for the most part, extremely friendly and proud of their homeland. There is no other culture that takes as much pride in themselves as the Irish do, and as a result, Irish people are almost always happy. I spent many of my first nights in one Dublin pub or another, drinking Irish stout and listening to the stories passed around the pub, treated by everyone as if I were a long-time friend. Leaving Dublin was hard to do, but I had already made up my mind to spend another few days before returning home.

I rented a car and traveled west from Dublin, leaving the city behind in favor of narrow, winding country roads that took me through the Irish countryside. I stopped for lunch at a cozy inn where I dined on Caraway and Fennel Crusted Loin of Lamb with a mustard sauce, set off with a potato dish made with kale and bacon, all of which I washed down with an Irish stout.

It was there I met Kaelee Broderick.

Blue eyes, long red hair, and skin as smooth and pale as fresh cream. She was all of twenty-two, which should have sent me running the opposite direction.

Not a chance.

She sat with me over a second Irish stout. We chatted for more than an hour. I learned that she lived with her mother and father on a farm a few miles from town, and that she sometimes worked at the inn for extra money. I told her a little about myself and why I had come to Ireland, and after listening to me describe my visit thus far, Kaelee invited me to come home with her.

"I couldn't possibly intrude like that," I told her.

"You wouldn't be intruding at all," she assured me. "My mother and father would love to meet you."

She wouldn't take no for an answer. I relented. Quite honestly, the thought of spending a bit more time with Kaelee gave me a pleasurable feeling.

Her parents, Peter and Aileen, were nice people, both several years my senior. Peter was still in good shape for his age, a big man with red hair and wide shoulders, and when he shook my hand, I felt the strength in his grip.

They lived in a stone farmhouse surrounded by fields of rich green grass and rolling hills. There was a crystal blue lake nearby, a barn, and a handful of cows, chickens, and pigs. It was all very quaint and serene—the sort of simple country life one often sees depicted in flea-market oil paintings.

The house was modest but comfortable. Kaelee showed me to the guestroom and said that I should feel free to ask for anything I needed. There was something suggestive about the way she looked at me when she said it, but at the time I simply wrote it off as wishful thinking on my part.

I looked out the window of the guestroom and felt immediately breathless. It's hard to believe such beauty exists in this world. I could have stood looking out that window for hours without moving, but I didn't want to leave my gracious hosts in limbo, and besides, I could hardly wait to be back in Kaelee's presence.

Kaelee intercepted me as soon as I came out of the room. She took me by the hand like an eager child and led me toward the front door.

"I'm going to show him around," she called to her parents, both of whom were sitting at a wooden table in the kitchen.

And out the door we went, Kaelee keeping a tight grip on my hand as she showed me around the farm. The last stop was the pond, fairly well hidden from the house by a stand of thick green trees.

"Let's swim," Kaelee said, and before I could ask what she planned to wear in the water, she began stripping off her clothes.

I glanced around nervously.

"Nobody will see," Kaelee said, stepping out of her panties and jumping into the water.

What the hell, right? I wasn't about to deny a young, gloriously naked Irish girl beckoning me to get naked with her. It didn't matter one bit that she was about half my age. I didn't give it a thought. I'd come to Ireland to fulfill one lifelong dream, and if I could add *this* moment with *that* girl to the dream, I was pretty sure I'd die a happy man.

The water felt like ice when I plunged into it. The shock of it took my breath away for a few seconds that stretched into eternity.

I lost sight of Kaelee until she popped up out of the water in front of me, giggled, and swam back toward the shore, the smooth curve of her bottom breaking the water, her feet kicking up a wake.

She swam over to a spot where she was able to stand, the water coming up to just below her breasts, causing them to float and bob on top of the water. Her nipples and the surrounding areolas, both such a light shade of pink that they were almost invisible against her milk-white breasts, were tight and covered with goose bumps from the chill of the water.

"Are you okay?" she called to me.

"I'll let you know when my heart starts beating again," I said.

I swam over to her, found my footing, and stood up. The sun shining down on my shoulders soon warmed the upper portion of my body.

"Doesn't this bother you? The cold water, I mean."

"I love it," she said. "It's very invigorating."

"It's very cold," I said. "And I think certain parts of my anatomy have shriveled up and disappeared."

She thought that was funny. She giggled, and then I felt her hand on my cock under the water. I responded with an immediate and enthusiastic erection.

"Come on," she said.

She let go of me and ran out of the water. I followed her. We fell to the ground beside a Rowan in full bloom. She grabbed hold of my cock again, closing her slender fingers around the throbbing shaft.

We kissed. She worked her tongue into my mouth as she slid her hand up and down the length of my cock, demonstrating she was no stranger to handling this particular part of the male anatomy.

She broke the kiss and moved down to lick one of my nipples. She continued stroking my cock as she circled my nipple with her tongue and then nibbled it with her soft, wet lips. Only one other woman had ever paid attention to my nipples. I liked the sensation, and it was a turn-on for me when Kaelee spent time going from one to the other.

She worked her way down and kissed my stomach, stretching herself flat on the ground between my legs. I leaned back against the trunk of the tree and watched as Kaelee brought my cock to her mouth.

She stroked my cock in slow, rhythmic fashion as she circled the head of it with her tongue and then flicked her tongue back and forth against the tip of it. When she started nibbling the head of my cock, she raised those beautiful blue eyes so she could look at my face.

She took my cock in her mouth and closed her soft, wet lips around it, sucking firmly and gently as she pulled it deeper into her throat. I pushed her hair back on both sides of her face and brought it to the top of her head, gathering it into a ponytail so I could watch as she moved her mouth down on my cock and then up again, over and over, bringing me to the edge more quickly than I wanted.

I gently pushed her away from my cock and kissed her, guiding her back onto the grass. I sucked one pale nipple into my mouth and worked it with my tongue, sliding a hand over her belly and through the damp, red curls covering her mound.

My finger slid between the plump lips of her pussy. I applied slight pressure to her clit and rubbed it in a circular motion, first clockwise, then counter. I explored a little further, sliding my finger along the velvet-slick folds of her pink inner lips and slipping it into her pussy.

She arched her back and offered herself to me, letting her legs fall open. She worked the muscles of her pussy on my finger, drawing it deep inside her. It was like having a hot, wet mouth sucking on my finger.

She kissed me hungrily, her tongue darting into my mouth. I pulled away reluctantly, took my finger from her pussy, and moved my head between her legs. She smelled of soap and female heat. I thumbed open the lips of her pussy and teased her opening, dragging my tongue inside her a few times, then I dragged my tongue between her pink folds and caught her clit between my lips to nibble it.

She pumped her hips, thrashed against me, rubbing her pussy in my face. I slid a finger inside her and pushed it in deep, wiggling it around inside her as I licked and sucked her clitoris, bringing her to the brink of climax before I stopped suddenly.

She fell back on the grass, gasping and panting, her breasts rising and falling with the uneven rhythm of her excitement. I took her by her hands and pulled her into a sitting position, then I leaned against the trunk of the tree and brought her down on my lap.

She reached behind her and lifted my cock, directing the tip of it between her plump lips. She eased down, forcing her wet pussy over the head of my cock, and suddenly I was all the way inside her and she started riding me.

She had a way with those hips. She rode to the tip of my cock and down again, then she rocked her hips back and forth, grinding against the base of my cock until I thought I would lose my mind.

I cupped her ass in both hands and bounced her up and down. She reached back and squeezed my balls. For the longest time there was nothing but her and me, the rhythmic slap of her ass as she came down on me, her breasts bouncing up and down in a sort of wild abandon . . .

. . . and then I couldn't stop the flood.

The sheer magnitude of the pleasure I felt at the moment of climax is beyond what can be described with a few simple words. I threw my head back against the tree so hard I nearly lost consciousness.

I held on to her ass and continued to bounce her on my cock. I could feel the walls of her pussy tight around my shaft, milking every drop of hot semen from me, and then she began to gasp and moan as she reached her own climax.

My cock stayed hard. I raised up with her clinging to me, her legs tight around my waist, and lay her back on the ground, never taking my cock out of her. As I began fucking her again, I leaned down and kissed her on the mouth, taking her sweet tongue into my mouth, pumping her pussy with less urgency this time.

We didn't make it back to the house until much later. I was concerned Peter and Aileen would know right away what

I'd been up to with their daughter, but if they did, they didn't give any indication.

Dinner that night consisted of Irish stew and bacon rolled in boiled cabbage. There were Irish coffees afterward while Peter, in true Irish spirit, regaled me with stories of his youth. It was late when the three of us finally turned in.

I couldn't have been asleep more than half an hour when the door to my room squeaked open on its hinges. The bed sagged slightly as Kaelee climbed onto it.

She slipped her hand under the covers and inside my sleep pants, grasping my cock and slowly jerking it to attention. Her lips brushed my ear and came around to settle on my mouth. She nibbled my lower lip, teased her way into my mouth with her tongue, then whispered for me to meet her in the barn.

She was gone as quickly as she'd arrived.

I sneaked through the house expecting to hear Peter's gruff voice come at me from out of the darkness. Once outside the house, I actually took a moment to breathe before I continued on to the barn.

Kaelee was waiting for me in the barn, clad only in a short pink nightie and matching panties. The material was sheer. Her pink nipples were hard against it.

She ran to me, throwing her arms around my neck as she pressed her soft body to mine, her nipples digging against my chest.

"I want you to do something to me," she said.

She took my hand and led me to the back of the barn. We settled in front of a stack of hay bales, one of which was partially broken down and scattered on the floor in front of the remaining bales.

She tugged off my pajama pants and underwear in one smooth motion, tossing them over her shoulder, and then she took my cock in her mouth and began sucking, working her tongue against my shaft as she did.

She pushed me back against the hay and settled between my legs, then she continued with my cock, nibbling the head of it, teasing the sensitive spot just beneath the head, and licking and sucking my balls.

She sat up suddenly, crossed her arms, and took hold of the bottom edge of her nightie, whipping it over her head. She played with her breasts. They were hardly more than a handful, but she made the most of them, kneading them and tugging her pale nipples.

She came up to me, pressing her breasts in my face. I licked one nipple and then the other. I sucked on them, teased them with eager flicks of my tongue.

"I want you to do something to me that's never been done," she said.

She stood up and removed her panties. I was staring straight up at her light red curls. She separated her pussy lips with two fingers and used the middle finger of her free hand to fuck herself.

She withdrew the finger and moved her hand between her legs, back behind her. She closed her eyes and gave a little moan and a sigh. I couldn't see what she was doing, but I had a good idea she was sticking her finger in her asshole.

She turned her back to me and bent over, confirming my suspicion. Her slender finger was indeed in her asshole, buried to the hilt. She drew it almost all the way out and pushed it in again.

"I've never had anything there before," she said. She was looking at me upside down between her legs. "I want to feel you there tonight . . . now."

She had a tiny asshole as pink as the opening of her pussy. Her finger seemed too large for it. I couldn't imagine pushing my cock inside her.

Still, it was what she wanted, and I knew that particular part of her anatomy would have no trouble opening wide enough for my cock so long as we took it slow and used plenty of lubrication.

Kaelee had thought it out ahead of time. She was at least knowledgeable enough about anal sex to know we'd need something to pave the way, so to speak, and she'd made sure to bring along some butter. It was all she could find, she explained, and I assured her it would do the trick.

I had Kaelee lie down on the hay. I pushed her knees back and spread them wide, and after eating her pussy and licking her asshole for some time, I smeared a good portion of butter around her asshole and worked it in with my fingers.

It's been my experience that a cock goes in easier and more smoothly in the missionary position, and this being Kaelee's first time, I thought it was a good idea to start as comfortably as possible.

I buttered my cock and began the slow process of working it into Kaelee's ass. It wasn't entirely pleasant for her at first. Despite the copious amount of butter, which quickly melted against the heat of our bodies, her tiny pink anus resisted my advances. When the head of it finally penetrated Kaelee, she moaned and whimpered in a way that sounded more like pain than pleasure.

She encouraged me to keep going. I went in about halfway, then I pulled almost all the way out again. I eased my cock back inside her, going a little deeper the second time around. By the fourth round of gradually working my cock deeper into her ass, I was able to fuck her without causing her pain.

I draped her widespread legs over my arms and held on to the outside of her thighs for leverage as I moved in and out of her ass with slow, even strokes. She looked up at me with wide, innocent-looking eyes, moaning, squeezing her tits and playing with her nipples.

She raised her ass off the ground, angling herself so I had deeper access. Every thrust of my cock forced warm, melted butter from her ass. It dribbled down her ass cheeks, onto the floor beneath her bottom.

I withdrew my cock and slipped it into her pussy, giving her a few good strokes there, and then I was in her ass again.

"Yeah," she gasped. "Oh yeahhhhhh . . ."

I pulled out of her again and turned her over, then I pulled her to her hands and knees, wasting no time getting back into her sweet, pale bottom. I reached around in front of her and rubbed her clit as I pumped her ass. I wasn't going to last much longer, and I wanted her to be able to come before I did.

She suddenly slammed her ass back, pushing herself all the way down on my cock, and started jerking her hips, rubbing her pussy against my hand.

"Yes,' she screamed. "I'm coming . . . don't stop."

I wasn't doing anything at that point, so I continued doing just that. I let her fuck my hand, keeping my cock buried all the way inside her ass. She trembled against me, gasping and moaning, and as the last shudders of her climax came on, I gave her ass a few more strokes and let myself go.

I wasn't sure I was ever going to stop. My cock jerked hard as I pumped hot squirts of come deep into her ass. I held her tight and groaned with each spurt. I could feel the sticky, warm mixture of butter and come soaking her thighs, running all over the place.

I slowly withdrew when I finished, releasing a flood of the slick mixture that ran down to soak her pussy. She looked at me over her shoulder, smiling, and reached back between her legs to stick a couple of fingers in her cunt.

We lay there a long time afterward, both of us basking in the aftermath of the experience, and then we sneaked back inside.

The next morning we sat down to an Irish breakfast—meats, eggs, soda bread, and black pudding. Kaelee and I couldn't keep our eyes off one another, and the simple act of her bringing a pork sausage to her lips was in itself suggestive.

We slipped away after breakfast. Our tryst lasted a good portion of the morning. I dreaded the time when I would have to say goodbye. Every moment spent with her was both a blessing and a curse, rich with pleasure, fraught with pain.

My time with Kaelee came to an end five days later. Early one morning, as the sun rose high over mist-kissed fields of Irish Clover, I bid farewell to Kaelee and her parents, leaving behind the rolling green hills of the Irish countryside in exchange for the urban insanity often found in Dublin.

The rest of my trip was pale in comparison, and as I boarded a plane in Dublin that would take me home again, I felt an emptiness that would haunt me for the rest of my days.

An emptiness where my heart should have been . . .

An emptiness softened only by the thought of my Rose of Tralee.

Kaelee , my wild Irish Rose.

A Kiss Goodnight

Joshua was on his way to the Cayman Islands. His latest novel was finished and off to the publisher. It was a habit he'd gotten into many years earlier. He'd spend six months to a year on a novel, take a month somewhere spectacular, and then come back to New York to start the next book. It was a pattern that had always kept him happy *and* productive.

Joshua was content. He was a bestselling author with plenty of money. He made his own rules and lived by them. The only thing lacking in his life was someone to share it with. He didn't dwell on it, but now and then the reality caught up with him and he'd find himself wishing he had someone.

Joshua checked into his hotel late in the afternoon. It was too late to hit the beach, so he settled in and then went out for a bite to eat. Fresh seafood was a weakness of his, and the seafood served in the hotel restaurant was some of the best he'd ever had. He chose Caribbean Lobster Medallions in Spicy Island Citrus Crust and served over white wine risotto, roasted cumin-crusted Striped Sea Bass with sautéed vegetables, and Shrimp Scampi over tomatillo garlic linguine.

The restaurant was colorful and crowded. Joshua had to assume that some of its patrons were not guests of the hotel and had come simply to enjoy the exquisite cuisine the restaurant served.

Joshua was a people watcher. It was part of a writer's job to be aware of the people around him, and Joshua could spend hours watching people. He'd make up stories about each of them and tuck away details that would later find their way into the characters in his books.

Joshua finished his meal and took a stroll along the beach just as the sun was beginning to set, painting the sky in various hues of pink and purple. These were the times Joshua wished he had someone in his life most.

Joshua stopped for a drink in one of the little cabanas along the beach. He usually drank scotch, on the rare occasions he did indulge, but tonight he was in the mood for something colorful and rum based. He was just about to motion the bartender over when someone said, "How about a Kiss Goodnight."

Joshua turned to the man who stood beside him. The man was in his thirties, highly tanned, with dark, wavy hair and eyes the color of the Caribbean.

"Excuse me?" Joshua said.

"A Kiss Goodnight," the man repeated. "It's a drink. You looked like you might be wondering what to order."

"As a matter of fact, I was doing just that," Joshua said.

"I watch people," the man said. "I'm usually fairly good at figuring them out." He studied Joshua a moment, then said, "You're a writer."

"You really *are* good," Joshua replied.

"Not that good," he said. "I've read your books."

"Ah . . ."

"I'm Alan, by the way."

"It's nice to meet you, Alan," Joshua said. "Would you like to join me for a Kiss Goodnight?"

"I think I would," Alan said.

That was the beginning of something Joshua had never expected to find. He and Alan spent the next several days together, parasailing, scuba diving, and sharing their love of fresh seafood. They took in the nightlife as well, drinking and dancing on more than one occasion until the sun came up.

A week went by and it became clear to Joshua that something was developing between he and Alan. They were in Joshua's room. Joshua felt an overpowering desire for Alan that he was sure he could no longer hold in. He knew Alan felt the same way, though neither of them had expressed it in words.

Joshua made the first move. They were on their way to dinner when he turned to Alan and said, "Why don't we order room service."

Alan's eyes met his and it was clear that he understood. Instead of ordering room service, though, they made their way to the bed, kissing and undressing one another as they did.

Alan's cock was thick and hard. Joshua knelt in front of him and stroked it a couple of times, then he lifted it and licked the head of it until Alan's breathing began to take on a deeper, heavier rhythm.

Alan lay back on the bed, his erection falling against his stomach. Joshua straddled Alan's legs and began massaging his dick with both hands, squeezing the length of it, cupping his balls, and stroking the crown with his thumb.

Finally Joshua concentrated his efforts on pleasing Alan with his mouth. He ran his tongue over Alan's balls and began working his way up, tracing the outline of blue veins that criss-crossed Alan's cock from the base of his shaft to just below the smooth mushroom-shaped helmet.

Alan moaned as Joshua nibbled the head of his cock and then took it into his mouth, sucking gently as he rolled his tongue against the underside of his shaft.

Joshua enjoyed the distinct taste of Alan's cock. He drew the hard, throbbing flesh into his mouth, gradually working his way down, pausing now and then to allow himself to adjust to the length of it.

Alan moaned as Joshua tightened his mouth around his shaft and came up again, letting the head of his cock slip out with a sloppy wet noise.

Joshua jerked his hand up and down the length of Alan's cock a few times, then he pushed it against Alan's stomach and ran his tongue along it until he came to the sensitive spot just beneath the crown.

A drop of pre-come glistened at the tip of Alan's cock and Joshua caught it with his tongue, then he took Alan's cock into his mouth again, slowly stroking his shaft as he sucked his cock.

Alan lifted his ass off the bed, pushing more of his dick into Joshua's mouth. Joshua could feel how close he was to release. He could taste the slightly salty taste of the pre-come that rolled across his tongue.

"That feels good," Alan said, groaning. "You'll make me come . . ."

Joshua jerked his hand faster, moving his fingers over the slick, hot skin as he worked his tongue against the tip of Alan's cock.

"Yesssss . . ." Alan groaned.

Joshua swallowed as Alan's cock jerked in his mouth and come hit the back of his throat. It was the first time he'd let anyone come in his mouth. He'd never even tasted his own come, which he thought most men had done at least once, but he found he not only liked the taste of Alan's come, he liked the way it felt in his mouth as well—warm with a smooth, slippery texture.

Alan was breathing deeply as Joshua finished and lifted his head.

"I take it you enjoyed that," Joshua said.

"That's putting it mildly," Alan replied.

He sat up and moved closer to Joshua. They shared a deep, hard kiss. Alan reached down to stroke Joshua's cock. He gave it a good squeeze, running his slightly rough thumb over the head of it.

"Stand up," he said.

Joshua stood on the bed, his knees a little shaky as the mattress sunk under his weight. His hands fell on Alan's shoulders for support. His dick bobbed in front of Alan's face, the tip of it brushing against Alan's lips.

Alan slid his mouth around it, pressing his tongue against the underside as he worked his way down, stopping when he had the full length of Joshua's cock in his mouth. The warm, wet sensation of Alan's sucking had Joshua on the verge of orgasm almost immediately, but he wasn't ready for it to end.

He stepped back, pulling his cock from Alan's mouth, and knelt in front of Alan. They kissed again, taking turns slipping their tongues into each other's mouth, and then he picked up the phone and called room service. He placed an order for two bottles of champagne.

"A man of taste," Alan said.

"I thought we might relax, slow things down a bit," Joshua said.

"Do you think we need to slow down?"

"I need to," Joshua said. "The way you were sucking my cock, I could have come in no time. Drinking dulls the senses. It helps me last longer."

"Why worry about how long you last?" Alan said. "We have the whole night ahead of us." He smiled. "We have the whole rest of our vacation, in fact. There's no rule that says we have to leave the room."

He pulled Joshua down on the bed and kissed him again, stroking his cock as he did. He put Joshua's hand on his own cock. Joshua was amazed to find him rock hard once again, eager for more action.

"I want to fuck you," Alan said.

Joshua shuddered with excitement at the blunt way in which the words came out. *I want to fuck you.* He'd never been with anyone so direct. He wanted to ask about condoms. He didn't have any. He hadn't expected to meet anyone, and he certainly hadn't expected to end up with a cock sliding into his ass.

As if reading Joshua's mind, Alan leaned over the side of the bed and took his wallet from his pants. The sight of his hard, tight ass when he bent over like that, with his balls dangling between his legs, gave Joshua the urge to be the one doing the fucking.

"I carry them just in case," Alan said.

Joshua had a feeling that "just in case" happened more often than not with Alan. He was too well practiced, too at ease with this situation, for it to be rare.

There was a knock on the door. Alan slipped on a robe and went to answer it. He rolled the cart with two bottles of champagne in ice buckets into the room and told the good-looking waiter to add an appropriate tip for himself to the bill.

Alan stroked his own erection as he watched Joshua pour the champagne. They clinked the glasses together.

"To good friends," Alan said.

"To good friends," Joshua agreed.

They finished off their first glasses quickly.

"I like the stuff," Joshua said, "but I've never been the kind of guy to sip and savor it."

"Me either," Alan responded, reaching for the bottle. "Let's get drunk."

It wasn't long before the first bottle was gone and the second was well on its way. The two men sat together on the bed, kissing and stroking each other. Joshua couldn't believe how thick and hard his cock was. It usually took more than a heavy petting to keep him aroused, but the sensations Alan gave him with just a little touching kept him as hard as steel. So hard, in fact, there was a dull throb that wasn't quite painful but a little distracting.

Alan set his champagne aside and went down on Joshua. He sucked gently at first, swirling his tongue against Joshua's shaft, caressing Joshua's balls with one hand as he did.

Joshua groaned his pleasure. He leaned against the headboard of the bed and watched as Alan worked on his cock. He liked watching Alan's mouth slide up and down on his dick, making it wet and shiny, and once again he felt the beginnings of an orgasm he wasn't ready for. This time, though, he was able to focus his thoughts elsewhere just long enough to circumvent it.

"I want your cock inside me," he said.

Alan brought his mouth away from Joshua's cock. He gave it a firm squeeze and then grabbed the condom from the nightstand. He tore the package open and rolled the condom down over his cock. Neither of them had any sort of lubrication, but a small bottle of lotion supplied by the hotel came in handy. Joshua retrieved it from the bathroom, handed it to Alan, and then moved onto his hands and knees.

Alan squirted a generous amount of the lotion in the palm of his hand and smeared it over the length of his cock. He squirted another dollop and massaged Joshua's balls, rolling them around in the palm of his hand.

"Are you ready for me?" he asked.

"Un-huh," Joshua said.

Alan reached up and wrapped his slippery hand around Joshua's cock. He stroked it slowly, grasping it firmly, moving the taut skin up and down.

"Are you sure?" Alan asked.

Joshua could not have been more sure. He wanted to feel Alan inside him now, more than he'd ever wanted to feel anyone.

Alan fingered Joshua's ass and massaged his balls, squeezing them with gentle pressure. He worked his finger in and out of Joshua's ass. He reached around and stroked Joshua's erection.

Joshua groaned as the head of Alan's cock met slight resistance and then slid into his ass. He felt pressure as the thick, hot length of Alan's cock filled him and then the pressure was gone as Alan withdrew all but the head of his cock.

Alan tightened his grip on Joshua then, sliding his cock all the way into him, withdrawing, and then sliding in again. Each thrust became harder. Alan's heavy balls swung against Joshua's, sending electric sparks of pleasure through him.

He felt Alan's cock swelling inside him. He could feel the heat of it through the condom. He felt it throbbing.

Alan's breathing quickened along with the speed of his thrusts. He groaned and pushed himself all the way into Joshua, digging his fingers into Joshua's hips as he exploded. Joshua felt the hot spurts of come even through the condom.

They collapsed together and Alan finally withdrew his cock. He removed the condom and dropped it over the side of the bed. They had more champagne while Alan lazily stroked Joshua's cock. Finally Alan went down on Joshua and skillfully brought him to an explosive climax that left Joshua gasping for air.

Paradise was a good place to be, but the vacation would eventually come to an end. Joshua had come alone, but he left with a friend—someone who he felt might be in his life for some time, in a meaningful way.

Life came at you like that sometimes. Good things had a way of showing up when you least expected them to, and for Joshua, the promise of a new beginning had started with a simple Kiss Goodnight.

A Little Too Eager

Caitlyn and I had just finished shopping at Wal-Mart. We were in the parking lot, loading our purchases in the trunk of the car.

"Excuse me . . ."

Caitlyn and I turned to the sound of the voice and saw a tall, fairly good-looking guy in his mid- or late twenties coming toward us. He approached us like a salesman, a big smile on his face, sticking out his hand to me. Being suspicious by nature, I chose to ignore the hand until I had more details.

"My name's Rob,' he said. He glanced at Caitlyn then back at me. "I've got a proposition," he continued. "If I'm out of line, let me know, I'll be on my way."

"What kind of proposition?" I asked.

"You two are married, am I right?" he said.

"That's right," I said,

Another quick glance at Caitlyn, then he looked at me and said, "I'll give you a thousand dollars if you let me fuck your wife."

The words tumbled out of his mouth as casually as if he were making an offer to buy my car.

"Are you out of your mind?" I said.

Caitlyn is a busty blonde. I was used to men ogling her. She was quite the looker. Still, though, this was the first time any man had made such an overt gesture toward her, at least in my presence, and my first instinct was to hit him. Believe me, that's what I was about to do when Caitlyn said, "Fifteen hundred."

I jerked my head in her direction, not believing my ears. "What the hell are you talking about?" I asked.

"He can fuck me for fifteen hundred dollars. No less."

"You . . . hold on . . ." I looked at Rob. "Excuse us a minute," I said.

"I'll be right over here when you're ready."

He walked over and leaned against a car parked across from where Caitlyn and I were parked.

"Are you serious?" I asked Caitlyn. "You'd let this dude screw you?"

"For fifteen hundred dollars. Why not?" she said.

"Why not? You don't even know him," I said.

"He'll have to wear a condom," she said, smiling.

"That's not the point . . ."

I was at a loss for words.

"You've always fantasized about watching me with another man," she said. "This is the perfect opportunity to do it. We'll get paid to live out your fantasy."

"There's a difference between fantasy and reality."

Her mind was made up. I could have argued with her all day. I could have thrown a fit, I could have refused to go along with the whole arrangement.

In the end, I went along with it because Caitlyn wanted me to. I always did what Caitlyn wanted me to do.

Rob paid for the motel room. He counted out the fifteen hundred dollars up front and gave it to me. I pulled a chair into one corner of the room, stuffed the cash in my pocket, and sat down to mind my own business.

Caitlyn stood next to the bed, All-American soccer mom, her blonde hair in a ponytail, her T-shirt nearly busting under the weight of her large breasts, and her jeans tight over her firm bottom.

Rob took her in his arms and started kissing her. She wasn't the least bit hesitant, and suddenly I felt a million miles away.

Caitlyn responded to him enthusiastically, opening her mouth to allow his tongue to explore its warmth. Her tongue danced back against his, and then she began to suck on it, bringing it deeper into her mouth.

Rob's hands slid over her hips and found their way to her ass. He squeezed her butt through the jeans, using the leverage to pull her even tighter against him.

They finally broke the kiss. She pulled her T-shirt over her head and tossed it aside, then she reached behind her back and unhooked her bra. The satiny cups came away and her breasts bounced invitingly free.

Rob liked what he saw.

Caitlyn kicked off her tennis shoes, slid out of her jeans, and sat on the edge of the bed, wearing nothing but white socks and pale blue panties.

Rob stood in front of her and reached for the button of his jeans. Caitlyn beat him to the punch. She undid the button for him, dragged the zipper down, then tugged his underwear down far enough to free his erection.

She ran her tongue around the fleshy pink tip of his cock and then flicked her tongue against the underside of it. She took him in her mouth next, tilting her blue eyes up to watch the reaction on his face.

The look in her eyes was the soft, seductive look she gets when she will do anything to please me, when her only desire is to make me feel good, only now the look wasn't for me at all, it was for this complete stranger who now had his cock in her mouth.

Caitlyn dragged his pants all the way down around his ankles, keeping his cock in her mouth as she did.

He managed to kick off his shoes and remove his jeans and briefs, all while Caitlyn continued to service his cock with her mouth and fingers.

She was eager to please him.

A little too eager.

Rob took off his shirt and tossed it over his shoulder, then he put his hands on the back of Caitlyn's head and guided her up and down on his dick. She went deep, taking every inch of him, coming away now and then to lavish his hard shaft with long strokes of her tongue. She worked her way down one side and up the other, then she pushed his cock against his stomach and started at the base of it, working her tongue against the length of his thick-veined shaft until she came to the purplish mushroom-shaped helmet.

She planted a wet kiss on the head of his cock, smacked it against her tongue a few times, then stood and kissed him, keeping her hand wrapped around his cock and giving it a hard squeeze. She gave his cock a couple of quick strokes for good measure, then she took off her panties and pressed them against his face.

He sniffed, taking in the scent of Caitlyn's pussy, obviously appreciating its aphrodisiacal properties. Something about this strange man being allowed to smell my beautiful wife's pussy was arousing and disturbing at the same time.

He backed her up until her legs hit the bed and she fell back on it. She wrapped her arms around his neck and tried to pull him down with her, but he broke free and knelt on the floor beside the bed.

Caitlyn drew her knees to her chest, opening herself wide. She reached between her legs and started fingering herself. That was completely unexpected. I can't tell you how many times I've asked her to masturbate, only to have her tell me she's too self conscious to touch herself while I watch.

Rob knelt beside the bed, slid his hands under her ass, and pulled her to him, easing his tongue between the slick pink folds of her vulva. His tongue slid through the slippery folds and disappeared inside her.

She moaned, softly at first, then with increasing intensity, pumping her hips against his face as he fucked her with his tongue.

"Eat me," she said.

The sound of those words coming from her mouth caught me by surprise. She is not normally verbal during sex. She's usually pretty straight laced in the bedroom, not much into anything that might be considered kinky or over the top.

"I'm coming . . ." she gasped.

She lifted her ass off the bed and pushed it against his face, grinding her pussy on his mouth, squealing with pleasure as she did. Her stomach quivered and the muscles in her thighs rippled. Her breasts rose and fell as her breathing quickened.

She screamed as she reached her peak, then she collapsed back on the bed, out of breath and fully satiated.

She turned around and got on her hands and knees, waving her bottom at him as he rolled a condom onto his cock. When he didn't get it on fast enough, she turned around and rolled it over his cock for him, then she was on her hands and knees again, looking at him over her shoulder.

"Fuck my ass," she said.

Just one more thing to add to the list of things she'd never done for me.

Rob rubbed the head of his cock up and down the length of her wet pussy, then he lifted it and placed it against the tight entrance of her ass. He held her by her hips and eased the head of his cock past her tight entrance. She groaned as it slowly disappeared inside her. He took his time, working his cock in a little deeper, and when he was halfway inside her, he grabbed hold of her ponytail and held on as he began fucking her ass.

I felt humiliated. Not only was I watching another man have sex with my wife, I was subjected to watching her do things she had never even considered doing with me. The worst part is, I was as aroused as I was humiliated. I wasn't sure if it was watching my wife in action with another man or the humiliation itself that turned me on more.

Maybe it was her own excitement that made it so good for me, I don't know. Maybe it was the fact that she was so eager to please him.

Rob groaned as he reached his climax.

Caitlyn came with him.

After Rob left, I asked Caitlyn if I could make love to her. We still had the room, after all, and why let it go to waste?

Long-Distance Love

The phone rang. Karen leaned over to the nightstand, raising an arm over Frank, who was casually sucking one of her nipples. She brought the phone receiver to her ear. "Hello," she said, and when she heard her husband's voice on the other end of the line, she sat up and said hello again, this time trying her best to sound composed.

She held a finger to her lips to let Frank know he needed to be discreet.

He smiled at her and went back to work on her nipple. "How's Chicago?" she said into the receiver. Frank continued working on her nipple, swirling his tongue around it, gently pulling it between his lips.

Karen ran her fingers through his hair, pulling him closer to her breast. She spoke into the phone again. "I was just lying in bed," she said. "Trying to watch TV. How was the meeting today?"

* * *

Greg sat on the edge of the bed in his hotel room, a drink in one hand, a cigarette in the other. He cradled the phone between his shoulder and cheek.

"Boring," he said. "I made my presentation. Don't know how it went over, though. The head honchos are half stupid. They have no idea what they want."

He took a gulp from his drink and set it on the table next to the bed, then he stood and began unbuttoning his shirt. "Anyway, I'll know more in the morning," he said. He stuck his cigarette in his mouth and unbuttoned his pants.

* * *

Frank had his head between Karen's legs. He licked her pussy, which she'd shaved bare earlier that evening. She could feel every stroke of his tongue.

"I miss you," she said into the phone.

Frank stuck a finger inside her, moved it in and out, all the while circling her clit with the tip of his tongue. She arched her back, rubbing herself in his face.

* * *

Greg took off his shirt and tossed it on the floor. He kicked off his shoes, pushed his pants to his knees, then sat on the bed and finished removing them.

"You feel all right?" he asked.

* * *

"Ummm, I'm fine . . . why?"

She moved her hips up and down on Frank's tongue. He pushed his hands beneath her ass and pulled her closer.

* * *

"You sound different, that's all, like maybe you're distracted, not all the way in the conversation."

* * *

"I guess I'm just a little tired . . ."

She held the back of Frank's head, fingers spread wide, holding him in place as he tongued her clit with light, teasing strokes that sent shivers through her belly, all the way up to her nipples.

He went to work on her breasts again, sucking one nipple, fondling the other, back and forth between the two.

Karen slid a hand between her legs to finger herself.

Frank came up on his knees, one hand grasping his thick penis. He stroked it, looking into her eyes as he did. She knew what he wanted. She motioned him closer, replacing his hand with hers, stroking him. He placed the purple crown of his cock at her lips. She turned her head slightly, just enough to enable her to reach his cock and still be able to talk into the phone.

"Wanna have phone sex?" she asked her husband. "Pretend you're here with me now, sliding your big dick into my mouth . . ."

She opened her mouth as Frank fed his cock to her. She sucked gently, working her tongue around the rim, curling it against the underside.

"Umph . . ."

* * *

Greg reached for his drink and slid back on the bed, resting his back against the wall, now wearing only his boxers.

Amber came out of the bathroom wearing a towel. Her blonde hair fell over her shoulders in wet, shiny rings. She let the towel fall from her body and climbed onto the bed, straddling Greg's knees. He lifted his ass so she could take off his boxers.

"Yeah," Greg said into the phone. "Suck my cock."

Amber grasped his cock with both hands, leaned down, and slipped her mouth around his cock. She began to pull and tug his thick shaft, sucking his dick deeper as she did. "That feels good, baby . . . suck it."

* * *

Frank pushed his cock to the back of Karen's throat, causing a slight gag reflex before she was able to recover and start sucking properly.

* * *

Greg listened to the noises his wife made on the other end of the line, hot and wet, sucking sounds, probably her fingers, or maybe her dildo. She wanted to complete his fantasy for him. She wanted him to believe she was there with him.

He reached down and tangled his fingers in Amber's soft blonde hair, caressing her scalp as she took more of him into her mouth.

The girl was good, he'd give her that much. It hadn't taken more than a couple of drinks to get her to come to his room. She was one of those girls that hung around, waiting for the big conventions, looking for some guy to spend money on her. It didn't matter to her that some of them were married, so long as she got what she wanted in the bargain.

"Ummm, deeper, baby," he said, gently pushing on the back of her head.

She locked her lips tight around the base of his cock and came up slowly, letting the head of his cock slip from her mouth with a wet smack. She gripped him at the base and watched the expression on his face as she circled his smooth pink knob with her wet, hungry tongue.

* * *

"I want you to fuck me," Karen said into the phone, and as she did, she turned over and raised her bottom for Frank.

Frank took up residence behind her, his big hands gripping her fleshy thighs as he pulled her toward him.

"Come on, fuck me," she panted . . .

* * *

. . . and Greg slid deep inside Amber's wet pussy, cradling the phone and supporting his weight with both hands on the bed.

Amber wrapped her legs around his waist, locking her ankles together. She pressed the heels of her feet down on his muscular ass, pulling his cock all the way inside her . . .

* * *

"God, I love your cock," Karen said. "Give it to me, come on, fuck me!"

* * *

Greg loved when Karen talked that way. Her nasty words, the way she begged for his cock even when he wasn't there, it was a turn on.

He slammed into Amber, shaking her tits like Jell-O. She bit her lower lip to keep from squealing. He'd told her up front not to give him away, that they were going to play a little game, and that she needed to be discreet. He was pretty sure the idea of taking his cock while he was on the phone with his wife appealed to the horny little blonde. She wiggled beneath him, lifting her hips up to meet each of his thrusts . . .

* * *

Frank's belly collided with Karen's ass cheeks. She rotated her bottom as Frank gave her long, hard strokes, taking his cock all the way each time, then filling her with it again.

"Ohhh, yeah, I'm coming," Karen squealed. "Come with me!"

Frank gave a few more thrusts and pulled out to jerk off on her ass.

* * *

Greg's hand was a blur as he stroked the length of his cock until he squirted thick, warm spurts of come onto Amber's flat, heaving stomach.

* * *

Karen reached back and ran her fingers through the sticky white mess on her bottom. Frank leaned up over Karen, his cock pressing into the crack of her ass. She turned her head slightly, allowing him to kiss her on the lips.

* * *

Greg pecked Amber on the cheek and fell on the bed beside her, adjusting the phone so he could talk to Karen.

"You there?" he asked. He could hear her heavy breathing. "Did you come?"

He stroked one of Amber's pink nipples.

* * *

"I'm here," Karen said, stroking Frank's semi-hard cock. "That was incredible. You wouldn't believe how much I came."

* * *

"I'll be home tomorrow," Greg said. "I love you."

* * *

"I love you too," Karen replied. "See you then."

She hung up and turned to Frank, ready for one more round. . . .

Love in Chains

Mariah sat at the bar and drank straight whiskey. Men approached her one by one, each of them vying for her attention. Some were smooth in that over-confident sort of way, others made complete fools of themselves, and still others were quite simply pathetic.

Mariah raised her hand and signaled the bartender for another drink. His name was Larry. He was a nice guy. She hadn't fucked him yet, but not for lack of trying. One night, after consuming way too much alcohol, she had come on to Larry, only to have him refuse her offer of a blow job behind the bar.

She watched Larry come to her now. He set a bottle of Jack Daniel's on the bar top. Mariah glanced at the bottle, then into Larry's eyes.

"Come on, Larry," she said. "Are you going to pour me another, or do I have to do it myself."

Larry shook his head. "Why do you do this, Mariah?"

"Do what, Larry?"

"This . . ." He indicated the bar with a wave of his hand. "Why do you waste your time with these losers?"

She took a long, thin cigarette from her purse and lit it, blowing a cloud of faint blue smoke from the corner of her mouth.

"We're all losers," she said.

Larry shook his head sadly, poured her whiskey, and walked to the other end of a bar to serve another customer.

"Can I buy your next round?"

Mariah turned to see the tall, good-looking man who sat on the stool beside her. Dark hair, a nice smile, white teeth, a bit of a tan.

"I don't think that'll be necessary," she said.

His smile wavered.

"I think we can skip right to the part where you fuck me."

She didn't ask for his name. He didn't offer. They went to her place. In her bedroom, dark except for a couple of candles. The two of them undressed. She opened the nightstand where she kept condoms and KY-Jelly. She rolled a condom onto his cock, smeared some of the lubrication up and down the length of his shaft, then rubbed some around the opening of her pussy.

She lay back on the bed with her knees pulled back and wide apart. He hovered above her, one hand groping his cock. He guided the tip to her slick entrance and slid inside her.

When he tried to kiss her, she turned away from him. She didn't kiss. Kissing was too intimate. She could be fucked, but there would be no kissing ever.

The man didn't seem to notice, and if he did, he didn't care. Fucking was fine with him. He would be happy as long as he was fucking her.

Fucking was good. She liked being fucked. It was the part that came after fucking—the part where they always left— that bothered her most. She was getting accustomed to it, though, and these days she expected it.

She'd been alone her whole life. Everyone, beginning with her father, had abandoned her. She had *always* been alone. She would *always* be alone.

Fucking was a reprieve.

"Fuck me," she whispered to the man from the bar.

For the next few minutes the only sounds she heard were the sounds of his raspy, uneven breathing and the steady slap of his balls against her ass.

He fell against her and grunted as he came, then he rolled away from her, removed the condom, and dropped it over the edge of the bed.

They lay there for several minutes without saying a word. She smoked a cigarette. He lay with his arms behind his head, staring up at the ceiling. She glanced at him a couple of times, watching the way the flickering light of the candles danced on his face.

He rolled onto his side and propped his head in his hand. "Are we going to exchange names?"

"Why?"

"It just seems, I don't know, appropriate."

"Did you enjoy fucking me?" she asked in a casual, nonchalant sort of way.

"Of course . . ."

"Did you need to know my name while you were fucking me?"

He didn't answer. He looked at her for a long moment, then he stood up and began getting dressed. She watched him. He gave her one last look after he had his clothes on, then he walked out of the room.

She listened to the front door open and close. A moment later she heard his car door open and slam shut. She heard the engine start, heard the car back out of the driveway, and a sharp squeal of tires.

Then came the silence.

* * *

The next night was the same. Another man, another quick fuck. This time he went down on her first. He used his tongue expertly and made her come, and then she rolled the condom over his cock and applied the KY-Jelly.

He climbed between her legs and slid into her. She locked her ankles behind his back and met each of his thrusts. He reached his climax and she came again, this time with him.

He stayed a little longer than most. She fell asleep with him beside her, but when she woke up early the next morning, she found herself alone again. He had slipped away in the middle of the night, but he'd at least lasted longer than most.

* * *

Johnny's Body Shop.

Piercings and custom tattoos.

Mariah entered the building. The unmistakable scent of marijuana hung heavy in the air. Fluorescent light cast a sickly glow over the place. A man with dirty-blonde hair and a beard was tattooing a vagina on the back of a bald man's head.

"Be with you in a minute," he said, glancing briefly at Mariah before returning to the job he was doing on the bald head.

Mariah sat and watched him work. When he was finished with the vagina on the bald man's head, the tattoo artist stepped back and proudly admired the job he'd done.

He turned his attention to Mariah. "What can I do for you?"

* * *

Larry poured bourbon for Mariah. She brushed a strand of her blonde hair behind one ear and picked up the glass, taking most of it down in two swallows. Larry watched her. She set the glass down hard on the counter, nodded at it, and said, "Give me another."

Larry poured another.

"I'll go easier on this one," she said.

Another customer called Larry down for a refill on his beer. Larry went down and took care of the customer, then he came back to Mariah.

"Larry, are you ever going to fuck me?" she asked.

He leaned on the bar, looked into her eyes, and said, "No, I don't believe so."

"Why?"

"Because I don't believe that's the kind of guy I am."

"What does that mean? Are you gay?"

"No, that's not what I mean. A nice girl like you, I just don't think I could fuck you and leave it at that."

"Nice girl?" She laughed. "Where do you get that I'm a nice girl? You've seen me leave the bar with countless men, even a few women. There's nothing nice about me, Larry."

"Sure there is. You just don't allow anyone to see that side of you."

She lit a cigarette, lost herself momentarily in deep thought, then said, "You'd want more than just to fuck me?"

"I'd want more," he said.

Another customer called out for a refill. Larry went to take care of it. When he returned to Mariah, she said, "Come home with me tonight. I have something I want you to see."

Larry thought about it. She sensed his hesitation.

"Please . . ." she said, letting her voice soften as much as she was capable.

"Sure, I'll go home with you," he told her. "But I won't be just another night for you. If that's what you're looking for, you won't find it with me."

She didn't believe him. She was sure he'd be like all the others. When he knew everything about her, when she told him the truth, he would run away.

But he would fuck her first.

They always fucked her.

* * *

"Did you mean what you said about wanting more than just to fuck me?" Mariah asked. They were standing in her living room.

"I meant it."

She smiled. "You'll have to excuse me if I have trouble believing you. My experience with people in general, and men specifically, is that they usually take what they want and then run away."

She turned and headed toward the bedroom, stopping long enough to give him a look of invitation. She continued into the bedroom. He followed her.

She stopped beside the bed and turned to face Larry as he came into the room.

"Why has it taken so long for me to get your attention?"

"You've always had my attention," he said.

She unbuttoned his shirt and slid it off. She knelt on the floor in front of him and reached for his belt, loosening it, undoing his trousers. She tugged his pants down to his ankles. His cock, already hard, made a tent in his boxers. She hooked her fingers in the waistband of the boxers and dragged them down.

226

His cock jumped out at her. She wrapped her slender fingers around the thick shaft and moved her fist along its length several times, then she leaned up and ran her tongue around the helmet, pausing long enough to flick her tongue against its tip before she finally took it into her mouth.

He was silent as she sucked his cock, save for the occasional groan. She worked diligently, almost methodically, her hand and mouth moving in unison.

She stopped suddenly, leaving him on the verge of coming. She stood up and sat on the bed. She removed her shoes one at a time, watching Larry as she did, keeping her eyes fixed on his.

She stood up and unfastened her jeans, stepping out of them, letting them fall to the floor beside where her shoes lay.

She was now wearing just her blouse and panties.

Larry kicked off his shoes and stepped out of his jeans and boxers. He moved close to her, reaching out to slide his arms around her waist. She grabbed hold of his wrists. "Wait," she said. "I want you to promise me something."

"What?"

"That you won't ask questions."

He hesitated, then said, "Okay, no questions."

She pulled her panties down and off, dropping them on top of her jeans. She stared into Larry's eyes and he held her gaze, looking for something there.

Larry was sure he saw her fear, but there was something else too— longing, maybe even a little hope.

She slowly undid the buttons of her blouse, letting the two sides cover her breasts until the final button was undone, then she slid the blouse from her shoulders, letting it drift to the floor in a whisper.

She watched for Larry's reaction. His eyes fell immediately to her breasts. Through each nipple was a large silver ring, and attached to each ring was a silver chain that swept down and around her ribcage.

She turned her back to him.

The silver chains curved up and attached to a pair of handcuffs that dangled between her shoulder blades. She gave him several seconds to take it all in before she climbed onto the bed on her hands and knees. She looked back at Larry, giving him as seductive a smile as she could manage.

"I want you to put the handcuffs on," she said. "Put them on and fuck me."

He hesitated.

"Please . . ."

The vulnerability in her tone made him do it. He climbed onto the bed and knelt behind her. He put his wrists in the cuffs and clicked them shut.

"Now fuck me, Larry," she said. "I want you to really fuck me."

She was looking at him over her shoulder. A strand of blonde hair fell over one eye. Her pink mouth was moist and sexy.

She reached back and lifted his cock, placing it between her pussy lips, angling the tip at her slick entrance. He pushed into her, filling her pussy with his dick, sliding in until his balls pressed against her clit.

"I'm not a nice girl," she said.

He withdrew his cock and slid into her again.

"Do you know I've been fucked in the men's restroom at the bar?"

She rocked herself back against him, swallowing his cock deep into her pussy.

"You didn't know that, did you?" she continued. "Well, it's true, I have. I stood with my hands against the stall while a stranger fucked me."

She pumped her ass back against him.

"I fucked my best friend's husband. She never found out . . ."

The slippery pink lips of her vulva clung to his shaft, folding in and out with every stroke of his cock.

The silver rings through her nipples swung back and forth, pulling her tits with them.

"I let two men fuck me on a train . . . I gave a stranger head under the table in a crowded café . . . I let one of my girlfriends fuck with me a dildo while her husband fucked her ass . . ."

She knew he wouldn't be able to stand the truth. There was no way he could love her. No one could love her.

He could fuck her, though. All men were capable of fucking.

Fucking required no emotion, no love, nothing but the need for release.

She gasped and began to grind herself against him, panting, her fingers clutching at the covers as she reached her climax.

He couldn't move his hands far with the handcuffs on, but he stretched his fingers out until they were just touching her shoulders.

". . . but I've never . . . *ever* . . . made love. . . ." she added, nearly in tears.

She came up on her knees then, leaning her back against his chest, and turned her head to one side, allowing him to kiss her.

As her tongue shot into Larry's mouth, his balls tightened and his cock jerked inside her as he came.

They lay together afterward, in the dark, him spooning her from behind, the handcuffs still on. He felt her fingers brush his hand and then she slipped something cold and metallic against his palm.

A moment later she heard the soft click of the key snapping the handcuffs open. Sometimes you had to follow your instincts. Sometimes you had to believe in someone other than yourself.

She closed her eyes and went to sleep, truly believing in her heart that Larry would be there in the morning.

Lube Job

Brooke was in her own little world, thinking about the guy she'd left behind. It pissed her off it had to be that way, but sometimes love wasn't enough. A girl could be expected to handle just so much before she had to open her eyes and see the truth.

Sex with Michael had been good in the beginning of their relationship. No, who was she kidding? Sex with Michael had been better than good. It had, in fact, been nothing short of mind blowing, and it had stayed that way for nearly two years, right up until his drinking had taken over his life and left his interest in sex nonexistent.

A nonexistent sex life was something Brooke had no interest in. She was a young woman with a healthy sexual appetite, and any man who wanted to be with her had better be able to pull his weight in the bedroom, or in the kitchen, or in the woods, or wherever else she felt the need.

She was heading south now, trying to put as many miles between her life with Michael as she could. Her parents lived in a small Texas town, and she was going home again at the age of thirty-five.

She caught herself thinking about Michael as she drove and that bothered her. She could easily recall the way he touched her and the way he made her pussy tingle with just a stroke of his finger.

And Michael knew how to eat pussy. There was absolutely no doubt about that. He knew just the way she liked to be licked, exactly when to put his fingers inside her, and how hard to suck her clit.

She felt her pussy starting to tingle and her panties getting damp. She had to clear her mind of her horny thoughts or she'd end up running her car off the road, but she couldn't stop thinking about Michael.

Damn him. Why wouldn't he go away?

She remembered the time they'd been doing it doggie-style. He'd been behind her, really fucking her, sliding his thick cock in to the hilt and all the way out again. She'd been caught up in the heat of it, loving the way his cock filled her, and suddenly he'd smacked her on the ass. She'd tried so hard not to laugh because she knew Michael liked to spank her, but she hadn't been able to help herself. She'd bit her lip until she nearly drew blood, but the laughter came anyway.

He'd sulked for a long time after that. She really hadn't wanted to hurt his feelings. It wasn't that she minded being spanked. She liked it just fine when she was in the mood, but that night she'd found it funny, not erotic.

She made it up to him a few days later. He was watching TV in the living room when she marched in wearing a transparent nightie and matching panties, demanding he spank her bottom because she'd been a naughty girl. Not only did he happily spank her ass, he fucked her like he'd never fucked her before, leaving her pussy swollen and sensitive for days.

She was smiling at the memory when an awful grinding noise brought her back to reality. She glanced down at her dash and saw the *check oil* light flashing at her. She knew enough about cars to know that if she didn't pull over now she'd blow up her engine.

She pulled over to the narrow shoulder of the road. She knew where she was. She was only a little way from Little Lake. She could easily walk the short distance, so she set out on foot, hoping she'd find an open gas station when she got there. It was Sunday, which meant fishing day for the good people of Little Lake, so the odds weren't in her favor.

At least she was dressed for the hike. She wore short cutoffs that accentuated longs legs, sexy hips, and a firm, well-rounded bottom, and her halter top did little to contain her firm, jiggling breasts. If she was lucky, maybe a male would drive by. No way in hell he'd pass her without giving her a lift.

No such luck, though, and she ended up walking the entire way.

She spotted a gas station at the only major intersection in town and headed straight for it. There was a very old tow truck parked on the side of the building. She hoped it was in running condition and could be used to bring her car to the station to be fixed.

Her heart sank immediately when she reached the gas station and saw the *closed* sign hanging in the window.

"Shit," she muttered, looking around for another station.

She didn't see one and she wasn't surprised.

"What now?" she asked, as if some magical answer would come to her.

She was about to start walking again when she heard what sounded like hammering coming from inside the garage. She went to the garage door and peeked through one of the dirt-smudged windows. She had to stand on her toes to see inside.

There was a guy inside. A nice-looking guy, late twenties or early thirties, wearing a plain white t-shirt and Levis. His hair was nearly shoulder length and black. His bangs fell across his forehead as he bent over a work table to examine what was probably some sort of car part. There was a car up on jacks, which Brooke figured belonged to the part the guy was looking at with such intense scrutiny.

She tapped on the window.

The guy looked up at her but made no move to come toward her. She waved him over. He set down the tool he was working with and came toward her at a casual pace. No way he was going to be rushed.

He finally reached the door and then dropped out of Brooke's sight. A moment later the garage door rumbled up.

"Can I help you?" the guy asked.

"I sure hope so," she said.

She noticed how he lowered his eyes to glance at her chest, and when he looked up again, he had a very slight smile on his lips. She looked down at her chest and saw that she'd perspired so much the shirt had become see-through, showing the dark circles of her nipples.

She looked up at him again, certain her cheeks were turning red.

"It's hot out here," she said, as if the words offered some justification for her tits being on very prominent display in front of a stranger.

"Sure is," he said in a laid-back Texas drawl. "About a hundred ten in the shade. You want something to drink?"

"Please," she replied.

He motioned her into the garage and dragged the heavy door down again. She watched as he crossed to an old-fashioned Coca-Cola ice chest and opened it up, reaching inside to draw out two bottles of soda. He opened the sodas and brought one to her.

"So, how is it I can help you?" he asked.

"Well, I think I ran my car out of oil a little way down the road," she said. "It started rattling and grinding and the oil light came on."

He took a drink of soda. "You pull over right away?"

"As soon as it happened," she said.

"Good."

He took another drink of his soda. When he said nothing else, Brooke asked if he thought he might be able to take a look at it.

"Depends," he said. "You think you can wait 'til I finish up here?"

He indicated the car on the jacks with a slight nod.

"Sure," she said.

It wasn't like she was in a hurry to get anywhere, and besides, she was sort of at his mercy.

He pulled out a wooden stool for her to sit on, then he went back to work on the car part. He finished with it and leaned into the engine compartment to put the piece back on. Brooke watched his arm muscles flex as he held the part in place and tightened it down with a wrench.

Next he lay on a flat wooden thing on wheels and rolled himself beneath the car. Brooke couldn't help but notice the size of the bulge in front of his jeans and she found herself squirming on the stool, fighting the urge to go down there and unzip his pants for a peek.

She was still staring at his crotch when he suddenly rolled out from underneath the car and caught her in the act.

"If you really wanna see it, all you gotta do is ask," he said.

She knew she was blushing again, but she didn't care. She really did want to see his cock, so she decided to go for it.

"Show me," she said.

There was nothing shy about him. He grinned as he set his wrench aside and slowly unzipped his Levis, slipping one hand inside his pants to withdraw his long, thick cock.

Brooke's eyes widened at the sight of it. It was so damn perfect, slightly paler than the rest of his deeply-tanned skin, with a slight curve to it. The head was smooth and had a deep pinkish-purple hue. Light blue veins criss-crossed their way up and down the length of the shaft.

"Do you like it?" he asked.

She could only nod and mumble something unintelligible. She was not normally this awkward around a man, but something about Mr. Mechanic had her all flabbergasted. She felt like a schoolgirl looking at her first cock.

He moved closer. She could feel the heat of his body as he pressed her back against the wall. His dark eyes fixed onto hers and she felt as if he were reading her mind.

He took one of her hands and placed it on his hard cock as he leaned in to kiss her, nibbling her lower lip before insinuating his tongue into her mouth. She opened her mouth to let his tongue explore. Her fingers tightened around his cock as she felt it growing longer and thicker, getting harder as she began to stroke it.

Her nipples were hard little points against the front of her damp shirt, hot and throbbing with the need to be touched. As if he'd read her mind, Mr. Mechanic slipped a hand beneath her top and ran it up to cup one of her breasts, gently applying pressure. His fingers sank into her soft, firm flesh and his palm pressed down on her nipple.

He massaged her breast, kneading it gently, then he ran a thumb slowly back and forth across her hard nipple, sending wild sensations through her entire body with every stroke. Their kissing became hotter, his tongue searching every inch of her mouth.

She released her grip on his cock and pulled away from him, going to her knees on the dirty concrete floor. His dick bobbed in front of her and she took it in her hand again, running her tight fist up and down the length of it as she ran her wet pink tongue around the tip.

He ran his fingers through her soft brown hair, pushing it back on both sides of her face, tilting her head up so he could look into her seductive eyes as she worked on his cock.

She took him into her mouth slowly, savoring the hot, hard smoothness of his cock as it slid across her tongue.

He pushed his jeans down a little further, giving her access to his balls. She cupped them in her hand and massaged them, rolling them around against her palm, stroking and caressing him the way she knew guys liked to be stroked and caressed.

A small moan escaped from the back of his throat, deep and slightly restrained. Brooke wasn't about to let him get away with that. If he was going to moan, she was going to make him moan like he meant it.

She took his cock deeper into her mouth and tightened her lips around it as she came up again, letting the head of his cock slip from her mouth so she could lick and nibble it.

She went down again, this time taking nearly every inch of him. This time when he moaned it was long and low, a deep moan of pleasure that was completely unmistakable.

She moved her head up and down, sucking his cock and working her tongue on it at the same time. She kept one hand tight around the base of his shaft and continued to massage his balls with her free hand.

He pulled her to her feet suddenly and kissed her urgently, taking hold of the bottom of her shirt, which he drew up and over her head, tossing it aside as he went to his knees in front of her.

He dragged her shorts and panties down to her ankles. She worked them over her sandals and kicked them off to one side.

Then she felt his fingers on the lips of her pussy, pulling them apart, the tips of them stroking and probing her until her slippery juices began to spill over them.

He ran his tongue around her wet entrance and then dragged it up the length of her pink folds, seeking her aroused clit and taking it into his mouth. He flicked his tongue over the top of it as he pulled it into his mouth with a gentle suction.

She squirmed against his face, rubbing her wet pussy on his mouth, and now it was her turn to moan.

He stood up and kissed her again, running his hands over her tits and leaving behind grease marks, then he carried her over to a work table and set her down on the edge of it.

She opened her legs wide as he knelt in front of her. Her fingers slid through the thick tangle of his hair, around to the back of his head, and she pulled his face to her pussy. He worked his tongue inside her, his nose pressed hard against her clit.

She moaned, arching her back as he fucked her with his tongue, pushing it deep inside her and occasionally drawing it out to lick her soft pink lips. When he slid a finger into her, she nearly screamed from the pleasure it produced.

He stood up, leaving her gasping and panting as he got undressed. A can of motor oil sat next to her and he picked it up, holding it above her chest for a long moment before tilting it.

The dense golden-brown oil spilled between her tits and ran in a thick river down to her belly, pooling around her navel before spreading out and continuing its slow trek into the dark curls of hair covering the mound of her pussy.

He set the can of oil aside and pressed his hands together on her stomach, slowly running them up until just below her tits where they went their separate ways, each hand sliding over an oil-slick breast.

She loved the satiny sensation of the motor oil—the way it made her nipples roll easily against his palms.

He brought his hands down again, over her belly, over the tops of her legs and along her inner thighs.

She held her hands out and he knew what she wanted. He picked up the can of oil and tilted it, pouring some into her palms. She wrapped both hands around his cock and smeared it with the motor oil, slowly moving her hands up and down, running one hand between his legs to massage the oil over his balls.

She leaned back and drew her knees up, opening herself wide for him. He moved as close to the edge of the table as he could get, watching her as she guided his slippery cock to the entrance of her pussy.

The head of it nudged against her, pushing its way into her opening. She felt it slipping into her one hard, slick centimeter at a time. He stopped about halfway inside her and slowly withdrew, leaving the head of his cock poised at her entrance for one teasing moment before sliding into her again, this time a little quicker, not stopping until his throbbing erection was buried deep inside her tight, gripping pussy.

He leaned down and captured one of her stiff nipples in his mouth, sucking hard on it as he began to pump his hips. He worked his tongue over the nipple inside his mouth, circling the goose bump-covered areola, flicking back and forth over the nipple itself, and then he moved over to work on her other nipple.

His thrusts were long and slow, each one filling her to the hilt, making her moan as her body responded with tiny electrical charges of pleasure.

She lifted her ass away from the table, wanting to open herself as wide as possible for him.

He gradually increased the speed and intensity of his thrusts until he was driving into her, slamming his cock in deep, his balls slapping against the cheeks of her ass in a rhythmic dance.

He seemed to know when she was on the edge and he would stop, letting her squirm and moan beneath him until she nearly begged him to put his cock inside her again. She finally locked her legs around his waist and kept him there, urging him to fuck her harder by using her legs to pull him back inside her each time he withdrew.

Her first orgasm was nothing less than explosive. She arched her back and pushed her wet pussy down on his cock. He stayed there, his cock trapped deep inside her as she came.

When she finished, she fell away from him, breathing hard, her cheeks flushed with the heat of her orgasm.

He kissed her.

"What about you?" she asked.

His cock slipped out of her as she sat up. She took hold of it and began to stroke him, moving her hand easily up and down his slick shaft. She liked the way it pulsed in her hand.

She watched his face as she jerked him off, letting his expressions guide her. When he closed his eyes and moaned, she knew she'd found the right pressure and rhythm and she kept it up.

She slipped off the edge of the table, not breaking the rhythm, and knelt in front of him. She leaned up to lick the head of his cock as she continued to give him a hand job. The look on his face—a slight smile, his closed eyes—let her know that it wouldn't be long.

She knew what he wanted.

"Does that feel good?" she asked.

She made her voice sexy—the harsh, excited whisper she knew turned a lot of guys on. "Do you want to come?"

He made a noise in the back of his throat. It was an unintelligible grunt, something more along the lines of animal lust.

"Would you like to fuck my tits?"

He made a soft grunt and nodded, opening his eyes to look into hers. She saw his desire and his need for release in those eyes. He may have been playing it cool, but he was on the verge of letting it all go now and giving in to the force of nature.

She leaned closer, placing his thick cock between her tits and pushing them together to seal his cock in their slick embrace. She started running her tits along the full length of his cock, flicking her tongue against the head of his dick each time it peeked up from her cleavage.

He put his hands on her shoulders to support his weight and began pumping his hips, taking charge of the situation, his eyes shut once again as he let the slick warmth of her breasts caress his hard-on.

She caught the head of his cock in her mouth on the upstroke and sucked hard, working her tongue around the edge of it, teasing the little opening at the tip, then she released it with a wet *pop* and he continued to fuck her oil-slickened cleavage.

She watched as he moved faster, thrusting his dick up between her tits, drawing it back again. The tip of it had turned almost purple, his shaft was red and the veins stood out. His balls were heavy with come, dragging against her slick skin just above her ribs.

"Close . . ." he said, forcing the word out with a grunt.

"Come on," she urged him. "Come all over my tits."

He groaned and his cock exploded. A thick spurt of creamy-white come hit her chin and dribbled down her neck. His cock jerked again, squirting hot spurts of come that soaked her neck and her chest.

He finally stopped coming, his cock still and satiated between her tits, the last of his come dribbling from the tip.

She looked up at him and smiled, moving her tits slowly on his cock, smearing his come up and down.

"If you're this good at lubricating cars," she said, "I might be on the road again before the sun goes down."

"Sorry, ma'am," he said in his slow Texas drawl, "but we're closed on Sunday. Looks like you'll have to wait around 'til morning."

She stood up and kissed him, feeling his hard cock standing up against her belly. If another night in town was the way it had to be, she figured she could deal with that just fine.

Maid for You

Samantha came home and found Brad sitting on the couch in front of the TV, drinking beer and watching a porno movie.

"Why do you watch that stuff?" she asked.

She glanced at the screen and saw a big-breasted blonde on her hands and knees, taking on two guys, one in her mouth and one in her pussy.

"That's just disgusting," she said, but she didn't mean it at all. What she really felt was insecure. How could she measure up to that sort of thing?

"Would you please turn it off?" she asked.

He didn't want to turn it off, but he wasn't in the mood to fight, and he knew that telling her no would upset her.

"Okay," he muttered, switching off the DVD player.

"Thank you," she said on her way out of the room.

Brad hated when she got this way. He knew her problem, and it wasn't that she was anti-porn. He knew, in fact, that she watched the stuff herself when he wasn't around. She even enjoyed it.

It all boiled down to self-esteem. No matter how many times he told Samantha how beautiful she was and how much he loved her, she had absolutely no confidence in her looks. In her mind, she was twenty pounds overweight, her hair was plain, and her tits sagged. She was always worried about something.

The constant insecurity drove Brad nuts. He liked her the way she was, and as far as her tits went, they were all natural. Sure, maybe they hung a little low, but that was because they were big and heavy. Samantha wasn't one of those air-brushed bimbos with plastic tits.

How he felt about her didn't matter, though. He could tell her night and day that no other woman could turn his head, but she'd never believe him.

Therein lay her problem with pornography. She couldn't stand the idea of Brad watching other women naked and having sex. She believed he had fantasies about those women, that he'd rather fuck a porn star than her.

Not true. Watching the sex aroused him, but it was his wife that he desired. He was as aroused by her these days as he'd been when they first met. When he watched the dirty movies, all he thought about was how lucky he was to have a woman in his life that he wanted to do those nasty, kinky things with.

Samantha was already in bed when he turned in for the night. She lay on her side, facing away from his side of the bed. He knew she was only pretending to be asleep. She wasn't going to talk to him. That was his consequence.

He kissed her on the cheek and rolled over, his back to hers, and eventually drifted off to sleep.

* * *

She was at the kitchen table reading the newspaper when Brad came down for his morning coffee ritual. Her hair was slightly mussed and she wore a short wrap-around silk robe. She looked inviting.

"Morning, babe," he said.

He bent down to kiss her. She turned her cheek to him. It was obvious she hadn't yet decided to allow him back into her good grace.

He poured a cup of coffee and carried it to the table. "How long do you plan to keep this up?" he asked.

"Keep what up?" she asked casually, her face hidden behind the newspaper.

"Crucifying me because I watched a *bad* movie," he said.

"I guess for as long as I feel like it," she said.

"Can you give me a round-about idea?" he asked. "You look really sexy this morning, and I'd like to clear off the table and fool around."

He felt her tension slide away. Although he couldn't see behind the newspaper, he would almost bet she was struggling not to laugh. She really couldn't stay mad at him when he set his mind to making her give in.

"Just give me a little action. You can go back to crucifying me later."

That was it. Her laughter finally came. "You're such a pervert."

She set the paper down as he came around the table and kissed her. She untied the sash of her robe, allowing it to fall open. He ran his hands over her breasts, rolling her nipples under his palms. They were already hard.

She pushed her tongue into his mouth as he lifted her and set her on the table. He pulled her ass to the table's edge. She opened her legs for him as he knelt in front of her and buried his face between them, one hand going down to pull her panties to one side, the other grabbing him by the back of his head to pull his face tight against her pussy.

He licked the plump lips of her pussy and worked his tongue through the kinky blonde curls until he found her slick, pink inner lips. He ran his tongue over the soft folds and slowly made his way up, taking her clit between his lips to nibble it. She moaned, pumping her pussy against his face.

He stood up and pushed his boxers down. His erect cock sprang out, alive and ready for action. He stroked his shaft a couple of times, then he placed it against her slick opening and eased it inside her. The plump lips of her pussy separated and her slippery inner lips folded back in wet welcome. His cock disappeared in one smooth thrust. He kissed her hard on the mouth and then caught one of her stiff pink nipples in his mouth.

She drew her knees back and opened them as wide as she could, watching as he pounded her pussy with deep strokes. He held her by her hips, keeping her steady, pumping into her until she started to gasp and moan.

"Don't stop . . . you're making me come!" Samantha screamed, panting.

Her pussy squeezed his cock, caressing the length of it as he continued fucking her. The hot grip of her slick cunt massaging his dick was enough to take Brad over the top with her. He groaned as his cock erupted inside her.

She moaned as the first wave of her climax washed through her belly, locking her legs around his waist. Her tits flopped up and down, nearly smacking her in the face. She shuddered against him, finally relaxing as the last of his hot cream squirted deep inside her.

He collapsed on top of her, his sweaty chest against her soft boobs. They were spent, breathing heavy, both of them completely satiated.

She finally mustered up a kiss.

"You're forgiven," she said.

* * *

Samantha poured another cup of coffee. Brad had gone off to work. She carried her coffee into the attic and began sorting through cardboard boxes, looking for Brad's stash of porn. She knew he had one.

She found what she was looking for and went through the box, checking out the glossy porno magazines. She'd known about them for some time now, and while she didn't like the fact that he looked at them, she didn't make a fuss about it so long as he kept them away from her.

She opened one of the magazines and thumbed through the pages, stopping now and then when something caught her eye. She had to admit, some of what she saw excited her. She enjoyed looking at other people having sex. Something about watching strangers fuck made her feel especially naughty.

Sometimes she got so mad at herself. On an intellectual level, she knew there was nothing wrong with looking, so long as it didn't have an ill effect on the way couples treated each other in the bedroom, and so long as there was never any infidelity involved. On a purely emotional level, though, she hated the idea of her husband looking at other women engaged in wild sex. She didn't like the idea of him looking at other women at all, for that matter.

Brad's interest in porn made her feel inferior. She couldn't help it.

She put the magazines away and looked through some of his videos. She wished he would throw them away, but there was no chance of that. He'd made it clear to her more than once, as much as he loved her, he saw nothing wrong with his collection, and he wasn't about to throw out his adult material just to appease her out-of-whack emotions.

While she was putting everything back the way she'd found it, a magazine fell out of the box. She picked it up and was just about to put it back when she saw an ad on the back cover for a company called Pornocopia Productions.

The ad heading read: So you wanna be a porn star?

Samantha examined the advertisement with interest. The company motto was, *"We turn the girl next door into a whore."* The company specialized in helping its customers create custom-made amateur porn films.

Would she dare consider such a thing? How would Brad feel about watching a movie made just for him, starring his own wife?

She called the number given for the company, initially only to inquire about the process, but by the time she hung up with the woman who'd answered the phone, she had an appointment the following Friday.

* * *

"Can I help you?" the young, attractive blonde behind the desk asked.

"I have an appointment," Samantha said, feeling a little nervous.

"Fill this out," the woman said, handing Samantha a clipboard and a couple of forms. "We'll be right with you when you finish."

Samantha took a seat and looked at the forms she was being asked to complete. One was a model release form, the other was a series of questions designed to help the director make the movie Samantha wanted to make. She read each question carefully and answered them as best as she could.

When she came to the questions pertaining to other actors and actresses she might want to include in the movie, Samantha began to have second thoughts. Until now, she hadn't really thought much about the fact that she'd be having sex with strangers. Although she was doing this *for* Brad, she wasn't sure how he'd react to seeing her with another man.

She hadn't come this far to back out now. She really wanted to make the movie. She had a hard time choosing between the French maid scenario or the cheerleader scenario. Brad had often mentioned how he'd like to see her in a French maid outfit, so she chose that scenario, eager to fulfill his fantasy.

The total cost of the shoot, which included two male co-stars, was $2,500.

"Just go right through that door," the girl behind the desk told her, pointing to the soundstage entrance. "Someone will take you to makeup, you'll be briefed on the script, and then you'll meet the director and your co-stars."

A cute, young brunette wearing blue jeans and a Rolling Stones T-shirt greeted Samantha on the other side of the door. She introduced herself as Michelle as she led Samantha down a narrow hallway and into a dressing room.

"I'll be helping you with makeup and wardrobe," Michelle told Samantha. "Take off your clothes and we'll get started."

"Take off my clothes?" Samantha asked.

"Sure," Michelle said. "Don't tell me you're shy?"

"Well, no, I just . . ."

Michelle went to the closet and took out a French maid uniform complete with fishnet stockings and black pumps. "You'll be wearing this, at least for a few minutes, and then you'll be naked."

Samantha suddenly felt silly. She was here to fuck strangers, after all, and getting naked was part of that. She just hadn't been prepared to take her clothes off in front of Michelle.

She nervously began to fumble out of her clothes.

"Here, let me help," Michelle said, sliding Samantha's bra straps from her shoulders.

The unexpected touch of Michelle's fingers against her skin gave Samantha a shiver of pleasure. She'd never felt sexually attracted to another woman in her life, but suddenly she imagined being in bed with Michelle, the two of them licking and kissing one another. When their eyes met, Samantha felt an overpowering urge to kiss Michelle, but she resisted the temptation.

"How do you want your hair?" Michelle asked. "We could put it in a ponytail or tease it up real wild . . ."

Samantha considered the question a moment. "I think a ponytail would be best," she said. "My husband likes my hair in a ponytail."

She was naked now except for her panties.

"Those too," Michelle said. "The costume has matching silk panties."

Samantha pushed her panties down around her ankles and stepped out of them, taking the panties Michelle offered her.

"Okay, let's do your makeup," Michelle said.

Samantha sat in front of the mirror. She felt a little self conscious at first, sitting there in nothing but her panties, but gradually she got used to it and relaxed.

"You're very pretty," Michelle said. "You won't need a lot of makeup."

"Thank you," Samantha responded, feeling her cheeks heat up as she blushed.

Michelle opened her makeup case and lightly applied makeup to Samantha's eyes, then she took out a thick brush and applied rouge to her nipples, making them appear a shade darker. The soft bristles made Samantha's nipples hard.

Michelle stepped back to admire her work. "Okay," she said. "Time to get into your costume."

Samantha put on the maid costume, adjusting her fishnet stockings as she slid her feet into the sexy pumps. She looked at herself in the full-length mirror. The transformation was complete. She no longer felt like a wholesome, down-to-earth girl next door. She was no longer the sweet, devoted wife. She had truly become, at least for the present, a slutty French maid ready to service two studs.

"Ready?" Michelle asked.

"I'm ready," Samantha said, taking a deep breath to prepare herself for the moment of truth.

The set resembled a fancy hotel room. There wasn't much of a script. The premise was simple. A French maid happens into a room where two businessmen are in the midst of discussing business. The two men invite her to stick around for a threesome. Dialogue was ad lib.

Samantha almost chickened out when she saw the two guys (a well-hung Italian stallion and a Conan wanna-be with shoulder-length blond hair) who would be fucking her, but she stood her ground and fell right into her role once they started kissing her and slipping their fingers under the elastic of her panties. Her pussy was so wet she could feel the insides of her thighs getting damp.

Conan laid her back on the bed and pushed her skirt above her waist, sliding his hands beneath her to lift her pussy to his face, pushing and probing his tongue against her silky panties.

The Italian Stallion straddled her chest, stroking his thick cock as he dangled his balls in her face. She rolled his balls around on her tongue and sucked on them one at a time, then tried to get both in her mouth at once. She forgot all about the cameras. All she wanted was to taste that big cock in her mouth.

The Italian Stallion slid his dick to the back of her throat. She managed to take it all without gagging, which surprised her, and as she sucked on him, she squeezed his heavy balls in the palm of her hand and massaged them.

Mister Conan Wanna-Be pulled her panties to one side. His tongue darted around between her pussy lips. He found her clit and teased it with soft, quick flicks of his tongue, then he caught it in his mouth and nibbled.

She moaned around the cock in her mouth, arching her back to press her hot pussy against Conan's face.

Her first orgasm came quickly, sweeping through her body like a tidal wave. The Italian Stallion continued to fuck her mouth, picking up the pace until he was pumping hard and fast.

Conan lifted his face away from her pussy. His cheeks were slick and shiny. He moved up and knelt beside her, sliding his cock into her mouth as the Italian Stallion withdrew his.

She worked on both cocks with her mouth, moving from one to the other, deep-throating and licking. She pressed the two smooth knobs together and tried to fit them into her mouth at once, with little success. When that didn't work out the way she planned, she rubbed their cocks against her tits.

Samantha sat up and the two studs pulled her short dress over her head. Conan dragged her panties down and off. She kept the fishnet stockings and fuck-me pumps on for effect.

The two men positioned her on all fours and took her from both ends, Conan plowing her pussy while the Italian Stallion fucked her mouth. She let them sandwich her next, with Conan fucking her pussy while the Italian Stallion pumped her ass. It was the sort of thing she'd seen a lot of the women do in Brad's movies, and if that's what turned him on, she wanted to make sure she was the one doing it to him.

Samantha finished them with her mouth, moving from one to the other, servicing them until they came on her face and in her mouth. She swallowed as much come as she could catch in her mouth, then she licked the remainder from their cocks.

When she finished, she felt dirty, but dirty in a good way. Dirty in a sexy way. She thought maybe she felt more alive than she'd ever felt before.

And now *she* was Brad's celluloid slut.

* * *

She turned out the lights, lit a few candles, and checked herself one last time in the mirror. She wore a white negligee, transparent enough to show off her nipples, and a pair of satin and lace panties. A bottle of champagne sat in a bucket of ice on the coffee table.

When Brad came home, he was surprised and nearly speechless. He set his briefcase aside and took Samantha in his arms, kissing her hard on the mouth. Her tongue danced across his lips and teased its way into his mouth.

"Did I forget something?" he asked. "It's not our anniversary, is it?"

"No . . . I just love you," she said. "And I want you, right now, right here."

She went to her knees and took out his cock, running her tongue around the head of it first, then taking it deep into her mouth to suck on it.

Brad was almost always the one to initiate sex, and once it was underway, Samantha would get into it and enjoy herself. This aggressive attitude was a side of his wife he wasn't used to seeing, and one he could easily get used to.

She took her mouth away from his cock and stood, wrapping one hand around his shaft and giving it a good squeeze. "I have a surprise for you," she said.

"A surprise?"

"Yep, a surprise, but first I want you to change into something more comfortable. When you're ready, meet me in the living room."

"You got it," he said.

He went to the bedroom and changed into comfortable sleep pants. He spritzed on a little Aspen almost as an afterthought, then he hurried to the living room, not wanting to waste time and risk a change in Samantha's mood. He found her curled up on the couch, waiting patiently for him.

He sat beside her. She leaned over to kiss him, reaching between his legs to feel his cock through the loose sleep pants. He had a hard-on already.

He slipped his hands beneath her negligee and over her breasts, rubbing his palms across her stiff nipples, feeling every little goose bump around her areolas.

She broke the kiss and pulled away. "Here," she said, reaching for his surprise, which she'd left beside the champagne bucket.

She handed him a wrapped package. "What could this be?" he asked, weighing the package in his hand as if trying to figure it out.

"Just open it," she said.

He unwrapped the DVD. There was a French maid on the cover, on her hands and knees, her short dress riding up to expose her panty-covered ass. Samantha had posed for the cover, but since Brad couldn't see her face, he had no way of knowing it was her. Above the photograph was the title *Maid for You*.

"A porno?" he asked, caught off guard by the offering.

"A *special* porno," she said, taking the case from him and heading over to the DVD player. "And I'm going to watch it with you."

She put the DVD in the player. Brad's eyes were fixed on the TV screen as Samantha snuggled up beside him and started rubbing his dick again.

It wasn't long before Samantha was strutting her stuff across the TV screen, getting naked with her two male co-stars. Brad watched in silence. Hard-on aside, he showed no reaction to what he saw on the screen.

Samantha took out his cock. She gave it a squeeze and began to give him a slow, lazy handjob, watching his face as she did, searching his face for some clue that he was enjoying the movie. She couldn't really tell. At least he had a hard-on. That had to be a positive sign.

The movie lasted almost a full hour. When it was over, Samantha climbed onto Brad's lap, slid her arms around his neck, and leaned down to kiss him. He turned his head to one side, just enough to avoid her kiss.

"What's wrong?" she asked.

"What's wrong? I just watched you fuck two strange men and you don't know what's wrong? How could you do that?"

"I thought you'd enjoy it."

"You thought I'd enjoy it?" he asked, full of indignation. "You cheat on me with *two* guys, you give me a souvenir DVD of the whole thing, and for some reason completely foreign to me, you think I'm supposed to be *happy* about it?"

"I thought it would be something special," she said, climbing off his lap. "Do you know how hard it was for me to do that?"

Brad laughed. "Yeah, it *looked* like you were having a hard time."

She winced at the stinging sarcasm, torn suddenly between tears and anger and giving in to a combination of the two. "Fuck you," she screamed at him, storming out of the room.

Brad poured a glass of the champagne and gulped it down, wincing at the taste. What he wanted was a fucking beer. He went to the kitchen for a Heineken and returned with it to the living room. He lit a cigarette, looked at the DVD case again, then grabbed the remote control and started the movie, rewinding, fast-forwarding, and pausing every so often.

The more he watched it, the more he appreciated it for what it was. Eventually he began to get aroused, especially by his wife's performance, which rivaled those of any porno actress he'd ever seen.

When he got right down to it, what bothered Brad the most wasn't seeing other men enjoy Samantha. He could understand that. What bothered him was seeing Samantha enjoy the sex so much, and that was simply ridiculous. Sex was, by its very nature, enjoyable. Samantha was clearly performing for him, and was it so bad that she was having a good time in the process?

He took out his cock, which was hard and throbbing with desire for the beautiful blonde actress in *Maid for You*. He jerked off in time with Samantha jerking off her two well-hung co-stars.

The old saying "have your cake and eat it too" had never made more sense to Brad than it did right now. He loved to see hot, sexy women perform wild sex acts for the camera, but he never, even in his wildest fantasies, imagined he'd have the opportunity to bang one of those sexy little fuck queens . . . until now.

This fuck queen was his for the asking. She was *his* fantasy girl, and she was waiting for him in the bedroom right now.

The title of the movie said it all.

Samantha was made for him.

Meat Me in the Middle

Debbie stood in front of the mirror and undressed. She caressed her big breasts, making her thick pink nipples stand up erect. She ran her hands up her belly, cupped a heavy tit in each hand, and squeezed them together, then she slid one hand between her legs and pushed a finger inside herself. She was soaking wet and hot. She needed to be fucked.

She put on a pink satin kimono-style wrap, tying the sash loosely in front.

She could hear the TV from the living room. A football game. Getting Jimmy to pay attention to her was going to be a trick, but she needed him now. She wanted him to want her just as bad. She wanted him to throw her on the floor in the living room and drive his cock into her. She wanted to wrap her legs around him and open herself to his driving thrusts.

She looked at herself in the mirror again. Hair the color of beach sand, blue eyes, her body still firm and flexible, even though she was in her late thirties. She was proud of the shape she'd kept herself in. She didn't work, she didn't have any kids to take care of, and she sat on the couch and watched TV most days. It was a wonder it hadn't caught up with her.

She hadn't planned her life this way, but that was the way it was, and at least she still looked good. No sign of the middle-age spread so many women her age seemed to complain about.

She went down the hallway and into the living room. Jimmy was sitting on the couch in his boxers, his feet propped on the coffee table, a beer in one hand and a cigarette in the other. His eyes were fixed on the TV set. The sound was turned up to an obnoxious level.

Jimmy glanced over at her briefly but took no real notice. She climbed onto the couch and moved up beside him, sliding her arms around him, nuzzling her face into his neck.

"I want you to fuck me," she said.

She kissed his neck and slid one hand down the front of his boxers. His cock lay limp against one of his thighs. She wrapped her hand around it and squeezed.

"Honey, come on . . ." Jimmy said, not taking his eyes off the screen.

She stroked up and down. His cock responded, growing thicker in her hand. She continued to masturbate him.

"Not now, please," he said.

She kissed his chest, circled her tongue around one of his nipples, then leaned over to lick his other nipple. "Come on, Jimmy," she said, tilting her eyes up at him and giving him a pretty pout. ""I really need to feel your dick inside me."

She kissed her way down his stomach, knelt on the floor between his legs, and pulled the front of his boxers down, exposing his thick cock. She slipped her fingers between his cock and his belly, lifting his dick to her mouth. She ran her tongue along the length of it, teased the sensitive spot just below his purple crown, then slid her mouth around the head of his cock and began sucking it.

Jimmy paid her no attention. He was caught up in the game. Debbie worked eagerly at his cock, nibbling the fleshy knob, flicking her tongue against the tip.

She watched his face as she did, looking for some sign of encouragement. He didn't even bother to glance down at her.

She sucked him for a few more minutes, then she released his cock and climbed back up on the couch, once again snuggling up to Jimmy. She slipped one hand inside her satiny robe and caressed a hard nipple. She squeezed her soft tit in her hand, massaged it, and tugged on her nipple. She dropped her free hand between her legs and slid a finger inside her pussy.

Damn, she was wet. She felt her juices rolling down her finger as she worked it in and out of her pussy. She fucked herself with her finger, paying special attention to her clit, exerting the right amount of pressure to make her moan.

"Shhhh," Jimmy said. "The game, honey."

As if she cared about his fucking game.

She straddled him, pressing her knees into the couch cushions on either side of him, letting her robe fall open so her jiggling tits were in his face. She reached behind her and extracted his cock, which had already gone soft again. She rubbed it between the lips of her pussy until it began to stiffen, then she sat back on it.

There, how could he resist that?

He leaned to one side so he could see the TV.

Debbie rode to the tip of his cock and down again. Surely he couldn't ignore her for long. What guy wouldn't want a beautiful woman on his lap, grinding away at him? She pumped her hips harder as she continued riding him.

One of the teams scored. It was apparently Jimmy's team, because suddenly he whooped like a wild Indian, shoving one fist in the air. When he did, his ass came off the couch and his cock slid all the way up inside Debbie's pussy, inadvertently setting off her orgasm.

"Ohhhhh," she screamed.

Jimmy pushed her aside at the peak of her climax.

"Not now," he said.

The shock of being pushed aside so suddenly disrupted her orgasm, leaving her angry and frustrated.

"What's wrong with you?" she asked. "You'd rather watch football than fuck?"

He looked at her then, as if he'd just realized she was in the room. "This is a big game," he said.

He said it with such seriousness that she knew it would be impossible to get through to him.

"Forget it," she said. She stood up, tying her robe. "Just go ahead and watch your precious game."

She stormed into the bedroom, fell onto the bed, and closed her eyes to sleep. She was still horny. Her interrupted orgasm had only made it worse. She tossed and turned for a long time, annoyed by the sound of the TV, agitated because she was so worked up, both physically and emotionally.

Jimmy still hadn't come to bed by the time she finally drifted off to sleep.

* * *

Debbie was sitting at the kitchen table with a book and a cup of coffee when Trish knocked on the door. Trish was her neighbor. Another bored housewife who spent a lot of time watching TV. Sometimes the two of them would get together and talk, sometimes they went shopping together, other times they sat and watched afternoon soaps.

Trish was a year younger than Debbie, with dark brown hair and green eyes. She was married to a man who, like Debbie's husband, took little interest in sex. Trish often came by just to chat, and more often than not they would joke about the lack of sex they were getting, mainly because complaining did no good.

Trish went to the coffeemaker and reached into an overhead cabinet, taking down a coffee mug. She filled the mug to the rim. She noticed an airtight package of Polska kielbasa lying on the kitchen counter.

"Dinner?" she asked, nodding at the lengthy sausage.

"Yep. I'm going to make it with sauerkraut. Jimmy likes it, although I shouldn't make anything that makes him happy."

Trish sat down at the table. "He's in trouble, huh?"

"I just can't get him to put out," Debbie said.

Trish laughed. "Join the club. Gary's the same way. He'd rather watch TV. I could sit on his face and not get a reaction . . . no, I take that back. He'd tell me I was blocking the TV."

"What happened to the guys we married? I remember when I couldn't keep Jimmy off me. Now I'm lucky to get him to look at me."

"I know the feeling," Trish said.

They drank coffee and talked about the neighborhood, which was always good for a little gossip. It didn't take long for them to go through the last of the coffee. Trish offered to make the next pot, and while she was preparing it, her eyes fell once again on the Polska kielbasa.

An idea struck her. She glanced over at Debbie, who was watching her as she made the coffee. "Have you ever noticed how sexy this stuff is?" Trish asked.

She held up the package of sausage.

Debbie smiled. "You're a pervert," she said.

"Don't tell me you've never thought about the sexual connotations of a sausage. Every girl has."

Again Debbie smiled. "Maybe once or twice," she said.

"Have you ever masturbated with one?"

"Have you?" Debbie asked, blushing.

"Sure. A girl's gotta do what a girl's gotta do."

"I never have," Debbie said.

There was an awkward moment of silence, then Trish said, "Wanna try it?"

"Are you serious?" Debbie asked.

"Sure I am." Trish took a knife from the silverware drawer and cut the package open. "You've already said Jimmy doesn't deserve his favorite meal. You can feed him soup. We'll put this to good use."

She held the sausage up and cut the little piece of skin that held the two ends together. When the sausage unraveled, it measured at least twenty inches.

"Holy shit," Debbie said.

"Imagine this inside you," Trish said.

"I am," Debbie replied, her eyes growing wide with excitement.

"Come on, let's play," Trish said.

Trish headed for the bedroom. Debbie was quick to follow. She wasn't exactly sure how far Trish wanted to take the adventure they were about to have, but it occurred to her she was willing to go all the way. She wasn't sure why she and Trish had never fooled around in the past, but the idea of doing it now gave her a rush and made her pussy tingle.

In the bedroom, Trish tossed the sausage on the bed and faced Debbie. They met each other's eyes for a moment, as if taking the time to make sure this was what they both wanted, and when there seemed to be no question, Trish slid her arms around Debbie's waist and pulled her close.

Debbie liked the way Trish's lips felt against her. She opened her mouth slightly, letting Trish work her tongue in. Trish worked Debbie's tank top up, exposing her breasts. She slid her hands up and over Debbie's tits, rolling them under her palms.

Debbie moaned.

They broke the kiss and began taking off their clothes, scattering them all over the place as they hurried to get naked. They fell together on the bed, Debbie on bottom with her knees bent and spread wide, Trish situated on top, grinding the mound of her pussy against the mound of Debbie's pussy.

Trish kissed Debbie again, thrusting her tongue into Debbie's mouth. Debbie sucked on it for a few seconds before releasing it.

Trish gathered Debbie's hefty tits together, capturing one hard nipple between her lips and pulling it deep into her mouth. She flicked her tongue over the tip of the nipple, gave it a little bite, then moved over to work on Debbie's other nipple.

She worked her way down, taking her time, running her tongue over Debbie's smooth skin. She teased Debbie's navel, running her tongue around it a couple of times, then dipping her tongue in the soft indentation.

Trish moved lower, pressing her mouth against the soft, curly hairs on Debbie's mound. Debbie spread her legs wider, arching her back to give Trish unrestricted access to her slippery pink slit.

Trish teased Debbie's clit from beneath its fleshy hood and nibbled on it with her lips, then she gently sucked it into her mouth and rolled it around on her tongue. She worked a finger into Debbie's pussy at the same time, working it in and out a few times before adding another finger.

Trish fingered Debbie for several minutes while she ate her.

"You've done this before, haven't you?" Debbie asked, moaning and stretching her body like a satisfied kitty.

Trish gave Debbie's heated pussy one more long lick before she slid back up face to face with her. "Only once, a long time ago," Trish said. "In college."

Trish rocked her hips, grinding her pussy against Debbie's pussy.

"I remember how freaked out I was when the girl kissed me, but wow, it didn't take long for me to get into it," Trish added.

"Let me eat you," Debbie said.

Trish sat up. "How do you want me?" she asked.

"Just Slide up here," Debbie said, reaching out to Trish. "Like this?"

Trish straddled Debbie, her damp pussy hovering just above Debbie's face. She lowered herself slowly. Debbie extended her tongue, flicking it between Trish's plump lips, running it along the fleshy pink folds within. For a beginner, she wasn't timid about the way she worked on Trish's pussy, spreading Trish wide with her fingers and exploring every inch of her vagina.

Trish turned around, keeping her pussy within Debbie's reach as she lowered her head between Debbie's legs. She spread Debbie's pussy and flicked her tongue over Debbie's clit, causing her to moan into Trish's pussy.

Trish reached over and grabbed the thick, lengthy kielbasa. She slid one end into her mouth and sucked on it, then she slipped it into Debbie's pussy and slowly began feeding it into her one inch at a time.

Debbie gasped with pleasure as the thick sausage filled her pussy.

"How's that feel?" Trish asked.

"It feels good," Debbie said. "Fuck me with it."

Trish pushed it in until almost six inches of the kielbasa was inside Debbie's pussy, then she withdrew it slowly, bending down to lick Debbie's clit as she pulled the sausage all the way out, then pushed it in again.

"Shit, Trish," Debbie gasped, pumping her hips on the thick meat.

Trish pulled the kielbasa from Debbie's pussy. She ran her tongue along the length of Debbie's pink slit for good measure.

Trish climbed off Debbie and told her to lie down with her head at the top of the bed. Debbie got into position. Trish grabbed hold of Debbie's ankles and spread her feet apart, then she sat facing Debbie, opening her legs between Debbie's.

She handed one end of the Polska kielbasa to Debbie and kept the other for herself, rubbing it against her pussy before inserting it. Debbie slid the other end into her pussy.

The two women inched their way toward one another, working their pussies down on the length of sausage until they met in the middle, clit to clit. They began to move their hips, working the meat between them, grinding their pussies together, and soon their moans filled the room.

"Oh, yeah," Trish said with a groan.

Debbie reached out and took Trish's hands in her own, lacing her fingers with Trish's, squeezing tight as she began to pump her hips. Trish picked up on her rhythm, and soon the two were pumping and grinding together faster, pussy to pussy, each filled with ten inches of Polska kielbasa.

"I'm going to come," Debbie said breathlessly, panting so hard that her breasts rose and fell in sporadic rhythm.

"Me too," Trish gasped.

The sausage was trapped deep inside them when they climaxed, one right after the other. They continued to fuck it, hips thrusting, the meat slippery between them.

Debbie suddenly leaned forward, kissing Trish passionately, and when she did, she not only pushed herself down further on the kielbasa, she pushed the other end deeper into Trish's pussy, intensifying both their orgasms.

They fell apart afterward, both of them exhausted and momentarily satiated, the sausage slipping out of their pussies to lay between them on the bed.

Trish moved up and lay beside Debbie, lazily stroking one of Debbie's thick, still-erect nipples.

"Jimmy can keep his football," Debbie said.

Trish leaned up and kissed her nipple.

"So can Gary," Trish said. "This was way more fun than anything he's done with me in bed for the last few years."

"Does this mean we're turning lesbian?" Debbie asked, only half joking.

There was a knock on the door. Debbie moved over to the bedroom window and peeked outside. She could see the front porch from that angle.

"UPS man," she said. "I'm expecting a package."

They exchanged a quick look.

Debbie said, "You're not thinking what I'm thinking?" she said.

Before Trish could respond, Debbie grabbed her pink robe and threw it on as she rushed to the front door.

The UPS man was on his way back to his truck when Debbie opened the door. "Excuse me," she called out.

He turned around to see what she wanted. His eyes widened when he caught sight of Debbie standing in the doorway, her robe open to reveal the slopes of her breast.

"Come here," Debbie said.

He was a big guy in his early thirties, a crew cut, wide chest and arms that were thick and muscular. Debbie looked him up and down, smiled, and said, "My friend and I have been having some fun, and we were wondering if you had some time to join us?"

"You serious?" he asked.

She untied her robe and opened it, flashing her tits and pussy. "Is this serious enough for you?"

She invited him into the trailer.

"Follow me," she said.

She led him down the hallway, into the bedroom. Trish was lying on the bed, her legs spread wide, one hand moving between her tits, working her nipples, her other hand pushing one end of the Polish sausage into her pussy.

The UPS man stood in awe.

Debbie dropped to her knees and unzipped his trousers. She took out his cock, running her fingers along the length of it, looking up at him as she did.

"Isn't it just awful what a couple of married women have to substitute when their husband's won't put out?" she said.

"Just a shame," he said, glancing down at Debbie just in time to see her slide her hot mouth around his hard dick.

Trish pushed the Polish sausage deeper into her pussy. Her vaginal lips stretched apart to accommodate the meat. She reached the halfway point and continued working the sausage inside her.

"Jesus," the UPS man said.

In all the years he'd been working for the company, he'd never been involved in anything like this. He'd heard stories, sure. A lot of the guys he worked with claimed to have been involved with a horny housewife at one time or another. If you believed those guys, this sort of thing happened all the time, but this was the first time he'd seen it, that much was a fact.

Debbie let go of his cock and stood up. She slipped her robe off and kneeled on the bed, climbing over Trish. She shifted her ass invitingly, and the UPS man didn't need a second invitation. He moved up behind her and slid his dick into her pussy.

Debbie leaned down and started kissing Trish.

Trish continued to fuck herself with the Polish sausage.

The UPS guy held Debbie by the hips and delivered long, deep strokes of his cock, filling her pussy, withdrawing, and then filling it again. Each thrust of his cock made Debbie's heavy tits jiggle. Debbie dangled them in Trish's face so Trish could suck her nipples.

Trish slipped out from underneath Debbie and knelt beside her. The UPS guy took his cock from Debbie's pussy and slid into Trish. He fucked her for a few minutes, then he slid his dick into Debbie again.

Trish took one end of the Polish sausage in her mouth and began to suck on it. Debbie took the other end, teasing it with her tongue, treating it just like she'd treat a man's cock. She opened wide and slid her mouth around the fat tip of the kielbasa.

The UPS guy was fucking Trish now, then he was back inside Debbie, then Trish again. He worked up a sweat, alternating between the horny housewives, one after the other. His breathing quickened. His balls slapped a steady rhythm against their pussies.

"Damn," he said with a grunt.

He couldn't hold back any longer. He jerked his cock out of Trish's pussy and wrapped his fist around his shaft, jerking up and down. He threw his head back, gasping and moaning, his fist flying up and down. His cock exploded, spurting strings of milky come across Trish's ass and pussy. He shifted slightly to the left, unloading the rest of his semen onto Debbie's ass.

Debbie and Trish turned around together, pulling his cock down so they could take turns licking him clean.

The UPS man went back to work happy.

Debbie and Trish took a shower, soaping one another up, kissing and playing around a little before they got out and got dressed.

Jimmy would be home in less than an hour.

"Looks like I'll be running to the store later," Debbie said, dropping the limp, well-used kielbasa into the trash can. "I'll need to stock up on meat."

"Shall I join you for lunch tomorrow?" Trish asked, smiling.

"You bet," Debbie answered. "Can you guess what's on the menu?"

Trish smiled. "Let's just say there's going to be a run on smoked sausage," she said, and the two of them couldn't help laughing . . . .

Mount Angel

I was flying over the Cascade Mountains in my new Lancair Columbia 350. She was a real beauty, constructed of aerospace composites, sporting a 310-hp Continental engine with a cruising speed of 185 knots. She'd cost me $346,000 before taxes, but it was money well spent.

There's nothing like flying. No other feeling in the world, except for the sweet sensation of sliding your cock into a tight, wet pussy for the first time, compares to the pure exhilaration of riding the clouds.

I checked my gauges. Everything was in order. I took a drink of coffee from the thermos I carried with me on all my flights. Had to have my coffee. Good, strong Italian Roast. Never left home without it.

It had been a clear day when I started. The sun had been shining bright, its rays bouncing light off the snow-covered mountains. The weather turned suddenly. The sun vanished. A blanket of gray fell over everything, and then the snow began to fall.

I banked to turn around and head back to the same small airfield I'd taken off from. Something thick rolled in front of me. A cloud, maybe, or some kind of mist. I don't know now what it was, and I sure as hell didn't know then. My gauges went wild. The next thing I knew, I was flying out of the mist, heading straight for the rock face of a mountain. I banked hard to the right and went into the sharpest climb I could manage. I almost made it. Another few feet and the wing would have missed the side of the mountain. As it was, the tip of the wing struck a piece of rock and tore away.

I was going down. No doubt about it. I braced myself for the landing. I closed my eyes and said a prayer to whoever it was that might be listening.

The ice-packed, snow-covered mountain top was coming at me fast.

The last thing I remember about the accident was the god-awful sound of my $346,000 aircraft striking the ground.

The first thing I did when I came to was check myself for damage. Looking out the front windshield, I saw a jagged wall of rock. The nose of the plane had stopped just short of smashing into the rock face, which would've most certainly left me dead.

I unbuckled myself and half climbed, half stumbled from the cockpit, falling to my knees as I hit the icy ground. I took a look at my prized airplane. I had fared much better than she did, that much was evident. I, at least, was still in one piece. The Lancair had her left wing almost completely gone, and she'd left bits and pieces of herself scattered across the frozen wasteland in her wake.

I looked around, overwhelmed by the severity of my situation. My best guess was that I was stranded somewhere between 11,000 and 14,000 feet high in some of the most rugged mountain country in North America, surrounded on all sides by sheer walls of snow-covered rock.

I was in deep shit.

The first thing I did was find my thermos. Thank God it was still intact, still mostly full of hot, steaming coffee. I opened it and took a drink, then I screwed the lid back on tight and set it aside. I'd make it last as long as I could. There was no doubt in my mind I was going to be here for a while.

It was snowing harder. I searched the plane for anything I might be able to use to start a fire. I kept a few supplies tucked away in the back of the plane: a small first aid kit, blankets, dried beef, instant coffee, and bottles of water. Not much, but if I was careful, I could make it last a couple of days.

I was hoping I'd be long gone before then.

I scoured the landscape for timber, doused it with some of the fuel from the wreckage, and sat by the fire with a blanket wrapped around me, counting the reasons why I shouldn't attempt to climb down the mountain.

One *very* good reason was all I needed. I was stranded 14,000 feet in mountains covered with snow and ice, and I had no climbing gear. That constituted a good enough reason for me.

* * *

I'm not sure when I stopped believing help would come. By day five, I was starting to see things. The food was long gone. I had a little water left. I was on the edge of consciousness when she appeared.

She was beautiful. Her hair was white-blonde, her eyes translucent blue with flecks of gray, and her skin was pale. She wore a wisp of transparent fabric that exposed the roseate glow of her nipples and the gossamer hair of her pubis.

She was an angel, no doubt about it. My angel, as a matter of fact.

She drifted to me across the jagged, icy wasteland that kept us apart. She straddled me and leaned down to kiss me. The electricity of that kiss spread warmth through my entire body. I felt my nearly frozen blood begin to boil.

She teased my mouth with her tongue, first licking my lips, then working her tongue into my mouth. She kissed me harder as she began to move her hips back and forth, rubbing her pussy against my crotch.

I felt heat spreading through my limbs. My arms began to thaw, then my legs, and soon I was moving with her, pulling her against me as I thrust my hips up to meet the movement of her hips.

Angel slid up so she was sitting on my chest, her sweet pussy a mere inch from my face. The scent of her wafted past my nostrils. I took her by her hips and pulled her onto my face. Her knees locked tight around my head, and she began to grind herself down on my mouth.

My tongue worked between the lips of her pussy. She tasted as sweet as honey. Her juices were warm and sticky as they flowed over my face. I flicked my tongue over her clitoris. She came up slightly, allowing me easier access to her wet, very heated opening.

267

I probed her with my tongue, pushing it just inside her, moving it from one side to the other. Her ass cheeks were soft and yielding in my hands. I feasted on her, sucking up the sweetness, fucking her with my tongue, pushing it in as far as I could go with it.

She turned around on me, not taking her pussy from my face, and fell forward, her slender fingers groping my crotch. She unsnapped my pants and tugged my zipper down, freeing my hard-on. Her mouth moved along one side of my shaft. She nibbled her way along the length of it until she came to the swollen tip, which she lovingly caressed with her warm, wet tongue.

She took me into her mouth slowly, letting her tongue work against my hot cock as she worked her way down on it. She tightened her lips as she came up, relaxed them as she went down again, all the while working one hand up and down on my dick at the same time.

I pushed the wispy gauze-like fabric up over her ass and marveled at how beautiful and full her cheeks were, how pink and wet the folds of flesh between her plump blonde lips were?. I pulled her to my mouth again, working my tongue between the lips of her pussy, teasing the entrance a little before pushing my tongue inside her.

I thought I heard her whimper, maybe even moan a little bit, but I couldn't be sure. I was so caught up in the taste of her on my lips and tongue, so taken aback by the euphoria caused by the intoxicating scent of her.

Then she was standing, her transparent dress caught in a slight breeze, her pale hair moving gently in that breeze. She brought her hands up to caress her breasts. She squeezed them, rubbing her palms across her nipples.

She slowly raised the wispy dress over her head and stood over me, her legs wide, one foot on either side of me. I propped myself on my elbows and stared up at her pussy, watching as she fingered her slick pink inner lips.

She brought her fingers to her mouth and licked the juices from each of them, then she played with her nipples, twisting them, rolling them between her thumbs and fingers. She did all this for me, never once taking her eyes from mine.

She held out her arms. I stood up. She kissed me again, her tongue snaking into my mouth, then she took a step back and started undressing me. I helped her, and soon I was as naked and vulnerable to the cold as she was.

She dropped slowly to her knees in front of me, wrapping one hand around my cock (a cock that felt as hard and heavy as a 2x4 despite the freezing temperatures). She ran her tongue from the base of it, all the way up to the head of it. She swirled her tongue around the pink helmet as if she were licking an ice-cream cone, and then she went down and took my balls into her mouth and sucked them, first one at a time, then the two of them together.

She took my cock into her mouth, slowly working it to the back of her throat, taking it smoothly. Every inch disappeared. She did things to it while it was in her mouth I'd never felt before, and then she pulled back, once again letting it bob in the icy chill of the mountain air.

She stood up, pausing halfway to kiss my stomach. She stopped again at my chest and placed kisses on it, then she teased my nipples with tiny, gentle flicks of her soft, warm, pink tongue.

I went to my knees next, sliding my hands over her hips, around to her ass, drawing her to me as I reached her cunt. I held her close, probing her slick folds with my tongue, nudging the tip of my nose between her lips and against her clit.

She held my head in her hands and twisted her fingers in my hair. She sighed with pleasure, and it sounded like a sweet melody, floating through the mountains, echoing back to me from jagged mountain peaks.

I ate her pussy, nibbling the lips, slipping my tongue deep inside her. My fingers sank into the soft flesh of her ass cheeks. The tips of my fingers rested in the tight crack between them. I let one finger tease her puckered asshole before I eventually worked it in.

We made love on the frozen ground. Angel straddled me and guided the smooth, fleshy tip of my cock to her slippery hole. She sat back on it, sliding down to the base of my cock, and then she began to ride up and down. She moved slow and easy at first, but gradually began to ride me faster, coming all the way to the tip of my cock and then slamming down hard.

I slid my hands under her and clutched her quivering ass cheeks in my hands so I could assist her in up and down motions. It was all I could do to hang on to her as she bounced on my dick. Her tits jiggled with her movement, her pale blonde hair whipped around her face.

Snow began to fall around us. Big, wet flakes that melted as they landed on our skin. I should have been freezing, but all I could feel was the exquisite heat generated by Angel and me.

She turned around on my cock, keeping it buried deep inside her hot cunt, and fell forward on her hands, presenting her backside to my view. I watched as she pumped her pussy on my cock, up and down, the slick pink folds clinging to my thick, hot shaft.

I squeezed the cheeks of her ass and lifted, pulling them apart, giving myself an unobstructed view of her pussy stretched wet and pink around my dick. She was wet and slippery, hot and gripping. She pumped her hips, riding me hard, taking me fully into her, riding all the way to the tip and down again.

She sat up like a cowgirl, her hands behind her for balance, and bounced on my cock. Her ass bounced against me, cheeks quivering. Her pussy gripped my cock like a tight hand, stroking, bringing me closer to the edge.

She stopped suddenly and stood up.

"Take me from behind," she said.

She got down on her hands and knees, panting and gasping as she reached back to help guide me inside her. I knelt behind her, running my hands over her round ass, up to her hips. My dick jutted out, slightly curved, glistening with her juices. I nudged the head between her lips, prodding the slick entrance, sliding into her with one smooth thrust. The slick heat wrapped around my cock, swallowing it, caressing it with what felt like a million tiny stroking fingers.

Hands on her hips, I fucked her with long, deep strokes. Her pussy opened to me, swallowing every inch of my cock. My balls swung back and forth, slapping away at her cunt each time I drove into her.

A blanket of snow lay around us now. It continued to come down, so thick I could hardly see Angel in front of me as I fucked her.

Wind howled through the mountain pass.

"Come with me," Angel whispered.

Her whispered words cut through the storm and seemed to echo off the walls of the rocky slopes around us.

I worked a finger into her ass. It was tight and warm and accommodating. I pushed it in deeper, working it in and out, preparing her for my cock.

I pulled out of her pussy and lifted my cock, resting the head against her puckered asshole, pushing slowly. The pink little opening stretched slowly, wrapping around the head of my cock, closing around it, drawing it in.

The wind picked up. I could feel the ground shaking beneath my knees. I held her tighter, sliding my dick all the way into her tight bottom.

Snow fell at an angle, blown to the side by sharp, cold wind. A distant rumble came like a freight train as snow began to slide down the sides of the mountain. The ground shook harder. I held Angel tighter, alternating between her pussy and her ass, concentrating only on fucking her while Mother Nature screamed her fury all around us. Through it all, I felt warm and alive. I was protected. Angel glanced at me over one shoulder, her half-closed eyes focused on my face, her mouth opened just slightly. She was beautiful in a way that stole my breath. A combination of innocence and lust.

The mountain rumbled beneath us; Angel moaned.

I fucked her harder, driving deep into the confines of her clenched pussy, then switching back to her asshole. I treated both openings with equal care. My fingers sank into the soft flesh of her hips as I held her steady against the ground-shaking fury of a snow slide.

Even as the mountains came down around us, I gave myself fully to Angel, unleashing my own torrent of white fury. My head spun, the world around me set in motion as I reached my climax. My cock jerked inside her, sending jets of thick, hot sperm into her cunt. I screamed my pleasure into the surrounding chaos. Fire and desire ripped through me as I continued driving into Angel, filling her pussy with my cock, pushing into her so deep I felt as if I were trying to climb inside her womb.

She moved with me, pumping her ass back against me, manipulating my dick with the slick, gripping walls of her cunt. She milked the come from me, taking it deep inside her, trapping me inside her until she knew I had nothing left to give.

Angel came up, pressing her back against my chest. I brought my hands up over her breasts, tugging her nipples. She moaned as she reached the peak, as she came with me.

Over her shoulder I could see the snow rolling toward us, a wall of white . . .

* * *

. . . light in my face.

Overhead lights, sterile white walls, the smell of medicine heavy in the air.

I looked around the room. It sank in slowly. I was alive, in a hospital, it seemed, warm under a heavy blanket. A nurse stood at the foot of my bed, her breasts nearly exploding from the top of her uniform. She was blonde, blue eyed, and very serious.

"What happened?" I asked.

The words came out in a jumble that sounded like a foreign language to me.

She looked up, the serious look on her face transforming immediately into a smile. "You had an accident," she said. "This is Cedar Point Hospital."

"My plane went down," I said.

"And you were lost for days," she added. "You're lucky to be alive."

She hung my chart back on the end of the bed and came around to one side, leaning over to feel my forehead. Her breasts fell against the front of her uniform, once again threatening to break loose. I may have been incapacitated, but my cock was still in working order. I felt the stirrings of an erection.

"A bad storm made it hard to find you," she said. "It's a miracle you managed to stay alive."

"I had a guardian angel."

"You must have," she agreed. "The doctor will be in to see you in a minute."

She turned to go. I watched her leave. Her uniform was short, just barely covering her plump bottom. It would have been nice if she'd dropped something on her way out the door.

I closed my eyes and recalled the image of my naked angel, her hair pale blonde, her eyes translucent and distant. I recalled the way she tasted, the way she smelled. Was it possible she'd been a figment of my imagination?

I didn't think so.

I fell asleep and dreamed of the nurse. In my dream, she did drop something, and when she bent over to pick it up, I got a look at the lacy white panties my mind had conjured up for her.

In my dream, where everything is possible, I stood behind her and tugged her panties aside, and I slid my cock into her pretty blonde pussy. She pressed back against me and rotated her sexy ass, working her pussy on my cock. She finished me off with her mouth, looking up at me with big blue eyes, licking her lips to show me how much she enjoyed the taste of my come.

* * *

Someone came into my room, disturbing my dream. I woke up, hoping to see the nurse. I had a bigger surprise instead.

"I'm Doctor Miller," she said.

Her hair was blonde, slightly darker than I remembered, and her eyes were a different shade of blue, but her facial features were the same.

"Do I know you?" I asked.

"Not that I know of," she said. "I don't believe we've met, and you haven't been conscious since you were brought in this morning."

"It's just . . . you look like someone."

"Oh."

"Well, how am I, doc?"

"You had severe hypothermia and frostbite when you arrived, but you're going to be fine."

"I still have all my body parts then?"

"Yes," she said, smiling. "You still have all your body parts."

"That's good."

She looked at my chart, hung it back on the end of the bed, and said, "I'll check back with you before I leave tonight."

"Thanks," I said.

She headed for the door.

"Hey, doctor," I said.

She stopped and turned around.

"Yes?"

"You ever been to the mountains?"

"Once or twice," she replied, smiling before she left the room.

I was released two days later. I tried to contact Doctor Miller, whose first name was Rebecca, a week after I was released. I was told there was no such person on staff at the hospital, nor had there ever been.

I still don't know what happened to me while I was stranded in the mountains. I dream about her still, my angel, the woman who took me in her sexual graces and loved me back to life.

Mount Angel.

That's what I call the place in the Cascades that nearly took my life. It's where *she* lives.

I plan to scale those peaks again, one day soon.
Maybe I'll find her there.
Maybe, though, she never existed at all.

My Dearest Belinda . . .

My manhood throbs with anticipation at the thought of your soft lips and pale skin. I can feel your breath on my ear as you nibble. I can taste the sweetness of your lips as you brush them across my own. I cannot wait until we meet yet again, in the secrecy we must for now, to join together in the passionate throes of ecstasy that our coupling brings . . .

Belinda's heart raced as she read the fancy cursive writing on the old, fragile sheet of paper she held in her hands. Her cheeks were flushed and she was damp between her legs.

This was the attic of the house she'd grown up in. It was the first time she'd ever been up here. It had always frightened her as a child. Now, as an adult, her curiosity had driven her up here.

She'd found the letter in the bottom drawer of a cherry wood dresser, tucked away under the liner. The dresser had belonged to her great great grandmother, just as this house had, and just as all the furniture in the house had. The house had been in the family for generations. It was Belinda's now. She'd considered selling the place, but in the end, she couldn't bring herself to do it. It belonged in her family. It was her destiny to stay here.

The letter had belonged to her great great grandmother as well, who Belinda herself had been named after.

Belinda sat beside the oil lamp she'd brought with her to light the way and continued reading.

. . . there is no doubt that you and I are meant to be together, if not in this lifetime, then perhaps the next. Until then, my sweet, we will continue to meet in the most out-of-the way places, the shadows, the nooks within which we can explore one another to the fullest . . .

Belinda let one hand drift between her legs. She slipped her fingers under her nightgown and touched the damp cotton of her panties.

. . . last night, my love, the intensity of our passion was almost too much for me to bear. The taste of you upon my lips, sweet and thick like honey . . . the way you moved beneath me as my tongue stroked the silken folds of your inner lips and lashed at the tiny pink pearl that is always so sensitive to my touch . . .

It was starting to rain. Belinda could hear it on the roof. Big, heavy drops at first, then a downpour. The wind picked up and began to howl. Lightning flashed outside the only window in the attic, followed by a crack of thunder that made Belinda's heart leap into her throat.

She continued with the letter.

. . . the way I slid into you, so deep, filling you with my hardness until you wrapped your legs around me. I held you there, my hands gripping your wrists and pinning them to the bed. You gave yourself so completely to me, surrendering to the heat of our lovemaking. I wanted so badly to allow myself release, to explode inside you, my dear Belinda . . . and I wanted that release to create a bond between us that would never be broken . . .

I wanted to, but I didn't allow myself that pleasure. I would not allow myself that pleasure until you had been satisfied completely. Isn't that the way it has always been between us, you thinking only of me as I think only of you?

The sound of your soft moans, the way you whimpered with each thrust I made into you . . . you breathing heavy . . . your creamy breasts, each topped with a roseate nipple, rising and falling. I could feel you clenching around me, caressing the length of me. It was so hard to hold back . . . nearly impossible . . .

We should leave this place, my dearest Belinda. I fear we will be caught and we will never be able to raise the child we conceived last night . . .

Surely, after our mutual climax, the way you arched your back to allow me to penetrate you ever deeper, the way you took my hot explosion, there could have been no other outcome than for you to have conceived . . .

The letter ended there, with the *d* in the word *conceived* veering off on a wild course across the page and morphing into what appeared to be a signature. She could barely make out the scrawl, but it looked like Samuel.

The wind whistled outside. It was pouring rain now, battering the house. More lightning fractured the sky. Thunder cracked like gunshots.

She felt a chill run along her spine. She was starting to imagine things. She thought, for instance, that she'd seen a shadow move on the far side of the attic. The logical part of her knew it was a trick of light, or lack thereof, that had caused it. The flickering of the oil lamp, the surrounding cloak of darkness, and maybe the residual effect of the lightning—all had combined to create something that wasn't there.

She set the letter aside and picked up the oil lamp, taking it with her as she moved among the dusty furniture and the trunks. She knelt in front of one rather large trunk and looked inside.

She wished there was a light. It would have been better to go through this stuff during the day. Not only would she have been better able to see things, but she wouldn't have been as creeped out.

She reached into the trunk and brought out a framed picture. The shadows played over it, making it hard to see clearly, but she knew the woman in the picture was her great great grandmother. She'd seen pictures of her before. She took a lot of her looks from her great great grandmother, which was why she had been given the name Belinda.

She set the photograph back into the trunk and picked up another. This one had her great great grandmother in it too, with a man she didn't recognize.

A cold breath of air swept over her then and she felt the hairs stand up on the back of her neck.

She quickly put the photograph back into the trunk and closed the lid.

There was one more trunk she wanted to go through before she called it a night. It was against the wall, wedged in between two very large antique chairs. She carried the lamp over and opened the trunk.

The trunk smelled of moth balls. It was full of clothes, all neatly folded. She removed an article of clothing and took it with her, taking care to retrieve the letter on her way downstairs.

It was unbelievable how intense the storm had become by the time she was downstairs again. She loved thunderstorms, but when they became this intense, she got nervous. There was a fine line between comforting and scary, and a raging thunderstorm was much closer to scary, even downright frightening.

She set the oil lamp on the night table and laid the dress from the trunk on her bed. It was beautiful. Dark red velvet with cream-colored lace trim at the neckline. She slipped the nightgown from her shoulders and let it slither to the floor, stepping out of it as it puddled around her feet.

Another wisp of cold enveloped her, just as it had in the attic. The house was old, but it had always been well insulated and not prone to cold leaks. She made a mental note to have someone come and check the place out.

She became aware of her nipples. They were erect. Painfully erect, in fact. Taut, straining. She cupped her breasts in her hands and gave them a gentle squeeze, then she rolled her thumbs over the tips of her nipples, causing herself to shudder with pleasure.

She turned and faced the dresser against the far wall of her bedroom. A huge etched mirror was attached to the dresser, affording her a full view of herself. She saw that her cheeks were flushed, that her straining nipples were like ripe fruit about to explode, that even her stomach had deepened in color.

She thrust one hand down the front of her panties and slipped a finger into the juicy heat of her pussy. How unbelievably wet she was. So wet she could almost hear her finger working in and out.

She stepped out of her panties and ran her hands over her body, exploring her curves, enjoying the smooth feel of her pale skin.

She picked up the dress. Why had she felt the need to bring this particular item of clothing downstairs, and why did she now feel the need to put it on?

She put the dress on, then she went to the dresser and brushed her hair with an ivory-handled brush. One hundred strokes, just as she had always been told by her mother, who had been given the same advice by her mother, and so on and so on, all the way back to her great great grandmother Belinda.

She set the brush down and began piling her long blonde hair up, letting soft silken strands of it hang loose and brush her cheek.

The lights flickered.

She felt another cold breeze brush past her.

Suddenly the lights went out. The oil lamp was still burning. She could see it behind her in the mirror. Its flickering light cast dancing shadows over the walls and around her reflection in the mirror.

She went over to the bed and put the dress on. The velvet felt cool against her skin. She turned to look at herself in the mirror and that's when she saw him standing behind her.

She whirled back around, her heart pounding in her chest, expecting to confront the dark-haired intruder, but she was alone in the room.

Again it had to be the shadows. That's what she tried to convince herself, but she knew what she'd seen. More than shadows.

A crack of thunder startled her. She was working herself up now. Every little flash of lightning, every rumble of thunder presented an imagined threat.

She wanted the lights to come back on.

Another breath of cold air swept by her. This time she felt something more. She felt light pressure on her right cheek, as if someone had touched her.

There was something about the touch that made her comfortable. Her fear dissipated. She couldn't explain it, but she suddenly felt very aroused. More so than when she had been reading the letter. There was no reason for it.

The air felt as if it were charged with electricity. The flame in the oil lamp wavered and went out, as if someone had blown it out.

She felt someone behind her then. She didn't turn. She was afraid to turn.

She felt someone take her by the wrists. Her arms began to rise, lifted by some unseen presence. Whoever it was, or whatever, brought her hands to her breasts. She thought briefly that she should resist, make a run for the door, and leave this house behind forever.

She couldn't do it.

She didn't *want* to do it.

She closed her eyes and closed her hands over her breasts, squeezing them gently through the velvet fabric of the dress.

She heard her name whispered.

"Belindaaaaaa . . ."

The sound of the voice came from everywhere and nowhere at once.

"Belindaaaaaa . . ."

She shivered.

This time the voice came from beside her, right in her ear.

"My dearest Belinda . . ."

She came to on the bed, completely naked. Her legs were open wide. Her nipples were erect and sensitive. She was so very wet.

The rain had stopped. There was no wind. The room was alive with preternatural silence.

The flame on the oil lamp came to life seemingly of its own volition.

"Samuel?" Belinda said in a soft whisper. "Are you here, my daring man?"

The mattress sank as someone unseen lowered his weight on it.

Belinda smiled.

"I can't see you, Sam," she said.

There was a flash of lightning outside the window and the electrical energy in the room began to build.

The figure of a man took shape beside the bed. Nothing solid at first. Just a misty shape that resembled a nude male.

"Come to me, Sam," Belinda said. "Come to me now . . ."

The vague human shape began to shimmer and then solidify.

She held her arms out to him. He climbed onto the bed and lowered himself down on her. They kissed. She reached down and stroked him.

"So hard . . ." she whispered into his mouth.

She felt him throbbing in her hand, swelling even more as she squeezed his shaft. He kissed her breasts and slowly worked his way down, kissing her belly and the mound of her pussy.

She ran her fingers through his hair and guided him between her legs, pulling him to her as she did. His tongue moved between the lips of her pussy and traced the outline of her vulva. She felt it circling her clit, teasing her into a near state of frenzy, and then his lips were on her, tightening around her clit. He began to nibble and suck at it, bringing her very quickly to the edge of climax and then backing off just before she found release.

He finally entered her, slowly easing the length of his cock into her and withdrawing. He did this again and again, teasing her with the promise of a good, hard, long-overdue fucking. She clawed at his back, digging her nails into flesh that was not quite there.

He gradually quickened the pace of his thrusts, going all the way inside her and pulling almost completely out.

"Samuel . . ." she said, moaning the word more than actually saying it.

He took her by the wrists and lifted her arms over her head, pinning them to the mattress, and continued to thrust into her. Each stab of his cock brought her that much closer to orgasm. She could feel it swelling inside her, insinuating itself into her as if it were intent on only her pleasure and nothing more.

Her belly quivered as the first waves of her orgasm began to build. She started breathing quicker and her legs wrapped around Samuel's waist as she thrust herself against him.

Samuel was breathing quicker now too, groaning with every thrust he made. She could feel the sweat on him. She tried to hang on to him, but her fingers slipped against his wet skin.

She was so close now.

"Ohhh, Samuel . . ."

She arched her back, forcing herself to take his cock all the way. He slipped his hands beneath her and held her close to him, bending down to cover her mouth with his as she reached her climax.

He came with her. The room became charged with static electricity and then explosions of light that appeared to be lightning inside the house rather than out.

Belinda reached her peak and then collapsed back onto the bed, clutching a pillow to her chest. Her legs were wide open and her breathing was deep and ragged. She felt exhausted and fully satisfied.

The room was dark. Not even the oil lamp was burning.

The last thing she remembered was putting on the dress, which now lay on the floor beside the bed.

It was raining softly. The room was cold. An occasional bit of lightning illuminated the bedroom. The shadows at the foot of her bed swirled and shifted, but she didn't feel afraid. She knew they were only shadows.

She seemed to remember something . . .

The trip to the attic.

A man.

She felt herself between the legs. She was wet and warm, even a little tender. She slipped a finger inside herself and brought it to her lips for a taste.

Nothing but her own juices.

She hugged the pillow close to her and closed her eyes. By morning the storm would be gone and the electricity would be on again.

She began to drift. She wasn't sure at first whether it was her imagination or not, but then she heard it again, distant and gentle.

"Sleep well, my dearest Belinda . . ."

And she knew that something extraordinary had taken place this night. . . .

My Doll

Anna woke me up with kisses on my stomach. I watched her in my half-groggy state as she took my cock in one hand and teased the tip with her pink tongue before she slipped it into her mouth. She never once took her beautiful blue eyes away from my face. She enjoyed seeing the pleasure she brought me.

I tangled my fingers in her silky shoulder-length hair and moved her up and down on my cock. She stroked the lower half of my shaft with one hand, moving it in unison with her hot mouth, and she worked her tongue around the head of my cock, concentrating especially around the sensitive spot just under the tip.

She came up and straddled me, raising her bottom as she reached back to lift my cock and sit on it. Her knees pressed into the bed on both sides of me and she leaned up, dangling her beautiful breasts in my face. Her nipples were dark brown and as hard as pebbles.

"Good morning," she said, her voice sweet and slightly hoarse the way it always was first thing in the morning.

"Morning, doll," I said.

That was my pet name for her. She was my doll. Beautiful and fragile.

She slowly began to ride me. I didn't have to do a thing. She moved up and down, slow and lazy. She worked her hips back and forth, bringing me close to the edge and then letting me slip back again. Finally she took me to the edge and beyond. I felt my cock jerk inside her as I reached a climax that was almost religious in its intensity.

We lay together for a long while afterward. She kissed me, got out of bed, and padded naked into the bathroom. I followed her. We made love again in the shower, her legs around my waist as I pressed her against the tile wall.

We dressed for the day. She had several errands she needed to run. She kissed me and told me to get some work done. She was always telling me to work. She was my driving force.

I'm a writer. Cheap paperback westerns with less plot than a Geico commercial. Nothing literary, I know, but I make a fairly good living at it.

I poured a strong cup of espresso, carried it up to my office, and sat at my desk in front of the old Underwood I still used to type my manuscripts. I hadn't yet, nor did I have any intention of entering the computer age.

It was October 31st. Halloween had always been my favorite holiday. Not an official holiday for most, at least as far as the working world was concerned, but my favorite holiday nonetheless.

This particular Halloween was a true nightmare.

By mid-afternoon, I had managed three chapters of my latest plotless western. I almost ignored the knock on the door, but there was something about it that seemed insistent. Two police officers stood on the porch in the crisp fall chill and told me my wife had been killed in an automobile accident.

* * *

Imagine, if you can, having someone reach into your chest and rip your bleeding, still-beating heart out and then telling you that you are sentenced to spend eternity walking around with the void left behind.

Can you feel it?

I sure as fuck felt it.

I did nothing for the rest of the year, nor did I do anything for the first four months of the following year. Nothing, that is, unless you count drinking myself to sleep every night as an accomplishment. I didn't write, I didn't go out, except on rare occasions to purchase food and plenty of scotch, and I didn't even sleep in the bed I had shared with my wife.

I did nothing but drink.

My agent, Kyle Weathers, called me quite often, at first to offer his condolences and his support, then to beg me to get back to work.

"Writers can't afford to take time off," he told me. "People forget about you. They move on. You get left in the dust."

And then, of course, he added the part about my being under contract and obligated to turn out two titles a year.

I told him to go to hell.

* * *

The one-year anniversary of Anna's death came and went. I continued drinking on a daily basis. I sat in the dark that night and tried to imagine her with me again. I would have given anything to have her with me again. I would have taken my life if I'd had some guarantee she'd be waiting for me on the other side.

The holidays went by in a blur. Another new year came waltzing in without my blessing. One morning in April I went up to my office. I don't know what drew me to it that day, but I went inside. Sitting on my desk was the manuscript I'd been working on the day I got the news of the accident.

I sat down in front of the typewriter and rolled a blank page into it. I stared for a long time at that blank page. The urge to write was fighting to break the surface. The urge to finish the manuscript Anna had told me to work on the day she died was trying to take control of me.

I tried to type, but my fingers wouldn't move. They hovered over the keys, motionless, my mind as blank as the sheet of paper.

I wasn't ready.

Not yet.

That night I didn't sleep on the couch. I went to sleep in the bed I had shared with my wife. It felt strange but comforting. The sheets had not been changed since Anna's accident. The pillows were the same. If I closed my eyes and imagined hard enough, I could still smell her on them. It was the first good night's sleep I'd had in more than a year. It appeared that maybe it was time to move on.

The next morning I sat at the typewriter and again stared at a blank page. This time the words began to flow. I typed for over an hour before I went to the kitchen for another cup of coffee.

I grabbed a half-empty bottle of scotch from the cabinet over the sink and poured it down the drain. I poured the coffee and went back to my office to write some more. I chain smoked and wrote. By the time I turned in for the night, I had completed the entire first draft of the manuscript.

* * *

I started writing again on a regular basis, saving my ass with my agent and my publisher. I also started dating again.

Nothing heavy, mind you. I wasn't interested in anything of substance on that front. There was no way I'd find a woman who could fill my emotional needs the way Anna had. I stuck pretty much with one-night stands, fucking beautiful women I met at book signings mostly, having a roll in the hay with a woman I'd met at one of the frequent parties thrown by my publisher.

There were plenty of women both willing and eager to wrap long legs around my waist and meet every thrust of my cock. There were plenty of women willing to lick and kiss me, plenty of women who would take me in their mouths and suck me until I was finished. Those women seemed to wait for me at every turn, and I was more than happy to take advantage of them.

But only for a while.

Sexual flings are fun, but the one-night stands began to inhibit me. Regardless of what many women claim in the beginning, most want more than they let on. Sex is fine for them at first, but then they look for more. I didn't have the time or the inclination to deal with women who required anything more from me than detached sex. I stopped dating altogether. All it did was put a damper on my ability to work.

I threw myself into my writing again. My secret lover, always there when I need comfort in the night or a friendly face in the morning. My writing demanded very little of me and had always served me well.

Sexual urges still came. I took care of myself, masturbating usually with a pair of my wife's panties. I still had her things. Her bras and panties, her nighties, her socks, stockings, and shoes, all still tucked away in their proper places.

I would close my eyes and take my erection in a firm grip, stroking it slowly, conjuring up the image of Anna, naked and wanton. My thoughts of her ran rampant. I would see her in my mind's eye, so beautiful and vivacious, her pale blue eyes and thick black hair, the heavy fullness of her breasts, the curve of her back and the smooth rise of her ass . . . those visions never failed to arouse me.

* * *

October 31st, the second anniversary of my wife's death, I woke up early and made coffee. I stepped outside to smoke a cigarette and enjoy the crisp coolness of Autumn. There was a very large package leaning against the door frame. I found no return address and no identifying marks of any kind.

I brought the package inside. I didn't open it right away. I was curious, of course, but a gut instinct told me to prepare myself for what might be inside.

When I finally did tear the package open, I thought I was going to faint dead away. Lying in the box, surrounded by a soft velvet wrapping, was one of those sex dolls you see advertised in the adult magazines.

But this wasn't just any sex doll.

This one looked exactly like my dead wife.

It was uncanny. She was made of realistic material. Her hair was full, soft, and shiny, her pale blue eyes looked moist and soulful, and her skin felt warm to the touch. Looking at her unnerved me. It was how I imagined she might have looked in her casket, except I hadn't been able to see her that way. Due to the nature of the accident, Anna's casket had been closed.

I was about to close the box, unable to take this sick prank any longer, but Anna's eyes seemed as if to plead. I looked at her for a long moment, forgetting that what I saw before me was nothing more than a replica, and then I leaned down and kissed her on the lips.

I went to bed that night with Anna quite naturally on my mind. I dreamed of her. In the dream we made love. We were on the beach, lying in the sand, hidden by a cove. I tasted the salt of the sea on her lips. She locked her legs around my waist and pulled me deep inside her . . .

. . . and then I woke up.

My bedroom was dark. It was raining outside. A flash of lightning and the crack of thunder startled me. I could hear something I recognized immediately as the clack of typewriter keys. My heart nearly seized in my chest.

I swung my feet over the edge of the bed and stood on shaky legs. I headed down the hallway, moving cautiously to my office. The door was closed. No light shone beneath the door. Someone was not only typing on my typewriter, they were doing it in the dark.

I took hold of the door knob. My palm was slick with sweat. I turned the knob slowly and pushed the door open, then I reached into the room and ran my hand along the wall, searching for the light switch.

The typing stopped.

I flipped the switch, flooding the room with soft yellow light. There was no one at the desk. The typewriter was silent. A piece of paper had been rolled into the platen. I read the words that had been typed onto the paper: *I ask you now to close your eyes, if you dare to fantasize. You will hear the gentle sigh of a doll with pale blue eyes.*

I read those four lines of text again and again, trying to make sense of them. Who'd written them? What did they mean?

I turned away from the typewriter and saw her sitting in a corner of my office. She was wearing one of Anna's nighties, a short see-through black number.

And I swear she smiled at me.

I grabbed the doll up and carried her back downstairs. The box was still where I'd left it. I tossed the doll inside and closed the lid. I planned to get rid of her first thing in the morning. She looked like Anna, true enough, but there was something unnatural about having her there.

I went back to bed. Sleep came gradually and fitfully. I dreamed of Anna again, dancing for me the way she often had when she was alive, wearing a thin negligee and panties, her hips swaying from one side to the other, hands behind her neck and on her hips and behind her back, grinding to the beat of old time rock 'n' roll. In my dream I tried to touch her, but every time I reached out, she slipped away from me . . .

. . . and then an explosion of thunder startled me from my sleep . . .

. . . to find her standing at the foot of my bed, a shadow wrapped in shadows.

Another flash of lightning and she removed the nightie, her dark hair catching on it as she brought it over her head, her breasts jiggling with the movement.

"Anna . . . ?"

The next flash of lightning illuminated her standing right beside the bed, reaching out to me.

It wasn't Anna, it was the doll.

She was alive.

The mattress shifted as she climbed into bed with me. She ran her hand across my chest, over my stomach, and slipped it beneath the covers. I felt her fingers slip under the elastic band of my briefs and encircle my erection.

"This is part of the dream?" I asked, but I knew the answer to the question. This was no dream. She was here, warm and real and alive.

She bent down and kissed me. Her lips were full and soft, her breath tasted sweet on my lips. She began to jerk me off, a nice slow rhythm, her fingers tightening with just the right pressure, her thumb concentrated on the sensitive spot just below my glands. She knew exactly what to do as only Anna would know how to do it.

She explored my mouth with her tongue. I sucked it, I took it as deep as possible, I tried to bring it inside me, tried to make it part of me. It was a kiss I never wanted to end.

When the kiss did finally end, Anna made her way to my chest. She teased my nipples with her tongue. She licked and nibbled them. She worked her way down, planting wet little kisses on my stomach, and then she pushed the cover away and straddled me, slowly backing up until her hard nipples dragged over my thighs.

She grabbed my briefs and pulled them down, exposing my hard-on. I watched as she teased the head of it with her tongue and then took it in one hand and brought it into her mouth. She swirled her tongue around the head of it and sucked at the same time. The warm, wet sensation drove me mad. She went down further, taking more of my dick into her mouth. It seemed as if she were sucking and licking and nibbling all at once.

She raised up and took off her panties. She held them against my face and I inhaled the heady scent I knew so well— the scent of Anna's pussy.

I slid my hands over her waist, over the curve of her bottom, lifting her up as she reached back and brought the tip of my cock to rest between the soft, plump, and very damp lips of her pussy. She didn't put it in yet. She rubbed the head of my cock between those lips, caressing it against the silky-slick folds.

"Do you want me?" she asked, her voice breathy and full of desire.

"Yes, I want you," I responded.

She came down and kissed me again, her lips just touching mine, and whispered, "I love you."

"I love you too, Anna."

She slowly sat back, pressing her wet pussy down on my cock, and then she grabbed the headboard for support as she began to ride me, working her hips in slow circles, grinding back and forth, her breasts bouncing and jiggling above my face in a tempting invitation.

I reached down and cupped her round, soft ass in my hands, squeezing my fingers into her cheeks so I could raise and lower her on my cock. I could feel the lips of her pussy against my fingertips, I felt my cock slick and hard as it moved in and out of her. I brushed the puckered entrance of her asshole and then slipped it into her, exploring that tight, hot little region.

She rode me hard, bouncing on my cock, panting and moaning. The cheeks of her ass slammed down on me, my finger plunged deeper into her tight bottom. She let go of the headboard and fell on top of me, covering my face with her tits. I caught one dark nipple in my mouth and sucked hard on it, bathing it with my tongue. I did the same to the other one, working my way back and forth between them, sucking and nibbling, teasing the rubbery tips with my tongue . . .

She raised up suddenly and lay back on the mattress, keeping my cock inside her as she did. She pulled her knees back and I grabbed her by the ankles, lifting her feet high in the air, spreading her legs wide apart. The lips of her pussy clung to my cock and folded in and out with every stroke.

I reached down and pressed my thumb to her clit. I manipulated it, rubbed it with a concentrated circular motion until Anna, my doll, began to gasp and pant and slam her hips up at me to meet every thrust of my cock.

"I'm coming," she said, barely getting the words out between gasps.

She pulled her ankles free of my grasp and locked her legs around my waist, pulling me deep inside her. I pumped faster, spurred on by Anna's fast-approaching climax. Her body shook beneath me. The slick, hot walls of her pussy tightened around my cock. Her muscles contracted, caressing the length of my cock, coaxing me to climax just as Anna reached her own. My cock jerked inside the tight confines of her cunt and unleashed a thick and creamy torrent of pent-up passion. I pulled out of her, releasing a flood that left the sheets soaking wet.

We didn't stop there. I pulled her to her hands and knees and entered her from behind, reaching under her to play with her tits, I twisted and tugged her nipples and slammed my cock into her come-flooded pussy.

We made love in the shower, we went down to the kitchen and I fucked her on the kitchen table. We went outside and had sex in the backyard as the wind howled, thunder cracked, and lightning fractured the night sky.

Back inside the house, Anna went to her knees and took my cock in her mouth. She used one hand to stroke my shaft and the other to massage my balls. She tightened her mouth around the head of my cock and sucked. I closed my eyes and let her take me to the edge one more time, filling her mouth with the last bit of come I was able to manage that night.

We took a long shower together. I ran soapy hands over her tits and slipped soapy fingers into her pussy. She soaped my cock and balls and worked up a thick lather. We stood under the hot spray of water and rinsed off, then we got out and spent some time drying one another with a thick, fluffy towel.

We went to bed naked. She snuggled up beside me. I draped one arm across her midriff and cradled her head against my shoulder.

"Will you be going away?" I asked.

"I'll always be with you," she promised.

We kissed.

"I love you," she said.

"I love you too, doll," I told her.

Those were the last words I ever spoke to my dead wife. . .

My Friend's Hot Mom

My buddy Chuck and me hang out at Starbucks because that's where the intellectual pussy is, and trust me, the intellectual pussy is the good stuff. Those chicks are so busy being intellectual that when they do finally drop their panties, it's completely over the top.

We were sitting at Starbucks and doing what we do best when Chuck brought up the fact that Spring break was coming and that he'd promised his mom he'd spend it at home. He asked me if I wanted to come along.

"Hell, why not?" I said, taking a sip of a large Café Latte. "What the fuck else do I have to do?"

Chuck knew what I meant. He had about as much going on in his life as I did, which was absolutely nothing. We were two college students majoring in beer and babes, with an emphasis on the beer.

Chuck was from southern California. I'd never been to California before, so I was looking forward to fun, sun, and chicks in bikinis. If I was *real* lucky, maybe a good portion of those chicks would be tanning their titties.

There was one slight problem I had to overcome. We were flying from Chicago to California. I hate planes. The way I see it, God gave birds the ability to fly, not people. You can talk about statistics all you want, but it doesn't change my mind one bit about air travel. Maybe there *are* more car accidents than plane accidents, but in an airplane crash the odds are pretty damn good it won't work out well for *any* of the passengers.

Chuck reminded me of the southern Cal girls and their sun-tanned tits. That's all it took to get me on the plane, and after a few rough moments at take-off, I started relaxing a bit. I closed my eyes and thought about that whole Mile-High-Club thing, drifting off to sleep, dreaming about the stewardess with the long red hair and baby-blue eyes, and oh man, what we did together in the cramped bathroom of that 747 . . .

. . . Next thing I knew, I was jolted awake as we touched down at LAX.

Chuck's mom met us at the airport. It was love at first sight for me. She was the hottest fucking MILF I've ever seen. Blonde hair, blue eyes, and very busty. She was wearing a pair of ass-hugging jeans, a tank top, and sandals. I later found out she was thirty-nine, but I'm here to tell you, girls half that age couldn't hold a candle to her.

Chuck was good enough to let me ride shotgun. I kept sneaking glances at Chuck's mom the whole way, trying to imagine her naked. I had to shift in the seat more than once because my cock was hard and threatening to pop my zipper. I was relieved as hell when we finally reached our destination and I could get out of the car to discreetly make an adjustment.

I followed Chuck into the house and upstairs, both of us lugging our bags. He left his stuff in his old bedroom, then showed me where the guest room was.

"The next room down is mom's room, the bathroom is at the end of the hall."

"Cool," I said.

He left me alone to settle in. I plopped down on the bed, slipping my hands behind my head, and stared up at the ceiling for a long time, thinking about Chuck's mom and how hot she was. Thinking about her bedroom being right next to the room I was in was enough to give me another hard-on.

Chuck pounded on my door a few minutes later. "Mom made us some sandwiches," he said. "You hungry?"

I followed him down to the kitchen, noting with disappointment that his mom was nowhere in sight.

"Where's your mom?" I asked, trying to sound as casual as I could.

"Went to get her nails done," he said, taking a bite from his sandwich. "You want something to drink?"

"Sure," I said.

He got a bottle of Coke from the refrigerator and poured two glasses full.

"Dude, you're mom is hot," I said, regretting the words as soon as they were out of my mouth.

"Like I've never heard *that* before," he said with a snort. "All my friends wanna fuck her."

"What about your dad?" I asked.

"They got divorced last year," he said.

"So . . . does your mom see anybody?"

He shrugged. "I don't ask."

I didn't want to push it, so I dropped the subject, although I couldn't stop thinking about Chuck's mom and wanted to know as much about her as I could.

"Wanna go out for some pizza tonight?" he asked. "I'll introduce you to some of the guys down at Barney's Place, we'll shoot some pool, drink a few beers . . ."

"Sounds good."

What I really wanted to do was hang around the house with Chuck's mom. That sounded way better than a bunch of sweaty guys, pizza, and beer. Hell, I wasn't even thinking about the bikini-clad babes anymore. Still, I didn't really have a choice. What was I supposed to do, tell my best friend I wanted to hang around the house hoping to catch a glimpse of his mom in the buff? I couldn't imagine that shit going over real well.

So I spent most of the night at Barney's Place. The pizza wasn't bad, the beer was good, and Chuck's friends bored the fuck out of me.

* * *

My head hurt like hell the next morning. Not that I can't handle my beer, but I'd really tied one on the night before. I sat up in bed, checked my watch and saw that it was almost noon, then pulled on jeans and a T-shirt and wandered downstairs to join the land of the living.

Nobody was home. A note by the coffee pot informed me that Chuck and his mom were visiting family members and wouldn't be back until later that night. I was to make myself at home and help myself to anything I wanted. The note was written in flowery, feminine cursive and signed Amanda.

Just seeing her name was enough to make me forget about my headache.

I poured a cup of strong black coffee and stepped out to the patio for a cigarette, then I went upstairs to take a shower. Amanda's bedroom door was wide open. I couldn't resist taking a look inside.

Her bedspread was soft and thick and covered with rose patterns, her pillows were big and fluffy, and there was a white teddy bear sitting against the headboard. White lace curtains covered her bedroom window. A vanity dresser loaded with perfume and makeup sat against the wall on the far side of the room, and there was a nightstand beside the bed.

A pair of track shoes lay on the floor at the foot of the bed with a pair of dirty white socks draped over them. Next to her shoes, partially hidden under the bed, was a pair of silky red panties.

I got a rush like taking a plunge down the last drop on a roller coaster. My heart pounded against the inside of my chest. My palms were sweating. I could feel every throb of my cock as it pushed against the front of my jeans. Being in her room was wrong. It was an invasion of her privacy and a violation of her trust, but goddamn, it was exciting as hell.

I picked up her panties and held them to my face, enjoying the cool feel of the silk against my skin. I sniffed the crotch. The smell of her pussy made me dizzy.

I yanked my zipper down so fast that it caught on the loose skin. I took a deep breath, corrected the miscalculation, and pulled my dick out anyway, wrapping the cool silk around it to soothe the pain.

I grabbed one of her socks and rolled it over my dick like a condom, then I laid her panties out on the bed and pressed my nose against the pussy-scented crotch, inhaling deeply as I jerked the sock up and down on my prick.

I licked her panties as I pumped the sock on my dick. In my mind I could see Amanda with me, spread out on her bed, naked except for the panties. I was eating her, licking her cunt through the panties, then I was fucking her, holding the panties to the side while I pounded her sweet pussy.

The fantasy was too much. My cock jerked quite a few times, pumping a creamy load of come into the sock, and pretty soon I felt it soaking through, making my fingers all wet and sticky. I licked her panties long after I finished coming, savoring the faint traces of Amanda's pussy juice.

I draped the sock back over her shoes and put her panties back where I'd found them, hoping the sock would dry fast and Amanda wouldn't find me out.

I couldn't leave the room without looking in the nightstand. There was no telling what I'd find. I wasn't disappointed. There was a bottle of K-Y Jelly and a long, thick dildo. I sniffed it, wondering if Amanda had used it recently. The thought of her fucking herself with that thing gave me another hard-on.

I jacked off in the shower. All I could do was picture Amanda in her bed at night, her legs wide open, two hands driving the dildo deep into her wet pussy. I squeezed my cock hard, leaned against the shower wall, and beat off until a hot stream of thick come crossed the width of the tub and splashed the sliding glass door that enclosed the shower.

I finished my shower, wondering what my chances were with Amanda. Could a woman like her ever go for a guy like me? For real, what did I have to offer her? She was older than me, definitely a lot more experienced, and able to get any real man she wanted. What chance did a college bum have?

* * *

Amanda went to bed early that night. Chuck turned in a little later, saying that he was going to try and get up early the next day and go hang out at the beach. I wasn't the least bit tired, so I made popcorn, grabbed a can of Coke, and flipped through the cable channels until I found a zombie flick that looked pretty good.

It wasn't good enough to take my mind off Amanda. I thought about her upstairs, wondering if she was sliding that huge rubber dildo into her pussy. I tried over and over again to focus my attention on the movie, but I kept thinking dirty thoughts about Amanda.

I soon found myself wandering upstairs, heading for Amanda's bedroom. I didn't expect to find her door partially open, and I sure as fuck didn't expect to hear soft moans coming from inside the room.

I couldn't resist a peek inside.

The room was dark, except for a few candles flickering on the nightstand and her dresser. Amanda was on her bed, naked and completely exposed, using the dildo on her pussy. Her head was turned to one side, looking away from the door, and her knees were bent and laid flat on the bed, totally exposing her pussy. She held the dildo with two hands, just the way I imagined, pushing it in and out of her pussy and pumping her hips to meet each thrust of the dildo.

I felt like a pervert for watching. If my behavior wasn't illegal (and I was pretty sure it was close), then it was at least morally questionable. Still, I couldn't get my feet to move. I couldn't tear myself away from the door.

My cock strained against the front of my jeans. I wanted to take it out and jerk off, but with Chuck's room right down the hall, I wasn't going to chance it. I sure as hell didn't want him to catch me jerking off outside his mom's bedroom.

Amanda moaned softly. It was music to my ears. I shuddered with pleasure at the sound of it . . .

. . . and then I coughed.

She stopped thrusting the dildo into her pussy and turned toward the door. I stepped to one side of the door and held my breath, sure I'd been busted.

Shit.

I rushed to the bathroom, praying she hadn't seen me and that she didn't know what I was up to. I took a deep breath, peed, and then stood for a couple of minutes, calming my nerves before going back into the hallway.

Amanda was waiting for me, standing in the bedroom doorway, one hand resting on the door jamb, her other hand on her hip. She was completely naked.

"I was, uh . . . the bathroom," I stammered.

"Right," she said. "The bathroom."

She smiled and motioned with her finger for me to follow her as she backed into her bedroom. I couldn't believe it. There wasn't a heartbeat of hesitation on my part. I followed like a trained puppy.

"Close the door," she said, climbing onto her bed.

I pulled the door shut and turned back to face Amanda. She was lying on one side, her head propped in her hand, looking at me with those sexy eyes. She motioned me over to her.

I went to stand at the side of the bed. I tried not to stare at her like I'd never seen a naked woman before, but damn, it was impossible.

"That was so naughty," she said, "watching me the way you were."

She leaned over and slid a hand up under my shirt. I felt her fingertips circle my nipples. The pleasure was so good it hurt.

"I know," told her. "I shouldn't have . . ."

"Well, don't worry about it," she said.

She withdrew her hand from under my shirt. I wanted it there again.

"Why don't you take that off," she said.

As I whipped my shirt over my head, she reached up and unzipped my pants, slipping her fingers inside to take out my cock.

"Very nice," she said, running her hand up and down my shaft. "Much better than my toy."

She suddenly let go of my cock and pulled away from me. "Take off everything," she said.

"What about Chuck?" I asked, glancing back at the bedroom door.

"Don't worry. He sleeps like a rock. Get naked for me."

I shoved my jeans to my ankles, pushing my underwear down with them, and stripped both off, dropping them on the floor beside me.

She reached up and stroked my cock again, then she swung her legs over the edge of the bed and sat up, scooting closer as she pulled me toward her by my cock. Her heavy tits swayed and jiggled as she settled in place.

"You look like you could use a little help with this," she said.

She squeezed my cock and leaned forward, flicking her soft, wet tongue against the tip of it. Her soft blonde hair fell around her face so I couldn't see what she was doing to me. It didn't matter. I could feel her tongue working around the head of my dick, teasing the sensitive spot underneath, and dancing around the edge of it.

She raised her head, brushing her hair from her face, and looked up at me with those sexy, seductive eyes. "Fuck my mouth," she said.

She opened her mouth and lowered her head, taking my cock to the back of her throat. She reached around and grabbed my ass, one cheek in each hand, and began pushing and pulling, drawing my cock deep into her mouth and out again.

"Shit," I groaned, sliding my fingers through her hair to grip the back of her head as my cock pushed in and out of her mouth.

I tried to take it easy on her, afraid my cock would choke her, but she wasn't having it. She encouraged me to pump my hips, to fuck her mouth with long, deep strokes, and that's exactly what I did.

She took my cock all the way down, sucking hard on it, using her tongue against my shaft. She came up, making her lips tight, holding like that for a few seconds before she finally let my cock slip from her mouth with a wet suction.

"Wanna fuck me from behind?" she asked.

Before I could answer, she turned around and got on her hands and knees, offering me her wide, pale ass. Jesus, I couldn't believe how fucking good it looked. I took her by the hips and eased my cock between her plump pussy lips, pushing through the slick pink folds.

She wiggled her bottom against me, working her pussy down on my cock.

"Don't be shy," she said. "Fuck me hard."

I held her hips tight and drove my dick all the way inside her, pulling right back out, then going in again. The tight, hot sensation of her pussy stroking my hard-on, the slick folds of her lips clinging to my cock—it was all I could do not to let myself go right then and there.

But I didn't do it. I wasn't about to disappoint Amanda. I wanted to last. I wanted to make her come again and again. I wanted to be the man to satisfy her wildest desires. I wanted to be the one she remembered.

"Harder," she cooed. "Come on, fuck that pussy."

Her heavy tits swung back and forth below her as she rocked up and down on my cock. I held on for the ride, driving her pussy hard, thrusting deep inside her.

I reached around her with one hand and caught one of her tits, squeezing the soft flesh and twisting a fat, hard nipple between my thumb and forefinger.

"Ummmmm," she moaned.

She rocked up and down on my cock, banging her ass back against me. Her cheeks quivered as they collided with my stomach. I could feel my balls swinging against her pussy, smacking her clit with every thrust. Then she threw herself forward, taking her pussy all the way off my cock. I stood there dumbfounded, feeling the cool air on the tip of my wet dick.

She rolled onto her back, spreading her legs wide, I climbed between her legs and reached down to guide my cock back inside her. She grabbed my ass and held tight as I fucked her.

"Hard," she panted. "Don't stop."

I pounded into her pussy, driving her down into the mattress. She pumped her hips at me, meeting my thrusts.

"Don't stop . . . make me come," she said. I fucked her harder and faster, pulling all the way out and going in again.

"Yes," she screamed. "Oh yeahhhhhh . . ."

She wrapped her legs around my waist and locked her ankles together, trapping me there. I felt her quivering tits pressing against my chest as her pussy clamped down around my cock.

"I'm coming," she gasped.

All I could do was hold on for the ride. I pressed my dick deep inside her and stayed put until she was finished.

We changed positions, turning on the bed so our feet were at the end of it. Amanda pushed me onto my back and mounted me, grabbing my dick as she sank her hot pussy all the way down on it.

She grabbed the headboard for support and started riding me. I couldn't believe how insatiable she was. She dangled her tits in my face and had me suck her nipples as she bounced on my dick.

It wasn't long before she was ready to come again.

"I want you to do it with me," she said.

She raised up, held the frame of the bed tight, and bucked wildly on top of me, up and down, back and forth . . .

She picked up the pace, bringing her hot pussy to the tip of my cock and then plunging down on me again.

"Shit . . . almost there," I groaned.

She fell over me, smothering me with her soft tits, grinding her pussy down on my cock. I felt my whole body tighten, then my dick exploded, squirting thick spurts of come deep inside her.

She came with me, moaning and panting, pressing her heavy tits against my face so I couldn't breathe. Fine by me. If I had to die of suffocation, between her tits was the way I wanted to go.

She finally sat up, allowing me to catch my breath.

She reached back behind her and stroked my balls with her fingertips. My cock was still hard inside her. I could feel my come leaking out.

She raised up off my cock and moved up until her sloppy wet pussy hovered above my face. The lips were swollen and glistening. My come dribbled out of her freshly fucked hole.

"Lick me," she said.

She lowered her pussy to my mouth, and before I had a chance to think about what she wanted me to do, I pushed my tongue inside her, feeling the hot, slick warmth of my own come rolling into my mouth.

Not that it bothered me. If licking up my come was the price I had to pay to have Amanda's sweet pussy on my face, I already had my wallet out. I used my thumbs to pull the lips of her pussy wide apart, and I pushed my tongue deep inside her, licking all around. I trapped her smooth pink clit between my lips and nibbled, then I washed it with the tip of my tongue, making her squirm and moan.

She scooted up so I could get to her tight little asshole. I worked my tongue around it, then pushed against the taut muscle, feeling it give just a little.

"Would you like to fuck my ass?" she asked.

She turned around and offered it to me.

"There's K-Y in the nightstand," she said.

I got the K-Y Jelly out and squeezed some on my cock, then I rubbed it all around her asshole, slowly working a finger into her. I didn't have any experience with anal sex. I was a little clumsy. She reached back between her legs and rubbed my balls as I eased the tip of my cock in her ass.

"Just push it in," she said, working her ass back against me.

I held her by the hips and pushed. My cock went in easy, filling her tight ass to the hilt. She gave a little grunt and rotated her ass, working my cock around inside her. I pulled back, nearly all the way out, then slid in again.

"Oh yeah," she groaned. "Fuck my ass."

I was never lucky enough to find a chick who'd let me fuck her in the ass, so doing it that way to Amanda was a dream come true. Her ass was unbelievably tight, clinging to my cock as I thrust in and out, my balls swinging hard against her pussy with every thrust.

When I came this time, I didn't think I was ever going to stop. My cock jerked into her ass. She pushed back against me and pumped her hips as I filled her ass with my hot, sticky come.

We stayed there in her bed for a long time after we finished, gathering our strength for another round.

I didn't spend much time with Chuck over the rest of Spring break. Most of my time was spent with Amanda. I'm not sure if Chuck ever figured out what was going on, and I sure as hell didn't tell him about it, but he never seemed surprised when I bowed out of some big party or beach blast he'd lined up for us.

By the time we headed back to school, Chuck was already talking about Ft. Lauderdale next Spring. I told him he'd be making the trip without me. I'd be heading back to California instead.

Who needs a bunch of hot college girls in bikinis when there's my friend's hot mom to keep me occupied?

New Year's Ball

Carrie listened in disbelief as her husband told her why it would be a good idea for the two of them to attend a sex party on New Year's eve. The party was being thrown by the CEO of the company he worked for. That was Jason's justification. It would be good for his image at work. Only high-ranking employees of the company were invited to these special events, and the fact that Jason had been included in the invitations this year meant that he would be moving up in the company.

"It's just sex," Jason said.

"Just sex?" she responded, barely able to hide the indignation in her voice. "You're talking about fucking other women, Jason. You're talking about other men fucking me . . . how can you say it's only sex?"

"It is," he said.

She looked at him for a long moment, considering seriously what he was asking of her. While she wasn't sure she could go through with such a thing, the more she thought about it, the more she liked the idea of trying. Maybe he was right, after all. Maybe it was just sex. If she could look at it like that, maybe she could bring herself to open up and enjoy the party for what it was.

"If you really believe we should do this," she said, "then I'm willing to try."

* * *

Jason whistled in appreciation when he saw Carrie dressed for the party. She had her dark hair pulled up on top of her head, with one curl falling against her cheek. She wore a black form-fitting dress with a plunging neckline that displayed plenty of creamy cleavage, sheer black stockings with lace patterns, and a pair of high-heeled pumps to round it all off.

"Wow," he said, "if you weren't already my wife, I'd ask you to marry me."

She smiled. "Are you sure you want to take me to this party then?"

"Why wouldn't I?"

"Well, if I look that good . . ."

"I know who you'll be going home with," he said confidently.

"That's true," she said, kissing him hard on the mouth.

He slid his hands up the backs of her legs and beneath her short dress and squeezed her ass through her thin panties, pulling her tight against him.

She broke the embrace. "We're not going to get there this way," she said.

He looked into her eyes for a long moment, then said, "I believe you're more excited about this event than I am."

She gave him a soft smile. "Maybe," she replied.

* * *

The CEO of Jason's company was Travis Martin. He lived in a ten-bedroom mansion on 100 acres of land in a secluded private development. The property featured iron gates and stone walls. Gas lamps lit the curved driveway. The house featured huge windows and every inch of the interior was lit up. There were cars lining the driveway.

"Wow, there are a lot of people here," Carrie said.

"It's a big company."

"I thought only the executives were allowed to attend."

"And anyone they care to invite, up to a limit," Jason said. "It is an orgy, after all, so the more the merrier."

Jason found a place to park. He and Carrie went inside. Travis spotted them as soon as they entered the living room. He waved and came over to greet them.

"You look lovely tonight," he said to Carrie.

"Thank you," she replied.

She couldn't help but notice how handsome Travis looked. He had dark hair, deep blue eyes, and an appealing smile. His nose was strong and his cheeks were sharp and well defined. She locked eyes with him and lingered there a moment, then Travis turned to Jason and said, "Good to see you, Jason. There's plenty to eat, open bars, and when you're ready to join the fun, there are some *special* events going on upstairs and out by the pool."

Jason and Carrie exchanged a quick glance. He was ready for this. He wondered if she might change her mind, but the look in her eyes told him all he needed to know. She was not only still in, she seemed more eager about it with each passing second.

They stopped by the bar for a drink, then Jason took her around and introduced her to some of the people he worked with. She'd met a couple of them, but most of the faces were unfamiliar.

Gradually, after she became bored with the business mingling, Carrie made her way to one of the tables serving food. She had an egg roll, which was very good, and then corn chips dipped in a white cheese sauce with crushed red pepper.

She looked for Jason on the lower floor after she finished eating, and when she couldn't find him anywhere on the lower floor, she wandered outside and through an entrance leading to the pool area.

Even though Travis had mentioned it earlier, Carrie was still caught by surprise when she saw what was going on around the pool. There were thirty or so people in various stages of undress, some chatting casually while others engaged in various forms of sexual activity in a number of combinations.

Carrie was no Virgin Mary, but she had only read about this kind of thing in her life. She'd certainly never seen it before, even depicted in any movie she'd ever watched, and up until tonight, she had never known anyone who engaged in this sort of behavior.

She stood for a long moment and watched women making out with women, men with men, couples, threesomes, foursomes, and more in every combination imaginable. She was about to turn around and leave when she saw Jason. He was on the far side of the pool, naked and in the midst of a pile of other naked people. She almost hadn't seen him, but he'd stood up suddenly, his erection sticking up hard and thick. A beautiful blonde with large, natural breasts was on her knees in front of him, stroking his dick as she licked the head of it.

Carrie considered going back inside. It didn't bother her so much to see Jason engaged in sex with a bunch of strangers. Not like she thought it would. She was, however, a little confused about her place in all this. Should she take off her clothes and join him, or should she go off and find her own adventure? She didn't have long to think about it before she felt a firm hand on her wrist and a deep, comfortable voice say, "Come on."

She turned to face the man who had taken the liberty of assuming she wanted to go with him. It was Travis. He was smiling at her. It was a sexy smile, very warm and reassuring.

"The best way to get used to it is to jump right in," he said.

He led her to a fairly unoccupied area just away from the pool. She watched him undress and then followed suit. She found herself looking over at Jason. He was now fucking the blonde from behind while she sucked someone else's cock.

She turned her attention back to Travis. She had removed her dress and now stood before him in panties, stockings, and her heels. He admired her briefly before pulling her to him and kissing her hard on the mouth.

He slid his hands up over her breasts, rough palms rolling her nipples, his fingers squeezing into her creamy, pliant flesh.

She broke the kiss and slowly went to her knees, hesitating a moment before wrapping her fingers around his thick cock and bringing the head of it to her lips. She flicked her tongue against the tip of it and swirled it around the spongy-soft head, then she slipped her mouth around his dick and took it slowly to the back of her throat.

His hands moved around to settle on the back of her head. Each time she came up, he pulled her down on him again, repeating the process until he was moving her mouth up and down on his cock at a steady pace.

She had always considered herself good at giving head. She'd never had any complaints, and in most cases, men had always been quite verbal in expressing their appreciation. Travis turned out to be no different.

"God, where did you learn to do that so well?" he asked, following the question up with a long, deep-throated moan.

She resisted the urge to take her mouth from his cock long enough to answer such a silly question. *Why, practice, Travis,* she imagined herself saying to him. *Sucking lots of cock is the best way to learn.*

She had to resist giggling around his cock. There would be something inherently unexciting about that. Most men, in her limited experience, did not take kindly to giggling of any kind during sex. Their insecurities kicked in. It made them uncomfortable. Not all, of course, but *most.*

Carrie took her mouth from Travis' cock and stroked it, using her saliva as lubrication, pushing the somewhat loose skin of his shaft up and down. A little pearly drop of pre-come leaked from the tip of his dick and she caught it with her tongue and let it roll to the back of her throat.

She liked the taste of come. A lot of women didn't. Jason had mentioned that to her several times early on in their relationship. It amazed him that she liked it as much as she did. He had never known a woman who would swallow. The fact that she made no fuss about it had definitely been a selling point for him.

She took Travis' cock in her mouth again, only this time she applied a firm, steady suction as she moved her hand up and down his shaft. She felt the heat and pulse of his cock against her tongue.

He tangled his fingers in her hair and drew her down on him, sliding more of his cock into her mouth. His hips began to move as he took control and fucked her mouth with long, easy strokes.

She reached up to caress his balls. They were loose, hanging gently against the palm of her hand. She closed them in her fingers and massaged them.

"Ummm, that's so nice," he said, groaning.

She moved her hand faster on his cock, wanting to taste his come. She could sense the nearness of his orgasm.

"Oh, yes . . ." he moaned.

He pushed into her mouth one last time, keeping his cock there as he exploded. His body tensed and he groaned deeply, wrapping her hair around his fingers. His cock jerked in her mouth and she felt the first hot spurt of come across her tongue. It hit the back of her throat and she swallowed hard, taking it all down. A second spurt came with just as much force. She gulped again.

When he finished, Travis withdrew his cock, letting it rest against her lips. She smiled up at him and then licked the remaining drops of come from his cock, then she took it into her mouth and gave the head of his dick a quick suck, making sure there was nothing left over.

He pulled her to her feet and kissed her. She slipped her sticky tongue past his lips and into his mouth. It excited her to know that he could taste his come on her lips and tongue, and even more so because he seemed to enjoy it.

She looked over to where Jason had been and saw that he was no longer there. She was curious as to where he might have gotten off to, but she was more interested in feeling Travis' cock inside her. She turned her attention to Travis again, reaching down to stroke his semi-hard dick.

"I want you to take me from behind," she said. "I want to feel your cock sliding into my pussy while I'm on my hands and knees."

She moved into position, offering her smooth, creamy bottom to him. She wiggled it invitingly and he settled in behind her, running his hands over the cheeks and opening her so he could get a good look at her pussy.

He slipped a finger into her moist opening and moved it around inside her. He slowly withdrew it and massaged her clitoris, then he lifted his dick and rubbed it against her pink folds a few times before inserting it.

He slid his hands over her ass and around to take her by the hips. She rocked back against him, pushing her pussy down over his cock as he eased into her. She felt the lips parting, stretching to fit around him. He slid into her completely, pressing his balls against her clit, and then he withdrew almost all the way before he went into her again.

She loved the way he felt inside her. Each stroke filled her completely. She could feel the weight of his balls slapping her pussy with every thrust, banging away at her and sending electric shocks of pleasure through her whole body.

She looked up and saw Jason approaching. He was alone now, still naked, his cock dangling against his thigh as he knelt in front of her.

She felt a little odd now, enjoying Travis' cock with her husband so near, but she felt aroused all the same. She made no secret about the fact that she was enjoying herself, and by the look in Jason's eyes, he was enjoying her pleasure almost as much as she was.

He stroked his cock and moved it within easy reach. She licked it and took it into her mouth, sucking hard as he slid to the back of her throat.

Travis dug his fingers into her soft skin and held on as he fucked her. She tightened her mouth around Jason's cock and sucked harder.

Another woman joined them. She thought it was the same blonde Jason had been with earlier, but she couldn't be sure.

Jason took his cock from her mouth and the blonde took over. She sucked Jason's cock for a minute, then she started kissing Carrie. It was weird for Carrie at first, since she had never kissed a girl in her life, except for one time in high school, and that had been nothing like this. She liked it, though, and soon she was returning the kiss, slipping her tongue into the blonde girl's mouth.

Jason moved around behind her and took Travis' place. He slid his cock into her slick pussy while Travis came around to kneel beside her. She reached up to stroke his cock as she continued kissing the blonde.

The blonde broke the kiss and gave her attention to Travis. Carrie guided Travis' cock into the blonde's mouth and jerked him off as the blonde gave him a blow job. It wasn't long before Travis was on the verge of another orgasm.

Someone else joined them. Another man. Carrie thought she knew him. Maybe someone she'd met at one of the company Christmas parties.

Jason came inside her and moved away. The new man immediately slid his cock inside her.

Two more women joined them. One was a brunette, the other had long blonde hair with purples streaks in it. The blonde with the purple streaks straddled Jason and settled down on his cock, bringing it back to life.

The brunette moved around behind Carrie and began to massage her clit as the guy she thought she recognized picked up the pace of his thrusts. He didn't last long and then someone else took over.

Later, after Carrie had some champagne, she found the blonde with the purple hair. Her name was Sheila. She was the girlfriend of one of the higher ups. She was twenty-four and still a bit on the wild side. Carrie liked her personality. They hit it off and found a quiet room upstairs. Carrie had never been with a woman fully, and after the round of kissing earlier in the night, she wanted to see just how far she could go with another woman.

Sheila started kissing Carrie as soon as they were on the bed. She ran her hands over Carrie's breasts as she guided her back. Carrie drew her knees up and Sheila climbed on top of her, settling herself between Carrie's legs so their pussies pressed together.

Carrie wrapped her legs around Sheila and arched her back. She slid her arms around Sheila's neck and pulled her down so they could kiss.

Sheila slowly made her way down, circling each of Carrie's nipples with her tongue, leaving a damp trail down to Carrie's belly. She put her head between Carrie's legs and licked Carrie's pussy. Her tongue danced across Carrie's clit and between the silky folds of her pussy, finally settling at the opening as Sheila worked it inside her.

There was something to be said for being eaten by another woman. Maybe there was something to be said about how one woman knows what another likes. Carrie wasn't sure she would know what might turn Sheila on, but she was sure Sheila had the instinct. The girl was skilled with her tongue, no doubt about it, and when she added two fingers, it was all over for Carrie. She reached an orgasm that tensed her muscles and made her scream. When it was finally over, she fell back on the bed, gasping and panting as she tried to regain her composure.

When it came time to return the favor, Carrie knelt between Sheila's legs and lowered her head tentatively. Sheila's pussy was completely shaved. She had a little heart tattooed on her bare pubic mound. Her outer lips opened to reveal the bright pink folds of her inner lips. Carrie hesitated and then kissed Sheila's inner thighs, first her right, then her left, gradually working her way to Sheila's pussy.

Carrie licked around the opening of Sheila's pussy and then worked her way up, bringing her tongue over Sheila's clit, which was engorged and peeking from beneath its hood. Carrie caught Sheila's clit between her lips and nibbled, trying to do something to Sheila that she knew she enjoyed. It seemed to work. Sheila's breathing became deeper and then faster. Her soft moans increased in volume until she was moaning so loud and with such intensity that Carrie felt the vibrations against her lips.

Sheila pushed up against Carrie's face and locked her knees together, holding Carrie against her as she reached her orgasm.

"That was incredible," Carrie said when they were lying together afterward.

"You were awesome," Sheila said.

"First time," Carrie admitted.

"Really?"

Sheila could hardly contain her amazement at the admission.

The party was still going full blast. A clock on the dresser read 11:59 in bold red letters. Carrie wondered if she should go find Jason for the traditional New Year's kiss. She glanced over at Sheila and decided Jason would be all right on his own tonight.

The red numbers flipped over. The new year had arrived. An explosion of noise erupted from various parts of the house and out by the pool.

"Happy New Year," Sheila said.

"Happy New Year," Carrie replied.

Then they embraced and brought in the new year with a hot kiss.

Not-So-Sleeping Beauty

My wife Jackie is beautiful. She's faithful, kind, and considerate. We have a good marriage. She is everything a man would want his wife to be.

Unfortunately, she was my second choice. It was her sister Gina I wanted more than anything. Gina is five years younger than Jackie. She's vibrant and sexy and full of life. She was the wild child of the family.

I never got a chance to pursue Gina. She married some rich guy and moved away. Jackie and I began a relationship that started with friendship and grew into something more romantic.

We were married a year later.

Gina came to stay with us last week. She was divorcing her rich husband, who, as it turned out, was an abusive alcoholic.

The day Gina arrived, I knew I was in trouble. All the old feelings I had for her came rushing back. Looking at her took my breath away. Wavy auburn hair, green eyes, long legs, and skin as smooth and pale as cream—she was a vision.

The flirting started right away. I told myself I was going to be a good boy, but when Gina turned on the charm, I fell immediately under her spell.

She wasn't so obvious the first couple days. A few subtle looks, a suggestive comment here and there . . .

But then she turned up the heat. It was a Friday morning. I was in the kitchen having a cup of coffee. Jackie was upstairs taking a shower. Gina came into the kitchen wearing a silky kimono-style robe cinched at the waist. The robe came down just far enough to cover the slight rise of her well-shaped ass.

I was sitting at the kitchen table. Gina went to the counter where the coffeemaker sat. She had to stand on tippy toes to reach the overhead cabinet where the coffee mugs were. When she did, the back of her robe rode up just high enough to give me a peek at her pale blue panties stretched snug over the well-rounded cheeks of her ass.

I turned my attention quickly to the newspaper, lit a cigarette, and tried to concentrate on my morning routine. It wasn't easy, believe me.

Gina poured coffee and sat across the table from me.

"You're awfully quiet this morning," she said.

"Just reading the headlines," I replied, trying to sound casual.

I glanced at her over the top of the newspaper. She was watching me. There was something in her eyes that told me she knew the affect she was having on me.

"Good coffee," she said.

"Starbucks."

I let my eyes fall down to where the robe fell slightly away from one breast. I could see the smooth curve of her tit and just a glimpse of pale pink aureole. I quickly looked away, but not before Gina caught me in the act.

"Shame on you," she said with a smile.

"Sorry," I muttered.

I lowered my eyes back to the newspaper.

"Don't be sorry. I'd wear more if I had a problem with it."

Before I could respond to that, Jackie came into the kitchen. She poured coffee and joined us at the table. She was freshly showered and ready for the day.

"I say we have a girls' day out?" she said to Gina. "We'll do lots of shopping, have lunch, catch a movie . . . what do you think?"

"Sounds like fun," Gina said. She finished her coffee. "Let me grab a quick shower first, okay?"

She got up and headed out of the kitchen. Even with my wife sitting right beside me, I caught myself checking out Gina's departing backside.

Jackie caught me too.

"You like what you see?" she asked.

I was embarrassed. Any attempt at justifying my behavior would've only gotten me into trouble, so I gave her a simple, "I'm sorry," and went back to reading the newspaper.

As soon as the girls left the house, I went upstairs to Gina's room. I wanted to find something of hers I could touch—something distinctly private and off limits.

I went into her bathroom. Her hairbrush lay on the sink, her make-up case was open, and a bottle of Charlie sat on the glass shelf above the sink, along with a tube of pale pink lipstick. I opened the lipstick and sniffed it. I touched it to the tip of my tongue, thinking about how Gina had run the lipstick over her full lips.

Something caught my eye. The short robe she'd worn this morning was hanging on the back of the bathroom door, and right there on the floor, in a silky little pile, were the panties she'd worn too.

I picked them up and rubbed my thumb over the crotch. They were still damp. I sniffed them, deeply inhaling the heavy, rich scent of Gina's pussy. My cock was hard. I unzipped my pants and took it out, still holding Gina's panties to my face as I stroked myself with my free hand.

I went back into the bedroom and went through her dresser. The top drawer contained shirts, all neatly folded, and a couple of pairs of shorts. The second drawer was panties, bras, and socks. There were pajamas and assorted negligees in the third drawer. I shuffled around through the negligees and found an ivory vibrator at the bottom of the drawer. It was modestly sized and shaped like a bullet.

I closed my eyes and imagined the smooth tip of the vibrator sliding into Gina's pussy. I wrapped her silky panties around my cock and jerked off. It felt good, and the more I thought about Gina, the more I became convinced I wanted to fuck her.

I groaned as I released my come into her panties. I wiped myself off, rinsed her panties in the sink, and returned them to where I'd found them, hoping she wouldn't notice I'd tampered with them.

Jackie and Gina wanted to stay up all night watching horror movies. They'd bought four classic horror DVDs, several bottles of wine, and cheese and summer sausage for snacking. I tried to bow out, but they insisted I stay up and participate in their little party.

Gina wore a halter top and a pair of loose shorts. When she sat just right, I could see up under her shorts. She wasn't wearing panties. She knew I was watching. I caught her smiling at me on more than one occasion. Jackie was oblivious to her sister's flirtations.

We finished off two of the bottles of wine in pretty good time. My wife said she wanted to put on something more comfortable. She went upstairs. Fifteen minutes went by and she still hadn't returned.

"I better check on her," I said.

I found her in our bedroom. She'd managed to change into her nightgown and fall across the bed. She was passed out. I grabbed hold of her ankles, lifted her legs onto the bed, and drew a cover over her.

Gina was pouring more wine when I got back downstairs. She handed a glass to me. I sat on the love seat. "Jackie's out," I said.

"Really?"

"Yep. I'm not surprised. She's never been able to drink much."

I glanced at the TV. A killer was stalking through the woods, pursuing a nearly naked college chick. The girl was running so hard she could barely catch her breath. The killer was simply walking fast, but somehow he managed to gain on the young blonde.

"I love this stuff," I said.

"Me too," Gina agreed.

She had shifted her position on the couch so I had clear view up her shorts. I could see the plump shaved lips of her pussy and even a little flash of pink.

I reached down the front of my jeans surreptitiously and adjusted my hard-on. She glanced over just in time to catch me in the act.

"Problems?" she asked, a knowing smile spreading across her face.

I felt my cheeks warm and I knew I was turning red. I felt like a pervert who'd been caught jerking off in a darkened movie theater.

She thankfully turned her attention back to the TV set. I followed suit, trying quite unsuccessfully to focus on the movie. I kept looking over at her, sneaking peeks between her legs, hoping to see more pussy.

"I'm horny," she said suddenly, her tone as casual as if she'd only suggested she was tired and going to bed. She faced me, her legs slightly parted. "Do you mind if I play with myself?"

She slid a hand between her legs and rubbed the front of her shorts. She moved her free hand over one of her breasts and caressed it. She watched me as she did, fixing her sexy green eyes on my face. I held her gaze for a long moment before dropping my eyes down between her legs.

She took off her halter, revealing small, firm tits with pale pink nipples. She took a nipple between the thumb and forefinger of each hand and began to tug and twist them until they stood fully erect.

She took off her shorts next, proving I was right about her lack of panties. She leaned back on the couch and brought her feet up to rest on the edge of the coffee table, letting her knees fall open. The pink folds of her inner lips were slick and protruding from between her plump outer lips.

Gina ran her hands over her thighs, brought them up over her belly, and then slid them between her legs. She pulled the outer lips of her smooth-shaven pussy open, giving me a good look at her wet pink opening.

Jesus, I wanted to bury my face between her legs and press my face into that sweet pussy. I could almost smell it from where I sat. The sight of it was certainly having a strained effect on me. I shifted a bit uncomfortably.

"Take out your cock," she said. "I want you to jerk off while you watch me."

I didn't need to be told twice. I unzipped and pulled my dick out. I wrapped my right hand around it and began tugging up and down.

Gina took the fat summer sausage from the coffee table, held it with two hands, and pushed the rounded uncut end against her cunt. No way she'd be able to push it inside her, but she didn't need to. She humped the sausage, rubbing her pussy against it, her head leaning against the back of the couch. She closed her eyes and enjoyed the sensation of the meat rubbing between her pussy lips.

I worked my hand on my cock. I wanted so badly to go over and fuck her. Part of me realized I was being unfaithful to my wife right now, just by doing what I was doing, and Gina was being unfaithful to her as well. I felt bad, but I couldn't help myself. I wanted my sister-in-law more than I'd ever wanted any woman.

"Let's go to your room," I said.

She shook her head. "We can't. It wouldn't be right."

"This isn't right either. We've come this far, why stop now?"

"This is as far as it goes. I'm turned on by you, but I'm not fucking my sister's husband. I won't do it."

She set the sausage aside and began fingering her pussy with one hand, massaging her tits and nipples with the other.

"Just let me eat your pussy," I said.

I was sure she heard desperation in my voice, and believe me, I *was* desperate.

"Nope," she said adamantly. She pushed two fingers into her pussy and pumped them in and out. I could see her juices flowing over the fingers, running out to soak the couch cushion. Her nipples were hard. She pushed a tit up and dropped her head so she could suck the nipple.

I jerked my cock faster. I could feel my balls tighten. I was so close, so ready to come, but I didn't want to do it all over my hand.

"Suck my cock," I said, breathing harder now. She shook her head. She continued to finger herself. Her eyes were closed. She wasn't watching me now. Her breathing quickened, her breasts rose and fell in an unsteady rhythm. I could see she was close to getting off.

Then I heard Jackie at the top of the stairs. Thank God she made noise before she came down. Gina just barely managed to get her halter top and shorts back on. I zipped my pants up and crossed my legs, hoping to hide my erection.

"I went out for a minute," Jackie said as she came into the living room.

"I was going to let you sleep," I said.

"I woke up dizzy. I really can't handle drinking."

She sat beside Gina on the couch.

Gina and I exchanged a nervous glance. I felt like Jackie could see right through us, as if she knew what we'd been doing and she wasn't letting on. She had no clue, as it turned out, but my guilty conscience had me thinking otherwise.

"Want some more wine?" I held the bottle up, ready to fill her glass.

"No way," she said, laying her hand over the top of her glass. "If I have any more wine, I'll probably pass out before I can make it upstairs again."

Gina poured more wine for herself and lit a cigarette. I couldn't keep my eyes off her. I was afraid Jackie would catch me checking her sister out, so I was careful not to be overly obvious, but all I could think about was her wet pussy and the way she'd stuck her fingers inside herself.

We watched the rest of the movie that was on, then Gina said she was tired and ready for bed. She kissed her sister on the cheek, said goodnight to me, and headed upstairs. She tossed me a look over her shoulder as she went up the stairs. I wasn't sure what she wanted, but there was a definite invitation in there.

I poured more wine. I was eager to get upstairs to Gina. That meant my wife needed to go to bed, but she had put another DVD in. I handed her the wine. She took it this time, drank most of it, and let me refill her glass. It wasn't long before she was starting to feel the effects.

She leaned over and kissed me. It was a deep, horny kiss. I ran my hands over her gown, feeling her heavy tits through the thin material. Her nipples were hard.

I knelt on the floor in front of the couch and pushed her nightgown above her waist. She fell back on the couch and opened her legs wide. I licked her cunt through her panties, which were nice and damp.

She moaned.

I tugged the crotch of her panties to one side, exposing her dark brown bush. I smelled the hot, thick scent of her aroused pussy. She was soaking wet. I ran my tongue between her cunt lips, over the fleshy pink hood that hid her clitoris. I whipped my tongue against the fleshy hood and coaxed her clit to life.

"Oh, that feels so good," she said, slurring her words together.

I knew she wouldn't last long. The question was, would she pass out before I made her come?

I reached up with two hands and grabbed her panties, tugging them down over her hips, under her ass, and down her legs. I thumbed open her pussy lips and probed her wet opening with my tongue, pushing it in deep, fucking her with it, and then I ran my tongue along her inner lips until I reached her clit again.

I drew her clit into my mouth and whipped my tongue against it. Jackie moaned and lifted her butt off the couch, pushing herself up to my face. I slipped my hands under her and cupped her bottom, squeezing her cheeks hard. I sucked her clit and pressed a thumb into her asshole.

"Ohhhh, yeah, make me come," she cooed.

I nibbled her clit and then ran my tongue the full length of her silky pink slit. She humped my face until her body

324

shuddered in climax, then she fell back down on the couch, gasping and trying to get her breath.

We drank more wine. I went to the bathroom. By the time I got back, Jackie was passed out on the couch. I got a blanket from the downstairs hall closet and covered her up, then I went upstairs.

The guest bedroom door was partially open. The room Gina was using while she was there. I paused outside the door and looked in. A small nightlight was on, casting just enough yellowish light to illuminate the bed and surrounding area.

Gina lay face down on the bed, presumably fast asleep. She wore a light purple camisole with polka dots. It was bunched up above her waist, exposing her sexy ass and naked pussy.

I stood there for a long moment, contemplating my options. My wife was passed out downstairs. I was fairly certain she was out for the night. Gina seemed to be sleeping, but I didn't believe she was. I had the feeling this was all part of her game. I could go to bed and possibly miss out on some action with my sister-in-law, or I could enter the room and take a chance that she might truly be asleep, in which case she might wake up and accuse me of taking advantage of her.

I decided I'd take the chance. I hated thinking I might pass up an opportunity I'd later regret, and while a part of me felt guilty for what I was doing behind my wife's back, my hard dick was all the inspiration I needed to continue on.

I slipped into the room and closed the door behind me. I wasn't sure she was really asleep, but even if she was only pretending, I wanted to play the game exactly the way she wanted to play it.

I moved to the right side of the bed and stared down at her. Her ass was gorgeous. Smooth cheeks with a perfect valley between them. I imagined what it would be like to spread those lovely cheeks apart and slide my cock into her ass.

Her eyes were still closed. I watched her for a moment, looking for some sign that she was only pretending to be asleep.

She didn't open her eyes and her breathing remained steady and shallow.

I stroked her smooth ass cheeks. She didn't even flinch when I dragged a finger along the cleft between her ass cheeks and teased her puckered asshole with the tip of my finger.

With my free hand, I unzipped my pants and took out my hard-on. I wrapped my fist around it tight and began jerking off. I needed to come badly. I had to fight the urge to climb on top of Gina and slip my dick into her sweet pussy. She'd made it clear to me downstairs that intercourse was off limits.

What did she have in mind? I remembered the look she'd given me on her way upstairs. It had been a suggestive look, an invitation to something further, or was I simply engaging in a bit of wishful thinking.

I continued to rub her asshole with the tip of my finger as I slowly jerked my dick. She shifted slightly but didn't "wake up."

I took off my clothes and climbed onto the bed with her, still pulling on my cock as I leaned down and put my mouth on her pussy. I kissed her smooth, plump lips and worked my tongue between them to lick her pink labia. Sweet juice dribbled from her tight little opening and I lapped it up, all the while steadily pumping my cock. I pulled one of her plump lips aside, exposing more of her pink flesh to my tongue.

She shifted slightly, rubbing her pussy against my mouth. I released my cock so I could use that hand to pull her other pussy lip aside. I eased the tip of my tongue into her pussy and fucked her with it, pushing it as far in as it could go, then back out again, taking time every so often to lick her asshole.

She made a little moan. I teased her pussy lips with gentle flicks of my tongue. My hard-on pressed into the bed. I began to hump, rubbing my cock against her satin sheets. My nose nudged her between her ass cheeks and pressed against her taut asshole. The sweet, musky scent filled my senses, making me dizzy with lust.

I sat up and straddled her legs. My dick jutted in front of me at a forty-five degree angle. The head of it was smooth, pink, and throbbing. I grabbed hold of my cock and rubbed it between her legs, pressing it between her plump lips. Her slick juices made the inner lips of her cunt feel silky and hot. I nudged my cock head against her wet hole and eased into her.

She lay completely still as I fucked her. Now and then she would moan or shift slightly, but she remained passive, still pretending to be asleep.

I opened her legs a little, allowing myself easier access. The tight, hot grip of her pussy brought me to the edge in no time. I pulled out, wrapped it in one hand, and jerked a creamy explosion all over her ass.

I dressed quickly. She was still carrying on with her charade, but there was a slight smile on her face now. We shared a secret.

I checked on Jackie. She was sound asleep. I looked at her for several seconds, feeling a slight wave of guilt, and then I saw something that made me wonder. Her eyelids fluttered just a little, and on her face was the same knowing smile I'd seen on Gina's face moments earlier.

I headed upstairs.

"Sweet dreams," my wife called out to me.

I paused on the first step, shook my head in bewilderment, and said, "Goodnight," as I headed off to bed.

Ocean Hideaway

I stood looking out at the tranquil surface of the Pacific Ocean. I had a perfect view of the sun glistening on the gently rolling waves as they washed over the white-sand beach in front of the ocean house Sara and I had rented for the weekend. It really was about as close to Heaven as you could get on Earth.

The trip had been free. I'd won a radio contest. A trip to paradise for two. I brought my friend Sara with me.

I pulled myself away from the view, went to the kitchen to pour coffee, and then carried it into the bedroom where Sara was just waking up.

She sat up and smiled at me in that sleepy way she does first thing in the morning. Her soft blonde hair was slightly mussed and she had that dreamy look in her eyes. The sheet slipped down to expose two perfectly-formed breasts.

"We're in California," I said, reaching down to brush a finger over one of her erect pale pink nipples. "I know you aren't cold."

I sat on the bed, brushed a kiss over Sara's lips, and handed her a cup of coffee. She sipped it.

"Ah, much better," she said. "My eyes are starting to focus."

She took another sip of coffee and wiped her mouth with the back of her hand, then she leaned over to set the cup on the nightstand. Her breasts fell forward as she did. It was a sight I couldn't resist. I cupped one and rubbed my thumb across the hard tip of her nipple. She faced me. Our lips met aggressively. Her tongue danced into my mouth and I gently sucked on it.

She pulled back, reached into the nightstand, and took out a bottle of baby oil.

"I need you to rub me all over," she said, tossing the oil at me.

She kicked the covers off the bed and rolled onto her stomach, completely nude and as beautiful as any girl I've ever seen. I tipped the bottle and squirted oil between her shoulders, watching as the clear, slick trail rolled down her back. I squeezed out more oil, covering the smooth, firm cheeks of her ass.

Setting the bottle aside, I knelt beside Sara, pressing my hands against her back to spread the oil all over her. I slid my hands over her shoulders and brought them down her back, then I brought them down and over her ass, letting my fingers slip into the crack between her cheeks.

I straddled her legs and continued rubbing oil onto her back, leaning down now and then to kiss the back of her neck. The sleep pants I wore were loose, which was a good thing. If they had been any tighter, I would not have been able to hide the fact that I had a hard-on out of this world.

Not that it mattered if Sara knew she turned me on. We were friends. There had never been anything sexual between us, at least on a physical level, but both of us knew the possibility existed. We were just good at fighting it.

I brushed her hair aside and kissed her neck again, this time on one side and then the other.

"You having a hard time with that thing?" she asked.

"Just a little . . ." I answered.

I slid backward, dragging my hands down her back, over her waist, and then up onto the sexy curve of her bottom. I cupped my hands over her cheeks and began to really massage them, digging my fingers into the soft skin. She shifted slightly and opened her legs a little wider, allowing me to get a peek at the slick pink folds of her pussy between two plump lips.

I went to work on her inner thighs, one hand on each, massaging the oil into her skin, the tips of my fingers curving inward and brushing the damp curls of soft hair around the lips of her pussy.

I grabbed the oil and squirted more in the palm of my hand, which I began to work up and down each of her legs. When I reached her feet, she turned onto her back, raising one foot to me. I took her foot in my hands and worked my thumbs over the arch.

She moaned. "Ummm, that's nice," she said.

I brought her foot to my mouth. She pointed her toes, which caused the muscles in her legs to flex. I ran my tongue over the tips of her toes and kissed the top of her foot, then I slid my mouth around her big toe and sucked it.

She giggled.

"Tickle?" I asked.

"It feels weird," she said. "Weird but kinda good."

I kissed the soft arch and then took her toes into my mouth one at a time.

"Where is all this leading?" she asked.

"What do you mean?"

"I know we're supposed to resist the temptation to sleep with each other, but really, this is all too much . . ."

I avoided answering her question. I felt the same way. I wanted to fuck her right then and there. I'd wanted to fuck her for a long time now.

I got between her legs and grabbed the baby oil, tilting it over her breasts and letting the oil spill between them. I drew slippery circles around her nipples, enjoying the way the pale pink turned dark rose as she became more aroused.

I ran my oily hands over her tummy and slid them over her ribcage, splitting off in different directions as I reached her breasts, rolling the slippery nipples beneath my palms.

My cock made a tent against the front of my sleep pants now, so hard and ready for action that I couldn't have hidden it in a burlap sack.

"I just can't ignore that anymore," Sara said. She reached down the front of my pants and took a firm grip on my cock, giving it a good squeeze. "You might wanna let that thing breathe," she added.

"You know, if I let it breathe, we're probably not going to turn back," I said.

"Would that really be such a bad thing?" she asked.

"We agreed it would be," I said.

330

She pulled her hand out of my pants.

"I'm not so sure anymore," she said.

"No?"

"Nope." She chewed her lower lip thoughtfully. "If we're such good friends, I don't think sex is going to change that."

"I don't know . . ."

A long moment of silence passed between us. She looked up at me expectantly, waiting for my answer. The decision was all mine.

She sighed. "I can't believe you're this hard to seduce," she said. "Really, what is it going to take to get you to fuck me?"

Most guys would have called me crazy. Most guys would have been in bed with her long before now, and I was starting to question my ability to know a good thing when it was staring me in the face.

She spread her legs wide, showing me her pussy, running one hand down to caress the slippery lips. "I want you to go down on me," she said. "I want you to eat my pussy. You know you want to."

She was right about that. I wanted it more than anything.

I slipped my hands under her, cupping her ass and lifting her toward me, lowering my head between her legs. As my tongue rolled over the folds of her inner lips, I tasted a mixture of oil and her natural juices. It was hard to tell where one ended and the other began. I slipped one finger into the moist heat of her pussy and moved it around inside her as my tongue sought her clit, teasing the little pink pearl from beneath the hood of flesh covering it.

The instant my tongue stroked the sensitive surface of her clit, Sara arched her back, pushing her excited pussy against my face. My finger disappeared inside her. I hooked it and found her g-spot.

"Jesus . . ." she said through clenched teeth. "That feels so good . . ."

She rocked her hips against my face as I ran my tongue in circles around her clit and continued to work my finger in and out of her. Her natural juices were as sweet and as thick as honey on my tongue. I pulled my finger out of her and hooked my thumbs against her pussy lips, pulling them apart so I could run my tongue between the pink, slippery folds of her vulva and lick her opening.

She started squirming and the oil all over her body made it hard to hold onto her. My fingers dug into the cheeks of her ass and I lifted her to my face to push my tongue deep inside her.

I fucked her pussy with my tongue and licked between the cheeks of her ass, teasing the taut opening of her bottom. When I finally let her go, she fell back on the bed, her oily breasts jiggling.

"Take out your cock," she said.

She didn't give me a chance to do it myself. She pulled the front of my pants down to free my erection, then she sat up and scooted closer, running her slender, sexy fingers along the length of my prick. She stroked the sensitive spot beneath the head of it, back and forth strokes that soon had me ready to explode.

"I bet you want me to suck it, don't you?" she asked, looking up at me as she continued to jerk me off. "You want me to put it in my mouth, huh?"

She stretched out on the bed and lowered her head to my lap, running her wet pink tongue around the head of my cock. The warmth of her breath and the cooling effect of her saliva sent chills through me. She slipped her mouth over the head of my cock and began sucking, drawing me deeper into her mouth a little at a time, using her tongue against my shaft as she did.

It wasn't long before she had me on the edge. I nudged her away from me. My cock slipped from her mouth with a slurping sound. She ran her hand up and down the length of it a few times, looking into my eyes as she did, and then she said, "Let's fuck."

She sat up and turned around, getting on her hands and knees, her sexy, shapely ass at my disposal. I ran my hands up the backs of her legs and over her ass, pulling the cheeks apart to expose her most intimate places.

I teased her asshole with the tip of my tongue and then licked up and down between the lips of her pussy. She was as wet and ready for me as she'd ever be.

Reaching back between her legs, she took hold of my cock and brought the head of it up to rest against the entrance to her slippery pussy. I eased into her, feeling her slick lips open around me and then the snug heat of her pussy closing around my thick cock.

I held her by her waist and pulled back, leaving only the head of my cock inside her, then I went in again. My balls slapped a steady rhythm against her clit with every thrust. She looked at me over one smooth, sexy shoulder, her eyes half closed, chewing her lower lip as she began moaning.

I brought my dick out of her and rubbed it up and down the length of her pink slit, teasing the slick folds of her vulva. I slipped the head of my cock into her once again, just enough to make her think I was going to give it all to her, and then I pulled it out. She pushed her ass back against me, desperately trying to get my cock inside her again.

"Don't tease me," she said. "Put it back in."

"Teasing's good," I told her.

"Not now . . ."

She turned around, gasping and panting, wanting nothing more than to have my cock inside her again. She climbed onto my lap and impaled herself on my cock, squirming her ass as she settled into position. She draped her arms around my neck and began riding up and down, kissing me hard on the mouth as she did.

Her belly tightened as she worked herself up and down the length of my cock, rotating her hips as she came up, thrusting at me as she went down. She pressed herself against me, flattening her breasts on my chest, her nipples biting into me. Her breathing quickened with her pace.

"Oh, Jesus, yes . . ." she cried out as she climaxed

She fell back on the bed, pulling me down on top of her.

"I want you to come all over my stomach," she said, gasping between the words. "I love come on my stomach."

I wasn't going to last long. I fucked her hard and fast, driving my cock in and out of her pussy. The muscles of her pussy milked the length of my cock, alternately caressing and squeezing. My cock jerked and the first hot spurt of come went inside her before I had a chance to pull out.

"My stomach . . ." she gasped.

I pulled out of her and straddled her thighs, sinking my knees into the bed on either side of her as I fisted my cock and jerked the rest of my come onto her belly, collapsing over her when I finished.

She wrapped her hand around my cock, which was just starting to lose some of its firmness. She rubbed it around in the come on her stomach, then she dipped her fingers in the come and tasted it.

"Come here . . ." She held her arms out to me. "Let me suck your cock again."

I slid up so I was straddling her chest, leaning up to let my semi-hard cock brush her lips. She licked around the head of my cock and then took it into her mouth, nibbling and sucking until I was hard again.

Grabbing the back of the bed for support, I angled my cock into her mouth. She grabbed my ass and pulled me to her, taking my cock all the way to the back of her throat. She relaxed her grip. I pulled back and went in again, filling her mouth with my cock. She tightened her lips around the base of it and sucked hard, keeping the suction as I withdrew again.

She let my cock slip out of her mouth. The head of it settled against her bottom lip. She teased it with her tongue, looking up at me with those seductive eyes. "I want you to fuck my mouth," she said. "Fuck it like you mean it."

She slid her mouth around my cock again, pressing her tongue firmly against the underside. I sat up and grabbed the headboard. I began moving my hips, easing my cock in and out of her mouth. She mumbled something around my cock and I took it from her mouth.

"Faster," she said, pulling my dick into her mouth again.

It was what she wanted and I was more than willing to accommodate her. I held onto the headboard and fucked her mouth with long, deep strokes. She tightened her mouth around me and worked her tongue all over my shaft. It wouldn't be long before I came again. I could already feel it building, starting in my balls and working its way up.

She took her mouth away from my cock briefly. "Come in my mouth," she said. "I want you to do it."

She pulled my dick back into her mouth and started sucking. I quickened the pace. I knew what she wanted and I was going to give it to her.

"No . . ." I groaned.

My cock jerked in her mouth. She gulped with each hot spurt of come, swallowing it as fast as she could. The pleasurable sensations her mouth created around my cock as I came made my legs weak.

She let my cock slip from her mouth, wiping it back and forth across her lips before giving the tip a soft little kiss.

We lay together for some time afterward, talking about what we had done and what it meant to us, then had a quick shower and went outside, both of us still naked. There was a secluded cove practically right outside our door. No need for clothes. We were on a deserted strip of ocean-front property, and even if someone happened by and saw us, it wasn't like being nude on the beach in California was something new.

Sara stretched out on a blanket and to let the sun darken her skin. I admired the view. It wasn't long before I was lying next to her, stroking her nipples and fingering her pussy. She was wet again.

We made love right there on the beach. Waves washed up over the rocks and sprayed us with saltwater. I licked the drops from Sara's nipples and then went down on her again, matching the movement of my tongue to the rhythmic lapping of the waves that washed over the sand.

This time we came together, my cock deep inside Sara, her muscular legs wrapped tight around my waist. She held me against her for a long moment. Nothing seemed to matter but the sound of her breath and the warmth of her skin.

There was no turning back. We both knew it. There was something more between us now—something deep and lasting.

We spent the rest of the day in our little cove, hidden away from the world, loving every moment we could steal away from it. . . .

One Night in L.A.

I was coming out of an art supply store when someone called my name. I turned around and saw a man coming out of the same store, hurrying to catch up with me. He looked vaguely familiar. I thought he might be someone who worked in the store.

"You don't remember me, do you?" he asked when he caught up to me.

I felt awkward, but I had to admit I didn't recognize him.

"L.A. The convention."

Then it came back to me. He looked a little different now. His hair was longer and his tan was a little darker.

"Gary, right?"

"That's me," he said, smiling. "What the hell have you been up to?"

"Not a lot. What brings you to Chicago?"

"I moved here, believe it or not. An L.A. boy like me living in the Midwest. It still hasn't sunk in all the way."

If he was having a hard time with the idea sinking in, I was really wrestling with the concept.

"You feel like going for a drink or something?" he asked.

I told him I was pretty well booked for the week, but I took his number and said I'd get in touch with him. It was a lie, of course, but what was I supposed to say? I never told him I had a wife. I hadn't expected to see him again. How was I supposed to know he'd pack his bags and move to the same city where I live?

"I'll look forward to seeing you," he said, handing me a business card with his phone number on it.

After dinner that night, I went up to my studio and tried to work on a few of my sketches. My mind wandered back to that night in L.A. I was in town for a convention of west coast artists. Technically I'm no longer a west coast artist, but I had been living in San Diego in my early twenties, and a series of paintings I'd done at the time were still sought after at local art shows. I needed a vacation and decided a week in L.A. would do me good, plus I'd have the opportunity to promote some of my older works.

I was sitting in the hotel bar on my third night in town. I'd spent a long day taking in museums and other attractions, including the zoo and the planetarium. I was tired and thought I'd have a couple drinks before I called it a night.

Gary was sitting at the other end of the bar. I recognized him from the conventions. After about fifteen minutes, he came over and offered to buy my next round. That was about 8:00 p.m. We left the bar two hours later, and by that time, I'd had more than a few drinks.

We went to his room to continue our party. He had a bottle of good scotch tucked away in his suitcase. He opened it and we continued drinking. I had a good idea where it was leading, but I'd already thought it through. This was the perfect opportunity to satisfy my bi-curiosity.

The alcohol had loosened me up considerably, but not so much that I wasn't aware of what I was about to do. When Gary casually suggested we take a shower, I followed him into the bathroom without hesitation. I watched him undress. It was an odd feeling. I'd seen naked men before, but never with the intention of having sex with any of them.

Gary bent over the bathtub and turned on the water, then he said, "You might want to take off your clothes before you climb into the water," he said.

I undressed awkwardly. He was already standing under the hot spray of water, lathering his chest with soap. I climbed into the bathtub and he turned his attention to me, running the slippery soap over my belly and up to my chest, working it in slow circles over each of my nipples before traveling down again.

My cock was hard. He dropped the soap and wrapped his soapy fingers around my erection, squeezing tight as he ran his fist up and down the length of my shaft. My eyes were closed. I could feel his breath on my cheek, then his mouth was pressing against mine and his tongue explored inside.

He pulled me toward him, under the shower nozzle, dropping to his knees in front of me. The soap rinsed away from my cock. Gary started licking me, running his tongue over my balls and up the length of my dick, nibbling the head of it, flicking his tongue back and forth across the tip.

He slowly went down on me, taking half my cock in his mouth, then he came up again, stroking me a few times before he went down yet again, this time to swallow the full length of my dick.

I leaned against the shower wall and watched him suck me, moving his head slowly up and down, occasionally stopping to lick my balls and run his tongue up and down both sides of my cock.

He worked his way up, licking my stomach, tracing a wet trail up to my chest, flicking his tongue over one nipple and then the other. I felt his hands on my shoulders, applying a downward pressure, and I knew what he wanted me to do.

I knelt slowly, gently nibbling the soft, satiny tip of his erection, knowing he was about to slide his cock into my mouth. This was it, the culmination of years of fantasy and curiosity. Now I would know what it was like to feel a thick, throbbing cock in my mouth. I was afraid I wouldn't like it, that I might want to back out at the last second, but then the tip of his cock nudged past my lips and slipped into my mouth. I felt it glide across my tongue and disappear to the back of my throat, sealing the deal for me.

I sucked deep and hard. He moaned. I figured that meant I was doing something right. I kept at him with the same intensity, pulling his dick deeper into my mouth each time I sucked.

The first spurt of come caught me by surprise. I jerked my head back, but I kept his cock in my mouth, swallowing hard as his salty semen pumped down my throat. When he finished coming, I squeezed his dick, milking the last drops of come into my mouth.

We went to bed after the shower. He went down on me again, sucking and jerking my cock until I filled his mouth with come. He licked it up, then popped my dick into his mouth and sucked it until I gradually began to go soft.

After another drink, he started to doze off. As soon as he was asleep, I got dressed and left. I saw him one more time before I left L.A.

And now he was here, in Chicago, living just fifteen minutes away from where my wife and I lived. The wife who knew nothing of my affair.

I took out Gary's business card and ran my thumb over the embossed phone number.

Beth knocked on the door.

"Yeah?"

She came into the studio. "Are you coming to bed soon?" she asked.

"I've got a little more work to do," I said.

She kissed my cheek. "Hurry," she said, closing the door on her way out."

I glanced at the card again and dialed his number.

* * *

"I'm married," I confessed.

Gary handed me a scotch.

"Okay," he said quietly, seemingly unaffected by the news.

"What we did, that was just a one-time thing. I'm not gay. I just wanted to . . . I don't know . . . experiment."

"That's fine."

"You don't believe me, do you?"

"That you're not gay? I believe you're not gay. It doesn't matter one way or the other. Did you enjoy the experience?"

"I . . . well, yes . . ."

"Then it worked out, right?"

I went home with him that night. We sat together on the couch. He put my hand on his cock. I felt the hard bulge pressing through his jeans. I tugged his zipper down. I reached

340

into his pants and withdrew his dick, stroking it up and down, caressing the soft head with my thumb.

He stood up, moving so that he faced me. My fingers were still on his cock. I pulled him toward me, licking the tip of it, sliding my lips over it, swallowing the thick, hot length until I felt the head nudge the back of my throat.

He undressed himself, then he pulled me off the couch and kissed me, his hands peeling away my clothes as his tongue probed my mouth.

He grabbed my ass and drew me against him, our cocks rubbing together, his chest against mine.

I offered no resistance as he turned me around and bent me over the couch. His lips and tongue moved down my back. His hands squeezed and lifted my ass, spreading the cheeks apart. His tongue darted around my anus and over my balls. He reached around me and slowly pumped my cock, his tongue simultaneously working its way inside my ass.

He left the room and returned with a bottle of oil. I watched him squeeze some in the palm of his hand and rub it over the length of his dick. The mere sight of seeing that increased my arousal. I wanted what he was about to give me.

He dribbled the oil down the crack of my ass. I felt it spread around my asshole, then I could feel him massaging it in and around my tight opening, working the tip of one finger inside me, slowly inserting it deep inside my rectum, moving it in and out.

He held my hips and stood behind me, letting his dick slip between my cheeks. The head of it pressed against my anus. I pushed backward, trying to get it past the ring of muscle. He seemed to be too large to fit, but after only a little more resistance, he was sliding deep inside my ass, stretching me apart, filling me with his hot, hard prick.

Gripping the back of the couch, I steadied myself for each of his thrusts. He moved slow at first, easing back and forth until I was used to the newness of having my ass fucked, then he fucked me more intensely, driving in and out, hard and deep, his balls banging away at mine with every thrust.

His cock jerked inside me, swelling against the walls of my ass. He grunted as he slid all the way inside me and kept his cock there, filling me with thick, hot spurts of come.

I drove home that night without questioning myself any longer. I didn't think I was gay, but I was most certainly bisexual. I loved Beth, but I had to confess to her that I enjoyed sex with men. How do you tell your wife something like that?

She was awake when I got home.

"We need to talk," I said to her.

I told her about L.A., about running into Gary at the art store, and about being with him that night. She listened without saying a word. When I finished my confession, she said, "Do you want a divorce?"

"No."

"Then invite him over. I want to watch."

"I don't . . ."

"I want to see you suck his cock."

My wife had never been so bold. Hearing her say that made me want to fuck her.

"Are you sure?"

"I'm sure. Invite him over this weekend."

That night I dreamed about sharing Gary's cock with my wife. I saw each of us licking his dick, passing it back and forth, both our tongues lapping at the head of his cock as a fountain of hot, milky come spurted between us.

I slept like a baby.

Friday night came. Gary had agreed to go along with anything Beth wanted. I was nervous, but I couldn't wait for him to show up. When he finally arrived, the three of us ate dinner and retired to the living room for drinks. Beth made sure that she and I sat together on the couch. I really had no idea what to expect. The game now belonged to my wife. Only she knew what she had in store for Gary and me.

Gary began to talk about his latest pieces of work. Beth watched him while he talked, but her hand was in my lap, undoing my zipper. She slipped her fingers inside and took out my cock, casually stroking it as she listened to Gary.

Gary unzipped his pants and took out his cock, stroking the hard length of it. Beth lowered her head and began sucking me, taking my cock all the way to the base, her lips closing tight around it as she drew back, then relaxing as she plunged down on me again.

The conversation was gone. The only sounds in the room were the wet sounds produced by Beth as she sucked, mixed with the uneven breathing of two aroused men.

Beth worked extra hard on my cock, as if she felt she had something to prove to Gary—as if she wanted to show him that a woman was still better at sucking cock than any man could be. She caressed the spongy head of my dick with slow, lengthy passes of her tongue, leaving behind thick, silky strands of saliva that she sucked back into her mouth. She licked my balls, teased the sensitive underside of my cock head, and placed wet kisses up and down both sides of my shaft, all while stroking me with her soft fingers.

Gary came over to join us on the couch, still stroking his dick, his eyes fastened on my glistening penis as it slipped in and out of Beth's mouth. He stood in front of me so I could take his cock into my mouth. Beth stopped sucking my cock and watched, fascinated for some time by the sight of me sucking on Gary. When she finally went back to sucking my cock, she sucked with even more skill than she had before, jerking with her fist as she used her lips and tongue over every inch of my erection.

I didn't want to come yet, so I had to push Beth away. I pulled her to me, letting Gary's cock slip from my mouth and pushing it into Beth's. She went halfway down on him, sucked gently for a few seconds, then came up and swirled her pink tongue around his cock head. I leaned up to join her, our tongues working together around the smooth, fleshy helmet of his cock.

Gary shucked off his clothes as Beth and I continued to work on him, then as she occupied herself with his dick, I took off my clothes.

We undressed Beth together, licking and sucking every inch of her as we took off each article of her clothing.

She sat on the couch with her legs open, her butt resting on the very edge, and offered me her wide pink slit. I knelt down and began licking her, teasing the soft folds of her vulva and nibbling her swollen clit.

On the coffee table, placed there by my always-prepared wife, was a tube of lubricant she and I had used one time for anal sex. Gary grabbed the lubricant and smeared it along the length of his cock.

Beth dragged my head between her legs. I slipped my tongue between the fleshy folds of her inner lips, parting them with a long sweep as I made my way up to her clitoris. I drew the little pink button into my mouth and teased it with quick flicks of my tongue.

Gary pressed his cock into my ass. It went in much smoother this time. I felt the warm sides of his thick dick forcing me open, stretching my ass around it as he went all the way inside me.

He fucked me with slow, even strokes, massaging my ass with his dick. The warm, full pressure of him inside me was exquisite. I moaned, but the sound of it was lost inside the damp heat of my wife's pussy.

Gary moved faster, his balls slapping against mine, each thrust of his dick pushing me harder against my wife's wet cunt.

Beth watched over my shoulder as Gary fucked me. I wondered what it was like for her, seeing a man fuck her husband in the ass. Did she feel any jealousy at all, or was it just a sexual charge for her?

"Fuck him," she encouraged Gary. She put her hands on the back of my head and pulled me tighter against her pussy. "Eat that pussy," she gasped.

Gary was pumping me hard, his belly slapping the cheeks of my ass. I felt his dick swell inside me. It felt like his cock was three times its normal size, and then suddenly I could feel the slick, hot spurts of his semen pumping into my ass.

Beth reached her climax then, lifting her hips, thrashing against my face as I slid my hands under her bottom and tried to hold her steady.

Gary pulled his cock from my ass. I turned around and leaned against the couch, my cock standing up like a piece of carved marble. Gary went down on me. Beth slid off the couch and knelt beside Gary. She took hold of my cock and jerked me off as he continued sucking me. I groaned as I reached my climax, filling Gary's mouth with come. He tightened his lips and gulped, swallowing every drop as Beth continued to jerk me off.

When Gary finally removed his mouth from my cock, Beth leaned over and kissed him. He hesitated at first, then he let her tongue slip inside his mouth, sharing the last of my come with her.

The three of us have shared many such nights since, but that first one is the experience I will remember best, and it all started with one night in L.A.

Piece of the Past

I loved Kate, but our difference of opinion on too many issues stood in the way of a future together. She called off our wedding a week before it was to take place. Just like that, she dumped me, and it broke my heart. Deep down I knew it was for the best, but that didn't take away the heartache.

A confession here. I still kept her white silk robe hanging on a hook on the inside of my bedroom door. I still had her pictures, several of them anyway, in the top drawer of my dresser, buried under my socks and underwear. I forced myself to look at them every time I went through that drawer.

She moved away, somewhere south, I don't know where. I expected never to see her again. Two years later, just as I was starting to function without her, she called and said she was getting married. Just like that, as if that information was something I needed.

"I'm happy for you," I told her.

"You don't sound happy."

"Of course I am," I said, and I think I really meant it.

"Does that mean you'll be there?"

"Be where?"

"At the wedding?"

"I'd like you to at least meet him," she said. "My fiancé."

I was, of course, stunned by the suggestion. I told her no, but she started in with that sweet little-girl voice she always used when she wanted to have her way, so I gave in and told her I would at least meet the guy, but that I would in no way consent to showing up at her wedding.

Before we hung up, I had directions to the house she and Mike shared. We arranged for me to visit the following weekend. I spent the week trying to talk myself out of the visit, but five days after my phone conversation with Kate, I showed up as scheduled.

Mike wasn't home. Kate led me to the living room and offered me a glass of wine. We sat together on the couch. She faced me, bringing one knee up and tucking her right foot under her left leg.

"I bet you're wondering why I wanted this, huh?" she asked.

"Crossed my mind," I said.

"Having a hard time with this?"

"Would it make you happy if I said yes?"

"Sure it would. Are you jealous?" she asked.

"Don't flatter yourself," I replied a little too quickly.

"I don't need to. The fact that you drove all this way is flattering enough."

I changed the subject. "Where is this wonderful fiancé of yours?"

"He shouldn't be long. He wanted us to be able to catch up."

"Sounds like a nice guy," I said, edging the words with a hint of sarcasm.

"He's sweet," she said.

"Say you're not going to ask me to give you away at your wedding." I said.

"I would if I thought I could get away with it," she said, and then she hesitated, weighing her next words carefully.

"I called you for another reason," she went on. "You know how we sometimes talked about fantasies and stuff, and how I always told you I liked the idea of being with two guys?"

"Yeah, I remember . . ."

"Well, I kinda brought that up to Mike, and he and I talked about it, and I've decided I want to do it before I get married. I want the two of you together, all three of us making love."

I was thrown through a loop. I sat in silence. How the hell do you respond to such a suggestion?

"You okay?"

347

"Fine," I said. "This isn't the reunion I expected, that's all."

"Disappointed?"

"I don't think disappointed is . . . I'm just surprised. What does your future husband think of all this?"

"He's okay with it. I don't think he was thrilled at first, but he loves me. He wants me to be happy. I think he knows this is something I need to do."

"You *need* to do?"

"I think so," she said.

I took a swallow of sweet wine, thought about her proposition, and then said, "I'll think about it."

A key jiggled in the front door.

"Think fast," she said. "Mike's home."

She met him as he came into the living room, brushing her lips over his, then she introduced us officially.

"I've heard a lot about you," Mike said.

I studied the guy with the sort of scrutiny only an ex-boyfriend could manage.

I had an immediate dislike toward him, mainly because I wondered what sort of guy would share his wife-to-be with her ex-boyfriend. He wore casual slacks and a polo shirt. His haircut was too neat, his aftershave a bit too heavy. He wasn't Kate's style. I couldn't imagine the two of them fucking.

"I'll get more wine," Kate said. " You two should get acquainted."

We watched her leave the room. If anything, I couldn't deny he looked at her with the same adoration as I did. He loved her, despite what I may have thought at first, and maybe he *was* doing all this simply because he wanted Kate to be happy. I know I'd done things in the past just to make her happy. I would have gone to almost any length to give her what she wanted. Question was, would I still go to any length?

Mike and I didn't have much to say. Hey, thanks for letting me fuck her one more time before she becomes your wife.

348

Instead, I congratulated him on the upcoming marriage. He asked if I planned to be there. I promised I'd think about it, and then Kate returned with the wine, letting me off the hook.

She filled our glasses and sat with me on the couch. Mike sat in a recliner beside the couch.

"Is it okay to smoke?" I asked, taking a pack of cigarettes from my pocket.

"Knock yourself out," Kate said.

She grabbed an ashtray from the table on her end of the couch and leaned across me to set it on the arm of the couch. One soft breast pushed down on my hand. I felt her hard nipple through the thin material. The scent of her perfume danced around me, wrapping me in its suggestive scent.

I smoked my cigarette and finished most of my wine. The three of us made small talk. It was an awkward situation. I could tell Kate wanted a sign from me, some sort of an answer to her proposal.

She got tired of waiting. She'd always been impetuous. She took my wine glass and set it on the coffee table. "I'm horny," she said, and the way she said it was so matter of fact that there seemed to be no room for debate. She was going to have it her way.

She leaned over and kissed me as she fumbled with my zipper. Her tongue slipped into my mouth. Her fingers found my cock and smoothly extracted it from the confines of my jeans. She began to masturbate me. I forgot all about Mike for the moment and laid Kate back on the couch, sucking her pink tongue as I set about the task of undressing her.

Her jeans were tight. I tugged them past her hips and down to her knees, and she kicked them the rest of the way off, raising her ass long enough so I could take her panties off.

She sat up and pulled her shirt over her head, shaking her wild blonde mane back into place. I reached around her and undid the clasp of her bra, then watched as she slipped the straps from her shoulder. Her tits, the size of ripe cantaloupes, dropped free, jiggling pleasantly as she leaned over to help me undress.

349

I laid her back on the couch again, sliding my hands along the insides of her legs, pushing them apart. The sight of her like that, naked except for white ankle socks, made me hot and hungry. The folds of her vulva glistened with excitement.

I lowered my head and slipped my tongue between the lips of her pussy, teasing her pink opening, capturing her wet honey, working my way up the length of silky folds of flesh. She made a noise somewhere between a whimper and a moan. I took her clit in my mouth and nibbled it. She grabbed the back of my head with both hands and held me against her as she undulated her hips, rubbing herself hard against my face.

"God, I miss that," she moaned, pressing against my probing tongue. "I miss the way you do that . . . lick me. . . ."

Mike came over to stand beside us, his erection thrusting out of his slacks. An impressive one, I noticed, and he was stroking it as he watched my tongue disappear into Kate's pussy.

He watched for a minute before he put one knee on the arm of the couch and turned so that his cock and his balls dangled over Kate's mouth.

She went to work on him, sucking and licking his balls. She reached up and wrapped a tiny hand around his thick shaft and jerked him off.

I stuck two fingers into Kate's pussy. She was sloppy wet, absolutely drenched with excitement. I turned them this way and that, pushing them in deep, keeping my lips and tongue on her clit. She moaned and humped against me as she continued to jerk Mike off and suck on his balls.

I had trouble watching at first. I concentrated on eating Kate's pussy. I didn't want to see her pleasing Mike the way she was, regardless of the fact that she was going to be his wife, that she would be pleasing him like that for the rest of their lives together, however long that might be.

Mike moved back and then up again, pushing his dick into Kate's mouth. She swallowed his cock as smoothly and effortlessly as if she'd done it hundreds of times before, and for all I knew, she most certainly had.

I straddled her and slid my hard-on between round, soft tits. She pushed them together, cradling my cock there, and I moved back and forth, slowly fucking her freckled cleavage. Now and then she took her mouth from Mike's cock to lick and nibble the head of my cock as it peeked over the creamy mound of her tits.

"I'm about to come," Mike announced.

I wanted to fuck Kate doggy-style. I turned her around and pulled her to her hands and knees. Mike's cock slipped from her mouth while we changed positions. He quickly pushed it back into her mouth. I grabbed her by her hips and steadied her as I slid deep inside her.

Mike climbed onto the couch so he was kneeling directly in front of her, making it easier to fuck her mouth while I fucked her from behind. He tangled his fingers in her hair and fed her almost all of his cock.

I'm a voyeur by nature, extremely visual, and watching my cock slip in and out of Kate's pussy as Mike's cock pushed deep into her mouth was a visual feast. I spread the cheeks of her ass so I had a better view of my cock disappearing between her plump lips and blonde curls. The pink folds of her inner lips clung to my cock, slick and shiny, folding in and out with every thrust.

Kate sucked harder on Mike's cock, suddenly taking a couple of deep gulps. Mike groaned, pulling his cock from her mouth, trailing a thick string of come. Kate stuck her tongue out to catch some of it as Mike finished off with his hand.

Kate squeezed the walls of her pussy around my cock, coaxing me closer to the edge, massaging the length of my penis. The tiny pucker of her pale brown anus winked up at me. Wetting a finger, I teased the outer edge of the opening and then slowly worked my finger inside her bottom. She moaned her approval as the finger disappeared past the first knuckle.

Mike was finished for now. He poured another glass of wine and leaned back in the recliner, still naked, lazily rubbing his semi-erect cock with one hand as he sipped his wine.

Kate turned around to face me, then laid back on the couch, spreading her legs wide. I climbed on top of her and let her guide my cock to her wet opening, then I pushed into her, all the way in, all the way out again, leaving her gaping and wet.

She grabbed me by the ass and drew me back inside her, pulling the full length of my cock all the way up to my balls.

"I want you to do it hard," she moaned. "Fuck me hard!"

I supported my weight on the arm of the couch for leverage and fucked her hard, just the way she wanted it. Her tits shook as I pumped into her. My balls swung back and forth, colliding with the cheeks of her ass, slapping out a steady skin-on-skin rhythm.

"Oh God, I'm coming, baby . . . I'm gonna come," Kate cried out.

She wrapped her legs around my waist and arched her back, moaning as she came. She fell back to the couch when it was over. I was almost there myself. I gave a couple more thrusts and pulled out, grabbing my cock in my right hand to jerk my come onto her belly. I squeezed out the last drops and fell over her, gasping until I could breathe again.

We stayed there for a few minutes, with me leaning over her and my cock against her belly, my come sticky between us. She was looking up at me, deep into my eyes. Her cheeks were flushed pink with passion, her eyes were full of desire, and maybe even a longing for what we'd once had, I don't know. That much could have been my imagination, wishful thinking on my part.

When we finally separated, Kate went for a towel. She came back into the living room wiping my come off her belly. She plopped onto the couch beside me, still naked except for the socks.

We drank more wine. Mike lit a joint and passed it to me. "I don't smoke," he said. "But you two can share it." I normally don't smoke marijuana either but Kate wanted some, so I shared the joint with her.

"You're not finished, I hope," Kate said, giving my cock a playful squeeze.

"Just getting started," I said. "What do you wanna do next?"

"Remember that thing you always wanted to do to me? You know, where you had your finger earlier?"

"Umm-hmm, I remember."

How could I forget. Anal sex. We'd tried it a couple of times, never with any success. Kate was never one to give up.

"I want you to do that to me," she said, a mischievous smile spreading across her face. "Come on, let's go to the bedroom."

I glanced over to see how Mike was reacting. I wondered if he even knew what we were talking about doing. They seemed to have an open sort of relationship, and Kate didn't seem the least bit hesitant about inviting me into the bedroom, so I assumed she had at least discussed it with him beforehand.

She gave Mike a kiss, then she took me by the hand and practically dragged me into the bedroom.

I watched with quite a bit of appreciation as she climbed onto the bed on her hands and knees, shifting her ass in an inviting manner. "Come and get it," she said, looking back at me over her shoulder, grinning like the horny devil she'd always been.

I slid my hands up over the cheeks of her ass, lifting and separating them so I could tease her asshole with the tip of my tongue. I first circled the tiny puckered opening, getting it good and wet, then I wiggled my tongue inside. She rubbed her ass against my face. I tightened my grip on her ass cheeks, digging my fingers in as I pushed my tongue past her sphincter muscle, straight into her ass.

"Oh yeah, I'm sooo ready," she cooed. "There's something we can use in the top drawer."

I found KY-Jelly in the drawer, squeezed some on the palm of my hand, and smeared it over the length of my cock, then I squirted some on my fingers and spread it around her asshole. I squeezed out a tiny bit more and pushed two fingers of the stuff into her bottom, twisting them one way as I went in, the other way as I withdrew them.

353

"All lubed up," I said. " Are you sure this is what you want?"

"Un-huh, I'm sure . . ."

I wiped my hand on the bedspread and grabbed Kate by her hips, pulling her back to me. The length of my cock slid along the crack of her ass. She rubbed against me as she reached back to first stroke my dick and then guide it to the tight pucker of her back entrance.

Taking my time, I worked the head of my cock in first, watching as she slowly opened for me. There was a slight resistance and then her muscle relaxed. She made a noise in the back of her throat that sounded like a painful groan, then she grunted and inhaled a short gasp of air. I stopped.

"No, don't," she said. "Just be easy."

I eased more of my cock into her ass, taking my time. She reached back and put her hand on my ass, pulling me to her, moaning as I invaded her from behind, putting the full length of my cock where no other cock had ever gone before.

Mike came into the room to watch. There was one of those deep, round chairs in one corner of the bedroom. Mike pulled it up close to the bed and sat down, keeping his eyes on Kate and me. His cock was hard. He wrapped his hand around it and jerked off as he watched me fuck Kate's ass. It was a little disconcerting at first, being scrutinized like that, but I focused my attention on Kate and soon forgot all about Mike sitting next to us.

"Oooo, God, oh yeah, it feels good now . . ." Kate moaned.

"You like that?" I asked. "You like how my cock feels in your ass?"

"Oh yeah, I like it a lot," she said.

She reached back between her legs and stuck two fingers in her pussy. As she pounded her fingers in and out, the palm of her hand smacked her clit. She made herself come that way.

"I want both of you," she said, her breathing intensely heavy now. "I want you both inside me at the same time."

Mike and I exchanged glances. He shrugged at me. I shrugged back. This was all about Kate, that much was clear. What she wanted, we were going to give her.

Mike climbed onto the bed and laid down. Kate straddled him, raised up so she could position the tip of his cock at her pussy, and then sat down on him. She bent down and kissed him passionately, bucking and grinding on his cock. I waited a few minutes, letting her ride his cock, and then I got up behind her. Mike pulled the cheeks of her ass apart for me. I used more KY on my cock before slipping back into Kate's ass, which felt much tighter with Mike's cock filling her pussy.

Mike couldn't really move with Kate and me on top of him. He was mostly still while I fucked her ass, but occasionally he'd thrust up into her and push his cock around in her pussy as best he could.

It didn't take me long to work up to an orgasm. Her anal muscles squeezed and milked my cock. I could feel the thick heat of Mike's cock through the thin wall that separated us. The two of us pressed into Kate at the same time, making a tight sandwich, and she came again, grinding herself on both our cocks.

"Me next," Mike grunted.

I could feel his cock jerk as he emptied his come into Kate's pussy. When he finished, I started fucking her hard, driving my cock deep into her ass and back out again, my balls banging against Mike's balls, my stomach smacking Kate's ass cheeks hard enough to make them jiggle, and then I came in her too. The three of us became one writhing, pumping, grinding mass of sweat, come, and flesh— Kate's past, present, and future all at once.

She lay still between us. Her breathing was slow and steady. Sweat cooled on our bodies as moments passed. I felt something at that moment. Something beyond sexual satisfaction. Maybe it was longing for a time that was gone. A wave of nostalgia swept over me like a warm blanket on a cold night. . . .

* * *

The familiar strains of Mendelssohn's Wedding March rose from the organ and settled over me like a thick fog.

I stood at the back of the church, watching Kate make her way down the aisle, her lace and satin wedding dress trailing behind her.

Sometimes all a man needs is a tiny piece of the past.

Sometimes it's all he can stand.

I watched the woman I would always love as she exchanged wedding vows with another man. Earlier I had wished them well. I even wrote a check to help with the honeymoon.

Kate had looked at me with a question in her eyes, would we see one another again?

I didn't think we would.

The Pink Place

I've been sexually attracted to other women since high school. I'm thirty-six years old. It wasn't as hip to be a lesbian then as it is now. Two women couldn't be openly in love without fear of ridicule, especially in the tiny Midwestern town where I grew up.

I had quite a few crushes back then. I kept them to myself. I felt awkward in the shower room after gym. I'd take peeks at the girls around me, fantasizing about what it would be like to touch one of them, to feel her lips on my breasts or between my legs, and then I'd quickly look away, afraid someone would see me looking and know what I was thinking.

Fantasy and masturbation were my sexual outlets all the way up to my senior year in school. That's when I met Sarah. We became fast friends, and it wasn't long before I let her in on my secret. To my surprise, she was completely comfortable with it.

Needless to say, I fell in love with her.

It was inevitable that Sarah and I ended up experimenting, but it wasn't me who initiated it. Sarah was spending the night at my house. It was the start of a weekend. I'd taken two bottles of wine from my dad's bar, with every intention of getting Sarah and myself totally drunk.

We sat facing each other on my bed, legs crossed, wearing T-shirts and panties. We told stupid jokes and passed one of the bottles back and forth. Neither of us had ever drank, so we were silly before we finished the first bottle.

We laughed and rolled around on the bed. That's how it started. Sarah was trying not to spill her wine. I ended up on top of her, staring down at her, losing myself in her soft blue eyes. We stopped laughing. The whole atmosphere was charged with forbidden electricity.

She brushed my cheek with her fingertips, bringing them around to rest gently against my trembling lower lip.

"What's it like?" she asked.

"What's what like?"

"You know . . . being with another girl?"

"I've never actually *been* with another girl." I said, blushing.

"What?" she said. "Then how do you know you're . . . that you like girls?"

"I just know, that's all," I answered.

There was silence that seemed eternal, then Sarah shifted so she could put her wine on the floor. She gave me a chaste kiss and climbed under the thick pink quilt that covered my bed.

"Come on," she said, motioning for me to join her. "Come snuggle with me."

She lifted the quilt higher and I crawled under it with her. She let it go. It drifted down over us like a warm, soft, pink cocoon. I felt protected and accepted in a way I never had before. Sarah and I were the only two people in our secret pink world.

Her clean, soapy scent made my head swim.

Her warm, sweet breath caressed my cheek.

Then we kissed, and oh God, it felt so good. Who kissed who first is still a mystery, and one that doesn't need to be solved. All that mattered was how it felt and how *she* tasted. A beautiful kiss, soft and tentative at first, then hot and passionate and full of hunger.

I draped one leg over her, pulling her close to me. She moved a hand along the back of one of my legs, slipping it under my shirt. Her fingers brushed my bottom and settled between my legs. She pressed her fingers into my panties, touching me the way only I had ever touched myself.

She slipped a finger under the elastic of my panties, teased my lips, and then eased her finger inside me. I arched my back. Her finger went deeper. She pressed her thumb against my clitoris, massaging it hard through my damp panties.

I buried my face against her as the first wave of pleasure started in my belly. My nipples were hard. I bit my lower lip, trembling against her, trying so hard not to make any noises that might bring mom and dad running.

We were still and quiet for some time afterward. An awkward silence. Sarah spoke first. She asked if she'd made me feel good. She asked if I would touch her the same way she'd touched me.

"Yes," I whispered. "And even more . . . if you don't mind."

She offered no resistance, verbal or otherwise. I climbed over her and leaned down to give her a long, deep kiss, lifting her shirt as I did. Her breasts were small and firm, capped with tiny dark pink nipples. I ran my tongue around each one before kissing a wet trail down to her belly.

Her breathing was slow and even. Her flat tummy rose and fell ever so slightly. I could see the pale blonde hairs there, almost invisible. I ran my tongue around her navel and dipped into it, licking tenderly, practicing what I would soon be doing between her legs.

I heard my heart thumping a crazy rhythm as I went lower, bringing my lips over the mound of her pussy. Her pubic hairs tickled me through the thin cotton of her panties. Her scent engulfed me, so much like my own but still different.

I pushed two hands under her and brought her to me, lifting her gently, as if taking water from a stream. I licked the damp cotton panties, feeling the soft firmness of her sex. I tasted cotton and pussy—a combination that arouses me even today.

She moaned softly, almost inaudibly, and then she sighed. I hooked my fingers in the waistband of her panties and pulled them down. She drew her knees back as her panties came away, then she opened herself to me.

I'd seen myself in the mirror enough times, but now I studied Sarah, taking in all the details. I opened her, my thumbs holding back the pink folds, and I kissed her there. I stuck one finger inside her and began to fuck her with it.

"Feels good . . ." she murmured.

She tasted like sticky pink candy. I licked her and pushed my tongue inside. She shifted under me, then arched her back so I could get all the way inside her. This was the moment I'd fantasized about for so long, and now the reality was here, so much more exciting than my wildest dreams.

Sarah strained against me as her body shuddered with release. I held her tight, digging my fingers into the soft cheeks of her bottom, and licked and sucked her until she collapsed on the bed, gasping and fully satisfied.

We stayed up most of the night, touching and kissing and giggling, wrapped in the protective warmth of the pink quilt. When we finally slept, our naked bodies entwined, I dreamt of Sarah and our pink place . . .

. . . and of the nights we would share in its warm embrace. . . .

"**M**an, I don't like that shit," Melvin said.

Melvin was black as night, with a head as smooth as a billiard ball. He stood next to Frank, who was navigating the *Mariah* through the choppy waters of the cold Atlantic just two hundred miles off the Florida coast.

"It fuckin' came from nowhere," Melvin continued, half panicked.

"Just a patch of fog," Frank said with confidence. "We'll be all right."

"I never seen fog like this," Melvin said. "It's like the shit's alive or somethin'. I'm callin' Griffen up to take a look."

"You don't wanna bother Griffen with this, I'm tellin' you. He pays us to pilot the boat and protect the merchandise. You disturb him over a little fog, you'll likely end up feedin' the sharks."

Melvin studied Frank a moment, trying to weigh his options. He decided not to push his luck.

Frank changed course to try and avoid the fog, but the fog band shifted and widened, preventing him from getting around it.

Melvin licked his lips nervously. "I told you we was in for a storm, but did anybody listen to Melvin? Hell no. Now look at us."

They were smack in the middle of the Devil's Triangle, running a forty-foot cabin cruiser with a belly full of illegal drugs, money, and weapons. The last thing they needed was to run into trouble that would draw attention from the Coast Guard, or worse, some of that voodoo magic shit that always went down out here.

"Maybe you need to find another occupation," Frank said, reaching into his shirt pocket for a cigarette. "This one doesn't seem to be good for your nerves."

"Fuck you," Melvin said.

"Yeah, whatever," Frank responded.

* * *

Griffen and Lucy were doing the nasty in Griffen's private cabin. She was on her hands and knees. Her long black hair was damp and clinging to her cheeks, her heavy tits flopped back and forth with every thrust of Griffen's cock as he pounded her from behind.

Neither of them noticed the unusual bounce of the cabin cruiser, and if they did, it only added to the overall experience.

"Oh yeah," Lucy squealed, slamming her bottom back against Griffen.

"Shit, baby," he grunted.

He held her by the hips, digging his fingers into her soft flesh to steady her so he could drive his cock deeper into her tight pussy.

The boat lurched forward, throwing Griffen against Lucy. The weight of him drove her face down on the bed. His cock stayed inside her. He rose up, balancing his weight on his hands, and started fucking her again. He had barely started when the boat lurched again, this time nearly throwing the two of them onto the floor.

Griffen got up and grabbed his pants, pulling them on as he headed for the door. He glanced out the window and stopped in his tracks.

"Son of a bitch," he muttered, looking out the window.

Lucy sat up. "What's going on?" she asked, her gaze following Griffen to the window.

"I can't see a fuckin' thing out there," he said.

The boat lurched again. Griffen grabbed the window frame for support. Lucy tumbled from the bed. She tried hauling herself to her feet, but the boat pitched and keeled. Griffen was already moving toward the door. "Stay put," he said, then he ducked out of the cabin, fighting his way through a solid sheet of cold rain.

* * *

"Oh, man, we're gonna die," Melvin called over the roar of wind. "I knew this was a bad idea. I don't fuck with supernatural shit."

The sky blackened and fog completely enveloped the boat. A flash of lightning cracked the sky. Thunder boomed like cannon fire.

"Shut the fuck up," Frank said. "Just *shut* the fuck up. It's a storm, that's all."

Melvin held tight to the base of the helm as waves crashed over the sides of the boat. Frank checked the navigational devices and found them going haywire.

Griffen came up on deck, doing his best to stay on his feet as the boat pitched, throwing him wildly from one side to the other.

"We gonna make it?" he asked, his voice nearly swallowed in the cacophony of Mother Nature's fury.

"I think so," Frank called back.

A blinding white light exploded around the boat. There was a crackle as static electricity permeated the air, causing each man's hair to stand on end . . .

. . . and then silence.

The storm was gone and the sun was shining again.

"Holy shit," Griffen said.

"What the fuck is that?" Frank added.

Melvin stood with his jaw hanging down and his eyes as wide as silver dollars.

A Spanish galleon with the word *Pirotica* emblazoned on its side drifted toward them like a behemoth.

"Tell me that's not what I think it is," Griffen said.

"Well, do you think it's a Spanish galleon?" Frank asked.

"Something like that," Griffen replied.

"Then I can't oblige you, partner," Frank said.

They were drifting alongside the galleon now, so close they could reach out and touch it. "Let's board her," Griffen said. "She looks deserted."

"I doubt somebody just left a Spanish galleon floatin' around unattended," Melvin said. "Somethin' ain't right."

"I better check on Lucy," Griffen said.

He went below deck and found her in bed, still naked but half covered with a sheet. He told her to put some clothes on.

"What's going on?" she asked.

"Not sure yet. Just put on your clothes and be ready for anything."

He opened the top drawer of a dresser and took out a .357 magnum. He heard a scream top side and rushed back up on deck, stopping short when he saw Melvin and Frank surrounded by women in pirate garb.

Two of the pirates held swords to Frank's neck. Another one pressed the tip of her cutlass against the soft part of Melvin's chin.

"Drop the weapon, mate," a sultry female voice commanded.

Griffen felt something sharp against his lower back. He didn't need to turn around to know that it was another of those curved swords.

"Join ye friends, mate," the sultry voice commanded.

The tip of the sword prodded his back, convincing him a fight was out of the question. He joined Frank and Melvin.

The woman who'd gotten the drop on him was a real looker. Her hair was long, curly, and black as oil. Her skin was smooth and olive, her eyes dark and smoldering. She wore a loose white blouse, brown bloomers, a bandana, and black pirate boots.

"What the fuck, is this a costume party?" Griffen asked.

"Ye show bravado for someone with his backside in a bind," the dark-haired woman said. "I be Esmerelda, Queen of the Seas, Captain of the *Pirotica*."

Griffen tried to suppress a chuckle. He found the tip of Esmerelda's sword at his throat. "Ye find humor in yer predicament?"

Griffen swallowed hard. Esmerelda motioned over his shoulder, and before any of the men could react, they were rendered unconscious with clubs.

* * *

The men awoke completely naked, shackled to the wall in the belly of the *Pirotica*. It was damp and hot. Griffen's arm muscles bulged as he tugged at the thick chains holding his wrists above his head.

"A waste of time, mate," Esmerelda said, entering the bilge.

A chubby blonde and a leggy redhead entered behind her.

"We're not laughing, bitch, Griffen said. "Take off the chains."

Esmerelda gave a hearty laugh. "Ye be in no position to give orders," she said.

She stroked Griffen's soft prick. "Perhaps I might find ye of some use after all." She turned to her crew mates. "Dress him and bring him to my quarters."

She strode out of the bilge, leaving her crew mates to handle Griffen. When she was gone, the buccaneer woman turned their attention to Melvin and Frank. The chubby blonde, Lady Jane, was fascinated by Melvin. "What a fine piece ye have here," she said, stroking his dark cock until it became thick and hard.

She squeezed his shaft and flicked her tongue over the purple-brown tip, then she took him into her mouth slowly and proceeded to stuff as much of him down her throat as she could manage without choking on it.

The redhead, Mary O'Malley, watched her mate for some time. She felt her pussy tingle. Watching excited her, but there was only so much watching a girl could do. She raised her dress and touched her pussy, finding it wet and hot. She pushed two fingers inside herself, moaning as she thrust them in and out.

Frank fully intended to resist, but he was aroused. Forget the fact he was strung up like Christmas lights, his cock was hard as timber. He watched Mary finger herself, licking his lips as he imagined what it would be like to stick his tongue in her hot little pussy. He'd never been with a redhead before. It had always been a fantasy of his, and now it looked like he might get his chance.

"Ye be like what ye see?" Mary asked in a saucy tone.

"I like it just fine," Frank said.

She placed her wet fingers in his mouth. He sucked and licked like a starving man. His eagerness to please her amused Mary. She untied the front of her bodice, letting her ample breasts tumble free. They were soft and flawless, the color of cream, topped with fat pale pink nipples.

Mary knelt in front of Frank and wrapped her breasts around his cock, then she lowered her head and took him in her mouth, masturbating his cock with her tits as she licked and nibbled the swollen helmet.

Lady Jane turned her backside to Melvin and took hold of his cock, guiding his dark meat to the lips of her pussy. She rose up on her toes and pushed back against him, moaning when his cock disappeared inside her.

"Now that's what I call swabbin' the deck," she cried out, bouncing on his cock enthusiastically, her fat boobs flopping up and down in a wild rhythm.

Mary jerked Frank's cock faster. "Ye better spill for me or I'll make ye sorry," she said.

Frank grunted and jerked his hips forward. A thick glop of come splashed Mary's cheek. She wiped it away with the back of her hand, took his cock in her mouth, and let him finish off there.

"Give it to me," Lady Jane bawled, panting as she banged her wide bottom against Melvin. "Make me a happy wench."

She squealed like a cat in heat when she came. Melvin grunted and pushed his cock all the way into her plump blonde pussy. The force of his thrust lifted her off the ground. He emptied himself inside her. Lady Jane slid off his cock and dropped to her haunches, taking hold of his cock with two hands while she cleaned it with her tongue.

Mary tucked her breasts back into her bodice. She licked one of Frank's nipples and gave his cock a good, hard squeeze. "I'll be back for ye later," she said, then she turned to Griffen, who'd been watching the proceedings with restrained interest. "Now we best be gettin' on with ye, mate."

The two vivacious vixens unlocked the shackles that held Griffen to the wall. Lady Jane pressed her cutlass to the small of his back. "Don't be gettin' any ideas," she said. "I'll run ye through."

"Wouldn't dream of it," Griffen said.

* * *

Mary and Lady Jane prodded Griffen into the captain's quarters. Esmerelda sat behind a desk made of fine oak. She motioned Griffen to take a seat in front of the desk, then she poured rum for herself and offered some to Griffen.

"Wait outside," Esmerelda instructed her mates. "This bilge rat and me have business to conduct."

Griffen felt his cock stir. Discussion was not what he had in mind.

Esmerelda came around to the front of the desk. She sat on the edge of it and propped one booted foot on the arm of Griffen's chair. He had a clear view of her crotch. Her tight pants clearly defined the lips of her cunt. He smiled.

"I suppose you need a man too," he said.

"Ha, ye wish it were so. I prefer the comfort of a woman, mate."

She took a gulp of rum.

"Then why do you need me?" he asked.

"I have a crew of seventy women, and not all of them are as easily satisfied by the female touch as I. Ye and yer mates will be at their disposal."

"You're kidnapping us?"

"Call it what you will," she said. "I doubt ye want to leave us. The *Pirotica* is a ship of pleasure. We have nothin' to live for but pleasures of the flesh, for we be damned to drift the seas for all eternity."

"And you want my friends and me to drift through eternity seeing to your needs? I don't think so, lady. I got my own life to get back to." He drank from his goblet, enjoying the smooth rum. "And what's with the pirate shit?"

"Aye, ye be in the company of the best buccaneers of the lot. 'Tis sixteen seventy-five. Ye got lost in the Devil's Triangle, mate, and ye ain't ne'er goin' home again."

Griffen digested the information. "What about my boat?" he finally asked.

"Ha, the little tub we be draggin' behind us? I won't be seen sailin' the likes of 'er, but she be safe for now."

Griffen wondered about Lucy. Where was she? What about his stash?

"Clear ye mind, mate,'" Esmerelda said.

She picked up the rum bottle, abandoning her drinking goblet altogether, favoring her spirits straight from the bottle.

"Have you taken anything from the boat?"

"There be nothin' on the tiny craft of interest to me."

"Gimme a break, lady. We're both pirates. It takes a thief to know a thief. "

"A pirate is honorable. A thief be not more than a bilge rat."

"Maybe so, but the question remains—did you take anything from my boat?"

She shrugged, drank more rum, and said, "I be done with ye now," then to the women waiting outside the door, "Remove him."

Mary and Lady Jane entered the captain's quarters with their cutlasses drawn.

"I don't think the blades are necessary," Griffen said.

"Ye can't be trusted," Esmerelda said.

The pirates led Griffen up on deck. An orgiastic party was just getting underway. Naked women roamed the deck. Many were engaged in lewd and lascivious behavior. Griffen spotted Melvin and Frank right in the middle of it, fucking like wild animals.

He called Frank's name and made a dash for him. Mary and Lady Jane tightened their grips on his arms and thrust the tip of their swords to his neck.

"Be still," Lady Jane commanded.

Griffen didn't move another inch. He stood for a minute and watched his buddies work their way through one buccaneer after another. No sooner would they finish with one of the pirate wenches, another would take her place.

"Would ye give all this up, mate?" Mary asked.

"The question is, do I have a choice?"

"None at all," Lady Jane said.

They forced Griffen back down to the bilge and kept him there for several days. He was chained to the wall again. They fed him well. Esmerelda came in periodically to ask if he'd changed his mind. Griffen knew it would be easier to accept his circumstances, but he'd never been anything but stubborn. He wasn't about to play sex slave to a bunch of chicks, pirates or not.

* * *

"Sex is the least important thing on his list," Lucy said. "He cares about money and material objects. Why don't you just let him go back?"

"He be of use to me crew," Esmerelda said.

She couldn't keep her eyes off Lucy. The woman had caught her interest the instant she'd been brought aboard. Esmerelda preferred Lucy over any of the wenches in her crew. Something about her spoke of wild abandon.

Lucy felt the same way about Esmerelda, though she'd never been attracted to women before. This whole lesbian pirate thing had her thinking about what it would be like to forget men altogether.

"What drives ye to plead for this man?" Esmerelda asked.

"I know Griffen," Lucy said. "He'll never change his mind. All you'll get if you keep him around is trouble."

Esmerelda considered Lucy's warning. "And what would you have me do with you?" she asked.

"I like it here," Lucy answered.

"And I like ye here," Esmerelda said.

Lucy was sitting in a chair in front of Esmerelda's desk. Esmerelda took her by the hand and lead her over to the bed. When Esmerelda kissed her, Lucy felt her knees go weak. Esmerelda's tongue teased Lucy's mouth open and snaked inside. She ran her hands over Lucy's hips, moving them up to cradle Lucy's heavy breasts. She guided Lucy back onto the bed, pushing Lucy's skirt up to expose her silky panties, then she knelt and licked the damp material before drawing Lucy's panties aside to lick her between the lips of her pussy.

"Has any man ever done it so well?" Esmerelda asked.

"Never," Lucy panted. "Don't stop,"

Esmerelda slipped her hands under Lucy's ass and lifted her pussy to her face, delving in with her tongue. She caressed Lucy's outer pussy lips with her tongue, spreading them apart so she could work her tongue in deeper.

Lucy moaned. Her breasts rose and fell in steady rhythm. She draped her legs over Esmerelda's shoulders and undulated her hips, fucking Esmerelda's face.

Esmerelda undressed. She caressed her nipples and watched Lucy undress. They lay together side by side on the bed, kissing and fondling. Esmerelda straddled Lucy's chest, sliding her pussy onto Lucy's face.

Lucy pulled Esmeralda's pussy lips open, exposing the slick folds of flesh. She flicked her tongue over Esmerelda's clit and teased it, then she sucked it into her mouth and nibbled it.

Esmerelda seated herself on Lucy's face. She dropped her hands on the mattress for support and rocked her hips back and forth, riding Lucy's tongue until she climaxed.

Esmerelda turned and lowered her head between Lucy's legs, delving into the moist pink valley between her lips, searching with her tongue. She licked around Lucy's wet opening and thrust her tongue inside.

Lucy ate Esmerelda until Esmerelda came again.

Esmerelda brought her cutlass out and slid the handle deep inside Lucy. The sword handle slipped in and out of Lucy's pussy.

"Oh shit . . ." she gasped.

She was going to come. Esmerelda ran her tongue over Lucy's swollen clit and that was all it took to send her over the edge. Her orgasm came as a series of little waves of pleasure that culminated in an explosive shudder.

They lay together for a long time after, kissing and fingering each other.

"Aye, but I feel good," Esmerelda said.

"Me too," Lucy said.

She climbed on top of Esmerelda and pressed her tits against Esmerelda's face.

"Let's do it again," she said.

* * *

Griffen lifted his head at the sound of a squeaking door hinge. He saw two shapes enter the bilge. He struggled against the chains once again, but he had lost most of his ability to fight. He wasn't sure how much time had gone by, but he was pissed off.

"Take the fucking chains off me, bitch," he said.

Esmerelda and Lucy came into the bilge, followed by Mary, Lady Jane, and three other pirates. Esmerelda drew her cutlass and put it under Griffen's throat. "Listen, mate," she said. "This be your lucky day. Ye wanna go back to yer own time? I know the way. I'll grant ye yer wish."

"She's sending you back for me, Griffen," Lucy said. "I asked her to."

"What about you?" he asked.

"I'm staying. So are Melvin and Frank. We like it here."

"You can't be serious," he said.

Esmerelda released his wrists and ankles from the iron bands that held him. Griffen rubbed his wrists to promote circulation. He popped his neck, looking from Lucy to Esmerelda and back again.

"You sure about this?" he asked Lucy.

371

"I'm sure. This is where I want to be."

He gave Esmerelda a hard look. "All right, get me the fuck out of here."

He found Frank and Melvin on deck. They were drinking and having a good time. Frank was sitting with a thin brunette on his lap. He had a goblet in one hand, and with his free hand he massaged the brunette's pussy.

"You sure you aren't going back?" Griffen asked Frank.

"Look around," Frank said. "All the pussy I can stand, sailing the seas day and night, free to do what I want. Why would I leave this?"

Griffen found Melvin at the front of the ship, occupied by several women taking turns sucking his cock. Griffen didn't even bother trying to talk to him. It was obvious Melvin was where he wanted to be.

The *Pirotica* was sailing at four knots, cutting through the smooth waters of the Atlantic. They were two hundred miles off the coast of Florida. Griffen stood at the stern, preparing to board the *Mariah,* eager to be on his way.

"A week here be a hundred years, mate," Esmerelda said.

"My point exactly," Griffen said.

"Ye point yer vessel toward land and go," she said. "You'll end up where ye want to be."

Griffen boarded the *Mariah.* He checked his cargo before getting on his way. He wasn't about to return home without his livelihood. After a quick glance to the deck of the *Pirotica,* Griffen turned the *Mariah* around and headed for Florida.

A flash of static electricity and white light exploded around the *Mariah.* She vanished . . .

. . . and sat adrift in the Atlantic just off the coast of Florida, rusty and corroded with a hundred years' worth of saltwater. A pile of decayed bones lay at the helm. Only a skull was recognizable as human.

Somewhere in another dimension the Pirotica sailed the seas and its crew engaged in an endless drunken orgy of pirate pleasure. . .

Plain Brown Wrapper

The package was the only thing in my mailbox that day. Plain brown paper, no return address. I carried it into the house, poured coffee, and sat on the sofa to open it up. Inside I found an unmarked videotape.

I put the tape in my VCR and hit the play button. A momentary black screen, a few flickers, and then the TV screen filled with snow. I could hear muffled voices as an image slowly came into focus: my ex-wife kneeling in the middle of a big bed, white sheets twisted all around her. She was naked except for black panties and white ankle socks.

It was the first time I'd seen her since the divorce. To say the tape surprised me is an understatement. I'd often wondered what it would be like to see her again, but in all of my wildest imagination, this was not the way I pictured it.

She was five years older and just as beautiful as ever. Blonde hair, blue eyes, pretty in a girl-next-door sort of way. She looked over her shoulder at the camera operator. I could tell by the way her eyes lit up that she was intimately involved with whoever was shooting the tape.

She faced the camera, spreading her legs wide as she lay back on the bed. Her panties stretched tight across her pussy, outlining her plump pussy lips. I could see a dark spot on her panties; she was soaking wet.

Seeing Ashley brought back good memories, but those memories seemed to fade away when I heard a man's voice on the tape, muffled in the background, off camera somewhere, directing Ashley to play with herself.

She slid a hand over one of her heavy tits and caught a stiff brown nipple between her thumb and forefinger. She tugged on it and twisted it, causing the nipple to expand between her fingers.

She slipped her free hand between her legs, pressing two fingers against her panties, slowly rotating her hips as she rubbed herself. Her eyes were closed. If she was at all affected by the presence of the camera, she didn't show it; she was having a good time.

I couldn't remember a time when she'd been as open with me.

She raised her ass and pushed her panties down over her ankles, dropping them over the edge of the bed, then she opened her legs again, pulling her knees back and dropping them flat on the bed, giving the camera, and the man behind it, a full beaver shot.

The camera zoomed in close, zeroing in on Ashley's pussy, which was now completely shaved. I'd asked her to shave for me once. She had refused. Said it would make her feel like a little girl. Now there wasn't a pubic hair in sight. My view of her smooth-shaven lips and pretty pink vulva was unobstructed.

Ashley slid her hand over her mound, extending her index finger along the length of her slit. The camera pulled back. She bent her index finger slowly, inserting it into her pussy, arching her back as she pushed the finger deep inside her wet pussy.

Ashley had always been a compulsive masturbator. That much hadn't changed. I recalled the private shows she'd given me. I'd watch her fuck her pussy with a new object every day; everything from dildos to household items. Sometimes we masturbated together, touching each other, touching ourselves; I'd jerk off all over her pussy and she'd continue to play with herself, rubbing my come deep into her pussy, then she'd take my hand and put it between her legs so I could feel how messy she was there.

That had been our private thing. She always told me she could masturbate in front of me because she felt more comfortable than she could ever feel with any other man, yet there she was, not only masturbating in front of another man, but allowing it to be caught on tape. The very idea of that pissed me off. I wanted to stop it now, to turn it off and forget about it, but I couldn't. The perverted side of me *liked* what I was seeing.

Ashley rolled over and came up on her knees, pushing her round ass back at the camera. She reached between her legs and peeled the lips of her pussy apart with two fingers. She stuck them in her cunt and pushed them in deep, twisting them deep inside her, then pulling them out to drag them over her clit.

A male voice, this one different from the first, asked Ashley if she wanted to suck his cock. She nodded. A tall, dark-haired guy came into frame. His hair was shoulder length; his cock was long, thick, and hard. He ran his fist up and down the length of his cock as he approached the bed, keeping it nice and hard for Ash.

The thought of my ex-wife sucking a cock that big made me sick. I wasn't with her, and I shouldn't have cared, but I didn't like it.

I watched anyway.

Ashley sat up and swung her legs over the side of the bed, then she scooted her ass to the edge, placing herself in front of the guy. She took his cock in both hands and pulled it to her, opening her mouth to let it disappear inside for a brief moment. When it came out again, Ashley worked her tongue around the plum-colored tip, then she opened her mouth and took him in again, looking up at him to gauge his reaction as she sucked. I had a sudden urge to throw something at the TV. I wanted to destroy the image in front of me; I wanted to destroy the memory of her.

Ashley jerked the man's cock as she sucked. She let his cock slip from her mouth every now and then so she could run her tongue up and down the length of it. She pushed it against his belly and licked his balls, then she sucked them into her mouth one at a time.

He twisted his fingers in her hair, pulling her mouth back down on his cock, feeding her more of his cock than she could handle comfortably. Her cheeks bulged as his cock slid to the back of her throat. She gagged on it. He jerked her up by her hair, allowing her to suck in a deep breath before he pushed her down on him again.

"Come on, suck it," he groaned. "Suck that cock."

She pulled her head back for another quick breath. A string of saliva hung between her lower lips and the head of his cock. She gave his cock a few strokes and then took it in her mouth again.

"Aw yeah . . ." he groaned. He took his cock from her mouth and rubbed it against her cheek. "You ready to fuck?"

Without waiting for her answer, he pushed her back on the bed, grabbed her by the ankles, and pushed her knees up to her chest, opening her pussy wide. He dropped to his knees and gave her pussy a few long licks, then he climbed between her legs and pushed into her.

Ashley moaned and shifted her ass on the bed to give him a better angle. She raised her ass and wrapped her legs around him, locking her ankles together and using her legs to pull him back into her every time he withdrew. She talked nasty the whole time, spewing slut talk, telling him to fuck her, to come in her pussy.

I was never able to get her to talk to me that way.

The camera repeatedly changed angles. First a close shot of Ashley's face, her eyes closed and her mouth open, then a close shot of her lover's cock filling her pussy, his balls swinging hard against her ass with every thrust.

The camera came back for a wide shot when Ashley reached her climax, then zoomed in for a close shot of her lover's cock slipping in and out of her as he came inside her, each thrust of his cock forcing come out of her pussy and down the cheeks of her ass.

My cock was in my hand. I'd been jerking off without realizing it. I could feel the initial stirrings of an orgasm. I shut my eyes and leaned back, propping my feet on the edge of the coffee table; I concentrated my efforts on jerking myself off. Suddenly I felt the hot rush of come spurt over my fingers. The release felt good, and for a moment I forgot what I was doing, or what had driven me to masturbate in the first place.

Then my eyes fell on the TV screen again.

The video wasn't finished. Ashley's lover straddled her and slid his big dick between her tits, right into her mouth. The guy behind the camera stepped into frame now. He was an older guy, maybe fifty, still in fairly good shape. He climbed onto the bed and knelt beside her, stroking his cock in front of her face. The first guy climbed off Ashley and knelt on the other side of her head.

She took a cock in each hand, turning to suck one then the other, back and forth between the two. She rubbed their dicks all over her face, then she tried fitting both in her mouth at once.

They switched positions then. Ashley straddled the cameraman, sliding her wet pussy down on his cock. He bounced her on it a few times, then he stretched the cheeks of her ass wide and the other guy got behind her and eased his cock into her ass. She smothered the cameraman with her tits and moaned as the two men established an easy rhythm.

The video was coming to a close.

The two men exploded, one after the other. The cameraman came inside her, the other guy pulled out and jerked off on her ass.

I watched every frame.

The surprise was no longer the video in the plain brown wrapper.

The surprise wasn't that Ashley had sent it to me for whatever reason.

The surprise was that I still cared about her.

The surprise was how my heart ached . . .

. . . my cock ached . . .

The video came to an end . . .

. . . the screen faded to black. . . .

Rapunzel's Escape

Isabella was Queen of the lost land of Sapphica, a beautiful country where no man was allowed to set foot. The queen was tall and slender. Her breasts were perfect globes of pale flesh topped with pink half-inch nipples. Her eyes were the color of walnuts, her hair thick and dark, falling over her pale-as-cream shoulders.

Queen Isabella's reign over the kingdom of Sapphica was complete. Any man who dared set foot on the sacred land was dealt with in a quick and sure manner. Queen Isabella detested men. Hers was a kingdom of soft breasts and wet vaginas, a kingdom where women loved women. There was no place for the male species.

One day while strolling through the lush hills of Sapphica, Queen Isabella came upon a small cave from which emanated the sounds of a man and a woman making love. The queen entered the cave and found them together, a beautiful blonde by the name of Cassandra, and Peter, the son of a prominent businessman in the Heterolands.

Cassandra was on her hands and knees, her heavy breasts swinging with wild abandon as Peter took her from behind. He was in the throes of orgasm when Queen Isabella interrupted.

Peter knew that his coming to the lost land of Sapphica would not only cause a scandal in his own world, the clandestine coupling would result in punishment for his beautiful blonde Cassandra as well.

He stood before Queen Isabella, his cock now shriveled and resting against his right thigh, a drop of its pearly come hanging from the tip. "Please, Queen Isabella," he pleaded. "Please let no harm come to Cassandra."

The queen scoffed. She could scarcely stand the sight of him.

"Cover yourself," she said.

He quickly dressed. The queen contemplated the situation at hand, and after some consideration, she said, "Very well, I will spare the two of you this time, on the condition that if this illicit affair results child, and that child is a girl, she will be handed over to me at once."

Both Peter and Cassandra agreed, for they were certain the gods would work in their favor and no child would come of their heated union.

Queen Isabella allowed Peter to return to Heteroland without consequence. Cassandra avoided consequence as well, though she was put under close observation until it was determined the state of her.

Cassandra became the charge of a dominant keeper. Cassandra resigned herself to the life of a woman who would spend the rest of her life in Sapphica. She even came to believe, as day turned into night and night into day, that she cared for her new lover.

Then it came to pass that Cassandra was determined to be with child. Queen Isabella had Cassandra moved into the castle so she could watch over her. Throughout the pregnancy, Queen Isabella kept Cassandra at her side.

The queen was a notorious voyeur. She quite enjoyed the sight of two women making love. The only thing that excited her more was watching a room full of women together in orgiastic delight, and that being the case, the queen employed an entire troupe for just such a purpose.

Cassandra sat faithfully by the queen's side for these almost-nightly lesbian performances. She even grew fond of the shows herself.

The women who performed for the queen and her expectant charge were always enthusiastic. They would gather in a large pit before the throne and engage in all manners of sex acts, employing everything from tongues and fingers to large dildos, anal beads, and a host of other creative objects.

Sometimes the queen would open her legs and masturbate herself. Sometimes she would ask Cassandra to masturbate her. Other times she would let members of the troupe perform oral sex on her, several of them taking turns running their tongues along the length of her wet slit until she climaxed.

In the ninth month of Cassandra's pregnancy, a baby girl was born into the world and named Rapunzel. The queen took charge of her. Cassandra was banished from the castle and warned never to reveal the truth to Rapunzel.

As the years passed, Rapunzel grew into a beautiful child with hair the color of spun gold and eyes as blue as the ocean. Rapunzel was an inquisitive and precocious child. Queen Isabella, fearing Rapunzel would learn too much of the world beyond Sapphica, locked the child away in the highest point of the castle on her twelfth birthday.

The queen never laid eyes upon Rapunzel again. Servants took Rapunzel her meals and told her of life outside the tower. When Rapunzel was nineteen years old, she took her first lesbian lover, a woman by the name of Maria.

Maria would spend hours upon magical hours with her face between Rapunzel's smooth, creamy thighs, licking the soft pink lips of Rapunzel's pussy. Maria was skilled with her tongue. She knew just where to put her tongue on Rapunzel to evoke the most exquisite pleasures.

In turn, Rapunzel asked that Maria teach her the ways of loving another woman, and Maria took her time giving detailed instruction. She was only too happy to demonstrate the technique again and again, and Rapunzel was an apt student who practiced often.

There were nights when Maria would sneak into the tower to make love to Rapunzel, and afterward she would talk of life beyond Sapphica.

"Help me escape," Rapunzel said to Maria one night.

"I could never do that," Maria replied. "Not only would I risk the wrath of the queen, but I would be doing myself an injustice, for I would never see you again."

Rapunzel was heartbroken when she realized Maria cared more for herself than she did for Rapunzel's happiness, so Rapunzel bade Maria to never return to the tower again.

And so it was that a new servant was put in charge of delivering Rapunzel's meals, and though she was quite pleasant to talk to, she was not much for the eyes, and so Rapunzel would not engage in lovemaking with her.

The years swept by. Rapunzel spent much of her days brushing her golden hair, which she refused to cut. She even brushed her pubic hairs, which grew at half the rate of the hair on her head. As she brushed her flaxen locks, she fantasized about a life far away from Sapphica.

There were other ways Rapunzel passed her time as well. Self pleasure was chief among them. She had learned over the years, primarily during her time with Maria, how to bring herself to climax in many ways.

One of her favorite ways to masturbate was with the leg of a small wooden chair. The end of it was shaped in a way that reminded her of the male organ, although she only knew of the male organ through descriptions and crude drawings Maria had given her. Still, the wooden chair leg pleasured her immensely.

Now when Rapunzel pleasured herself, which was often, she would moan, and her moans were like a melodious symphony. Unbeknownst to the queen, the gentle sounds of her pleasure were carried on the wings of the wind, far into Heteroland, and they were heard by a young man named Devon Devonshire.

Devon could not resist the sweet call of Rapunzel. One day he followed her soft moans and gentle sighs until he stood at the foot of the tower.

"Hey," he called out, and then the moaning stopped, but for some time after there was nothing but silence. "Is anyone up there?" he called, and then Rapunzel peered from the window of the tower, looking down upon a real man for the first time in her life.

Devon was a fine, strapping young man, just one year older than Rapunzel. Rapunzel told him to go away lest the queen catch him and have him punished in the worst way.

Devon left, but the very next night, when once again he was drawn by the sweet, musical sounds of Rapunzel at the height of her pleasure, he returned. Rapunzel again begged him to leave, and so this went on for years. Rapunzel would bring herself to climax and Devon would arrive at the foot of the tower, only to be chased away by Rapunzel.

When Rapunzel was in her twenty-seventh year, Devon appeared once again at the foot of the tower. "Rapunzel, let down your hair," he called up to her, for he knew she had refused to cut her flowing blonde locks for all the years of her life.

"Please," Rapunzel begged, "go away and do not return."

But Devon Devonshire would not go away. He called up to her again, "Rapunzel, let down your hair."

This time Rapunzel, now driven nearly mad with her lust for this young man, slowly lowered her long hair to the foot of the tower. Devon grabbed hold of Rapunzel's flaxen locks and began his long climb to where she had been held captive for so many years.

Devon drew himself over the ledge of the tower window and fell into the room, breathing quite heavily from the climb. He stood slowly, his eyes wide in surprise as he took in the sight before him.

The room was quite literally filled with mounds of silken blonde hair. Rapunzel could just barely be seen beyond the curly forest of her pubic bush. The hair on her head lay spread about her now, covering the entire stone floor of Rapunzel's tower room.

Devon wasted no time getting naked. His cock stood thick and hard, jutting from his belly at a forty-five degree angle. The head of it was purple and throbbing. A tiny glistening drop of semen dribbled from the tip. He had waited so long, and now, with the object of his desire so close, Devon was not going to be kept from Rapunzel any longer.

He dove between her legs and began working his way through the thick, silky curls of her pussy. He could smell the rich, excited scent of her. He caught the scent like a bloodhound and let his nose be his guide. When at last he reached the gaping wet entrance of her pussy, Devon slipped his hands beneath Rapunzel's ass and brought her to his face, pressing his tongue between her slippery folds, driving it deep into her pussy.

"Oh yes," Rapunzel said, gasping. "Ohhhhhh . . ."

She locked her thighs around his head and began to bounce, fucking herself against his face, riding his tongue in a mad rush to reach her climax. She screamed as waves of pleasure washed over her like none she'd felt before.

The two lovers continued to go at it. Rapunzel took Devon's cock in her mouth and sucked it. She choked herself at first, but soon she had a knack for it, and as she massaged his heavy family jewels with one hand, she stroked his thick shaft with the other, all the while allowing her tongue to dance around the plum-shaped head until Devon could hold back no longer.

He let loose in her mouth with a flood of come so thick and sticky that Rapunzel was caught unaware. Some of it escaped her mouth and dribbled from her chin, but after swallowing as much as she could, she greedily licked her lips and ran her tongue over her wet chin.

They made love with unrestrained passion then, with Rapunzel riding atop Devon, her large breasts dangling in his face. He caught her plump, pale nipples in his mouth one at a time, working each with his tongue, using his teeth to nip at them, and then he pushed her fleshy breasts together and worked them at once.

Again the couple reached climax, this time nearly together, and Devon rolled Rapunzel onto her back and pounded into her like a man who had lost his mind.

When it was over, Devon insisted Rapunzel go with him to Heteroland. He produced a small knife from his trouser pocket and told her he would need to cut her hair so that they could use it to climb out of the tower, and with some regret, Rapunzel agreed.

Devon cut her hair and tied off one end, then he pitched the golden locks out the tower window and climbed down to the ground. He stood at the bottom of the tower, watching as Rapunzel came down next, though he could see nothing but the thick blonde bush between her legs.

When Rapunzel finally reached the ground, she and Devon embraced and shared a long, deep kiss. It was then that the queen appeared. She had with her several of her strongest women.

Devon took Rapunzel by the hand and they ran off. The queen's soldiers gave chase, but Devon knew many shortcuts between Heteroland and Sapphica. The couple eventually eluded the queen's soldiers, but just as they were about to cross into Heteroland, Devon's ankles became tangled in Rapunzel's long pubic hairs. He lost his balance and tumbled headlong over a dangerous precipice, bouncing like a heavy sack of potatoes against the jagged edges of the rock face.

Rapunzel fell to her knees and cried. She leaned over the edge of the cliff and saw that Devon's body lay at odd angles. She called to him to no avail. Her lover was gone, she knew with every beat of her heart, and now she could never forgive herself for this misfortune.

She stood on the edge of the cliff, her arms spread like the wings of a dove, and slowly she leaned forward until she could feel the wind on her face, blowing through the now-shortened locks of her hair, and she called Devon's name just before she reunited with him. . . .

Road Trippin'

1969.

There was groovy shit happening all over the country.

Everywhere, it seemed, except in the small Ohio town where Leslie was living out her youth in oblivion.

Leslie was all of nineteen years old, a slip of a girl with long brown hair, soft brown eyes, and not more than a handful of tits. The local boys loved her, but she had bigger plans for herself than to be barefoot and pregnant for some schmuck with a minimum wage job and no future.

Leslie wanted to see the world.

She hooked up with a twenty-five year old dude named Larry. He was a drag for the most part, but he did have a rusty 1964 VW bus, a folk guitar, plenty of grass, and even some LSD.

Lucy in the Sky with Diamonds.

Love to Suck Dick.

To Leslie, LSD stood for Love Some Day.

But not with Larry. When Leslie fell in love, it would be with someone who could teach her the meaning of life. It would be with somebody who could bring her something deep.

In the meantime, though, there was Larry, a tall skinny guy with long brown hair worn back in a ponytail, and a thick moustache that tickled Leslie's pussy whenever he went down on her.

Larry knew about this place in California. Some sort of movie ranch where a bunch of hippies lived together in harmony. Free sex, free drugs, and freedom from the restraints *The Man* laid on the average citizen on a daily basis.

It sounded like a real righteous gig, so Leslie went along for the ride.

Their first day on the road was uneventful. Leslie got high on the primo grass supplied by Larry and played with the radio dial, singing along whenever a good song came on. She wore cutoffs and a tan halter. She'd taken off her sandals and kept her bare feet propped up on the dashboard.

Larry went on and on about the movie ranch. "No rules, no heavy trips, just sex, drugs, rock 'n' roll, and even more sex."

"Sounds groovy," Leslie said, taking another hit from her joint.

Larry glanced at her bare legs. His eyes traveled up and settled on the crotch of her blue jean shorts. They were tight. The seam pressed into her slit, causing her pussy lips to bulge on either side.

"Play with yourself," he said.

"You should pay attention to the road," Leslie replied.

She really didn't feel like playing with herself, but she knew she would end up doing it anyway. It was what Larry wanted, and for right now, he was her ticket away from Ohio. If she had to play with her pussy to keep him interested, then she would play with her pussy.

"Come on, do it," he insisted.

She shrugged and dropped her feet from the dash. She raised her ass off the seat and slid her shorts down and off, then she put her feet on the dash again, bending her knees slightly and opening her legs wide. Her pubic hair was thick and dark, and even with her legs wide open, Larry could barely make out the dark pink folds of vulva hidden beneath the thick curls.

Leslie dropped her hand between her legs and stroked her pussy in a lazy fashion, working her fingers through her dark forest of curls in search of her clit. Her eyes were half mast as she manipulated herself with an air of slight disinterest.

She used her fingers to separate the lips of her pussy, giving Larry an unobstructed view of her red, glistening vulva. She circled her hard, swollen clit with the tip of one finger, then she went lower, curling her finger and pushing it deep inside her pussy.

Despite her initial lack of interest, Leslie found herself responding to her probing finger. She added two more fingers and pushed all three deep into her pussy, then she began to grind herself down on them, pressing her thumb against her clit for even more stimulation.

Larry had a hard time keeping the VW on the road.

Leslie came, gasping and moaning as she pumped her fingers into her pussy, and when it was over, she put her shorts back on and casually rolled a joint.

"Far out," Larry said.

Leslie shrugged. "If you say so."

She lit the joint and sucked hard on it, drawing smoke deep inside her lungs.

"Where's the acid?" she asked, passing the joint to Larry.

"In back, behind the panel with the smiley face on it," he told her, grinning as if it were the most clever hiding spot in the world. "And there's a jug of wine back there somewhere."

Leslie's cutoffs rode up to expose the smooth lower half of her ass cheeks as she climbed into the back of the bus.

"Groovy," Larry said, smacking her on the bottom.

"Watch the road, Larry," she said, barely able to hide her irritation.

She knelt in front of the panel and pulled it loose, then she reached in and came out with a small baggie of tablets. She replaced the panel, found the jug of wine, and climbed back into the front seat.

Larry found a turn-off onto a narrow dirt road. He followed the road deep into a field of corn and parked. They climbed out of the bus, wine and drugs in tow.

"You sure this is cool?" Leslie asked, looking around. "What if, like, some farmer decides to shoot us for trespassing?"

"We're cool," Larry said with confidence. "The owner of this shit probably lives a hundred miles from here."

Leslie took Larry's word for it. She sat indian-style on the ground between two rows of corn and opened the jug of wine. Larry sat across from her. They took some of the LSD and passed the wine back and forth.

Twenty minutes later they were flying . . .

. . . and Larry was being chased by a giant vagina.

387

"Groovy," he heard himself say, but he kept running, glancing back now and then to see the hairy outer lips of the giant pussy open and the inner pink folds flap like giant wings.

Leslie was lost in strawberry fields forever, naked and rolling around among the massive fruit. She straddled a large specimen and rode it, rubbing her pussy against its rough exterior until sticky red juice mingled with her own sweet nectar.

Huge butterflies with dazzling, colorful wings hovered overhead.

"Far out," Leslie said.

She smeared strawberry juice around her tiny, hard nipples.

Meanwhile, Larry had given up on escape and now lay back to let the monster vagina take him. The massive pink lips opened wide and closed around him, drawing him deep into the slick, pulsating darkness . . .

. . . that surrounded both of them now.

Several hours had elapsed.

"Wow, that was some trip," Leslie said.

"Dig it," Larry said.

He stood up, brushed himself off, and extended his hand to Leslie. She took it and allowed him to help her up. The wine jug lay on its side, completely empty. Beside it lay the plastic baggie containing what was left of the acid. Larry picked up the baggie and shoved it into his pocket.

They got back on the road and remained quiet for a long while, each of them basking in the residual effect of the LSD. Leslie was the first to speak up. "How long before we get to the ranch?"

"Guess it depends on how many more side trips we take," Larry answered.

"Oh," Leslie said, turning her gaze out the window.

"You ever been away from home?"

"Nope," she said. "Not far, I mean. My parents took me to see my grandmother when I was younger. That was out of Ohio, but I hardly remember."

He nodded emphatically, as if her answer held a deep truth he fully understood. "I was a little younger than you when I first hit the road," he said.

Leslie started rolling a joint, listening to him without really paying attention. Sometimes she hated to hear him talk. He was one of those guys who never knew when to shut up, and sometimes Leslie just wanted to be inside her own head.

She lit the joint. Larry was still babbling. He didn't even realize she wasn't listening. She found that an occasional nod or a well-placed half-laugh was enough to keep him happy.

"I've always been an outcast," he droned on. "A real rebel, you dig?"

Leslie propped her feet on the dash and sank down in the seat as she smoked the joint. It was maybe half an hour later when Larry decided he was too tired to drive any further. He pulled into a roadside park, shut the engine off, and got out to take a leak.

Leslie climbed into the back of the VW, found a blanket, and lay down to go to sleep. She was almost out of it when Larry lifted her blanket and crawled in beside her. She felt his hard cock pressing against her bottom.

"You awake?" he asked.

She didn't say anything, hoping he would leave her alone. She wasn't in the mood to fuck. A moment passed. Larry sighed and rolled over. She heard his zipper slide down, then the rhythmic slap of his hand on his cock.

She closed her eyes and drifted to sleep.

* * *

They had breakfast at a greasy spoon the next morning, then hit the road again. Larry started talking about Woodstock, claiming he'd been right up front through the whole thing. Leslie played with the radio dial. She came across *Honky Tonk Woman* by the Stones and turned it up.

"I met a gentle barroom queen in Memphis . . ." Larry sang over the radio.

"Gin-soaked," Leslie said matter-of-factly.

"Huh?"

"He sings gin-soaked, not gentle," she said.

"Oh."

He started singing again but stopped suddenly. "Check it out," he said, pointing out the front window.

A blonde wearing a short dress and knee-high boots stood on the shoulder of the highway with her thumb stuck out and a duffel bag at her feet.

"Let's give her a lift," Larry said.

He pulled onto the shoulder fifty yards or so ahead of the girl. She picked up her duffel bag and ran after the bus, out of breath when she reached it.

"Hop in," Leslie said, jabbing her thumb at the side door.

The blonde tossed her duffel bag into the bus and climbed in. "You guys are righteous," she said, pulling the door shut.

"No problem," Larry said.

He pulled back onto the highway. The blonde leaned up between the seats. "My name's Suzanne," she said.

"I'm Leslie, that's Larry," Leslie said. "Wanna get stoned?"

Leslie lit a joint, took a hit, then passed it to Suzanne.

"Where you heading?" Suzanne asked.

She took a hit of the joint and inhaled deeply, holding the smoke in her lungs for maximum effect.

"Some hippie hangout in California," Leslie said.

"A real groovy place," Larry added.

"You should come with us," Leslie suggested.

"Right on," Suzanne said.

Larry concentrated on driving while Leslie and Suzanne chatted and got more and more stoned. It was a real trip for Larry to listen to them, especially when they started talking about sex.

"You ever do it with another girl?" Suzanne asked Leslie.

"No," Leslie answered. "I always wanted to, but the vibes were never right."

"What about you," Suzanne said to Larry. "You ever had sex with a man?"

Larry's face turned red. "I let a friend suck my dick once, but only because he really wanted to, and I figured, hey, a blow job's a blow job, right?"

"That's one way of looking at it," Suzanne said.

Leslie rolled another joint and passed it to Suzanne.

"So," Suzanne ventured, looking at Leslie seductively through half-closed eyes, "how are the vibes now?

Leslie smiled lazily. "I like the vibes," she said.

She climbed into the back of the bus and sat facing Suzanne. They passed the joint back and forth. *Aquarius* came on the radio. The girls sang along as loud as they could. It was the happiest Leslie had felt since she'd left Ohio.

Suzanne leaned up and kissed her. It was soft and tentative. Leslie responded eagerly, opening her mouth to let Suzanne's tongue slip inside.

Suzanne lay down and pulled Leslie down beside her. They entwined their legs and made out. Suzanne slipped her hand down the front of Leslie's shorts and stroked her pussy lips.

Leslie moaned.

Suzanne took her hand from Leslie's shorts and licked her fingers. She raised up and peeled her dress over her head. Her breasts, considerably larger than Leslie's, bobbed gently as they came free of the dress.

Suzanne straddled Leslie and leaned over her, letting her tits hang down in Leslie's face.

Leslie gathered Suzanne's tits together and started on one pale pink nipple, giving it a thorough tongue bath before she moved on to the other one.

Suzanne raised up and took off her panties, then she helped Leslie out of her shorts while Leslie took off her halter.

Leslie lay back on the floor with her legs wide open. She rubbed her fingers between the lips of her pussy and inserted her middle finger, moving it in and out.

Suzanne moved between Leslie's legs, slipping her hands under her, bringing Leslie's pussy to her as she leaned into it.

Suzanne flicked her tongue over the slippery pink folds of Leslie's pussy and teased her tongue between them, slowly working it into Leslie's wet opening.

Leslie cried out softly, arching her back so Suzanne's tongue could go deeper. Suzanne squeezed each handful of Leslie's ass cheeks, digging her fingers in the soft valley between them. She let the tip of one finger tease Leslie's asshole until the taut opening relaxed, allowing Suzanne to slip a finger into Leslie's bottom.

Suzanne knew how to use her tongue. She pushed it in and out of Leslie's pussy, occasionally bringing it out to tease the little pink nub of her clit. The combination of Suzanne's finger in Leslie's ass while Suzanne licked her was enough to take Leslie over the edge. She squealed in pleasure as she came, her feet pressing hard against the floor of the bus and her body quivering. When her orgasm subsided, she dropped her ass back to the floor, gasping and panting as she struggled to regain a measure of composure.

"Wanna do me?" Suzanne asked.

Leslie nodded. Suzanne straddled her chest and slid her pussy up to Leslie's face. Leslie gripped Suzanne's ass and held tight as she buried her mouth against Suzanne's damp blonde bush. Lack of experience aside, it wasn't long before the curious probing of her tongue had Suzanne gasping and moaning.

"Yeah, lick me . . ." Suzanne said.

She pumped her hips back and forth, rubbing her pussy on Leslie's face. The beginnings of an orgasm stirred in the pit of her stomach and rushed to her head, making her so dizzy with pleasure that she nearly fainted. Afterward, she stretched out beside Leslie and they kissed and fondled each other as they passed another joint back and forth.

Another acid trip followed. Colors exploded and swirled around the two girls as they scissored their legs and rubbed their pussies together. Suzanne's big, soft tits pressed against Leslie's chest, eclipsing her tiny tits. They kissed, taking turns sucking each other's tongue.

Larry appeared in the midst of the action, grinning and waving his cock at the girls. He managed to wedge his cock between the kissing girls and they worked on it from both sides, kissing up his shaft until their tongues met at his knob.

Suzanne raised up and turned around to offer her ass to Larry. He buried his tongue in her taut asshole and fucked it, then he moved down and slid his tongue inside her pussy, all while Leslie continued lapping at the head of his dick.

Larry popped some of the acid. His cock, which was only of average size (on a good day) was suddenly a monster. He had his way with the girls at the same time, which had always been his biggest fantasy. Two wet, eager pussies at his command. Leslie was face down, singing along to whatever came on the radio, and Suzanne lay on top of her, face down also. Larry took turns with their pussies, alternating his cock from one to the other, tripping on the acid but equally high on the smell of sex that permeated the air around him.

When he came, his soul left his body and flew above the groovy dreamscape. His massive cock jerked. A thick stream of come spurted in slow motion, splashing across Suzanne's back and all over the cheeks of her ass.

Larry closed his eyes and rode the electric rainbow. Shades of Jimi and Janis and some crazy bunch of beatles being chased by a rolling stone.

Then Suzanne took something from her duffel bag. A cock. Larry saw that it was attached to a harness of some kind. She strapped it around her waist and fucked Leslie first, then she told Larry to bend over, and hell, why not? He was hip to a new trip and groovin' on a Sunday afternoon.

Suzanne eased the rubber cock into his ass. He went down on Leslie and teased her pussy with his tongue. Suzanne reached around and jerked him off as she fucked his ass with slow, deep strokes.

It was far out.

They found a place to eat later that night, long after the buzz had worn off, and then they stopped to gas up. Leslie and

Suzanne sucked off the attendant for the gas, not because they had to, but because they were *free* to do it, you dig?

Larry and Suzanne took turns behind the wheel. When Suzanne was driving, Larry tried to fool around with Leslie, but she was never as interested in him by himself as she was when Suzanne was involved. She let Larry fuck her once, hoping to shut him up, and one time she gave him a half-hearted blow job, but then she told him to go beat off.

They stopped at a roadside stand and Leslie bought incense that made the bus smell like sandalwood and the ocean, and when Suzanne wasn't doing driving duty, she was getting high in back with Leslie and the two were fooling around.

They camped at a roadside park their last night on the road. Larry played his guitar and sang folk songs while Leslie and Suzanne made love.

The next day, right around noon, they arrived at the ranch in Chatsworth and found a sprawling utopia that looked as if it might have come straight out of the old west. Wooden buildings nestled among rocky hills and rolling sagebrush formed the core of the hippie commune. A buckboard wagon sat in stark contrast to the scattered, busted-down buses and cars that littered the landscape.

Two young girls greeted Larry, Leslie, and Suzanne. They wore colorful pheasant dresses. One was blonde with flowers in her hair. The other had dark, braided hair. The blonde introduced herself as Patricia and her friend as Becky.

"We're tired of all the heavy trips society lays on us, dig?" Larry said.

The girls nodded with deep, righteous understanding.

"No heavy trips here," Patricia assured him.

There was dancing and singing and lots of celebration. There was wine and grass and sex with whoever happened to be convenient at the moment.

It was everything you'd expect to find when you weren't living by the rules of a society that promoted unjust wars and laws designed to keep the average man and woman down.

. . . And then he came out to introduce himself. A short man with black hair, a beard, and beady black eyes full of hate and impending doom.

Suzanne felt a cold shiver along her spine. She wanted to run as fast and as far away as she could. Larry felt it too, but not Leslie.

Leslie's heart pounded and her stomach fluttered. There was something scary about him, sure, but his eyes burned through to her soul, and she knew in an instant that he was the one she was searching for.

He was the one who would bring her something deep.

LSD.

Love Some Day.

"I'm Charlie," he said, fixing her with his poison eyes.

And Leslie loved him already.

Santa's Stockings

Ed had been walking up and down the street for five hours now, dressed as Santa Claus and drumming up business for Haglemeyer's Department Store. Snow had begun falling three hours earlier—the wet, heavy shit. Ed's balls were freezing. He slipped into one of the many strip clubs along the boulevard, hoping to roast his chestnuts over an open fire before he had to get back to work.

"Hey, Saint Dick," a buffed-up bald bouncer greeted Ed at the door.

Ed shot the bruiser a dirty look. "I'm checkin' my list, motherfucker," he grumbled, "and you ain't on it."

Guys like that really irked Ed. The big, dumb son of a bitch collecting a paycheck and probably getting his fill of pussy on the side, and what's he do? Instead of smiling like a good boy, he stands at the door with his arms across his barrel chest, waiting to beat up some poor schmuck who's just trying to get laid.

The club was smoky. Loud, bass-heavy rock music shook the building. A big-breasted blonde cowgirl was riding a stick pony onstage. Her large, swaying breasts changed colors under the house lights.

Ed went to the bar and ordered a beer. He carried it to a table right by the stage and sat down. The cowgirl spotted him and immediately started playing up. She leaned over the edge of the stage and dangled her boobs in Ed's face.

Ed dug a couple bucks from the pocket of his Santa suit and stuffed the bills between the cowgirl's ample boobs. He even managed to get a finger under her bra cup so he could sneak a quick feel of her stiff nipple.

"You gonna be naughty or nice?" he asked, grinning through his fluffy beard.

"Keep the cash flowing, Santa baby, and you'll find out," she teased.

She turned her back to him and bent over to touch her toes. Her skirt rode up to expose tight pink panties stretched over a firm, wide ass. Ed dug out a five-dollar bill. It was all he had. He hated parting with more than a buck at a time, but timing was everything here. While he had her attention, he planned on keeping her around. He slipped the five bucks under the elastic of her panties, again with a quick finger, only this time he brushed damp pubic hair.

The pretty blonde cowgirl continued to dance for Ed, lifting her breasts, pushing them together, and sucking her nipples. Ed watched with wide-eyed wonder. Occasionally she leaned over until her fat nipples were just out of his reach, and when he tried to grope them, she'd pull away, having a laugh at his expense.

A waitress in a short skirt, fishnet stockings, and a barely-there top brought Ed another beer. He gave her a big tip and followed it up with a smack on the ass.

A sexy, long-legged brunette in a leather body suit came onstage to replace the cowgirl. She strutted across the stage like a caged tiger, shaking her ass and collecting tips like the Salvation Army collects donations.

Ed pulled another big bill out and waved her over. She reached for the money, but Ed pulled it back, keeping it just out of her reach.

"What's in it for Santa?" he asked. "Missus Claus ain't been puttin' out like she used to, what with all those elves runnin' around."

She rolled her eyes, trying to humor him, but she was going to have to work a little harder to get the money, and Ed could see she was formulating her plan. She leaned down to give him a kiss, but that wasn't good enough for Eddie boy. He was one greedy bastard. He grabbed at her, trying to get his hands on her tits and ass. She was too fast for him, snatching the money and moving off to another half-drunk dude flashing a handful of cash before Ed even realized she was gone.

"What a cockteaser," he mumbled, signaling to a half-naked waitress for another beer.

One way or the other, Ed was having a good time tonight. He'd drink, maybe get a little pussy, and then head back to the department store for his paycheck. That was the way it had worked so far, that was the way he intended to keep it.

He got up and made his way through the crowded club. Right now his dick was confused. It was hard to keep a stiff dick when you had to piss.

The bathroom was at the end of a long, narrow, dimly lit hallway. He wandered through the door and down to the last urinal. As he stood with his dick in his hand, making little smiley face drawings with his piss stream, he heard a man groaning in one of the stalls to his left. *Please don't let him be jerking off,* Ed thought. *I don't need no guy thumpin' his dick while I'm tryin' to take a piss.*

He heard a woman moan next, which made him feel better. He could handle the thought of some couple balling nearby, but he couldn't handle some pervert pulling his dick in public. A thing like that just wasn't right, no matter which way you looked at it. Some things just weren't for public consumption.

He stuffed his dick back in his pants and zipped up. He moved down the row of stalls. The first was open and empty. The second was closed. Ed peeked through the crack of the door and found it empty too.

The third one was a different story altogether. He looked through the crack and saw the backside of a man, his hairy ass pumping away as he pounded his dick into a skinny brunette. He couldn't see much of the brunette because the guy was blocking his view.

He had to get a better look. He went into the stall next door and climbed up on the toilet seat. He gripped the top edge of the stall and peeked over. He could see the top of the guy's bald head and the swell of the skinny girl's ass, and he saw the guy's dick sliding in and out. The couple was so engaged in what they were doing that they didn't notice him.

At least, not until one foot slipped from the edge of the toilet seat. His fingers came away from the stall. He groped at it, trying to catch himself before he fell. His knees slammed hard against the side of the metal wall of the stall. The metallic bang echoed through the bathroom.

He fell off the toilet and landed on the dirty linoleum floor. He was barely on his feet when the guy in the next stall yelled, "Get outta here, ya fuckin' pervert."

Ed hurried out of the bathroom before the guy had a chance to get his pants up and come after him. He stumbled back to the bar and found another seat, this one just as close to the stage as his original seat had been.

The strippers (okay, dancers or whatever they liked to be called) came out one after the other. Some of them did some pretty amazing stuff. Ed in particular liked the chick that could lick her own pussy. Jeez, the things he could do with a babe like that in his bed. It just boggled the mind, that's what it did.

Ed called for beer after beer as he watched a variety of girls do their stuff. This was much better than playing Saint fuckin' Nick in the goddamn snow. Tits, ass, pussy, and brewski, that's what it was all about for Ed.

He wandered over to the bar and got change (enough one-dollar bills to keep the entertainment cheap and continuous), then he bought a pack of cigarettes from the vending machine. He didn't smoke all the time, only when he drank, and tonight he was going to do a lot of drinking.

He reclaimed his table just in time to see a naughty blonde inserting the second of three tapered candles into her pussy. The candles were lit. She inserted a fourth into her asshole. Damn, he really loved this shit.

He caught movement over in one of the darkened corners. The cowgirl was on her knees in front of some guy with a mohawk. Her head bobbed up and down. The guy with the mohawk had a big, goofy grin on his face.

A lot of money, that's all there was to it, Ed thought. *A guy like that ain't getting' head from a chick like that without cold, hard cash.*

Ed had to envy the guy, though. Sure would be nice to have that babe slobberin' all up and down on his dick right about now.

After the candle babe disappeared from the stage, a busty dark-haired chick wearing a leather corset and matching thong, with boots that came all the way up to her thighs, took the stage. A naked man crawled across the stage on all fours, his dick sticking straight out in front of him. The brunette held a riding crop in one hand. She straddled the naked guy's back and began to grind herself against him, really getting into it. She threw her head back and closed her eyes, humping her pussy against his back, pretending like she was having the wildest orgasm of her life.

Any one of these babes would be nice to get hold of, Ed thought. He'd let a woman like the one on stage now use that riding crop on him all night long just for the chance to sniff her panties.

She smacked the naked man's bottom as she rubbed her pussy up and down his back, and then she reached down and grabbed his pecker, jerking him off until he shot his load in front of the cheering crowd.

What a life that had to be! And the guy was probably gay to boot. Ed had heard that somewhere, that most of the guys who stripped didn't really dig chicks all that much. He didn't know if it was true or not, but he'd pretend to be gay of it got him a gig like this.

There was a brief interlude after the busty babe in leather rode the naked guy offstage. The room went dark, and when the lights came up again, there were two beautiful blondes in Catholic schoolgirl outfits onstage. They did a nasty bump and grind to *Only the Good Die Young,* helping each other out of their schoolgirl uniforms as they kissed and fondled.

Ed's dick stood right up and saluted. He particularly liked the Catholic schoolgirl angle. He knew all about those Catholic chicks. Not that he ever actually had one, of course, but he had a good idea what it'd be like to have one.

The girls kissed, letting their sweet, pink tongues touch briefly before they took turns sucking each others' tongues into their mouths. Their bodies pressed together so tight you couldn't slip a dollar bill between them. Their big, soft titties flattened together nipple to nipple as they groped and fondled each other.

They lay down on the floor, pussy to pussy, two different shades of blonde pubic hair mingling, and then they maneuvered until they were belly to belly. After a little more kissing and humping, one of the girl's went down on the other one, sinking her tongue into her partner's pink clam.

That was just too damn much for Ed, and when the two women started humping each other again, Ed could no longer contain himself. He dug the last of his money out and climbed right up onstage, pushing his way in between the two carpet munchers. They continued with the show despite his interference.

Ed managed to stuff a few bucks between one girl's tits and cop a feel of the other one's ass before the beefed-up bouncer from the front door got his meaty paws on him and pulled him off the stage.

It wasn't a pretty sight at all. Ed's head bounced off the floor a couple times. He saw stars. He heard some of the rowdier patrons hooting and hollering as the bouncer dragged him toward the exit.

"That's it, Saint Dick," the bouncer said. "Rudolph's waitin.'"

"Where the fuck's your Christmas spirit?" Ed asked, slurring the words.

"I'm the Grinch," the bouncer told him, "And I'm just about to steal your fuckin' Christmas."

Then the big man did what he did best. He used Ed's head to open the door, and then he tossed him out on his fat Santa Claus ass.

A yellow cab was parked at the curb. The cabbie leaned out his window, looking over the top of his cab. "You goin' north, Santa?" he asked.

Ed felt like someone had caved his head in with a bat. He struggled to his feet and stumbled over to the cab. It took him a minute, but he finally managed to give the cabbie his address. He slid into the backseat of the cab, leaned back, and closed his eyes. He was dead-ass tired, drunk as a sailor on shore leave, and broke as a cheap promise.

The cabbie took one look at Ed in the rearview mirror, shook his head, and said, "You disgust me, Santa, stinkin' like a brewery. We get to where we're goin,' you better be able to pay for this ride, you got that?"

"On the first day of Christmas, Santa gave to me . . ." Ed sang in an off key tone, flipping his middle finger at the cabbie.

The cabbie parked at the curb in front of Ed's apartment building and waited while Ed went upstairs to get money. Ed jiggled the key in his lock and let himself into his ramshackle apartment. A gorgeous blonde stood next to his bed, naked except for a Santa hat, red panties, and white stockings with red stripes.

"I'm your Christmas present, Santa," she said in a smooth-as-honey voice. "You can call me Candi Kane. Wanna lick?"

Candi Kane stretched out across the bed and opened her legs. Her thin red panties stretched over the plump mound of her pussy. Ed forgot all about the cabbie as he dove between Candi Kane's legs, burying his face in the lush wet heat of her panty-covered pussy.

"Don't be greedy, Santa, we've got plenty of time," Candi Kane purred. "How do you feel about doing a sixty-nine?"

Ed climbed onto the bed. Candi straddled him in the sixty-nine position, wiggling her bottom in his face as she unzipped his Santa suit. She took out his stubby penis, jerked it a few times, then popped it in her mouth to suck on it.

"Don't forget to deck my balls," Ed said just before Candi Kane settled her ass and pussy back against his face.

Ed could hear Candi's wet mouth smacking on his cock while her long, soft fingers stroked his balls. She stopped sucking long enough to look back at him with a pout. "Lick me, Santa, please. I've been such a good girl this year."

How could Santa refuse? He pulled her panties to one side, uncovering the slick pink folds of her vulva. Ed pressed a thumb down on either side of her pussy and spread the smooth-shaven lips apart. His tongue danced its way inside her. She shifted her ass to assist him, and then she returned her focus to his cock, taking it to the hilt.

Damn, she did things with her mouth that had to be illegal. Ed's cock was harder than he could remember it ever being. No surprise there, considering the remarkable skills this babe possessed. She worked both sides of his cock with her wet tongue, then she jerked him off as she concentrated sucking and nibbling the head of his cock.

Much as he didn't want it to end, Ed was pretty sure he wasn't going to be able to go the distance with this babe. She must have read his mind, though, because just about the time he was ready to pop, Candi spun around on him and dropped her ass onto his lap.

"I wanna ride Santa's pole," she said, rotating her hips as she slid down on his throbbing cock.

She threw herself forward, hanging her pale, heavy tits in Ed's face. He devoured them, sucking each of her fat pink nipples into his mouth and whipping his tongue over them. He concentrated on her nipples to avoid thinking about how good her pussy felt gripping his cock, or how the silky edge of her panties caressed his dick until he thought he was going to lose his mind.

"Bite 'em, baby," Candi Kane panted.

Ed slipped his hands under her ass and bounced her up and down on his cock as he caught her nipples between his teeth and chewed them.

"Ohhh, Santa . . ." she squealed.

"Santa Claus is comin' to town," Ed said with a grunt.

He flipped Candi over and pulled her up on all fours, her creamy ass wiggling invitingly, her panties all askew. Ed wrapped a fist around his stubby cock and guided it into Candi's pussy doggy-style. He pulled his Santa coat up and out of the way so he could watch his dick slipping in and out of her soggy snatch.

His hands found her hips. He dug his fingers in, pulling her back against him and holding tight as he began thrusting, banging away at her for all he was worth, his belly rolling and jiggling as it smacked her ass with every thrust.

This was too much. A girl like this could make it Christmas every day of the year. Ed loved the way her smooth ass jiggled as he pumped her pussy. His dick slipped in and out of her, the wet lips clinging to his shaft. Her inner lips folded in and out with every stroke of his dick, and ho, ho, ho, this girl was too much.

"Do my ass, Santa," Candi insisted.

Ed pulled his cock from her pussy and took aim. He pushed his dick against the taut opening of her bottom, groaning as she opened up to him. His cock slid right into her ass, the tight heat gripping his cock and sucking it deep inside the confines of her back passage.

Ed wasn't used to this kind of treatment from women. The only pussy he ever got was pussy he paid for, and even then he'd been turned down a few times. To have a chick like Candi Kane giving it up to him this way, letting him have her in any way he wanted her, was definitely a Merry Christmas to remember.

He held her hips and pumped into her with tight, jerky motions, stabbing his dick into the tight channel of her sweet ass. He could feel the dark little passage fitting itself around his pud, and oh Lord, this was going to be one hell of a Christmas light display.

He wanted to finish off in her pussy, so when he got his fill of her sweet, hot bottom, he let Candi climb on top of him again. She reached behind her and shoved a hand down between Ed's legs. She gave his dick a good squeeze and it was all over for him. His dick jerked in her hand and she began milking him as he filled her dripping honey pie with a thick coating of Santa's eggnog. He lifted his wide load off the floor, driving his stubby dick up inside her, grunting and groaning until he lay panting on the floor, fully drained.

Candi continued to milk Santa's nuts until his cock jerked inside her for the last time and then went limp. She slid back and knelt between his legs, taking his limp cock in one hand and slipping her mouth around it. Before he knew it was happening, Ed felt stirrings of another erection.

"Jingle balls," he groaned . . .

* * *

. . . looking up through a heavy blanket of wet snow, right up between a pair of sexy legs encased in white stockings and decorated with cute little candy canes.

Ed shook his head and tried to focus his vision. Between those legs was a strip of almost-sheer panty covering a plump blonde mound. A few wispy blonde pussy hairs stuck out around the lacy edges of those panties. He could see the dark cleft through the thin material.

"Are you all right, Santa?" the blonde asked. "Here, let me give you a hand."

She squatted beside him and her legs opened wide, giving Ed a nice beaver shot. Did they still call it that? Whatever, Ed could see right up her skirt, and Merry fuckin' Christmas, he couldn't help but feel the Christmas joy spreading through his bright red trousers. . . .

Snowbound

I remembered the sight of my wife in bed with another man. Although weeks had passed since I'd come home early and caught the two of them, I still saw the image of Rebecca on top of him in our bed, riding his cock with her head thrown back in ecstasy. It isn't a sight easily forgotten.

I took some time off work. I thought, mistakenly, that running away was the thing to do, so I ran like hell. I ended up in another state, living in a cabin in the mountains, pretending to be happy to be alone.

Alone isn't such a bad thing, after all, especially when you're healing from the wounds left by the woman you expected to spend the rest of your life with.

The solitude did me good. I was able, after a few days, to get back to work on the novel I'd been writing for some time. The deadline was approaching, and having been betrayed by Rebecca, I had neglected to sit down and write.

The snow was piling up outside. The windows were frosted. I sat at the kitchen table in front of my laptop, staring at the screen, envisioning the next chapter. A cup of coffee sat steaming beside me, a cigarette smoldered in the ashtray, and I drew a blank.

I turned the radio on and found a talk show. That usually inspired me, listening to some voice in the night discussing off-beat topics and callers debating them. I always wondered about those callers. What were they doing up so late at night, and were they as lonely as I was? What prompted someone to call into a radio program in the first place? Was it the need to feel that someone is listening?

I sat down and sipped my coffee, listening to the lonely, somehow hollow voices of the night, and continued to try and squeeze out the words I needed in order to finish the job that produced the money that would allow me to continue my self-imposed exile.

A weather announcer came on and announced a blizzard. I was sitting in a cabin in the mountains in the direct path of that blizzard. If being cut off from the rest of the world was what I was after, I had surely picked the perfect time for it. I glanced out the window and saw the snow picking up, swirling and blowing around like a huge white blanket.

I turned off the radio, lit another cigarette, and leaned back in my chair to stare at the computer screen without really seeing it.

The voice was faint, almost an auditory illusion. I wondered if I had even heard it, or was my lonely mind allowing my imagination to run wild?

A female voice.

It came again, this time a little louder. If there was someone outside the cabin, she had to be freezing.

I went to the door and opened it. A burst of snow blew into the cabin and dusted the floor. Outside, the snow blew so hard and thick I couldn't see more than a few feet down the slope running in front of the cabin.

"Anybody there?" I called into the blizzard.

"Help," a disconnected female voice answered from the swirling white shroud blowing through the night.

I wasn't dressed for the elements.—jeans, t-shirt, and bare feet.

But she was out there, and from the sound of it, she needed assistance.

I went outside, my feet sinking into drifts of snow.

"Where are you?" I called.

"Over here . . ."

The voice was closer, somewhere just ahead and to my right.

I found her leaning against a tree, out of breath, bundled up in a coat but still obviously cold. She wore a cap. Her cheeks were bright red.

I put my arm around her and led her to the cabin, closing the door behind us. She began taking off her coat. I went to the fireplace and threw on another log.

She was soaked throughout. I showed her to the bedroom and told her to pick something from my closet she could wear while her clothes dried. She disappeared into the room and I poured coffee for her.

She came out wearing one of my long-sleeved dress shirts. Her shapely legs were the first thing I noticed, and then the way her full breasts pushed against the front of the shirt, threatening to pop the buttons. She was blonde, maybe in her late twenties, with green eyes and a beautiful smile.

I realized I was looking and turned back to the fireplace to stoke the flames.

"Come sit by the fire," I said. "There's a cup of coffee on the table. I wasn't sure how you took it."

"Black is fine," she said. "Thank you."

She took the coffee from the table and came to sit on the stone ledge in front of the fire. She was still shivering.

I excused myself, went into the bedroom, and returned with a thick blanket, which I wrapped around her shoulders.

"That should help," I said.

She thanked me again, looking at me with genuine appreciation.

"I got lost," she said. "The storm came so fast, my car broke down, and I thought I could walk somewhere safe . . ."

"There aren't many people up this far," I said. "What were you doing in the mountains with blizzard warnings out?"

"Some friends of mine have a cabin," she said. "My fiancé and I were there with a few others and . . ."

She blushed.

"Well, I caught him with someone else," she finished.

"Join the club," I said.

"You too, huh?"

"My wife."

"Oh . . ."

We looked at one another for a long moment. It was clear there was sexual attraction between us, and the fact that we shared betrayal only made the connection stronger.

I leaned over and kissed her on the lips. A tentative kiss at first as I tested her willingness to take it further.

She responded enthusiastically, parting her lips, allowing my tongue to slip into her mouth. Her tongue darted out to meet mine. I ran my hands up her arms, to her shoulders, slipping the blanket off and going to work immediately on the buttons of the shirt.

Her breasts were full, the nipples hard and flexible at the same time. I cupped a round, pliant breast in each of my hands and ran my thumbs over the nipples.

She fumbled with the snap of my jeans.

I kissed her once again, then I stood and began removing my shirt as she tugged my jeans down around my ankles.

She looked up at me as she leaned up to slip her soft, wet lips around the head of my cock. She took my shaft in her hand, stroking it with slow, easy movements as her tongue flicked the tip of my cock and her lips nibbled.

I ran my fingers through her long blonde hair, pushing it back on both sides of her face so I had a better view.

I watched my cock disappear into her mouth gradually. My knees weakened as she sucked and licked at the same time, covering every inch of my shaft.

She cradled my balls in her free hand, squeezing them gently.

"Ummm, that feels so good," I said, easing my cock from her mouth. "Now it's my turn."

I took her hands and brought her to me, kissing her one more time before helping her out of her shirt and guiding her to the thick rug in front of the fire.

She spread her legs wide, bending her knees slightly. She slid one hand across her belly and down between her legs, opening her pussy with two fingers to expose the soft pink folds of her labia. Little drops of moisture glistened on the edges of the folds and especially around her opening.

I knelt on the floor and lowered my head. The scent of her was intoxicating, wafting up to meet me long before I reached my destination.

I slipped my hands beneath her and cupped her ass in them, lifting her to me as I continued toward her. My tongue met her opening and slid into her with no effort whatsoever, releasing a rush of her juices as it disappeared inside her.

She moaned.

I worked my tongue around inside her, then I moved up, working it against her pink folds until I reached the slick little bud of her clit.

I watched her facial expressions as I teased her clit with light strokes of my tongue, swiping it back and forth and then in a circular motion. Each stroke of my tongue brought a soft whimper of approval.

"Turn around," she said in an excited rush.

I continued to eat her pussy as I changed positions, giving her access to my cock, which she immediately took into her mouth once again.

She placed a hand on my ass and pushed down firmly, forcing my cock deep into her mouth. I resisted, not wanting to make her gag, but she insisted, pushing down even harder, taking my cock all the way.

I withdrew all but the head of my cock. She pushed down again, forcing it all the way to the back of her throat again. It only took a couple more times for me to understand what she wanted, and I began to fuck her mouth, moving slow but with long, deep strokes, pushing my cock in and out of her mouth.

She was getting wetter by the minute, her juices sweet and slick on my cheeks. I used my lips and tongue, and I slid one finger inside her and worked it around, pushing it in and out, working her into a frenzy.

Her mouth was warm and wet around my cock. She pulled my cock in and out of her mouth with a firm suction and something she did with her tongue, bringing me to the edge several times and then letting me settle down before she started up again. It was the most skillful blowjob I'd ever had.

I reluctantly took my head from between her legs and my cock away from her hungry mouth. There was no need for lubrication. She was soaking wet and my cock was slick with her saliva. She climbed onto my lap and settled down, sinking all the way to the base of my dick in one smooth motion, the cheeks of her ass slapping hard against the tops of my thighs.

I cupped her ass in my hands and began moving her up and down, each time bringing her nearly all the way off my cock before setting her down again. The sounds that filled the room were sounds I hadn't heard in a long time and hadn't expected, before tonight, to hear anytime soon.

Skin on skin, gasping and panting, heavy breathing, soft moans that escalated into deep groans of pure pleasure—the sounds of sexual heat.

Her tight pussy opened to accept my cock, then closed around it, squeezing and caressing and customizing itself to me. It was more than just a pussy. It was a living, thinking thing that took control of my cock and did everything in its power to give me more pleasure than I'd experienced in my whole life.

My wife was a memory. I swear to God, I couldn't have remembered a single pleasant moment with her even if I'd wanted to, and remembering anything about Rebecca while this beautiful woman, whose name I didn't even know yet, rode my cock was the last thing in the world I wanted.

She threw her head back and lifted her breasts, pushing one nipple into my mouth, begging me to suck on it, and then she fed me the other, all the while moaning and panting with pleasure as she bounced on my cock.

"Yes," she screamed, suddenly pushing herself all the way down on me and staying there, thrusting her hips and grinding her clit against the base of my cock.

She shuddered as she came. I held on to her, bringing her close to me. Her soft breasts flattened against me. Her stiff nipples pressed against my chest.

My cock jerked inside her. I came with her, pumping my cream up into her pussy. It seemed like an endless supply, spurting hot and thick inside her and running back out, making a sticky wet mess in our laps.

She finally collapsed against me, her breath coming in uneven bursts as she slowly recovered from her orgasm.

She lay her head on my shoulder for the longest time, and then she climbed off my cock and lay back on the rug, reaching out to me with both arms.

I moved to her, allowing her to hold me close. I wrapped my arms around her and found the warmth I had been missing.

We kissed again.

We had both been betrayed.

We'd found one another.

We were snowbound.

The Sexy Parts

I'd known her only since the day before. We'd met while I was signing copies of my new book at a local bookstore. Kim had pushed her way to the front of the line and tossed her copy on the table. She told me to sign it, "For the girl who gave me the hottest night of my life."

Five feet tall, blonde hair, blue-green eyes, she was the stuff of wet dreams.

"But I'd be lying," I said.

"Not after tonight," she said, confident.

* * *

We were in my hotel room, starting the second night of a one-night stand. She reached for the champagne, running her long, sexy fingers along the neck of the bottle, curling them around it when she reached the tip.

Sexy.

She was naked except for white ankle socks with lace. I'd asked her to leave those on. She popped the champagne cork and slid the tip of the bottle in her mouth, letting the thick foam spill over her lips and fingers.

She licked foam from her fingers, then she filled tulip-shaped glasses and handed one to me, straddling my chest as she did. She slid up until her knees came to rest on either side of the bed, her pussy within licking distance.

"Wanna eat me?" she asked.

Her angelic face was almost enough to make me feel guilty for the thoughts running through my mind, but her naughty grin reminded me she was all woman.

I set my glass aside, slid my hands under her ass, and pulled her to me, working my tongue between her damp blonde curls to tease the pink pearl of her clit. I ran my hands up over her freckled breasts, caressing her pale-brown nipples with my thumbs.

She tilted her champagne glass between her breasts. A sparkling trail ran down her belly, past her navel, then ran down through her pubic hair and onto my tongue.

She dropped her empty glass over the edge of the bed, then she slid back and leaned over me, dangling her wet breasts in my face. I pushed them together and licked her champagne-flavored nipples until they stood out hard.

Her damp pussy brushed the tip of my cock. She wiggled back until the head of my cock just barely penetrated her outer lips.

"Wanna fuck me?" she whispered. She pushed back some more. "Tell me how bad you want it."

"More than anything," I said.

She stroked my balls and slid her hand up my cock the same as she'd done to the champagne bottle earlier. She rubbed it between the plump lips of her pussy, caressing the soft, wet pink folds, teasing it against her opening.

She turned around suddenly, taking her pussy away from my cock, putting it in my face. I spread her ass, digging my fingers into the soft flesh and pulling her wide, fully exposing her pretty pink pussy and taut asshole. She moaned with pleasure as my tongue slid inside her.

She enclosed my cock with her breasts and jerked me off, catching the tip of my dick in her mouth every time it peeked above the creamy slopes of her breasts.

She would suck and lick it a few seconds before releasing it again.

While she busied herself with my cock, I ventured up and circled her taut anus. She looked at me over her shoulder, moaning, and said, "Ummm, I like when you lick me there."

We shifted positions again. She lay down on the bed. I kissed her neck, then brushed my lips over her nipples. After tracing the faint blue veins of her milk-white breasts, I went to work on her belly button.

She fingered her pussy and then stuck it in my mouth. I licked it clean, then I dipped my head and kissed her pubic mound. She opened her legs wider, took my face in her hands, and directed me to the spot she wanted me to lick.

"Oh yeah, right there . . ." she gasped.

She pumped her hips, rubbing her pussy against my face. I nibbled her clit, then I kissed my way down one leg, leaving a trail of kisses all the way. I took her socks off with my feet, kissed her ankles and sucked her delicate toes. I did the same with her other foot.

By the time I reached her pussy again, she was fingering herself. I replaced her finger with my own as I nibbled her clit.

"Fuck me now," she insisted.

She guided me inside her. The walls of her pussy closed around my shaft until it felt like I was being sucked into her. She opened her legs wide, then she lifted her ass off the bed as I entered her with a single smooth thrust.

She grabbed my ass and wrapped her legs around my waist as I fucked her.

"Suck on my tits," she panted.

I hooked my mouth over one nipple and sucked. She pumped her hips harder as I drew a good portion of her breast into my mouth. She was athletic. Her muscles rippled as she twisted and turned and arched her back.

We devoured each other. She moaned and gasped, her fingers clawed the sheets and tore red marks down my back, and we slipped together in a sweat-drenched dance of skin on skin.

She came first, arching into me and shuddering as the pleasure overtook her. I pushed all the way into her, reaching my own climax only seconds later.

We took a shower afterward, where Kim locked her ankles behind my back and held tight as I fucked her against the wall.

We had room service for dinner—a bottle of wine and seafood—then made love again before falling asleep in a tangle of arms and legs.

She woke me up the third morning by sucking my cock. A bowl of strawberries and whipped cream sat on a cart next to the bed.

"Breakfast in bed," she said.

I plucked a strawberry from the bowl. She came up to give me a long, deep kiss. I turned her over and painted her nipples with sticky red strawberry juice. Next I rubbed a handful of the sweet, plump fruit into her already-wet pussy, then topped it off with mounds of thick whipped cream.

I went down on her, lapping up the sweet berries and whipped cream, tasting her pussy with every swipe of my tongue.

She turned over and raised her bottom, sliding a hand between her legs to open her pussy with two fingers. I entered her from behind, effortlessly slipping my cock into her sticky-sweet pussy. Her tits jiggled with every thrust, my balls kissed her clit in rhythm.

"Ohhhh . . . I'm coming, yeahhhhh . . ." she cried.

She pulled away, turned on her knees, and jerked me into her mouth.

We lay together afterward, satiated for the time being.

"You never told me which part of my book you like best," I said, holding her close to me.

She kissed me. I tasted everything in that kiss— strawberries, whipped cream, our combined juices . . .

"That's easy," she said. "The sexy parts."

Slippery

The clerk at the grocery store had looked at Amanda like she was from another planet when she'd wheeled her cart through the line not once, but twice, each time with her cart completely filled with gallon containers of cooking oil.

Carrying all of it into the house had worn her out.

She emptied the gallon jugs of oil into her bathtub until it was full, then she went into the bedroom and covered the bed with a piece of clear, heavy plastic.

Mark was due home any minute.

She lit candles all around the house and turned off all the lights, then she carried a bottle of wine and two glasses upstairs to the bedroom.

She undressed and stood before a full-length mirror, admiring her long legs and high, firm breasts. Her nipples were pink and puckered. She ran her hands over her boobs and squeezed them, letting the thumb of each hand brush her nipples.

She dropped one hand down and fingered her pussy. She was already hot and aroused. Her juices were flowing freely, lubricating her opening so that she easily slid two fingers inside herself.

Tonight was the night she would make Mark's fantasy come true. He'd always wanted her covered in oil and completely at his disposal. Tonight was his birthday, and her gift to him was his fantasy.

She went into the bathroom and stepped into the tub of oil, careful not to slip and fall. Breaking her neck would never do. The fantasy would be spoiled if Mark came home to find her in a tub of oil with a broken neck.

She squatted slowly, enjoying the way the oil engulfed her, lapping at her thighs and pussy. She stretched out her legs until her feet touched one end of the tub, then she leaned against the back of the tub and sank even deeper into the viscous liquid, watching it flow heavily over her belly and her tits. She continued to submerge herself, going down until the oil slid past her chin and over her face, until finally she was beneath the surface.

She sat up so that her head and shoulders were free of the heavy, slick liquid. Her blonde hair was darker now, clinging in heavy strands against her cheeks. She wiped her hair back and wiped the excess oil from her eyes.

She ran a hand over her belly and between her legs, spreading her legs apart as she did. She pushed two, then three fingers into her pussy. She couldn't believe how easily they went in. She slid her other hand beneath her and worked a couple of fingers into her asshole. The oil made penetrating her ass seem effortless.

She closed her eyes and rested her head against the back of the tub, luxuriating in the smooth caress of the oil. It felt so relaxing, like she was being held down by a gentle force. There was a weight to the oil not present in water, but a weight that gave her a strange sort of comfort.

She fingered her pussy and her ass, unaware of how many fingers she used on each, not really caring. It felt too good.

She was nearly lost in orgasmic bliss when she heard the front door open downstairs and Mark calling out to her.

"Up here," she called back.

A moment later he came into the bedroom. He knocked on the bathroom door.

"Don't come in," she said. "I want you to take off your clothes and climb into bed."

She could hear him move away from the bathroom door. She waited for his response to the plastic covering the bed.

"Honey, there's plastic on the bed," he said in a confused tone.

"Just get naked and lie down on it," she called back to him.

She stood up, watching as the oil ran down her body in thick rivulets. She felt like a candle, with the oil representing melting wax. She ran her hands up her slick belly and over her shiny-slick tits. Her nipples were slick little points now, sensitive to the touch. She captured them between the thumb and forefinger of each hand and twirled them between her slippery fingers, tugging on them until they stood out swollen and proud.

She opened the bathroom door. Mark was lying naked on the bed, looking her way. She caught a glimpse of herself as she passed before the mirror. She looked like something out of a horror movie, hair plastered to her face, oil running down her body, and the candlelight flickering on her glistening skin.

"Wow," Mark said with sexual reverence.

She crossed the room and climbed onto the bed, straddling him, her knees slipping against the plastic bed covering on either side of him.

He ran his hands over her hips, sliding them across her oily smooth skin, moving up to her breasts, one of which he cupped in each hand. He ran his thumbs around her slick nipples, then pressed down, enjoying the way each slippery nipple bent beneath the pressure.

She slid her ass back until her well-lubricated pussy met the tip of his cock. Her hard, slick nipples pressed against his chest as she leaned down to kiss him.

He cupped her oily ass cheeks in his hands, then brought them around to grip her slick waist, holding on as best he could.

"I can't believe this," he said, still in awe.

"I'm your well-oiled fuck machine," she said. "All my parts are lubed for easy entry."

"Yeah," he groaned, thrusting his hip at her, sending his thick cock deep into the confines of her slick-as-hot-butter pussy.

He held tight, his fingers slipping and sliding against her skin as he began to thrust in and out of her.

"You like that?" she asked in a teasing tone.

"Does that even require an answer?" he replied.

The only sounds filling the room for the next several minutes were the sounds of their bodies colliding with wet smacks and the combined sound of their soft moans and heavy panting.

Amanda came up off Mark's cock suddenly, and when she dropped down again, it was her warm, tight asshole his cock slid into.

"Jesus . . ." he said, following it up with a deep, guttural groan that seemed to swell until it engulfed them.

He couldn't believe how easily her ass had swallowed his dick. His cock had, without any resistance whatsoever, filled her ass as easily as it penetrated her pussy. The tight, slick heat surrounding his cock was almost an instant orgasm. He had to focus on something of a nonsexual nature to keep from delivering a shot of come this early in the game.

"Baby . . ." he cautioned.

She wasn't making it easy. She rode his cock like a wild woman, bouncing up and down, rotating her hips and squeezing her tight anal muscles around his swollen cock. The oil heated with the friction of their bodies and the ride was smooth.

He lifted her up and rolled her onto her back. She drew her knees up and let them fall open. The oil-slickened folds of her pussy lay open, exposing the glistening pink wink of her eager pussy. He pressed two fingers inside her and found that she could easily take two more.

She rocked her hips at him, working her slick cunt up and down on all four fingers, lifting her ass off the plastic sheet as she raised herself off his fingers, dropping down hard as she plunged all the way down on them again. He turned his hand slightly and applied pressure to her clit with his thumb, working the swollen little nub free of its hood.

She sucked in a gulp of air and her belly quivered from the pleasure his fingers gave her. He pushed them in deep, curling them to press the spot behind her clitoris. She raised

420

her ass off the plastic sheet and cried out as the first waves of orgasm shot through her body.

Her muscles tensed and her thighs shook as she pushed herself against his fingers. He closed them inside her, making a fist, and her pussy, slippery as it was, went over his entire hand. She found herself drawn into a chasm of exploding colors so deep she thought she might never come back from it.

She fell way from Mark, gasping and panting, every nerve ending on fire, the pleasure center in her mind overloaded to the point where she thought she might simply black out.

Mark knelt between her widespread legs, running his hands over her greasy belly, up to her oil-drenched tits. He squeezed the soft, slippery mounds of creamy flesh in his hands, pushing them together as he moved up to slide his dick between them.

She held her tits in place as he dropped his hands to the mattress for support and raised his ass for the first stroke.

"Come on, fuck those tits, baby," she said.

He pumped his hips, sending the full length of his cock through her slick cleavage. The head of his dick bumped her chin. She opened her mouth and ran her tongue around it.

He pulled back and then slid his cock between her tits again, this time pushing it into her mouth. The angle was awkward for taking his cock in her mouth, so Amanda raised up to rest her back against the headboard.

Mark grabbed the headboard to support himself as he began to fuck his wife's beautiful tits. His cock was now slick with oil too. It moved easily between Amanda's boobs. She ran her tongue around the head of his cock each time it peeked up from between her tits, occasionally letting a good portion of his meat slip into her mouth, where she would trap it and suck.

"Oh, yeah, suck it," Mark moaned.

Amanda tightened her lips on his cock and sucked hard. Mark slowly pulled back, drawing his cock from the wet suction of her mouth and back through the slick valley between her tits.

She wrapped a hand around his cock and lifted it, bringing it over to slap it against one nipple, then over to the other. She leaned up and took him into her mouth again, running her hand up and down the length of his greasy cock as she concentrated her efforts on the swollen knob.

She teased the sensitive rim of his cock head with her tongue and nibbled at the tip, then she sucked hard on it, her fingers tightening on his slick meat as she jerked his thick shaft.

"Wanna come?" she asked, breathing heavy, pulling his cock faster, letting the tip of it just barely touch her lower lip.

"Not yet," he said.

He could have. He was that close. Another ten seconds of her hand, another couple of swipes of her tongue, and it would have happened.

He pulled away and moved down to kneel at her feet. She smiled knowingly. This was one of his kinky little fetishes.

His dick stood up hard and needy, the thick veins running along his shaft pulsing with the flow of blood, his balls swollen with come.

She turned her feet sideways and trapped his dick between the oily soles of them, squeezing his cock between them until the head of it turned crimson and seemed about ready to explode.

"You like that?" she asked teasingly.

"Yeah," he groaned.

She began to slide her feet up and down on his cock, curling her totes around it as she did. He grabbed her ankles, one in each hand, and took control, moving her feet up and down, quickening the pace.

"Come on my feet," she urged, though it wasn't necessary because he intended to do just that.

She pulled one foot away and slipped it between his legs, pressing her toes up against the underside of his balls. She put her other foot against his cock and pushed it against his belly, trapping his dick between her big toe and second toe, and then she started working both feet in unison, stroking his cock and massaging his balls until he thought he would pass out from the sheer oily pleasure of it.

He took her by the ankles and pressed her feet around both sides of his shaft, pressing hard to keep up the pressure as he began to rock his hips, sliding his slippery cock back and forth between the bottoms of his feet.

Amanda raised up, resting her weight on her elbows, watching with casual curiosity as he fucked her feet. She never really understood that particular fetish, but it turned Mark on, so she was willing to indulge him.

As Mark fucked her feet, Amanda lifted one of her tits and flicked the tip of her tongue around the nipple, then she took it in her mouth and began sucking on it. That was another thing that turned him on, watching her suck her own tits. That was fine by her. She liked doing it. She liked feeling her nipple in her mouth, especially like this, all hard and slippery.

She pumped her feet as he clung tight to her ankles, and between the two of them, her feet moved so fast on his cock it was almost a blur. His wrists beat a steady rhythm against his thighs. He closed his eyes, letting the sensation of her smooth, oily feet take him closer to the edge.

"Not long," he said through clenched teeth.

She raised herself a little more, preparing for what she knew would happen next. The first shot of come *never* landed on her feet. She'd done this enough times to know how far it would go and how to control where it landed. If she raised up just so, his come would splash her tits; if she sank down low enough and opened her mouth, she could catch it on her tongue.

She wanted it all over her tits now.

"Come on," she encouraged, rubbing a hand over her tits and pinching her nipples.

He liked to hear her talk. She didn't have to say much. The sound of her voice when he was on the verge of climax was enough to take him there.

"Ohhhh," he groaned, forcing his cock between her feet one last time and holding his position as a thick spurt of come erupted from his cock, making a high arc that reached all the way to her tits.

She liked the way it felt splashing her skin. It was warm and as slick as the oil that covered her. She watched it run down between her breasts, making a beeline for her belly.

Mark's cock jerked again, sending another creamy splash of come to join the first, and the little trail of come on its way to her belly became a flowing river of semen.

She ran her fingers through the smooth white cream and stuck them into her mouth, smiling up at him as she made a production of drawing the fingers from her mouth, sucking the come from them.

He was still coming, only now it was running all over her feet.

She smeared his come around the head of his cock, then sat up to lick it off. She teased his sticky wet cock with her tongue, then took the head of it in her mouth and sucked gently, still flicking her tongue against the tip.

He brushed her hair from her face so he could watch. She tilted her eyes up at him as she took his cock deeper into her mouth. With one hand she stroked his balls, with her other hand she stroked his shaft, all the while keeping her mouth and tongue working on him.

There wasn't time for his cock to get soft. She knew how to keep him rock solid, even after he'd been thoroughly satisfied. After all the years she'd been sucking his cock, she knew all the right spots to lick, exactly what kind of pressure to exert, and where to do it.

It wasn't long before she had him on the edge and moaning again, but she stopped suddenly, leaving him with a confused look on his face.

"Follow me," she said, sliding off the bed and going into the bathroom.

He hurried after her, and by the time he reached her, she was already sinking down into the tub of oil. He grinned and climbed in after her.

She opened her legs wide as he settled between them. She reached down and gripped his cock, tugging him to her, raising her ass just enough to get his cock into her pussy.

He pressed his hands flat against the bottom of the tub and slowly rocked his hips, sinking his dick to the hilt. He withdrew just as slowly, bringing the head of his cock to rest just inside her, then he entered her again, making her shudder with pleasure as he filled her.

The oil rolled across their bodies in thick lapping waves as he increased the tempo of his thrusts, pushing his cock in and out of her. Her ass slid across the bottom of the tub with every thrust.

He slipped out of her pussy, and in his haste to get back inside her, he slid his cock up her ass. She gasped sharply, then groaned as his cock filled her bottom. The unexpected penetration sent shockwaves through her. She tried to wrap her legs around him and sank deeper into the oil.

He pulled out of her and got on his knees, groping her slippery waist to raise her up and turn her around. She held tight to the front of the tub as he slid his cock back into her ass and started pumping.

His balls slapped heavily against her pussy. He sank his cock all the way into her and came all the way out again, each stroke stretching and filling her ass. The oil pushing into her ass with each thrust of his cock, creating a smooth, warm sensation that drove her insane with pleasure.

She pumped her ass against him, trembling as his cock came out of her and went in again. Her breathing quickened. She wanted the glorious release she knew this climax would bring, but she wanted to prolong the build up as well.

Mark held her tight around her waist. She looked back at him and saw that his eyes were closed in deep concentration, the way he always became when he was trying not to come too soon.

"Don't hold back," she said. "I want you to come for me."

"Yeah?"

"Yeah, I'm ready. I want us to come together."

He fucked her harder as he reached around to rub his fingers against her clit. She pushed her ass against him and started to grind, trapping his cock deep inside her pussy.

"Shit, babe, I'm so close now . . ."

"Come for me," she panted.

"Now," he groaned, and as he pushed into her one final time, his knees slid across the bottom of the tub and he fell backward, his arms groping for the sides of the tub as his cock slipped out of her pussy.

The sudden departure of his cock and all the noise Mark made as he toppled backward caused Amanda to turn sharply to see what the problem was, and when she did, her hands slipped off the bathtub and she fell forward, cracking her head against the faucet.

Despite his fall, Mark was coming. Amanda saw the come spurting from his cock even through the hazy cloud the blow to her head had caused. She scooted toward him, moving as if she were drunk, and took his cock in one hand, jerking him off as she took him in her mouth to finish him off.

The look of stunned confusion on his face was priceless. Amanda tried hard not to laugh, but she felt her smile spreading across her face even as she bit her lip to stop it.

Suddenly she broke into a fit of laughter. Mark looked momentarily chagrined, and then he was laughing with her as she fell on top of him and they let the bathtub full of oil take them under.

So Rachel

I let myself into an empty house. The hardwood floors echoed under my feet. The silence was overwhelming as I tried to take it all in.

This was so Rachel.

Everything had to be a big production with her.

The first time we'd made love, just shortly after meeting at one of those parties no one truly wants to attend, she'd taken me to her place for a night of over-the-top lovemaking. All candles and champagne and passion.

So Rachel.

Her hair, jet black and long, fell over me as she climbed on top of me and kissed her way down. Her pale skin caressed me, her hard dark nipples dragged across my skin, giving me goose bumps. She took my cock into her mouth and licked every inch of its hard flesh. She drew it deep into her mouth, hands and tongue working together to bring me to a climax I thought would never be topped.

So Rachel.

She sat up and guided me into her, sliding down on me, the smooth heat of her enveloping me as she moved up and down, pale breasts dangling in my face. She kept at me until I came again and again, even when I thought it would be impossible to go another round.

One transgression on my part.

In the bedroom, written on the mirror in pink lipstick: I hope she was worth it.

So dramatic.

So Rachel.

Lying on the floor, a pair of silky panties. I picked them up, held them to my face, and inhaled the aroma.

So Rachel.

She'd left the panties behind on purpose, you could bet money on that.

Everything Rachel did came with a blueprint. Everything she did was intense.

Everything she did was so Rachel.

Joelle waited anxiously for Derek to arrive. They hadn't seen one another since college. Derek had called her after seeing her on a talk show where she'd been promoting her new novel.

Joelle thought about how much she'd changed since college. Her relationship with Derek had been both brief and exciting, but she wasn't the same girl now as the she'd been in college.

Not the same girl at all.

She couldn't predict how tonight would go. She wasn't sure she even wanted to. She'd even been a little hesitant when he'd asked her to dinner. How often did he recall the times they'd spent together those many years ago? Had he read her book all the way through, as he claimed he had? Did he recognize himself in some of the heated passages?

Headlights flashed through the front window as a car pulled into the driveway. She heard the slam of a car door. A moment later came the knock. This was it. She hadn't seen Derek in more than a decade. She wondered if he would still have the same effect on her as he'd had back then.

She checked herself one last time in the mirror. Dinner was going to be casual, so she'd opted for a semi-casual blouse and dark pants. No dresses this evening.

She answered the door. Derek stood there wearing jeans and an Abercrombie and Fitch like only he could wear them. As had always been his custom, he had a five-o'clock shadow that made him look sexy as hell. His dark blue eyes pierced her soul the instant he looked at her. She did her best not to blush, but she wasn't sure she managed to pull it off.

"You look wonderful," he said.

"Thank you," she said.

Dinner was at a place called Villa Diego. They started with oysters and followed it with boiled shrimp in butter sauce, lobster tail, and scallops, served with toasted French garlic bread and chardonnay. The meal was delicious and the conversation was even better.

They decided to call it an early night, though. Actually, calling it an early night had been Joelle's idea. The more she thought about it, the more she understood why she had insisted on it. She was afraid of him. Afraid of losing control if she was near him for too long.

Admitting fear to herself had been a hard thing. She was sure she could handle being with him these days. She was, after all, a different girl than she'd been in college. She was strong and successful. The layers of self criticism she'd covered herself with back then had been peeled away by the years. Her books were bestsellers, her fans adored her, and she was self sufficient in every way.

Why, then, did she feel herself melting whenever he brushed by her? Why did she feel like the lost little girl in need of direction?

Derek was gracious about it. He took her home immediately upon her request, and although she could tell he wanted her to invite him in, he didn't push the issue. He did ask for a kiss, which she gave him, and he asked if he could call her again, which she gave him permission to do.

The kiss had been a simple one. On the lips, yes, but quick and without any sort of sexual connotation.

Or so she'd thought. Once she was inside her house and tucked away in the safety of her bedroom, she had begun to let her imagination run wild. She felt a chill travel along her spine as she remembered the touch of his lips on hers. She thought about the times in college when they'd slipped away for their secret sessions of light bondage and, in particular, the spankings.

Her new book recalled many of their adventures. She remembered writing the book—the sleepless nights she'd spent feeling wet between her legs with the memories. She'd even thought many times about looking Derek up again during the writing of the book, just so she could revive some of the old feelings she'd had for him during school.

She never did, of course. It had always been her belief that some things were better left in the past.

She couldn't believe how horny being with him again had made her. She climbed into her bed naked, feeling the cool touch of her sheets as she slipped beneath them. Her nipples hardened under the soft caress of the Italian silk.

She kept a long, slender pink vibrator in the nightstand beside her bed, along with a tube of extra-slippery lubricant. She took those things out and laid them beside her on the bed, then she drew her knees up under the sheets and opened them wide, allowing her fingers easy access.

A lot of women touched themselves only when there was no man available. Masturbation for a lot of the girls she knew was simply an act of sexual release, done as quickly and efficiently as possible.

Not for Joelle. She loved touching herself. She liked to trace every curve of her body with the tips of her fingers and tease her nipples until they were so taut they almost hurt. She loved the way it felt when she slipped a finger deep inside herself so she could feel her juices building.

She had, over the years, become quite experienced at giving herself an orgasm, but she had become adept at the build up as well. She was good at teasing herself, bringing herself to the brink, and then finally, when she could take the delay of her release no more, allowing herself to go over the edge.

She closed her eyes and pushed her finger deep inside herself, feeling the walls of her pussy clench around it. She withdrew her finger slowly, bringing it up and pressing it against her clit. She applied the right amount of pleasure to stimulate herself. When she was near the edge, she reached over and brought the vibrator to her pussy. She was dripping with her juices and wouldn't need the lubrication tonight.

She eased the slender pink vibrator inside herself and continued to finger her clitoris, thinking about Derek as she did. She remembered the way she had given herself to him when they were in school together. How many times had she offered up her behind to the stinging glance of his palm?

Her body began to quiver. She felt a tingling sensation in her belly, building slowly, spreading downward to encompass her pussy and upward to set her nipples on fire with electrical pulses of pleasure.

She arched her back and sank the slender vibrator deeper into her pussy. She pressed her fingers down on her clit, rubbing them in a circular motion.

Her release was explosive. She screamed as she reached the peak of her climax and then rode the subsiding waves of pleasure all the way down.

When it was over, she lay in bed naked, her vibrator beside her and her fingers still damp with her juices.

She closed her eyes and recalled a night with Derek, so long ago, back when they were young and full of fire.

She had only known him a week. She had gone on one date with him. That was all it took. A single date and she was his.

That night, after dinner and a movie, he had asked her to accompany him to his apartment. She'd gone, believing him when he told her his intentions were not to seduce her. The truth was, she'd already been seduced. She wanted him to want her in that way, and as it had turned out, he had.

The sex that night was nothing kinky. It had been hot and passionate, but there had been none of the special acts they shared later on.

Derek had eaten her pussy first. He'd gone down on her for a long time—longer than any man ever had—and he'd made her see stars with his tongue.

When he finally got around to fucking her, she had been so ready for his cock that she had orgasmed almost the instant he slid into her.

It was with these memories that Joelle fell asleep.

She woke the next morning with the phone ringing. She reached over and answered it, trying her best to sound more awake than she was.

"I'll see you tonight," Derek said.

"Huh?"

"Tonight," he repeated. "Wear something very short, no panties."

He hung up on her.

The nerve of him to hang up on her like that.

The nerve of him to give her a *command* and then hang up on her like that.

Who did he think he was? They weren't still in college, and she wasn't the shy little girl she'd been then. She wasn't about to get caught up in those submissive/dominant games again. Not unless she was the one in control.

She went into the bathroom, turned on the shower, and stepped under the hot spray of water. As she began to soap her body, she let her thoughts wander to the phone call from Derek. How hot and commanding his voice had sounded.

She shook the memory of the phone call from her mind. She was not going to allow him to draw her back into his need to control.

She soaped her breasts, running her palms over her hard nipples, and then she touched her pussy, which she found slippery with her arousal. She silently scolded herself for allowing thoughts of Derek to heat her up so quickly, even when she tried forcing herself to feel otherwise.

She slid two fingers into her pussy and fucked herself with them, turning her hand so she could press her thumb against her clit as she did. She didn't waste time with the build up this morning. She made herself come quickly, pressing one hand against the wall of the shower for support.

When she finished her shower, she put on a pair of shorts and a t-shirt. She made a pot of coffee, poured a cup, and sat down in front of her laptop to work on her next book. She found, as she tried to get into the groove of writing, that her mind kept wandering to Derek.

Damnit, why did she allow it to happen?

She grabbed her cell and started to call him back. She would tell him not to come over tonight. She'd make it clear that she wasn't interested in playing his silly games anymore. That would teach him to be so sure of himself.

She set the phone down instead, and she went back to work, this time managing at least a little bit of the chapter she was working on.

* * *

He would be here in fifteen minutes. She was wearing a very short skirt and a tight top that emphasized her breasts. Her feet were bare, the way she knew he preferred them, and she wore no panties.

Her pussy was already soaking wet. She wanted so bad to touch herself, but she decided to wait for Derek. She'd given up trying to deny her need to be dominated by him. The overwhelming desire had come back the moment he'd called her on the phone and *told* her he was coming over.

And now she waited, a slave to her desire. She knew where this would go. She'd been here before, many times over, and she knew exactly what would happen. He would be demanding and she would resist, but only playfully so, and only just enough to force him to punish her.

Punishment.

That was the name of the game between them. She was the bad girl and he meted punishment as he saw fit, usually in the form of a couple of stinging blows across the soft, yielding flesh of her ass.

She hadn't been spanked since their days in college because she'd never found another man to whom she could give herself to as completely as she could Derek.

No other man was worthy.

A copy of her book lay on the coffee table. On the cover was the picture of a very svelte blonde lying across the lap of a man with dark hair and smoldering eyes. The man almost captured the essence of Derek. Joelle had actually found a way to get in touch with the model for the book cover, and she'd given him a call. They'd met for dinner, but it hadn't taken her long to realize that the model, whose name was Tim, didn't possess the strong personality Derek possessed. He'd been a boring conversationalist with a weak, almost prima donna way about him. A shame, really. Such a waste.

Joelle never saw him again.

Headlights flashed through the front window. She heard the car door and waited, her heart beating hard with anticipation.

The doorbell rang.

She answered it.

Derek came inside. He stood in the foyer, looking her over, his eyes taking in every inch of her but betraying nothing of what he might be thinking.

She stood there on display, vulnerable and waiting for his command.

"Have you been naughty?" he asked.

Her eyes were downcast when she replied, "Yes, I have."

"Come with me."

He walked past her and moved into the living room. She followed, feeling the last vestiges of the strong, independent woman she'd become slip away. She was now that same uncertain girl she'd been back at school.

She was lost in *his* world.

Derek faced her, once again letting his eyes caress her from top to bottom.

"Lift your skirt," he said.

He smiled his approval. Not only was she not wearing panties, she'd shaved her pussy completely smooth, just the way she remembered Derek liking it.

"You haven't forgotten," he said.

"No . . ."

He glanced down at her book on the coffee table, then he picked it up and quickly thumbed through the pages, pausing now and then to read a passage to himself. "You haven't forgotten many things," he said.

"No, I haven't," she said.

435

"Tell me something, Joelle . . . how many men have there been since you and I? How many men have had the opportunity to tame you?"

"None," she said.

"I find that hard to believe," he told her. "You have always had a hard time believing it, but you were always a woman in need of taming . . ."

"There have been no other men." she repeated.

Derek set the book down on the coffee table. He stepped up to Joelle and took her face in his hands, tilting her head slightly to the side as he bent to kiss her lips. She felt like she would melt in his hands.

He pulled away then, indicating with a slight nod of his head that she should sit on the couch.

She did.

Derek unbuttoned his shirt and removed it. He folded it neatly and laid it over the back of a chair, then he took off his shoes and socks and set them aside.

Joelle watched his muscles bulge and flex with every move he made. She wanted him so badly at that moment that she almost could not resist the temptation to make a move.

Derek moved over to stand in front of her. She looked up at him, feeling like a little girl who had been caught with her hands in a cookie jar. She felt vulnerable and unable to maintain even a shred of resistance to him. She knew, with a certainty, that she would do anything he asked of her.

Anything at all.

"Go ahead, unzip my pants," he said.

She reached up and unzipped his pants, hesitating a moment before reaching inside to extract his cock. She ran her thumb along the underside of his shaft, feeling the veins running along its length. She felt the blood coursing through his cock, causing it to expand in her grip.

Just when she was about to take him into her mouth, Derek pulled away from her and pushed his cock back into his pants.

"That's mean," she said.

"Mean? Why is that mean?"

"You know what I wanted to do."

"And you'll have your chance," he promised.

He held out his hands to her. She gave him her hands and he pulled her to her feet, then he took her place on the couch and patted his lap.

She resisted. She knew the effort would be useless, but she did it anyway. She wanted to prove she had some degree of control, that she wasn't completely at his mercy. What she showed him was the exact opposite.

She lay across his lap, lifting her skirt before she did, exposing the soft, gently curved swell of her bare bottom to him.

He laid his hand on her ass and caressed it, moving his palm over the soft flesh in a circular motion.

He brought his hand up. She drew in a sharp breath as she waited for the blow to come. The time between when he raised his hand and it landed on her bottom seemed like an eternity. The blow stung. Not too much, but enough to cause her to tighten her cheeks, which only made it sting worse.

He brought his hand down on her bottom again. The sound of his palm against her skin was like a firecracker.

She squirmed.

He smacked her ass again. This time she whimpered, biting her lower lips to keep it to a minimum. She felt the cheeks of her bottom warming and knew that he had probably left an imprint of his hand on her tender flesh.

"I read your book," he said.

He brought his hand down on her ass.

"Very sexy . . ."

He slapped her ass again.

"It's so clear in those passages how much you missed me."

This time he brought his hand down harder, making contact with her ass hard enough to cause her to cry out.

"Get up," he said.

She stood up, facing him, and reached back to rub her sore bottom.

He reached for the book and opened it to a random page.

"I loved to feel his hand hard against my ass . . ." he read. "When he spanked me, I knew it was because I had disobeyed him, that I had acted without his consent, and that it was for my own good."

He looked up at her and smiled.

She looked away, knowing she was blushing.

"Let me see your tits," he said.

She hated that word. She hated it when he referred to her breasts as tits. He knew how she felt about it, which was why he did it. He wanted a reaction.

She didn't give him the satisfaction. Instead, she took off her top, exposing her breasts to him. Her nipples were hard and a deeper pink than usual, the way they always got when she was turned on.

Derek cupped her breasts and squeezed them, gently at first, then harder. She looked him in the eyes as he did it, standing her ground, making sure he knew that she could take whatever he wanted to give her.

He leaned in for a kiss. His lips brushed hers. She opened her mouth and let his tongue dance inside.

He pulled her close to him. Her nipples bit into his smooth, strong chest. He stroked her hair and then stepped back, motioning for her to turn away from him. When she did, he kneeled behind her and pushed her skirt up over her bottom. She felt his kisses on her ass, soft and warm and slightly damp, soothing away the sting of his blows. He brought his hands down and around, sliding them over her cheeks, nipping at her with his teeth.

His tongue darted between her cheeks and found her anus. The touch of it there made her knees weak.

He stood up, turned her around so she was facing him, and gave her another kiss, more passionate than any he'd given her so far.

"Take off your skirt," he said.

She removed her skirt and stood before him naked, waiting for him to fuck her. That was what she wanted now more than anything else. She wanted to feel his cock sliding inside her.

Derek took her by the hand.

"Show me your bedroom," he told her.

She led the way. He told her to lie down across the bed, face down, and then he placed two pillows under her, propping her ass up. He ran his hands over her cheeks, lifting and separating them. His thumbs drew the outer lips of her pussy apart, and then he pressed the tip of one thumb inside her.

"You're wet," he said. "Being told what to do arouses you."

Derek dropped his pants and climbed onto the bed, lowering himself on top of Joelle. The head of his cock nudged against her pussy, pushing the lips apart. He inched his dick inside her.

"Is that what you've been waiting for?" he asked. "Is that what you've missed all these years?"

He slid all the way inside her.

"Yes," she said, moaning her response.

This was exactly what she'd been missing.

Strapped for Cash

Adam was strapped for cash. It was as simple as that. He opened his wallet and stared inside, as if staring would change the fact that he was flat broke. It pissed him off to no end. A bunch of his friends were hanging out at the beach this weekend and he had no money. No money meant no fun, no action, and that was what Adam considered a bum deal.

He was sitting on the couch when his sister's friend Becky came from the kitchen. She stopped and said, "Why the long face?"

"Money problems," Adam said. "Big party at the beach this weekend and I don't have any cash."

"Bummer," Becky said.

"It sucks."

"I bet it does," she responded. "Ever think about getting a job?"

He looked at her and rolled his eyes.

"Seriously, Adam, you're twenty-three years old, you live with your sister, and you're unemployed."

"I didn't ask for your opinion," he said.

Adam secretly had the hots for Becky. She was two years older than him, slim, with small breasts and shoulder-length brown hair. Her eyes were green and she had the sexiest smile he'd ever seen. The only problem was, she was a sarcastic bitch most of the time. He'd never asked her out because he knew she would shoot him down in a heartbeat, and he wasn't about to give her the satisfaction.

"I'm just stating facts, Adam. You need to grow up."

"Get lost, will ya," he said. "I don't need the grief."

Becky shook her head in wonder. She started for the door and stopped. "I'll tell you what," she said. "If you want to earn some money, I might have a proposition for you."

"What kind of proposition?" he asked, not quite trusting her motives.

"Come by my place tonight," she said. "I'll tell you then."

* * *

Becky held the strap-on dildo in one hand and stroked it with the other, admiring the length and thickness of it. She loved the detail, right down to its realistic flesh tone and the thick blue veins running along the length of the shaft. She squeezed it, enjoying the firm but pliant feel of it in her grip.

Adam was cute. A bum, yes, but cute nonetheless. She had a fantasy, and Adam was perfect for it. She had a good feeling he would be willing to go along with almost anything for money, and besides, she could tell he had the hots for her. Even without getting paid, Adam would probably do anything she asked, but she was willing to help him fund his weekend adventure anyway, so long as she got what she wanted from it.

She stripped down to her panties and lay in bed, still caressing the strap-on cock. She'd been at the mercy of it more than once, most often using it on herself, two times with Adam's sister Jill. They weren't lesbians by any means, but they'd fooled around a couple of times, and Jill had strapped the cock on to fuck Becky.

Now it was Adam's turn. Would he submit to her wicked fantasies? She was almost certain he would.

She slid her mouth around the cock and made it wet, then she spread her legs and pressed the fat tip against her opening. She pushed it in slowly, loving the way it stretched her wide open, the way the lips of her pussy separated as the thick dildo disappeared inside her.

She moaned and lifted her butt, allowing the cock to slide deep inside her. She pushed it in until the balls pressed against her ass, then she withdrew it almost completely before sliding it in again.

The dildo had kept her happy during many lonely nights. It was making her happy now, and it would make her happy when Adam finally arrived.

The anticipation was almost too much for her. Her muscles tensed and her belly quivered as she exploded with pleasure, pushing her body up in an arch and holding it there until the waves of her orgasm subsided and she crashed back down on the bed, temporarily satiated.

* * *

Adam stood at the door, smiling nervously. Becky invited him in. She wore very short cut offs and a halter. Her small nipples were erect and clearly outlined through the thin material of the top.

Adam couldn't take his eyes off her. He was doing everything but drooling.

"Come on in," she said.

He came into the apartment and she closed the door. She led him into the living room. He sat on the couch and she sat beside him, drawing one leg up as she turned to face him.

"I'll be direct," she said. "I have a fantasy. It's a bit wild, but if you're willing to help me with it, I'll give you five hundred bucks. How's that sound?"

"Five hundred bucks?" he said. "What would I have to do for that, suck somebody's cock?"

"For starters," she said, smiling mischievously.

His eyebrows furrowed. "You're joking, right?"

"Not really," she said.

She leaned over and kissed him. He didn't react at first, still stunned by her announcement. She teased his mouth with her tongue until he responded, allowing her tongue to slip into his mouth. He was a little inexperienced, she could tell that right away, but she would soon take care of that.

She took his hand and guided it into her halter, moving his fingers over her hard nipple. She moved it for him, circling her nipple until he got the idea and took over for her.

She reached down and rubbed his dick through his pants. He was already rock hard. She unzipped him and extracted his cock, giving it a few strokes before she slid from the couch and got on her knees in front of him.

She had never considered herself very good at giving blowjobs, but she'd always been good enough to get the job done. By the way Adam moaned, you would think he'd never had one in his life.

She liked his cock. It was smooth and thick. She opened wide and took him halfway into her mouth, tightening her lips around him as she sucked. She wrapped her hand around the base of his cock and moved it up and down as she worked her tongue against the underside of his shaft.

"Wow, that's good," he groaned.

She looked up at him, taking her mouth from his cock. "Just getting you worked up for what I have in mind," she said. "You might want to take a few pointers."

He frowned at the comment, but he was so turned on by her attention that he let it go by without response.

"Take your clothes off," she said.

He kicked off his shoes and stood. As she tugged his pants and underwear down, he took off his shirt, then he sat again and removed his socks.

"What about you?" he asked.

"I'll get undressed when I'm ready," she said.

She knelt in front of him and took his cock in her mouth again, taking the full length of it into her mouth and sucking. He was at her mercy now. She knew it. If there had been any doubt in her mind that he'd go along with what she wanted, that doubt had long since vanished.

"Follow me," she said, standing up, leaving his cock wet and sticking up from his lap like a flag pole.

He followed her into the bedroom. She told him to lie down, which he did without hesitating, and then she began undressing. When she was naked, she climbed onto the bed with him, straddling him, and moved until her pussy hovered just above his face and out of his reach.

"You wanna lick me?" she asked.

"Yes," he responded, unable to hide the enthusiasm in his voice.

"Tell me you want to lick me," she said.

443

"I wanna lick your pussy."

She lowered her pussy until he could just reach it. He stuck out his tongue and wiggled it against her clit. She enjoyed the hungry flick of his tongue for a moment before she pulled away, again just out of his reach.

"Does that taste good?" she asked.

"Oh, yeah . . ."

"Do you like it?"

"I love it," he responded eagerly.

"You want me to sit on your face, don't you?" she said. "Tell me how much you'd like to have me sit on your face."

"Sit on my face," he said."I want you to sit on my face."

She lowered her pussy to his face, settling her full weight on him. He worked his tongue around until he was able to find her opening and slip it up inside her.

"Yeah, fuck me with that tongue," she said. "God, that feels so good."

She leaned up and grabbed hold of the headboard, using it for support as she began humping his face, grinding her pussy back and forth, moving up and down.

"Stick that tongue in there," she said, moaning. "Fuck me with it."

He pushed it in as far as he could and worked it around inside her.

"Ummm, that feels so good," she said.

She raised up and turned around, keeping her pussy on his face as she leaned down and took his cock in her mouth.

Adam spread the cheeks of her ass and pushed his tongue inside her. She rocked backward, pressing down on his tongue, shifting against him until she found a comfortable position.

His cock pulsed against her tongue. She rubbed his balls and jerked his shaft until she could hear his muffled moans against her pussy. The vibration of his moans along with his probing tongue brought her to orgasm.

She sucked his cock harder, jerking her fist up and down on his shaft, and suddenly he exploded into her mouth, filling it with what seemed an endless supply of come. She couldn't swallow all of it and pulled away, jerking the last of it over her breasts.

She climbed off him and off the bed. He watched her. The look on his face was nervous, as if he was worried she was finished.

She opened the drawer of the stand beside the bed and reached inside. She withdrew the strap-on and a bottle of lubrication. She set the lubrication on the nightstand and attached the strap on.

Adam's eyes widened as the slow realization of her intentions came to him.

"Suck my cock," she said.

He didn't move.

"Come on, you know you want to," she urged him.

His hesitation slowly melted away and he sat up in front of her. She stroked the rubber cock as she guided it to his mouth.

"Come on, baby, suck it," she said.

He wrapped his hand around the strap-on cock and took it into his mouth. Becky watched with fascination as he bobbed his head up and down on it. She saw none of his earlier hesitation. He seemed to be enjoying himself.

She pulled the dong from his mouth, holding it just out of his reach. "You like that?" she asked.

"It's all right," he said, trying his best to be nonchalant.

"It looks more than all right," she teased. "It looks to me like you're pretty good at it. Is there something you're not telling me?

"Ungh-uh," he said. "I'm trying to earn a little cash, that's all."

"Sucking my cock is only the beginning," she said. "Turn around."

He hesitated this time. She thought at first that he was going to refuse, but then he shrugged his shoulders and turned around, pointing his backside at her.

She picked up the lubrication. Slik-Hot. She squirted a generous amount into the palm of her hand. She assumed this was his first time and that there would be no such thing as too much lubrication.

She used some of the lubrication around his anus. She smeared it around the puckered opening and then worked first one, then two fingers inside him, being gentle as she loosened him up to prepare him for the dildo.

She remembered a friend had once told her she had penis envy. She'd thought her friend was crazy at the time, but later on, when Becky was a little older, she began to see what her friend had meant. She'd lain awake many nights wondering what it would be like to have a cock, to slide into a tight, warm pussy and pump into its slick confines until she came.

The strap-on was a poor substitute for the feeling part, but it gave her an idea what it felt like to be the one in control. Most women didn't see it that way, and neither did most men, for that matter, but Becky thought that having a penis gave its owner a certain amount of control.

It wasn't that she was a control freak or anything, but she had to admit, even if it was only to herself, she liked the feeling of being in control every once in a while, and if a lot of men thought about it, they would probably come to the realization that they enjoyed being controlled as well.

"Do you want me to fuck you?" she asked Adam.

He didn't answer.

She rubbed the head of the dildo against his balls and then between the cheeks of his ass. He made no effort to object.

"Tell me you want me to fuck you," she said.

"I do," he said.

"No, I want to hear the words," she demanded.

"I want you to fuck me," he said, but the words came out meek.

"Louder," she insisted.

He said it again, this time with more conviction.

She rubbed the tip of the cock up and down between his cheeks and settled it against his asshole. He groaned as she leaned her weight forward. She grasped the strap-on firmly at the base and held it as she eased it into him.

"How does it feel?" she asked.

She only had about two inches of the dildo inside him.

"It hurts," he said.

"Want me to stop?"

He shook his head.

She eased another inch or so into him, then she took him firmly by the hips and held him steady as she applied even pressure. The lubrication made her efforts substantially easier. It wasn't long before his anal muscle relaxed and she was able to fit almost all of the dildo in on the first stroke.

She withdrew about halfway and went in again, this time sinking the cock into his ass to the hilt. He moaned as she withdrew, but he showed no signs of wanting her to stop. She dug her fingers tighter into his hips and picked up the pace, keeping an even rhythm, sending the cock all the way into his ass with each thrust forward and drawing it almost completely out on every backstroke.

"You like that, don't you?" she said.

He looked back at her over his shoulder and she knew she was right. He was enjoying the hell out of it.

"Maybe this is what you've been wanting all along, huh?" she said.

She pulled the strap-on cock from his ass and rubbed the head of it around his asshole a few times, then she inserted it again. He was nice and loose, taking it easily, and each stroke brought a deep-throated groan of pleasure from him.

She reached around and felt his cock. He had a hard-on. She squeezed and stroked him as she continued thrusting into his ass.

She wished she could feel the tightness of his ass . . . she wanted to feel herself coming inside him.

She ran her thumb over the tip of his cock and smeared a silky-smooth drop of pre-come around him.

"Don't you come yet," she said.

She withdrew the dildo from his ass, took a condom from the nightstand, and tore the package open. She rolled the condom over his cock and lay back on the bed, spreading her legs wide. "I want you to fuck me," she said.

She didn't bother taking the strap-on cock off. She pushed it to one side and slid a finger inside her pussy. She couldn't believe how wet she was, how turned on by this whole situation she was.

Adam climbed between her legs and slid his cock into her. She tightened her legs around his waist and drew him all the way inside.

"Yeah," she groaned. "Come on, fuck me."

He pulled out and went in again, long and deep, each stroke filling her pussy to the hilt. He grunted with each thrust.

"Ohhhh, shit, this feels so fucking good . . ." he said.

She knew he wasn't going to last. He was pumping away at her, driving his cock in and out, almost crying with gratitude. If she had to bet on it, she'd say his sexual experience was limited at best. He was like a kid just learning to walk.

"I'm coming," he groaned.

She could feel it through the condom.

She was close to the edge herself. Her body was responding. She felt the rollercoaster effect in her stomach, the tingling sensations building deep inside her as each stroke of his cock brought her nearer to the ultimate explosion.

She clung to him and arched her back, cupping his ass and bringing him deep inside her. The walls of her pussy melted around his cock. She suddenly feared that she might strip the condom from his cock. Adam was fun, but there was no way in hell she wanted to make the mistake of getting pregnant by him.

Waves of pleasure swept over her. She screamed, she moaned, she called out his name over and over . . .

"Adam . . ."

The spasms seemed endless.

"I'm coming . . ." she screamed at the top of her lungs, pressing herself hard against him, wanting now to feel him inside her, not just his cock, but all of him. She wanted him to climb inside her, literally, and if it were possible, that is exactly what she would have had him do.

They lay together afterward, his arms around her, the used condom lying next to the bed on the floor, right along with the strap-on cock. It took the two of them some time to regain their composure. Her breath came in a slow, deep rhythm. She felt secure and warm and satisfied.

It frightened her. What was she thinking? This was all a game. She owed him five hundred dollars, but when she reminded him of it, he told her to keep the money. She knew then. This was more than a game. This was something special. This was something she had not bargained for.

"Where do we go now?" he asked.

He felt it too.

"I don't know . . . this isn't what I expected."

"Me either."

They lay in silence for several minutes, then she said, "Come with me to take a shower?"

He followed her into the bathroom. She turned on the shower and stepped in. He got in with her, taking her into his arms. His cock was hard again. He leaned her against the wall and kissed her. She guided him into her, draping one of her legs around the back of his.

"How's your ass?" she asked.

"Sore," he answered.

"Poor baby."

She gave him a swat on the ass.

There was no condom this time. It was crazy, she knew that. She was letting her emotions run wild. She was allowing good sex to dictate her future.

She felt confident about their future. She felt sure that Adam was confident too. Maybe she'd known all along. Maybe the attraction had always been there.

He moved inside her. She felt the same familiar flutterings as before. His kisses were different. His tongue sought her mouth and her tongue danced against his as he worked his cock in and out of her, this time at a more relaxed pace.

They were married three months later. Adam had a good job working with computers, they were buying a house, and they were expecting their first child.

The honeymoon was on a tropical island on Panama's Pacific coast. They were barely settled into bed the first night when Becky reached under her pillow.

"I brought along a surprise," she said.

Adam poured two glasses of champagne. He fed her a strawberry dipped in chocolate. "What surprise?" he asked.

She pulled the strap-on cock from under her pillow. "Our friend," she said.

Adam grinned. He was no longer strapped for cash, but that didn't mean he couldn't give into her every now and then. It was her fantasy, after all, and he had every intention of spending the rest of their lives making her wishes come true.

He gulped his champagne, gave her a kiss, and assumed the position.

Sweet Shoppe

He walked into the Sweet Shoppe on the corner and bought a box of expensive chocolates, a dozen roses, and chocolate-covered strawberries.

The girl behind the counter rang his purchase.

"Someone really special, huh?" she asked.

"Yes," he replied. "Someone special."

"Well, she's a very lucky girl," she said. "To have someone who cares about her as much as you do, I mean."

"Well, thank you."

He started to go, paused at the door, and turned back to the girl behind the counter. She'd already gone back to reading the romance novel she'd been reading when he came into the store.

"Do you have anyone special?" he asked.

"I'm afraid not. I'm always single on Valentine's Day."

He thought about that a moment.

"What's your name?" he asked.

"Rebecca."

"Well, Rebecca, these were for my wife . . ."

He gave her the chocolates, the roses, and the strawberries.

". . . I believe you might enjoy them more."

Life was for the living. His wife would understand. He'd been alone since she passed away. Maybe he would be a little rusty, but he'd never find out if he didn't open up to the possibility.

He thought he'd like to get to know Rebecca better, and just maybe she could help him love again.

He thought of her full breasts pushing against her sweater and tried to imagine her nipples. Would they be small or large, pale pink or brown?

What about her pussy. Was it shaved or covered with curly blonde hairs? Were the lips plump or thin? How would it feel to slide into a beautiful woman after so long?

There was time for all that later. For now, he thought maybe they could keep one another company on this very special day. . . .